THE BOLD, THE STRONG, THE PASSIONATE —FROM SPANISH ARISTOCRACY TO NEW WORLD PIONEERS—THEY FOUGHT FOR FREEDOM IN AN UNTAMED AMERICA.

John Cooper Baines—The rugged and headstrong American frontiersman whose code of honor drives him to protect the proud heritage of his family—a duty he would die for.

Catarina Baines—The robust and noble wife of John Cooper who has borne him three stalwart children. Her Castilian dignity and warm heart provide the flame for her husband's blazing mission.

Carlos de Escobar—Catarina's reckless brother, who is unable to control his raging torment when the thing he values most, his wife is snatched cruelly away.

Apache wife, whose happiness on the new frontier are vicious act of selfishness.

Don Diego de Mengez—A wealthy and ruthless land baron, who lusts after both possessions and women with equal evil.

General Santa Anna—A liar, thief, corrupt opportunist and traitor, who leads his men into battle not caring which side sheds the most blood. His vulture-like greed soon turns John Cooper Baines's closest friend into an enemy.

A Saga of the Southwest Series
Ask your bookseller for the books you have missed

A Saga of the Southwest
Book III

REVENGE
OF
THE HAWK

Leigh Franklin James

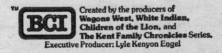

BCI Created by the producers of
Wagons West, White Indian,
Children of the Lion, and
The Kent Family Chronicles Series.
Executive Producer: Lyle Kenyon Engel

BANTAM BOOKS
TORONTO · NEW YORK · LONDON · SYDNEY

REVENGE OF THE HAWK
*A Bantam Book / published by arrangement with
Book Creations, Inc.*
Bantam edition / December 1981

*Produced by Book Creations, Inc.
Executive Producer: Lyle Kenyon Engel.*

*All rights reserved.
Copyright © 1981 by Book Creations, Inc.
Cover art © 1981 by Bantam Books, Inc.
This book may not be reproduced in whole or in part, by
mimeograph or any other means, without permission.
For information address Bantam Books, Inc.*

ISBN 0-553-20096-8

Published simultaneously in the United States and Canada

Bantam Books are published by Bantam Books, Inc. Its trademark, consisting of the words "Bantam Books" and the por-
trayal of a rooster, is Registered in U.S. Patent and Trademark
Office and in other countries. Marca Registrada. Bantam
Books, Inc., 666 Fifth Avenue, New York, New York 10103.

PRINTED IN THE UNITED STATES OF AMERICA

0 9 8 7 6 5 4 3 2 1

*To the Americn public who believes
in the primal honesty and decency of
this strong, young country with whose
views I am in enthusiastic accord,
I personally dedicate this book.*

Acknowledgment

The author appreciatively acknowledges his literary debt to Marla and Lyle Engel and the rest of the inspired Book Creations team including Philip D. Rich, editor in chief, and Bruce Rosenzweig, senior editor.

The author also wishes to express his indebtedness to his transcriber-typist, Fay J. Bergstrom, whose ability to read what she is transcribing has often helped him avoid error.

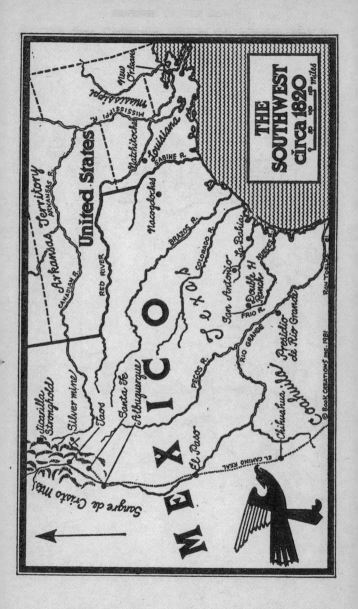

HACIENDA DEL HALCÓN

DOUBLE H RANCH

© Book Creations Inc. 1981

Ron Toelke '81

Prologue

For as far as the eye could see, the Hacienda del Halcón spread out across the fertile lands of the province of Texas. Located on the Frio River in Uvalde, the ranch had been founded six years earlier, when Don Diego de Escobar, an exiled Spanish nobleman, had followed the advice of his American son-in-law, John Cooper Baines, and had moved his family, his household staff, and his workmen here. Formerly intendant—or administrator—of the province of Taos in New Mexico, Don Diego had despaired of the Spanish yoke of restrictions, high tariffs, and prohibitive orders transmitted from the arrogant viceroy in Mexico City. When John Cooper Baines had discovered this unclaimed, fertile land west-southwest of San Antonio, Don Diego was glad to reestablish his homestead in the Texas country, raising with his son and son-in-law, cattle, horses, and sheep.

But even now in 1820, only six short years after the de Escobars and Baineses had moved to the Texas country, the Hacienda del Halcón—known also as the Double H Ranch— was a prosperous, sprawling homestead. There was the spacious hacienda, constructed of hewn timbers and adobe mud, which the trabajadores had recently completed, and here John Cooper, Don Diego, and Carlos lived comfortably with their wives and children. Each family's living quarters were connected to the main house by a spacious courtyard, where the children played or the adults took their siestas or had their refreshment before the sun went down. But the heart and soul of the large, Spanish-style edifice was the enormous oak-paneled dining room where the families would meet and

1

discuss the events of the day while Tía Margarita, the de Escobar cook for over a decade, served them the sumptuous meals on which she prided herself.

Then there were the outbuildings of the ranch, dozens of them, including the huge bunkhouse for the trabajadores, and the little cottages for the married workmen and their wives. There were the stables that housed the magnificent Arabian palominos—now numbering ten—which John Cooper had bought for breeding purposes, and there were the stables for the other horses of the remuda. There were also two large barns for the cattle that Miguel Sandarbal, loyal foreman of the Hacienda del Halcón, and John Cooper had bred from the wild longhorns they had found roving in this vast valley. So the Hacienda del Halcón grew and prospered, and in the years to come, John Cooper and Don Diego believed the ranch would become the greatest in the Texas country. Eventually there would be a school and a hospital and even a beautiful church for all the families of the community, in addition to the little chapel the trabajadores had built as soon as they had arrived here. Also, as the ranch grew, more living quarters would have to be built for the workmen and the household staff, as well as for the Baines and de Escobar families.

Back in Taos, Don Diego's post as intendant had been taken by his old friend, Don Sancho de Pladero, while Don Esteban de Rivarola, the sworn enemy of Don Diego, had replaced Don Sancho as alcalde mayor to administer local justice in Taos.

But those who remained in Taos, as well as those who had gone on to Texas, knew little of what was happening beyond this vast, still virtually uncharted territory. The year after John Cooper Baines and Catarina had joined Don Diego in Texas had been a year in which there was no summer in New England. In the first week of June, there had been snow ten inches deep in the Berkshires, Vermont, and New Hampshire, and in July and August, the ice had been half an inch thick. Almost no corn had ripened along the Eastern Seaboard.

In that same year of 1816, James Monroe, a Republican, had been elected President, and Indiana had entered the Union without slavery. A year later, the Alabama Territory had been formed out of the Mississippi Territory, and the first steam navigation on the Mississippi had definitely commenced. *The Seminole War had begun with an attack by the whites upon the Indians just above the Florida border, followed by Indian depredations on Georgia backwoodsmen. Mississippi had entered the Union as a slave state. In 1818, the United States flag, which had been adopted by Congress, showed thirteen alternate red and white stripes with a white star for each state on a blue background.*

In 1819, financial panic was felt along the East Coast and in the Midwest, a product of business readjustment, banking expansion, and land speculation following the return of an unsettled peace between the British and the United States. And just this past February, a treaty with Spain had been signed, in which Florida was ceded to the United States, the limits on the western boundary of the Louisiana Purchase were fixed, and all claims to territory north of the 42nd Parallel were relinquished.

In this year of 1820, Maine entered the Union, and Congress declared that the slave trade was piracy and punishable by death. And by the year's end, James Monroe would be reelected President. Also, as the year drew to its close, there would be a Connecticut-born frontiersman named Moses Austin, who, having gone bankrupt in the depression of 1819, believed that the frontier would be his salvation, and turned to the broad expanse of Spanish Texas. . . .

One

On this warm, late-October afternoon in the year of 1820, Catarina Baines and her handsome brother, Carlos, were in the courtyard of the *hacienda*, laughing and playing with their children.

Catarina, the daughter of Don Diego de Escobar, was now twenty-six and superbly beautiful. Since their move from Taos to their grand new ranch in Texas, she and her beloved *esposo*, John Cooper Baines, had reveled in the outdoor life,

and the sun had bronzed them so that, indeed, the blond
young mountain man looked almost as Spanish as his exquisite wife.

Their first child, Andrew, was now seven, but Catarina
had borne John Cooper another son, whom he had named
Charles, in honor of his brother-in-law. There was also a little
daughter in the Baines family, whom John Cooper had named
after his late mother, Ruth. Charles was five, Ruth two, and
Andrew looked after them protectively, much to the maternal
gratification of the serenely content Catarina Baines.

Playing with these children were two of the three children of Carlos and his lovely Apache wife, Weesayo, whose
name in Apache meant "light of the mountain." Their son,
Diego, named after Carlos's father, was a month older than
Andrew and inclined to take the lead in suggesting, and even
directing, the games all of them played. Weesayo had borne
two girls for her Spanish husband, the older being named
Inez, after Carlos's kindly aunt, and the younger, now only
eighteen months old, Carlos had named Dawn in tribute to
his wife. At present, Dawn was in the *hacienda* with her
mother.

Catarina turned to Carlos and uttered a happy sigh: *"Mi
hermano,* it seems so natural to be with our children, doesn't
it? And yet it wasn't so long ago that you were scolding me
because I was such a willful, spoiled child."

"I've forgotten that, *querida."* Carlos smiled as he lifted
four-year-old Inez into his arms, kissed her forehead, and
then turned back to Catarina. "I swear, I feel reborn here in
this wonderful land of Texas. All this country around us,
thousands of acres of rolling meadows, a fine river that gives
plenty of water for the *hacienda,* as well as for our sheep and
cattle and the horses—and all our loyal *trabajadores,* who
have become a family to us. This is the life I've dreamed
of."

"I, too, *mi hermano.* And who would have dreamed that
my John Cooper could have brought all this about? If you
hadn't brought him home to our *hacienda* in Taos after he
saved your life in the mountains, I might never have met the
man I could love. I might have married some disgustingly old
hacendado or *rico* in Taos and been bored to death."

"This is true," Carlos said. "And it was because of him
that I met my Weesayo, when he brought me to the stronghold of the Jicarilla Apache." He now looked over at Francesca, the six-year-old daughter of Don Diego and Doña Inez.

Carlos's father and aunt had been married six years after Don Diego's first wife died in Spain, just before the family had begun their journey to Taos. The middle-aged couple had found great joy in each other, and their happiness had grown immeasurably with the birth of their daughter. Now Francesca was sitting primly on a little bench, her hands folded in her lap, watching the other children play. "See," Carlos said, "Francesca is like a little mother, all dressed up and unwilling to get her clothes dirty." Raising his voice, he called, *"Holá, Francesca, come play with the rest of the children. They want you."*

"Sí, Uncle Carlos," the grave, dark-eyed little girl responded with a curtsy to them both. Carlos and Catarina smiled at each other and came to greet her. Esteban Morales, assistant foreman of the sprawling *hacienda,* had whittled toys for all of the children, and they were playing soldier now, squatting down and placing their battalions in order to prepare for a battle or perhaps a military parade.

As the shadows of the setting sun began to fall over the courtyard, Weesayo, exquisite in her buckskin garb, came out of the house, holding Dawn in her arms, her face drawn with anguish. She called out, "Carlos, *mi esposo,* the little one has a fever—it came upon her suddenly, and it frightens me!"

"Querida, I'll ride to San Antonio for a *médico,"* Carlos declared as he hurried to her.

But Weesayo, shaking her head, replied, "No, my beloved, it would take too long. And besides, you could not be sure the *médico gringo* would have skill enough. My mother taught me when I was a child to find barks and herbs that cure quickly. Last week, when I went riding to the east, I saw a clump of trees with the bark of the cinchona. I will ride there and bring back what will make our little one well again."

"And I'll care for Dawn till you come back safely," Catarina volunteered as she gently took the fretful little girl from Weesayo's arms. "I will put cloths dipped in cool water on her forehead—they will help the fever go down."

Weesayo sent her a grateful look. *"Gracias,* Catarina. And now I'll saddle my horse. Do not worry, Carlos, *mi corazón,* Tasumi will ride with me. I'll be in no danger!"

The Jicarilla Apache escort who had accompanied the de Escobar family to the Texas country so many years earlier had returned to their stronghold a few months after the journey had been completed. But Tasumi, an older man in his fifties, had remained in Texas, deeply devoted to Weesayo. He had insisted on staying to look after the "Beloved Woman."

"Wait at least till morning," Carlos urged. Again Weesayo shook her head: "No, the fever will grow worse as the night progresses. Tasumi and I will ride, and I shall bring back the bark which will cure Dawn's fever. Do not fear, my beloved husband!"

They kissed, then stood apart for a moment holding hands, looking into each other's eyes. Finally Carlos released Weesayo's hand, and the young woman headed for the stables.

Seven years ago John Cooper Baines had purchased his white palomino stallion, Fuego, and three mares from a horse breeder living outside Santa Fe, and he had bred these magnificent Arabians. Out of friendship for Carlos and his admiration for the latter's wife, John Cooper had made Weesayo a gift of the very first colt, a brown mare now six years old, whom Weesayo had named Esperanza, Spanish for "hope."

It was this docile, unswervingly obedient mare that Weesayo now saddled, while Tasumi swiftly readied his own wiry mustang. The mature Apache brave gloomily declared, "I do not like this, Beloved Woman. There is danger riding off to the east, where the *mejicanos* live. I will take my musket and my hunting knife. Your mother made me swear that I would look after you, though I did not need her bidding to wish to do so."

"You talk like an old woman, Tasumi," Weesayo smilingly teased him. "I ride as well as you, and I, too, have my hunting knife. Besides, I do not know that there are any *gringos* or *mejicanos* off to the east where we go for the bark that will cure my little Dawn. Stop grumbling, for the sooner we ride, the sooner we'll be back."

With a philosophical shrug, Tasumi nodded and let his beautiful young mistress precede him on her palomino mare, then mounted his mustang and rode at a respectful distance behind her. Twilight was already falling, casting grotesque shadows along the valley, and on the scrub and live oak trees and the clumps of mesquite. Catarina had gone back into the *hacienda* to care for Dawn until Weesayo's return, and Carlos went out to the front yard to watch his lovely wife ride off.

She saw him standing there in the distance, alone in the deepening shadows of the evening, and she smiled and waved her hand to him and called out, "I will return soon, my beloved." But as her horse headed to the east, she lost sight of him, and her voice was drowned out by the pounding of the horses' hooves.

Weesayo, daughter of the dead Descontarti, former chief of the Jicarilla Apache and blood brother to John Cooper, was now twenty-five and, to Carlos's mind, more beautiful than the day he had first seen her emerging from her father's wickiup. Her softly rounded face had a gentle, ethereal beauty to it, and she was slim, delightfully made, and lithe. As she rode Esperanza, she leaned forward, encouraging the eager mare onward, long strands dangling from the sleeves and seams of her buckskin jacket and leggings. At the ends of these strands were silver amulets shaped like little bells. And she wore around her neck the heavy turquoise necklace her father had given her at her ritual of acceptance as the "Beloved Woman." Her blue-black hair was plaited into a thick braid that descended almost to the middle of her back. To denote her marital status she wore, instead of the white eagle's feather, the black feather of Carlos's tamed raven Fortuna, which symbolized both marriage and motherhood.

Tasumi rode behind her, his eyes admiring her, his mien resigned and yet anxious; despite Weesayo's confidence, he feared that gringos or mejicanos did indeed live nearby. He knew the site to which he was riding, about a two hours' journey from the hacienda; yet he recalled that, to the south and about a mile and a half from that clump of cinchona-barked trees, a mejicano rico had built a large hacienda with several jacales for his trabajadores. He looked up to the darkening sky and murmured a prayer to the Great Spirit that whoever this hacendado was, he and his men would take no notice of gentle Weesayo, who sought only a panacea for her feverish little girl.

After two hours, Weesayo drew in the reins and brought her mare to a halt, turning back to wave her hand to Tasumi, since she had found the clump of trees with the medicinal bark. "It is as I remember, Tasumi!" she called. "Remain there on guard; it will not take me long."

"I hear you and obey, Beloved Woman," the middle-aged Apache brave declared as he halted his mustang and again, as an instinctive precaution, put out his hand to make certain that his musket was beside him, primed and ready for use.

Weesayo dismounted, tethering her mare to the thick

branch of a scrub tree, and hastened toward the clump of dark-barked trees. Drawing her hunting knife, she swiftly began to cut away strips of the medicinal bark and drop them into a leather pouch that she wore strapped to the belt of her buckskin leggings. Tasumi stared round, strangely apprehensive, though there was no sound to be heard, save the chirping of cicadas in the distance, and the occasional faint call of a night bird. The moon had hidden behind a cloud, and the soft darkness enshrouded the land.

Suddenly, there came from the east the clatter of horses' hooves and the hoarse voice of a man calling out, "¡Los indios! ¡Cuidado, hombres!"

Tasumi groped for his musket, drew it out of the sheath, and then suddenly three horsemen rode upon them, two carrying torches of pinewood in their right hands, as their left hands held tight check on the reins of their mustangs. The foremost rider uttered an oath and, drawing a pistol from the holster in his belt, fired at Tasumi. The Apache brave uttered a groan as the ball grazed his skull; tottering, he sprawled from the saddle and lay on his belly, arms outstretched, unconscious, his musket dropping with a thud beside him.

"There is another, hombres!" the hoarse voice bellowed again, and the second rider, a dour-faced, thickly mustachioed peón, rode forward at a gallop toward the startled young Apache woman, his musket raised to shoulder height, as he aimed it with one hand.

"¡Cuidado, hombre! ¡Yo soy mujer!" Weesayo cried as she straightened, lifting her arms in the universal sign of peace, dropping her hunting knife to show that she did not come armed as an enemy.

"A woman, is it, Hernando?" the hoarse voice sniggered. "Bring her to me, hombre, pronto!"

The two men with the torches rode up and surrounded her. They dismounted and approached her, holding their torches high. The man with the hoarse voice now rode up slowly on a piebald gelding, a stocky, middle-aged man in his forties, with a crisp black beard and a waxed mustache. His sombrero was rimmed with silver braids, the cuffs of his trousers were similarly decorated, and his paunchy middle was circled by a superb handcrafted black leather belt with a silver buckle on which appeared, in a monogram, the letters "P de M."

"You are right, Hernando," he growled. "More of these thieving indios!"

Weesayo, who spoke Spanish fluently, indignantly retorted: "Señor, I did not come here to steal. My *niña* is ill; I rode here to bring back the cinchona bark that will cure her. And there was no need to shoot Tasumi, who rode to protect me. He had done nothing to you."

"Listen to the *india puta, hombres,*" the bearded *hacendado* sneered. "What airs she gives herself, but she is dressed like an Apache, and she has a hunting knife." Then, staring appraisingly at Weesayo, he jibed, "I say that you are trespassing on my land and wishing to spy, perhaps even trying to murder my servants."

"But that is not true, señor! I am the wife of Carlos de Escobar, and I come from the Hacienda del Halcón, which is to the west of here."

"You, the wife of a Spaniard! At least, *india puta*, you have an imagination. We shall see how it serves you when you are put to the question in my dungeon. Hernando, Ruiz, bind her hands behind her back and bring her. And the other one?"

"He's dead, *patrón*," Hernando chuckled. "My ball sped true; I saw him fall from his horse and not move again."

"And the palomino, *patrón?*" Ruiz, a tall, scar-faced *peón* in his late thirties, inquired. "It's a fine horse, one worthy of so renowned a grandee as yourself."

Don Pedro de Menguez chuckled, pleased by this unctuous flattery, as he watched his two servants seize Weesayo, force her wrists behind her back, and bind them tightly with a rawhide thong. "You become more intelligent daily, Ruiz. You shall have your reward—when I've finished questioning this *puta* and have had my fill of her, you may take her to your quarters."

"You have no right to treat me thus, señor!" Weesayo protested, her face drawn and pale, but her shoulders straight with dignity. "You have only to send one of your men to the *hacienda* that I have named, and you will find that I speak the truth—I am the *esposa* of Carlos de Escobar and the mother of his children."

"There will be time for you to embellish this fabrication of yours under the lash, *puta*. Put her on your horse, Hernando. Ruiz, tether the palomino to your own. And now, let's ride back; I'm famished for food and wine!"

Tasumi had stirred a few moments ago, as consciousness gradually returned to him. He could vaguely hear the words of the three Mexicans and then his young mistress's indignant replies. His mustang had galloped off about thirty yards but now stood placidly waiting for its master to retrieve it. As his strength returned, he heard Don Pedro de Menguez's last words, and he dug his fingernails into his palms at the outrageous affront to the Beloved Woman, the daughter of a great Apache chief. But it was futile to try to help her now. His musket lay on the ground at a distance, and he was still weak from the wound. He held his breath and lay as still as he could, feigning death. And he prayed to the Great Spirit to give him strength to ride back to the mate of the Beloved Woman, who would save her from this accursed *mejicano*.

He watched, until he could no longer see in the darkness, the three men escorting the captive young Apache woman southward, and then he slowly rolled over onto his back and, staring up at the sky, murmured a fervent prayer. With one hand groping toward his throbbing head, he ascertained that the ball had creased his skull but left no dangerous wound. Yet he was still dazed and without strength. Summoning his forces, he rolled over onto all fours, staggered to his feet, and stumbled haltingly toward the mustang. Putting his fingers to his lips, he emitted a faint whistle, and soon he heard the mustang's hooves nearing him. When the animal stood before him, he wanly flung an arm around its neck and tried to hoist himself into the saddle. But the effort was too much, and he fell on his knees, groaning with pain and frustration. The docile mustang waited patiently as again he tried to mount it. Clasping it around the neck, his cheek pressed against its neck, he gasped, "Go back, go back to the *hacienda, pronto!*"

The mustang turned its head and circled back toward the west with a leisurely lope as Tasumi fought the waves of blackness that threatened to engulf him.

Night had fallen on the Hacienda del Halcón, and all the families of the community were in their houses, resting after their hard day's labor. Only John Cooper Baines was abroad, accompanied, as always, by his wolf-dog, Lobo, who trotted a few paces ahead, his ears alert, looking this way and that to make sure all was safe and secure on the ranch.

Even in these early decades of the nineteenth century, the Hacienda del Halcón enjoyed great success as a cattle ranch. Esteban Morales had already driven several small herds of cattle via the La Prior crossing and over the old Nueces bridge to Mexican markets along the Camino Real, as well as on to New Orleans, there to be shipped on cattle boats to the East Coast or to the West Indies. Esteban had sold many head of cattle to some of the Spanish settlers in San Antonio as well, and on occasion, when friendly Indian hunting parties neared the *hacienda*, he and Miguel had parleyed with them and given them gifts of several head to ensure peace. And in this way, John Cooper had been able to acquire some superb mustangs to interbreed with the horses of the remuda, in exchange for a few head of sheep or cattle. As blood brother to the Jicarilla Apache, John Cooper Baines wore a wampum belt that signified his friendship with the Indians, and thus, even the Apache and the Comanche, the traditional enemies of the settlers on the Texas frontier, did some trading at the Double H Ranch.

As he and Lobo took their after-dinner constitutional, John Cooper couldn't help thinking, as he always did when he gazed upon the peaceful, sprawling ranch, that he had indeed finally found a home. It had been thirteen long years since that fateful day in Shawneetown, Ohio, when he had witnessed the savage slaughter of his family by renegade Indians. In those days his companion had been his beloved Irish wolfhound, Lije, who, with the fifteen-year-old John Cooper, had crossed the North American continent, living on their own in the wilderness and with friendly Indians, finally arriving in the mountains of New Mexico. There, John Cooper had become blood brother to the chief of the Jicarilla Apache, who had given him the name *El Halcón*—the hawk. And then fate had decreed that the twenty-year-old John Cooper would meet the family of Don Diego de Escobar, a nobleman who had been exiled from his native Spain on trumped-up charges of treason, and had been appointed intendant of the province of Taos in New Mexico. John Cooper fell in love with, and married, Don Diego's beautiful daughter, Catarina, and with the de Escobars, John Cooper had made his home. Now in Texas they had found the peace and freedom they were all looking for.

Nor had John Cooper forgotten the hidden cache of silver he had found in that distant mountain not far from the Jicarilla stronghold. Twice during the past six years he had ridden there on his palomino Fuego to bring back silver ingots. Five of them he had deposited in the largest and most dependable bank in New Orleans, where, fortunately, she discreet bank officer had not asked John Cooper any questions about their source. Drawing on his account, John

Cooper had been able to buy new cattle from some of the wealthy ranchers in San Antonio, even importing some eastern cattle via a commission merchant in New Orleans. In addition, he had procured the latest guns, pistols, and hunting knives for the *trabajadores*, as well as new farming equipment, since the wives of the *trabajadores* raised the produce consumed on the ranch. John Cooper had also been able to use the money to import certain luxuries for the *hacienda*, as well as gifts for his beautiful Catarina and presents for his father-in-law and his gracious wife, Doña Inez. And, too, he had seen to it that Padre Moraga received some silver to give to the poor of Taos, a secret that the ailing old priest shared with him alone.

John Cooper smiled, not without some sadness, as he watched Lobo prancing a few steps ahead of him, content that all was well. The wolf-dog, now about eight years old, was the offspring of Lije and a South Dakota timber wolf. The Irish wolfhound had been killed by an arrow while defending John Cooper from a group of hostile Sioux braves, but Lije lived on in Lobo. The wolf-dog, though aging, was still as strong and powerful as ever. Yet John Cooper had trained him so well that he accepted even the smallest infant who stretched out a hand to pet him, and he would make a contented purring sound when his ears were scratched by any member of the household, including the young *criadas*, or maids, and the *trabajadores*.

Now, as John Cooper and Lobo strolled through the nearly deserted grounds of the Double H Ranch, they were joined by John Cooper's father-in-law, who had also come out for a pleasant stroll in the cool night air. Don Diego's hair was white now, but his step was sprightly and he carried himself, as always, with great dignity.

"Ah, it is a beautiful evening, is it not, John Cooper?" the older man exclaimed.

"That it is, *mi padre*."

"Do you mind if I join you and Lobo in your stroll? There is something I would like to discuss with you."

"By all means," John Cooper said eagerly. "What is it you wish to tell me?"

"Well, as you know, my son," Don Diego said as he fell into step with the younger man, "we have talked often about helping the Americans settle in this wonderful land of Texas. So long as the dear God permits me to enjoy life with my beloved Doña Inez and to watch my six-year-old Francesca grow each day more intelligent and more like a little woman who will, one day, be sought out by the finest suitor—perhaps a man like yourself, if God so wills—I propose to help more *gringos* establish themselves here in Texas. For in that way, you see, John Cooper, it will be possible to get trade into Santa Fe and to Taos, and to break away from the high tariffs and the exclusions which the viceroy and his government imposed upon us for so many years. Besides, it will not be long before Mexico rises against Spain and declares herself independent. Then, of course, Nueva España, as we knew it, will be entirely freed from the strings of the mother's apron, and we will need good men like yourself to help build a new country, where people can be free and self-sufficient."

John Cooper nodded, flushing a little at the flattery his father-in-law had just paid him. He remembered how Don Diego had helped the Texans who had escaped from the Battle of Medina, and how he had also helped the two young St. Louis traders, Matthew Robisard and Ernest Henson. Don Diego had defied the governor of New Mexico in upholding the latters' visit as men who came as survivors and not spies, and surely not as agents of war between the United States and Spain. Once the two men had paid their fine and prepared to go home, Don Diego had even given them money and horses.

In the last thirteen years, John Cooper had lived more adventurously than he could ever have dreamed back in that log cabin near the bank of the Ohio River. He had seen the American frontier being gradually pushed ahead into lands still dominated, on the one hand, by hostile Indians and, on the other, by equally hostile Mexican and Spanish officials. And yet, if he had met only the two St. Louis traders, he still would have concluded that the hope of the future would be to broaden this vast frontier by allowing it to be settled by just such men as those. Yet at the same time, since he had learned to respect Indian ways and customs, he would never agree that the frontier should be extended by exterminating those people who had first come upon this land and learned the bounty of the good earth, the water, the forest, and the elements. Indeed, John Cooper Baines vowed that, in whatever way he could, he would help to overcome the intolerance and prejudice of people who spoke different tongues, and see to it that this vast frontier belonged to everyone: Indian, American, and Spanish alike.

So the young mountain man was well pleased to hear of

his father-in-law's renewed pledge to help Americans settle in this great land of Texas. He and Catarina were more in love than ever, and he had watched Catarina grow into not only his passionate lover, but a mother intensely devoted to her children and to the welfare of other children. It was a good life, since they had their love, their family, and their dear friends and relatives in this complete little world. There was no shadow at this moment over the hawk.

And yet a month ago there had been the hint of a shadow. A band of Comanche, some twenty in all, had, without warning, attacked some of the *trabajadores* working with the cattle and killed two of them before John Cooper, Carlos, and Miguel, hearing the sounds of shots from the Comanche muskets and the cries of the wounded and the dying, had ridden out with Esteban and three other *trabajadores* armed with rifles. Lobo had run alongside his master, eager for the fight, baring his fangs and growling angrily as John Cooper sighted "Long Girl" and fired a shot which brought down one of the foremost Comanche riders. After killing a dozen of the Comanche band and driving off the rest, the men had dismounted and bent over the corpse of one of the marauders. John Cooper had scowled when Miguel said, "I recognize the tribal markings of Sarpento."

Sarpento, a venal, cruel Comanche war chief, had many years earlier killed the Texas husband of Miguel Sandarbal's wife, Bess, and had brought the young woman to the annual Taos fair to be sold as a slave. But through the intervention of Don Diego and Miguel, Bess had found a new home and a new husband.

Picking up the arrows with the red and yellow war markings of Sarpento's tribe, John Cooper had hurried over to a wounded Comanche and demanded, "Did Sarpento send you against this *hacienda?*"

The Comanche, grimacing with pain at his fatal stomach wound, had shaken his head, coughed, and gasped, "No, *gringo* dog. We left Sarpento's band many moons ago, and we saw your *hacienda* and thought there were many horses and *mujeres* for the taking—*aiii!*" And then he had slumped in death.

Miguel had breathed a sign of relief. "I was frightened there, *mi compañero*. I had thought that perhaps after all this time Sarpento had sought to take Bess back from me. Well, we drove them off, and I'll pray at the chapel tonight and thank the good *Señor Dios* for His mercy to us all."

Now Don Diego spoke up again, interrupting John Cooper's introspection. "You know, my son-in-law, everyone here is grateful for all you have done for us. It is truly fitting that our new home be called Hacienda del Halcón. You were the one who discovered it, you were the one who convinced us all to come here, and that is why I proposed that the new *hacienda* bear the name the Apache gave you: *El Halcón*, the hawk. When I see what you have accomplished here, a peaceful little community that owes no allegiance to the hidebound tradition of a dying Old World Spain, I believe that the ranch truly deserves your name, and certainly not mine, my fine son-in-law."

Then, with a broad wink, he added, "In case my old enemy in Taos, Don Esteban de Rivarola, still seeks me—and I know that he will not soon forget the grudge he believes he had against me—it is just as well that my name not be associated with this superb community."

"Well, thank God we also have some friends in Taos."

"Ah, John Cooper, I thank Him daily. Padre Moraga is truly a saint on earth, and Don Sancho has been wonderful, too. As you know, it was Don Sancho who smoothed the path for me when I left Taos, feigning ignorance as to my whereabouts, and to this day he has not told anyone of the location of our ranch. Indeed, it was your idea that he have his couriers take a circuitous route when they travel to us here with messages or the latest news, thereby throwing off the trail anyone who might be seeking to learn our whereabouts to do us harm."

"It's a shame, *mi padre*, that this is the state of affairs. But as long as there are greedy, intolerant men in power, there will be trouble in the land."

"That is why, John Cooper, it will be difficult for more Americans to establish themselves here in Texas. But my work henceforth will be to help them as much as I am able."

Carlos de Escobar had been restless all evening, and now John Cooper and Don Diego came across the young man pacing back and forth near the palominos' stables. As soon as Carlos saw the others he blurted out, "I'm worried. Weesayo should have been back by now."

John Cooper put his hand on his brother-in-law's shoulder and tried to reassure him, saying, "But she has Tasumi with her, Carlos, and she's an expert rider. They're armed, and besides you have to allow at least two hours in each direction, and then some time for her to collect the bark. She wouldn't want you to fret. And Dawn is being cared for by Catarina. She's doing everything that's possible. Now try to relax."

But Carlos, growing apprehensive, shook off this advice and walked by himself along the dirt road where he looked up at the night sky. He encountered Miguel Sandarbal, who was out for an evening stroll with his wife, Bess, and their little daughter. "You're worrying youself unnecessarily, *mi compañero*," Miguel said, trying to comfort Carlos as best he could. "She'll be back anytime now. There aren't any hostile Indians off in that direction, so far as the *trabajadores* know, and when the Apache were here with us, they scouted the terrain for many miles in all directions."

But by ten o'clock that night, Carlos's anxiety was so unbearable that he strode back to the stable and began to throw a saddle over his aging but still-durable stallion, Valor. John Cooper had given his brother-in-law the second colt born from the studding of his Fuego and one of the mares, but out of loyalty Carlos still preferred to ride Valor.

By the time an hour had passed, Carlos could wait no longer. He buckled on his rapier, the one he had bloodied while defending his father, Doña Inez, and Catarina when they had journeyed from Mexico City on the last part of their journey from Spain to their new home in Taos, and put into the saddle sheath his Belgian rifle.

Then, turning Valor's head to the east, he galloped off, the silence of the night only adding to his mounting concern over the prolonged absence of his beloved Weesayo.

A few miles farther on, he drew in Valor's reins and waited, leaning forward in his saddle, cocking his head and listening intently. It seemed to him that he had just heard the distant sound of a horse's hooves. He waited for a moment, and then, with a suppressed cry, urged Valor on to a full gallop.

The moon had come out from behind a cloud, and as Carlos strained his eyes, he made out the vague outline of a man on horseback, a man who seemed to crouch in his saddle and whose arms were locked around the neck of his mount. Kicking his heels against Valor's belly, he quickened the faithful stallion, and as he neared the unknown rider, he uttered an agonized cry, recognizing Tasumi.

"Tasumi, what has happened to you? Where is Weesayo?" he cried as he reined in Valor. The middle-aged Apache, his scalp smeared with clotted blood from the superficial wound, wanly tried to sit up in his saddle and spoke with effort: "I prayed to the Great Spirit to keep me alive till I could reach you, *hombre.* They fired at me, and I lay as one dead to learn why this was done. They took Weesayo and her palomino."

"They? They?" Carlos echoed in an agony of rage and fear. "Who dared shoot at you and make my wife a prisoner?"

"There were two men with their *patrón.*" Tasumi fought for breath. "They said that the Beloved Woman had come to steal or to spy on them, that perhaps she would bring *los indios* to attack them. They tied her wrists behind her back—I saw with my own eyes—and they put her on the horse of one of the servants of this *patrón* and they rode to the south."

"Dios, don't let anything happen to her! Tasumi, have you strength enough to show me where it was they took her? You need not come with me beyond that—I will find her. And if they've harmed her—" He clenched his fist and bared his teeth in savage fury. In his mind's eye he saw again the lovely, round, sweet face of the girl who had given him reason to live, such joy as he had never dreamed a woman could give a man, and had borne him three beautiful children. He shuddered with an ungovernable hatred for these three unknown assailants.

"I—I will try, *hombre.* Some time has passed—I think it has been more than an hour that I have been riding back to the Hacienda del Halcón," Tasumi laboriously explained.

"Forgive me, Tasumi, but I cannot rest till I find my Weesayo. Perhaps it would be better if you rode behind me and held on to me—you are so weak from your wound. Come, I'll help you get down and put you on Valor. Let your mustang find its way back."

"Perhaps you are right," Tasumi reluctantly agreed. "In my eagerness to return to you to tell you what happened, I forgot to bring back my musket. But it is still there, and it will mark the place where they took her a prisoner."

"Good! There we are now. Hold on tightly to me, Tasumi; you will point the way. Now let's go! We must find Weesayo!" So saying, Carlos clucked and snapped at the reins, and the obedient stallion sped forward.

Two

"Patrón, I have heard that there is a large *hacienda* far to the west of us, though I have not yet seen it. Can it be that this *india puta* tells the truth?" Ruiz asked.

"You are a fool, *hombre,* and that is why you are only a *peón,*" Don Pedro de Menguez scornfully retorted. "Besides, what Spaniard of noble blood would stoop so low as to take an Apache woman as his wife? No, I will persuade her to tell us the truth. But the palomino is a fine catch. I would have preferred a stallion, but what would you? *¡Vámanos!* I am famished, I told you!"

Two years ago, in return for favors done, as well as a large contribution into his own exchequer, Juan Ruiz de Apodaca, who had succeeded General Calleja as viceroy late in August of 1816, had given the dissolute hidalgo, Don Pedro de Menguez, a grant of land near the Mexican border. There, with some thirty *peones* who had toiled for his father on the latter's estate near Córdoba in the days before Napoleon, Don Pedro had built himself a feudal castle. A bachelor, notoriously sadistic, he had often had his men abduct attractive young girls from tiny villages just beyond the Rio Grande and forced them, under torture, to become his *criaturas.*

Weesayo remained silent and stealthily tried to work loose the bonds at her wrists, while Don Pedro, riding ahead of his two men, glanced back at the lovely young woman and lecherously licked his lips. She had spirit, he reflected, and judging by the costume which outlined her flanks and bosom, she would be indeed a tasty morsel for his private *calabozo.*

Dismounting in front of the wide frame building that was his *hacienda,* he barked an order to the two men, who obediently lifted Weesayo down from the mustang and, each gripping one of her elbows, dragged her forward into the house. Without a word, they strode toward a wide room in the back near the kitchen, and Hernando squatted in order to

18

lift open a trap door, then lit a candle. A flight of stone steps was revealed, and as he went ahead to light the way, Ruiz, standing behind Weesayo, gripped her upper arms and forced her down the steps, muttering lewd epithets into her ear: "Apache bitch, you'd best make up your mind to tell the truth to the *patrón, ¿comprendes?* He knows how to make stubborn bitches like you tell the truth, *¡es verdad!* And *Dios,* you're well made—perhaps when he's finished with you, Hernando and I can enjoy you. I've never yet had an Apache *puta,* did you know that?"

Grinding her teeth, Weesayo closed her eyes and tried to remain impervious to the salacious remarks. Yet inwardly she was trembling, and what she feared most was the loss of her beloved Carlos and her children. Little Dawn needed the bark so badly—she had done nothing wrong, why did the Great Spirit allow this?

At Don Pedro's order, the two *peones* forced Weesayo to the center of the stone-walled dungeon, and while Ruiz maintained her, Hernando lowered a thin, strong cord that passed through a metal ring hanging from the ceiling and tied it to both her thumbs, then hauled it up till she was forced to stand on tiptoe, her face drawn with pain. After he had secured the other end of the rope to a ring on the opposite wall, he and Ruiz were ordered out of the dungeon, as Don Pedro commanded, "Send in Soledad and Marquita to strip down this *india puta* for me! I'll delay my dinner—this lying slut must be taught a lesson in humility at once!"

Then, moving to a nearby taboret, he picked up a black leather quirt with a silver pommel and drew it through his pudgy fingers as he leered at Weesayo. "You persist in your lie, *puta,* that you came here for cinchona bark for your little one, do you? Well, I, Don Pedro de Menguez, a friend of His Excellency, Viceroy Apodaca, do not believe you. In my opinion, you mouth the name of this de Escobar from where, perhaps, you heard it over some campfire. And I have no doubt that you stole the palomino on which you rode. You and the brave who came here doubtless thought to prepare for an attack by your savage friends—we are too well fortified here for that to succeed, for as you see, we patrol regularly."

"Señor, I do not lie; I have never lied in all of my life," Weesayo softly retorted. "You have only to send one of your men to the Hacienda del Halcón to learn the truth. My little girl is ill with fever, and when I rode out this way last week, I saw the bark that will cure her fever. I have done you no harm, and my people, the Jicarilla Apache, of whom my dead father was chief, are at peace with both *gringo* and *meji-cano.*"

"So you say," Don Pedro de Menguez sneered. "Ah, now, my lovely *criaturas,* strip naked this thieving, murderous savage. And remain here to watch the good lesson which will profit you, if either of you ever try to lie to me, ¿*compren-den?*"

The two Mexican girls approached the shuddering young Apache woman and tore off her buckskin jacket and the long leggings, till she was naked in her moccasins. The *hacendado* sucked in his breath as his eyes devoured the firm, high-perched breasts, the slim waist which flared into resilient, agilely rounded hips, and long, lithe thighs. Shuddering with supreme shame, Weesayo closed her eyes and arched herself, trying desperately to ease the atrocious traction of the rope which cut her tender thumbs and drew her arms high above her head. Now, truly, she was afraid for her life.

"So you wish to show me how brave an Apache *puta* can be, now do you? We shall see, but Marquita and Soledad here will tell you that the quirt is stronger, ¿*no es verdad, mu-chachitas?*" He laughed cruelly as he drew back his right arm and slashed Weesayo just below her bosom with the leather quirt.

She stiffened, her head tilting back, but she forced herself to suppress any outcry and to keep her eyes tightly closed. Inflamed by her proud, stoic beauty, Don Pedro struck again and again, slowly circling her, till her buttocks and thighs and back, and even her belly and her breasts were violently streaked with darkening welts from the leather whip.

Dull groans of anguish were torn from her at the end of the flogging, which was more brutal than any the girls' master had ever administered to them. With horrified eyes, and hands at their mouths, they watched Weesayo's body jerk and strain under the whistling, smacking kisses of the leather quirt until, at last, she sagged, nearly fainting.

With a sadistic chuckle of triumph, Don Pedro de Menguez flung down the quirt and, advancing to the sagging, naked young woman, dug his fingers into her welted buttocks as he violated her with a ruthless violence. When he had finished, he turned to the two cowering *criadas,* clad in sandals and thin cotton dresses whose skirts descended only to their knees, and roughly ordered, "Now come with me, *muchachas*. We'll let Ruiz and Hernando enjoy what's left of this Indian bitch. And what you've seen should make you more nimble and eager to please me the rest of the night, isn't that so?"

"*Sí, p-patrón,*" Marquita faintly stammered, giving her companion a terrified look as she followed the brutal *hacendado* up the stone stairway.

He did not even bother to cover himself, and with a lewd laugh, he remarked, "*Hombres,* you deserve a reward at least for finding that superb palomino. You may both enjoy her. Don't kill her yet, though. Perhaps she can still amuse me tomorrow, when I have another session with her to learn what was behind her riding out to my estate."

"A thousand thanks, *patrón!*" Ruiz grinned, doffing his sombrero and bowing low with a sweep of it almost to the floor. Then he and Hernando hurried down the steps, as Don Pedro, with an uproarious laugh, put an arm around the shoulders of each of his maids and urged them on to his bedroom.

The light in this eerie underground dungeon came from the pinewood torches which the two *peones* had thrust into metal brackets set into the sides of the walls. They illumined the bleeding, dark-welted nudity of the almost-unconscious Weesayo, and they made the leering faces of the *peones* those of grotesque satyrs, as they doffed their sombreros and opened their breeches, arguing over who should be first.

At last, Ruiz prevailed, arguing that he had been the one who had suggested bringing back the palomino mare to the *hacienda*. Grudgingly Hernando agreed: "All right then, *hombre*, but be quick about it. My *cojones* are bursting—she may be an Apache savage, but she has the *tetas* of a real *mujer!*"

As Ruiz grinningly approached, Weesayo slowly lifted her head and blinked her eyes to clear them of the miasmic fog of agony and shame which nearly blinded her. "*Agua, por piedad, s–señores,*" she hoarsely gasped.

"Well, then, *querida*, if you'll be nice to us, we'll give you some water. I'd rather have you willing than fight you—I've heard how Apache women fight in battle beside their men and against us *mejicanos*," Ruiz sneered. Turning to Hernando, he barked, "Go fetch a gourd of water. It'll revive her, and she'll have more life for both of us, don't you understand that, *hombre?*"

"All right, all right, I'll get it. But hurry with her," Hernando grumbled as he hastened up the stairs.

Weesayo drew a long, shuddering breath and then, forcing herself to stare at the leering *peón*, entreated, "I cannot resist you—my strength is gone—your *patrón* used the whip too well—in the name of mercy, untie me; my thumbs are swollen and they pain me greatly—I—I promise I will submit willingly to you, if you'll grant me this mercy." As she spoke, her eyes entreatingly fixed on the smirking *peón*, Weesayo prayed with a despairing anguish:

> *Great Spirit, let this ignoble brute, who is only the tool of his cruel master, free me, Then I can avenge the dishonor done me. Yet, soiled as I am, I am not worthy of my beloved Carlos. Only in death can my spirit be freed—and if You grant me this prayer, I will sacrifice this* mejicano *dog to You as well!*

"All right then. But no tricks, mind you, *puta!*" Reaching above, Ruiz expertly cut the rope, and Weesayo crumpled to the floor with a cry of pain.

In his lustful haste to possess her, Ruiz dropped his knife, knelt down, his fingers biting into her bare shoulders, and turned her over onto her back. But as he did so, she had just enough time to reach out for the knife and to grasp the handle. As he mounted her, she put both hands on the handle of the knife and drove it with all her strength into his back.

The *peón* uttered a gurgling cry, half lifted himself, and then sprawled inert in death. With a supreme effort, Weesayo rolled his heavy body off her and staggered to her feet, just as Hernando came down the stairs.

"You damned, accursed Apache bitch, you've done in my best friend!" Hernando hoarsely cried as he dropped the gourd of water and thrust his hand toward his own knife. But Weesayo turned, her eyes huge and bathed in tears, as she whispered, "To you, Spirit of the Sky, to my father, I yield my life—*mi* Carlos, *mis niños*—forgive me—I cannot live after the shame of what has been done to me!"

And even as Hernando, mouthing obscenities, ran toward her, Weesayo lifted the bloody knife in both hands and plunged it into her heart.

Carlos and Tasumi had ridden for more than an hour. Though the moon was shining brightly now, Carlos despaired of ever finding the spot where his wife had been abducted. Then suddenly Tasumi uttered a cry and exclaimed, "There is the musket, as I told you! And do you not see the hoofprints of the horses those three men rode, who shot at me and took the Beloved Woman?"

"Yes, and they go directly southward. I'll follow them." Again, Carlos looked up at the sky and prayed silently. Then, his face purposefully grim, he quickened Valor's gait till they reached the imposing wooden gate that marked the *hacienda* of Don Pedro de Menguez.

"Keep your musket ready, Tasumi," Carlos urged. "I shall go to the *hacienda* and demand to see its owner, and I shall bring back Weesayo, or he will answer to me."

"May the Great Spirit bring her safely back to you," Tasumi murmured.

Dismounting, Carlos drew the Belgian rifle out of its sheath, inspected it to make sure that it was primed, put his left hand to reassure himself that his rapier was in its scabbard, and then pushed open the gate and strode forward.

He was challenged by the call of one of the *peones* who guarded the *hacienda*: "¡Holá! Who goes there?"

"I wish to see your *patrón*. Tell him it is Carlos de Escobar!" Carlos called out.

"Very well. Wait there. I am ordered to let no one come to the *hacienda* until my master gives his consent," the heavily set, bearded Mexican sentry querulously called back.

Turning his back on Carlos, he strode toward the *hacienda*, knocked at the door, and was admitted. Carlos could see that there were lanterns behind the curtains that covered the foremost windows on each side of this imposing house. It surprised him to see the house, since he didn't know there were any neighbors so close to the Hacienda del Halcón, nor had the *trabajadores*, in all this while, ever mentioned its presence. On the other hand, there was no reason for them to have done so: most of the fine grazing land that the cattle and sheep used lay more to the west than to the east in the magnificent valley.

A few moments later, Don Pedro de Menguez presented himself on the threshold of the door, flanked by the leering Hernando. There was a surly expression on his face, and he was clad only in his dressing robe over his *camisa* and *calzoncillos*, and was wearing *zapatillas*. "I do not understand why you wish to see me at such an hour, Señor de Escobar," he grumbled.

"Rest assured, sir, that I should not be here if it were not that I believe my wife was taken prisoner by you and your men," was Carlos's angry retort.

"Come now, Señor de Escobar, surely you're jesting! Why should I and my men make your wife prisoner?"

"That's what I'm here to find out. I do not have the courtesy of your name, señor."

"I am Don Pedro de Menguez, a friend of His Excellency the Viceroy," the *hacendado* sneered, drawing himself up.

"Very well then, Don Pedro. My wife is named Weesayo. She came to this area to look for cinchona bark to cure the fever of our youngest child, and she rode with a brave of her father's tribe, named Tasumi. He told me that your men shot at him and left him for dead, and that as he was recovering from his wound, he saw your men tie my wife's wrists, put her on a horse, and ride back to this *hacienda*. Moreover, the tracks of four horses lead here—and that other horse must have been the palomino that Weesayo rode. Now, Don Pedro, you'll do me the courtesy of releasing my wife and bringing her here, and then you will owe us both an apology, as well as an explanation for your barbarous conduct!"

"You are impetuous to imply that I am guilty of these things—" the *hacendado* began, with an impatient gesture of his pudgy hand, and Carlos saw a huge ruby ring upon the median finger. Realizing that the young Spaniard had noticed this, the *hacendado* smirked and explained, "I see you have noticed the gift of the viceroy to me for services rendered. And it was he who gave me this fine land where I have come to live in my declining years."

"Your ring does not concern me, Don Pedro. My wife does. Have the decency to bring her to me at once!"

"Gently, Señor de Escobar! You come here with a rapier at your side and a rifle in your hand late at night and—"

"In the name of God and all the saints, I will kill you if you don't bring her to me at once!" Carlos hoarsely cried, beside himself.

"I—er—I regret I cannot comply with your wish—believe me, Señor de Escobar, it was not of my doing or desire—"

"What are you trying to tell me?" Carlos's voice had a dangerous softness to it as his eyes fixed the *hacendado* with a burning intensity.

"Please be careful with that rifle; you have the advantage of me—as you see, I had retired for the night, and I am unarmed—Hernando, perhaps you can explain to Señor de Escobar," Don Pedro de Menguez stammered, glancing nervously at the *peón*.

"Why, señor, it's as my *patrón* says, it wasn't his doing at all—"

"Where is Weesayo? What have you done to her? Why can't you simply bring her here before me?" Carlos interrupted. He lifted his rifle in both hands, which made the *hacendado* shrink back with a stifled cry of fear. The latter babbled as he glanced again at Hernando, "By all the saints, you idiot, tell him what happened—he's got the look of a madman to him—"

"But it's true, señor," Hernando wheedlingly tried to explain, inclining his head in an abject bow to Carlos, wishing to prove that he recognized nobility. "How could we know that an *india puta* could be married to a handsome nobleman like yourself, Señor de Escobar? We thought she had heard your name somewhere, perhaps on a raid by her tribe and—"

"Enough of your simpering speeches, man! I'll put a bullet through you if you don't tell me this instant where she is—if she's alive, bring her to me!" Carlos was trembling, his voice nearly cracking with the strain of his agony and his mounting premonition.

"She—she killed herself—yes, you must believe us, señor—the *patrón* will tell you—we tried to question her, and she persisted in saying—"

"You mean you tortured her—and she—she killed herself—and God knows what else you did—you along with your master. But as God is my judge, I mean to avenge her!" Carlos cried.

The *hacendado* saw the look in Carlos's eyes and fearfully exclaimed, "How did I know she would try to kill herself—I only whipped her a little—oh, God—no—no, let me have a priest first—*ayúdame*—oh, *Dios!*" Don Pedro de Menguez turned to flee, his voice hysterically breaking. Stepping back a pace, Carlos grimly lifted the rifle to his shoulder and triggered it. The *hacendado* lifted his arms aloft, staggered, and then fell forward on his face and lay still.

Horrified by the turn of events, Hernando put his hand on his knife. But Carlos swiftly reversed the rifle and swung the heavy butt against the hand of the *peón*. The knife fell with a clatter, and Hernando grabbed at his hand and held it to his chest, whimpering like a baby: "You've broken my hand, señor; oh, how it hurts, you've broken it, you've broken it!"

In almost the same motion, discarding the rifle, Carlos had drawn his rapier and now pressed the sharp point against the man's breast. "Tell me everything!"

"If I do, you won't hurt me? I'm suffering so—my hand's broken, I know it is—"

"I'll disembowel you, *hombre*, if you don't tell me!" Carlos panted, his face a mask of agonized fury.

"It's as the *patrón* said—how were we to know she was telling the truth? I mean, señor, a handsome nobleman like you—we didn't expect an Indian girl—that is to say—I mean—"

"Out with it, by all the demons of hell!" Carlos almost screamed, and the *peón*, sweating profusely, felt the point of the rapier pierce his *camisa*.

"No, no, don't, I'll tell you! He—he had his *criadas* strip her, and she was tied in his *calabozo*, that's in the cellar, señor! And he, as he said—he whipped her—and then—and then—"

"I want to know everything!"

"Well—he's a man, he's the *patrón;* we couldn't stop him—oh, God in heaven, señor, don't kill me—it wasn't my doing, I swear by the Holy Virgin it wasn't my doing—he—he took her—you understand—I couldn't stop him—"

"And then?"

Hernando had backed against the wall where there was no further retreat, his eyes bulging and glassy, fixed on the deadly length of steel whose sharp point pricked his flesh through the thin shirt. "And then the *patrón* said—said we could have her—you understand, señor, I didn't mean to and I wasn't going to—and she asked for water, and I went to get some—and when I came back, the next thing I knew, I guess Ruiz had cut her down and she'd taken the knife and killed him—and then before I could stop her—she took the knife and—and—she killed herself, and that's the truth, I swear it by the Holy Virgin!"

The sentry had heard the rifle shot and came running now into the *hacienda*, calling out, "¿*Que pasa aquí?*" Whirling, Carlos ran him through with the rapier as Hernando, eyes bulging, stared in horror. Swiftly disengaging the bloody blade, the young Spaniard pressed the tip back against the chest of the *peón,* and uttering a sob from the very depths of his being, hoarsely declared, "Take me to my wife!"

"Oh, yes, yes, at once, señor," Hernando babbled, trembling so violently that he could scarcely stand. "It's as I told you, I didn't touch her—it was the *patrón* and Ruiz—"

"Not another word—take me to her or you'll die this instant!"

"I will, in the name of mercy, señor, don't kill me—I'll take you there right now!" Hernando gasped, drawing in his breath as he felt the point of the rapier prod him again.

As he stumbled down the stairway of the *hacendado's* dungeon, he quaveringly repeated, "I swear to you, señor, it wasn't I who harmed her—I'm not that sort, truly—don't kill me—"

The pinewood torches still flared in this silent, underground stone chamber, and Carlos shuddered as his eyes fixed on Weesayo's naked, sprawled body, her slim hands still gripping the handle of the knife that was imbedded in her heart. Beside her lay Ruiz.

After a long pause, during which Carlos fought for self-control, he roughly demanded, "What was done with the palomino she rode?"

"I put it in one of the stable stalls, señor; it's safe—"

"You'll get it for me so I may carry my wife home for proper burial! Not so fast!" he shouted, as the *peón* turned to ascend the stairway. "Stand where you are—I swear, if you try to run, I'll kill you slowly!"

"I—I won't run—oh, señor, be merciful—you must believe I didn't do this to her—"

"Say your prayers, *hombre;* out of respect for my murdered wife, don't try my patience with your cowardice!" Carlos fiercely interrupted. Lowering the rapier, he thrust it back into its scabbard, then stopped and bent down beside Weesayo. Tears nearly blinded him at the sight of the dark weals on her satiny skin, at the sight of the knife handle, which he carefully removed from her body and cast aside on the earthen floor, as he dabbed at the wound with the corner of his linen shirt. It was only after a long moment that he could rise, gently lifting Weesayo's body in his arms, and move toward the stairway and ascend it. Hernando, crossing himself and muttering prayers, followed him, his senses too congealed by terror to think of trying to escape.

"Now get the palomino—and if you dare to give an

alarm, you'll die the instant you raise your voice," Carlos directed. Outside the entrance to the *hacienda,* he carefully stooped again and retrieved his rifle, while still retaining a tender hold of his wife's lifeless body.

Hernando, wincing with pain from his broken hand, hurried to the stable and brought out the mare. "Get a blanket to cover my wife, and straps to bind her to her horse," Carlos ordered, and the *peón* swiftly obeyed.

He watched as the young Spaniard gently laid Weesayo across the back of the horse and securely bound the straps around her after having first wrapped her in the blanket to conceal her nudity. Esperanza looked back, tossed her head, and whinnied, and Carlos groaned aloud in his desolation.

"There, señor, I've done everything you wanted—let me go now—my hand is very bad—please, señor," Hernando whined. Then he staggered back with a strangled cry of terror as he saw Carlos draw his rapier: "No, *piedad,* oh, señor, have mercy, I told you I didn't do those things to her!"

Carlos crossed himself with his left hand. "Make your peace with God. And I, I'll account to the devil himself in hell for what I now do—"

Before Hernando could utter another syllable, Carlos, his lips tightening, thrust the rapier through his heart. He drew out the blade as the *peón* crumpled to the ground, then he wiped the blade clean on the dead man's shirt and sheathed it. Then he looked up at the sky and said aloud, "May *el Señor Dios* forgive me for taking the innocent life of the sentry. And if this man, too, was innocent, then let it be weighed against me on the Day of Judgment."

He bowed his head, took the reins of the docile palomino, and went back to the waiting Tasumi. When the Apache saw the blanket-covered body, he uttered a mournful cry, "*Aiieee!* I have failed the Beloved Woman. I should have died in her stead!"

"Let us take her home and bury her where she can see the sky and the peaceful valley she loved, Tasumi," Carlos said as he tethered the palomino's reins to Valor's tail, then mounted in front of the Apache who clung to him, his wrinkled face bleak with sorrow.

Three

It was nearly dawn when Carlos and Tasumi neared the ranch, with the slow, soft sound of the palomino's hooves a kind of funereal march to Carlos's ears. He wept unashamedly as he guided Valor back to this new home in which he and his beloved Weesayo had known the happiest years of their marriage watching their little children grow.

As Valor, sturdily enduring the weight of his two riders, moved slowly toward the stable, Carlos halted his mount and turned to look back at Tasumi. "Does your wound still trouble you, *hombre?*" he gently asked.

"It is nothing. The wound in my heart and in my spirit is incurable. I have thought all this way that we have come back with her"—the Apache closed his eyes, and his lips moved in a kind of silent prayer—"that it was I who brought about her death by not defending her. I failed in my duty to her."

"This you mustn't think, Tasumi," Carlos hoarsely interrupted as he fought a new onslaught of tears. He had kept himself from looking back at the palomino with its tragic burden, but now he did so, and he groaned aloud in the realization of his bereavement. "I should have gone with her. It was my doing, not yours, Tasumi."

"I will rest a little, señor, and then *con su permiso,* I will ride to the stronghold. They must be told that the Beloved Woman has gone to join her Great Father," Tasumi gravely declared.

For a moment Carlos willed himself to think of his stoic, wounded companion: *"Hombre,"* he said as he tried to force a compassionate smile to his trembling lips, "before you undertake such a journey, you must sleep and also have one of the *trabajadores* clean your wound and bandage it. And then you must take provisions with you. Go into the bunkhouse and rest till the time that it is daybreak and the men waken, and they will help you."

"So be it. Do you mean to bury the Beloved Woman now?"

"Oh, *Dios,* help me bear this burden of torment, this loss of my very own soul, for she was this and more to me," Carlos cried out, beside himself, as again tears ran down his cheeks. "I would to God there was a priest here—oh, Padre Moraga could conduct a proper service for my sweet Wee-sayo. Yet I, who was closest to her, will do what must be done. It is fitting, since she was my very life, that I give her the comfort of burial after I go to the chapel and pray." He dismounted now and held out his hand so that he could help the weary Tasumi down.

"You have spoken of the *padre* in Taos," the Apache said as he stood somewhat unsteadily by Valor. "My people know him and his kindness to the *indios.* Once I reach the stronghold, I will see that word is sent to him of the death of our Beloved Woman. And I am sure that he will come here to say the words that will comfort you."

These words, so compassionate, once again struck through the young Spaniard's defenses. He covered his face with his hands, and his shoulders heaved with muffled sobs. Tasumi merely watched him, for the Apache did not show such outward signs of grief, yet inwardly the middle-aged brave understood and shared Carlos's torment. At last he put out his hand and touched Carlos on the shoulder and said, "The Great Spirit gave you three children. They will have the spirit of the Beloved Woman in them; that must comfort you in the days ahead. I will do as you have bidden me, señor. And, in a few hours, when I have my strength back, I will ride to the stronghold."

Carlos nodded, dropped his hands to his sides, took a long breath, and murmured, "May your God and mine bless you for being beside me in this black, hideous night, Tasumi. Let me be alone now, that I may do what has to be done."

The Apache stared steadfastly at him, then put both his hands on the young Spaniard's shoulders. A look of profound understanding passed between them, and then Tasumi made his way to the bunkhouse. Carlos waited until he had entered, and then led Valor to the stable, unharnessed him, and gave him a ration of oats. The stallion nickered and shoved its muzzle against Carlos's hand, and once again Carlos was drawn to tears by this show of compassion; it was as if the stallion understood its master's torment and sought, as best it might, to alleviate it.

This done, Carlos went back to the palomino, took the reins, and walked toward the chapel which the *trabajadores* had built a few hundreds yards away to the east of the bunkhouse. The elegant little chapel to which he and his father and Doña Inez, as well as Catarina, had gone to commune and to seek divine guidance in their days in Taos, had been faithfully restored in one of the rooms of the new *hacienda*. But this chapel building, which had three rows of pews and could accommodate some twenty worshipers, was for the workers and their families. Carlos tethered the reins of the palomino to a hitching post not far from the chapel. He bowed his head, crossed himself, and opened the door—it was never barred at any hour of the day or night.

The rosy light of dawn had illumined the almost cloudless sky, and as Carlos entered, he had to accustom himself to the dark interior. Then he stopped short and uttered a stifled gasp.

Before the altar he saw a young Mexican kneeling, devoutly bowed, and, indeed, almost prostrated before the exquisitely hand-carved cross which Esteban Morales had made out of cedar wood and tinted with vegetable oils to give it a glossy patina. And as Carlos saw that sublime cross, created by a raw talent that was more eloquent than a practiced, commissioned craftsman might have wrought, he uttered a stifled sob again and sank down on his knees to pray for the soul of his murdered wife.

The young Mexican rose, crossing himself for the last time, and started with surprise to see Carlos at the doorway of the chapel. "Señor, forgive me, I did not mean to disturb your prayers—I did not know that you were here," he stammeringly began.

Carlos recognized the young Mexican; it was Jorge Pastronaz. He had come to the Hacienda del Halcón from San Antonio about a year ago, after his ailing parents had died. Young Jorge was twenty, and Miguel Sandarbal had found him to be an exemplary and dedicated worker with the cattle and with the sheep.

"It is I, rather, who have disturbed you, Jorge," Carlos gently said, rising. And then, desperately seeking in casual speech to block out the enormity of this tragic night, he added, "But surely, you're too young to have sins to confess at dawn, Jorge."

"Forgive me, Señor de Escobar." The young Mexican was tall, rawboned, and beardless, with an ingenuously appealing face. Carlos had noted with approval that whenever he spoke to anyone, he never shifted his gaze but was frank and outgoing, as Carlos himself preferred to be. "I beg your pardon—I have had a great feeling for Mother Church ever since I was a little boy, you see, señor. My parents were poor *peones*, but they were very devout. Now that they are dead, I have no family, but *el Señor Dios* has become my father and cares for me."

"You are drawn to the need of your religion then, and perhaps you yourself are destined for the calling," Carlos gently suggested.

"*Sí*, Señor de Escobar," Jorge Pastronaz agreed. "But there is no priest here, and although I know much of the mass and many of the prayers from memory—you see, I went with my father and mother as often as they would take me, when our *patrón* allowed us a Sunday off, for he was a greedy man and himself not a good *católico*—I am not educated enough to take the vows. So I say to myself, 'Jorge, do your work with the animals in the field, for *el Señor Dios* looks down upon these flocks as he does those of men, surely. And then when you have time, kneel in thanksgiving to Him who brought you here to work with such good people.' And that is why I am here now, Señor de Escobar, to thank Him for looking after me now that I have no family—for you see, I have everyone here on this ranch and everyone is my friend. You are the son of my *patrón*, and yet I feel a warm friendship for you."

Once again, Carlos could scarcely suppress the tears that sprang to his eyes. Mastering himself, he asked, "Do you know the prayer for the dead?"

"Of a certainty, Señor de Escobar," Jorge replied in wonderment.

"It is Weesayo, my wife—"

"Oh, no, Señor de Escobar—it cannot be—it would be too cruel—"

"It was that and more." Carlos's face hardened at the thought of Don Pedro de Menguez and his henchmen. "I have brought her back, and I mean to bury her now. If you will aid me, Jorge, and if you will say the right prayers, it would be of great comfort to me. Although we were married by Apache ritual, we were wed also by Padre Moraga in the faith, and she cherished it as much as I do." Even as he spoke, tears again rolled down his cheeks.

Jorge Pastronaz came to him, made the sign of the cross, and said sympathetically, "I am not worthy; I am a humble *peón,* I am not even ordained. But I loved and respected Weesayo, and what I will say, even if I do not remember all of the words that would be said in Mother Church, they will be from the heart and out of my own sorrow for you, Señor de Escobar."

"*Gracias, hombre.*" Carlos could not trust himself to say more as he turned and left the chapel.

He stood beside the palomino and stiffened, clenching his fists and muttering to himself, "Give me courage, O *Dios,* to endure this sorrow—it is too great for me; I cannot trust myself. And I cannot stay at the *hacienda* for much longer—the memories will be too terrible to endure—I'll see Catarina and John Cooper, my father and Doña Inez, and they'll be happy in their lives while I—I'll have no one, except the children she gave me—Why, *Señor Dios,* did she have to die? What sin had she committed—no—what sin had I committed in Thine eyes to offend Thee, to take her from me?"

Jorge Pastronaz had come out of the chapel, gone to a toolshed, and as quietly as he could, taken a spade from it, then hesitantly approached the grief-stricken young Spaniard. "If it pleases you, Señor de Escobar, I—I'll dig the grave. Tell me where you want it."

"*Sí.* She would love to see the sky and the valley, and to be near the river. The river that gives us the water of life. It is a ways from here—"

"I'll gladly go with you, Señor de Escobar."

Carlos nodded, reached for Esperanza's reins, and walked slowly toward the south. The *hacienda* was still dark, though by now he knew that Tía Margarita would be going to the kitchen to prepare the *desayuno* for the members of the household, as well as for the *trabajadores.* And this thought again brought new tears to his swollen eyes, for he remembered how many mornings he had gone out to banter with the fat, good-natured cook and to wheedle her into preparing a special breakfast for his beautiful young Apache bride.

He led Esperanza nearly a quarter of a mile to the south, near the river bordering the lands of the Hacienda del Halcón, and there, on a gentle slope that looked down onto the broad expanse of valley, turned to the young Mexican worker and said hoarsely, "She would like it here."

"At once, Señor de Escobar." The young Mexican crossed himself and then assiduously began to dig into the earth. Carlos could not bear to watch. He turned to look toward the east, watching the sun slowly rise above the

horizon with purplish and rosy hues that characterized a crisp
fall dawn. Beyond, everywhere the eye could see, there were
vast expanses of grazing land, of bushes and trees and even
verdant flowers in their wild clumps. All this was the domain
of his family. It was peaceful and serene—an eternity away
from the dreadful nightmare of the reality he could never, in
his wildest dreams, have conjectured. His lips compressed, he
stood straight, holding the reins of the palomino. From time
to time he crossed himself as he heard the thud of earth
which Jorge Pastronaz swiftly and deftly flung to one side.

"It is ready, Señor de Escobar."

"Gracias." Carlos took a deep breath and forced himself
to turn back to Esperanza. Then, very gently, he unfastened
the thongs which bound his young wife's lifeless body to the
mare, lifted her up in his arms, and made sure that the
blanket was wrapped protectively around her.

Then he moved to the large, deep grave the young
Mexican had dug, and even more carefully laid her down into
it. Emerging, he reached down for a handful of earth and
held it in his right hand as he stared for a last time at
Weesayo's face. Her death mask was one of agony and
despair, and he burst into heartrending sobs as he opened his
hand and let the earth fall upon that tortured visage, which
had once been the dearest in all the world to him. "Farewell,
Beloved Woman, Light of the Mountain," he murmured as
his voice choked in the unnatural silence of the dawn. "Go to
Dios, and may He keep your unprofaned soul in heaven."

Then he turned his back and let Jorge fill the grave. He
did not turn again until the Mexican hesitantly murmured, "It
is finished. *Con su permiso,* Señor de Escobar, I will say the
prayer I learned."

"I thank you for it, *amigo.*" Carlos sank down to his
knees, folding his hands and bowing his head beside Weesayo's grave.

Jorge began, in a hesitant Spanish, trying to express
himself in the pure Castilian that would be expected of the
son of a hidalgo such as Carlos de Escobar, but using mostly
the everyday Mexican idiom to which *trabajadores* were most
accustomed: "Be mindful, O *Dios,* of Thy servants who are
gone before us with the sign of faith, and sleep in the sleep of
peace. Oh, most merciful Lord Jesus, give unto them eternal
rest. We pray here for Weesayo, the wife of Carlos de
Escobar. We pray that her soul will be received by Thee, pure
and stainless as she was in life and in death. . . ."

"Amen," Carlos said half to himself, his eyes tightly closed as a spasmodic shudder ran through him.

"To her, O *Dios,* and to all that rest in Christ, grant, we beseech Thee, a place of refreshment, light, and peace. Through the same Christ Our Lord, Amen," the young *trabajador* concluded. He made the sign of the cross and knelt down beside Carlos.

After a long moment Carlos turned to him and said in a voice that shook with emotion, "Even Padre Moraga could not have done better. I bless you, and I am grateful to you for this comfort, Jorge Pastronaz. And now leave me. I shall pray at her grave and then go back into the *hacienda* and tell them what has taken place."

Kneeling beside his young wife's grave, his hands clasped in prayer, Carlos had no awareness of time. The sun had risen, the day was bright and pleasantly warm despite the autumnal season, yet Carlos felt drained, hollow, and lifeless. As he stared at the freshly formed mound of earth that marked Weesayo's final resting place, his mind was tortured by a thousand visions of her: as he had first seen her emerging from Descontarti's wickiup; as he had watched her about the tasks she performed for her father and mother, much as any obedient young daughter would; at the ceremonials of dancing and ritualistic worship in which she had appeared as the Beloved Woman, and finally, when she had taken him to their secret honeymoon wickiup, which she had helped fashion and decorate with her own soft hands, providing food and drink so that they need not stray for those ten magical days and nights that were allotted by Apache law.

He saw her again in his mind's eye in the little chapel in Taos, as he married her in the Catholic faith, to which she had acquiesced so eagerly in order to please him and his father, Don Diego. And then there was the joy of the three children she had borne him, and the pride Carlos had felt in this intermingling of their Apache and Spanish blood. In every way, though she had adhered to the code of her people, she had adapted herself with a winning ease to the Spanish way of life. In all things, she had been truly the Beloved Woman: everyone at the *hacienda* had loved and respected her, as assuredly as did her people back in the stronghold. To be permitted to share life with this gentle, serenely wise, and beautiful young woman had seemed to him to be the very epitome of life's meaning.

He was dazed with the full realization of his loss. Only now, seeing this fresh grave, did he begin to comprehend that for the rest of his days he would never again see that sweet face, nor those dark, earnest eyes, searching his. He would never again hear her lilting voice or the exquisite silences between them, which were more than words. He would never again feel her touch and all her womanly tenderness. Suddenly he was bone-weary, and he flung himself face down upon her grave and wept aloud, "*Dios*, Holy Virgin, and all the saints, what harm did she do anyone, why did she have to die so horribly, so uselessly? And now, I am bereft; I must begin again to take up my life—I have our children, true enough, but when I look at them, I will see only my Weesayo, and yet I shall never see her again in this life. Merciful *Dios*, master of the world and of all of us, give me courage, for I have none left now. . . ."

"*Mi hijo*, come, let us pray in the chapel. And you must take something to eat—you are exhausted; she would not have wanted you to neglect yourself this way!" the hoarse, choked voice of Don Diego de Escobar broke through his agonized nostalgia. Slowly, Carlos knelt up, wanly rose, and turned to see his father holding out his arms, his lips trembling, tears misting his eyes. And Doña Inez was beside him, a handkerchief to her eyes, her head bowed.

"Oh, my father, my father, it's too much to bear!" Carlos cried out as he flung himself into his father's arms.

"That is right, my son, cry it out. Those are not tears to be ashamed of, by the bones of all the saints!" Don Diego gruffly declared as he hugged Carlos in a convulsive grip and looked at Doña Inez, shaking his head in his own overwhelming sorrow. "Come, Carlos, you must take some nourishment—a cup of chocolate and a biscuit. The young *trabajador* Pastronaz went to the kitchen and told Tía Margarita—that is how we knew—and we rode out to where he said you were. Oh, my son, my son, I would to God you could have been spared this grief!"

Carlos groaned, but finally he straightened and fought for self-control. "How is little Dawn?"

"The fever seemed to break about midnight," his father gravely responded. "Catarina was so good with the little one. And she would not sleep until she was certain that Dawn was better. She was up all night with her."

But Carlos was staring at Weesayo's grave now. "Can I ever blot it out of my mind?" he finally said. "Will it sear my brain and scar it for the rest of my life?" His voice rose in almost a shout, and he clenched his fists. Then, trying to recover himself, he murmured dully, "I must make a marker—"

"Of course, *mi hijo*, of course. I shall have Estéban Morales begin work on it this very day."

"You're very kind, my father. Forgive me—and you, Doña Inez—"

"*Querido* Carlos, there is nothing to forgive. Only in your heart you must try to forgive those evil ones who took her life. Do not forget what Christ Himself said upon the cross, 'Father, forgive them, for they know not what they do.' You must keep that thought with you, Carlos." Doña Inez was very close to tears as she put her hand on Carlos's shoulder.

"I know, I tell myself that, Doña Inez. And yet how can I, a mere man, have such capacity for forgiveness?" His voice was bitter, then he closed his eyes a moment and again sought to regain his composure. "Tasumi said that he would ride to the stronghold to tell them there what happened to the Beloved Woman. And they will send a runner on to Taos to bring back Padre Moraga. I want him to give a memorial service at her grave." He turned away swiftly, unable to speak anymore. Don Diego and Doña Inez exchanged a compassionate glance, and then the latter came to him and gently took his arm and said, "Come, we shall have *desayuno* together. It will do you good to be with people who love you. We want to share your grief, for she was as beloved to us as if she had been our own daughter. Come, dear Carlos."

Four

For the next several weeks Carlos was disconsolate. John Cooper, as well as his lovely Catarina, had learned of Weesayo's tragic fate the morning the young Spaniard returned, and they had done their best to console him. Catarina had insisted, "My brother, I want to take care of your three children. It's my duty now." At this, the handsome young Spaniard had forced a wan smile to his bleak face. "And I swear to you they'll be brought up to remember her always," she avowed.

He had taken her hand and kissed it, as he would have done that of a duchess, and with tears in his eyes he had said hoarsely, "I have no words to thank you, my little sister. And you, John Cooper, who saved my life. And yet at times I say to myself, what if I had not gone riding in the mountains and hurt my leg? Then you'd not have taken me to the Apache stronghold, and then—" John Cooper, understanding his brother-in-law's unforgettable anguish, had simply gripped his hand and interrupted, very gently, "You mustn't think such things. Think only what happiness she gave you, and that her spirit will be in the children she bore you, *amigo*."

So, as best he could, Carlos de Escobar went through the motions of occupying himself during the endlessly long days. At times he worked with Miguel Sandarbal, but his heart was scarcely in his labors. Don Diego, greatly concerned over the diffidence which his stalwart son now showed, even though he understood it well, at last received a letter from Don Sancho's courier that made him brighten and say to Doña Inez, "At last, by the will of our dear Lord, I have news of something that may give Carlos a new reason for living."

"And what is that, my dear one?" His handsome, gray-haired wife had been sitting with their little daughter on her knee, reading to her from a book of Arabian Nights adventures. Now she looked up anxiously at her husband, her finger marking the place in the book where she had left off.

Don Diego beamed at her and his daughter, shook his head, and sighed, "Even in tragedy there is some joy, my Inez. Do you remember those two young Missourians, Matthew Robisard and Ernest Henson, who came to trade and were dragged at horse's tails to Santa Fe?"

"I shall never forget, nor the kindness of that sergeant who allowed them to spend some time at the *hacienda* before they were banished," Doña Inez promptly replied.

"Yes, and the romantic ending of that story—young Henson asked if he might take our *criada* Carmelita with him to St. Louis, and how the two of them were married before they set out for Carmelita's new home."

"Indeed I do! And how kind you were to them—God

blessed you for that, and He blessed me in giving me to you."
His wife blushed and lowered her eyes.

"*Querida,* young Henson now has two fine sons by his
Carmelita. Not knowing our whereabouts, he sent a letter to
Taos, which Don Sancho has forwarded to us, inquiring after
not only my health but yours and that of the rest of our
family. He writes that his partner, Matt Robisard, has sent
John Cooper a gift, which should be arriving here at any
time. But he also writes to say that he thought I might be
interested in the arrival of a man who wishes to bring
American colonists into this area. Henson still believes, as
does Robisard, that there must be peace between our two
nations, and that open, free trade is the safest way to achieve
this."

"I believe that myself, Diego."

"Just so, my dear one. At any rate, he named this man,
Moses Austin. It appears that Austin was born as a frontiersman on the far East Coast and has great ability, except
that fortune has slipped through his fingers. He has moved
repeatedly, as Henson informs me, and after the War of 1812
and the failure of a bank in which he was interested, he was
virtually bankrupted. So he turned again to seek a new
frontier and is now convinced that the broad expanse of
Spanish Texas will be the place, not only for his new fortune,
but also for the amity between our two countries."

"He is an idealist, as you are, my dear one."

"You flatter me too much, dear Inez. All the same, since
Henson knows that Don Sancho and I are Spaniards of liberal
outlook, he told Austin about us. Now what I propose is that
since Austin plans on arriving in San Antonio early next
month to meet with Governor Antonio de Martínez to seek
permission for an American settlement, I should very much
like to meet him and to give him some of my ideas as to how
he may approach these stubborn Spanish officials."

"I am sure, with your experience at the court of Spain,
dear Diego, you can instruct him well," Doña Inez said,
smiling.

"Again you flatter me too much. No, but we know from
my own son-in-law, John Cooper, that Americans are forthright and often too plainly spoken to suit the devious temper-
aments of many an official. Especially those who have great
power and bask in the knowledge that they alone can dispense it. So I will send one of the *trabajadores* to San Antonio

to greet Moses Austin and invite him to journey here before
he undertakes this interview with the governor."

"That is a wonderful idea, Diego!"

"In my old age," the gray-haired hidalgo murmured
"nothing would please me more than to bring about an
alliance between this old world and the new. Have we not
seen how well it has worked out in my own household, with
John Cooper making my Catarina the perfect husband, and
helping her become a considerate, thoughtful, and devoted
wife and mother? See what she has done with Carlos's three
children. She has been most capable in explaining to them the
news of Weesayo's death, and already they began to take to
her as if she were their own mother."

"I think more of her now than I have ever done before,
to be truthful with you, Don Diego. And you think this
Moses Austin will come here and that, perhaps, Carlos will be
interested in the idea of American settlements?"

"Decidedly. Why, it is even possible that Carlos might
wish to escort this man to the governor. It will give him
something to do, a challenge for his mind. I see how he frets
himself, riding horseback, going out in the fields with the
cattle and the sheep, always with that sad look in his eyes.
And I have cautioned the *trabajadores* not to allude to the
tragedy, for it would only upset him."

"You are a good, kind man. I knew that from the first
day my sister became your wife, Diego. I have always known
it, and I cherish you for it."

"My dear one," Don Diego said. Then he took a chair
and put out his hand to his daughter. "Come now, Francesca,
sit in my lap and tell me a story."

"But, *mi padre,* you can tell better stories," the little girl
saucily replied, at which both Don Diego and Doña Inez
burst into laughter, as they hugged their daughter.

The day after this conversation, Esteban Morales, who
was working with the *trabajadores* out in the grazing fields,
spied five riders coming from the west and alerted his men.
During the years at the Hacienda del Halcón there had been
few visitors, mainly hunting parties of Indians who had been
friendly and traded horses for beef. As the riders neared, the
assistant foreman joyously cried out, "Why, it's Padre Moraga,
amigos! Now we shall have a real service in the chapel, so
that we may obtain the mercy of the loving *Señor Dios!*"

Four of the Jicarilla Apache braves flanked the white-haired, frail priest who rode on a gentle mare. Esteban was the first to greet him and bowed his head as he kissed the priest's hand, then eagerly ordered one of the workers to ride back to the *hacienda* to tell Don Diego and John Cooper of the priest's arrival. Meanwhile, he asked another of the workers to escort the Apache braves to the bunkhouse, where they would reside for the duration of the priest's visit.

"How good of you to make the long, tiring journey here, Padre Moraga," Don Diego exclaimed as he hurriedly approached the old priest. He knelt and kissed the man's hand, then rose and crossed himself. "You come at a time when you are most needed. My son, Carlos, is beside himself with grief over Weesayo."

"I wept when the news was brought to me from the Apache stronghold," the old priest murmured, crossing himself. "That same day, I said mass for her sweet soul. Our just God, I feel certain, received her soul and knew that she was as truly a good Christian as any one of you here."

"Amen to that, Padre. Carlos is out riding with Miguel. It has grieved me all these weeks to see how he struggles within himself, how he tries to find something to occupy his time, and, also, which concerns me the most, how seldom he plays with the children. It is as if he were punishing himself for having been guilty of her death," Don Diego soberly declared.

"I will see him alone before I give the service. I shall do my best to comfort him. Yet his grief shows how deeply he loved this sweet, wise young woman who, in no way, offended any of God's creatures."

"Thank you for coming, Padre Moraga. There is a young worker here, Jorge Pastronaz, who comforted my son that terrible night when he returned with his wife's body. He helped Carlos bury her and said the prayer for the dead. And he told Carlos that he wishes to serve our dear Lord and to be a communicant."

The old priest's face was aglow. "That is a wonderful thing. I shall talk to him, too. If he is earnest in his desires, I have within me the power to consecrate him as a lay friar. He will then be able to hold mass for you and your family, as well as the *trabajadores*."

"It would be good to have such a man among us who could relay your kindliness and concern for our souls, Padre Moraga," Don Diego told him. "You will take some refreshment and rest a little after so wearying a journey."

"It is kind of you, Don Diego. I confess I am beginning to feel my years."

"And what is the news from Taos?"

"I fear there is unrest. Nueva España is threatened with revolution—even to the point of breaking away entirely from the monarchy and declaring its independence. In Taos the people feel themselves cut off from Nueva España, and their loyalties begin to be divided. Also, there are those who, as you well remember, were enemies to you and who still hold vindictive grudges. One of them, especially, has sought to find your whereabouts, which as yet the trustworthy Don Sancho de Pladero has not betrayed."

"Yes, I know him to be a good friend, and I am grateful for that," the hidalgo said, nodding. "I think I can guess the name of my most steadfast enemy. It is the man who replaced Don Sancho as *alcalde mayor,* Don Esteban de Rivarola."

"Just so, my son," Padre Moraga concurred. "I have sought in the confessional to try to instill within him a gentler spirit—but I fear my poor efforts have been in vain. And though the church does not mingle with the affairs of state, I sense from his remarks, and also from his actions in Taos, that he is impatient for the independence of Nueva España, in order to further his own ambitious ends."

"He will be very dangerous, then. But come, I keep you from your refreshment and rest. I have a room for you, and Tía Margarita will bring you *el almuerzo.*"

Padre Moraga knelt before the altar in the little chapel, praying aloud, while Carlos de Escobar, his face drawn and his eyes red and swollen from incessant tears, knelt in the first pew row.

"Merciful Lord of our fathers, and of all mankind from the beginning of Thy inspired creation, grant Carlos, Thy son, peace of heart and an easing of his grief. Let him find solace in the mercy of Thy judgment on his innocent wife, Weesayo. Let him take new purpose in life, for he is young and strong and a true believer in Thy eternal wisdom and justice. Amen."

The priest rose with an effort and turned, his face grave with concern. "My son, you cannot persist in this grief. It will destroy you, and she would not have wished that. Your father and sweet Doña Inez, as well as your sister, Catarina, and your good friend John Cooper, are distressed for you. They are helpless to assuage your sorrow, and they fear lest compassionate and soothing words will only serve to reopen the grievous wound you have suffered. Can you not turn your mind to a healthy purpose, my son?"

"I've tried, Padre Moraga. I don't doubt the infinite wisdom of *el Señor Dios*—I'm not a blasphemer. And you know that I just confessed to you and told you how I said that I'd account to the devil if I'd taken the lives of innocent men—that sentry, and then Hernando, who swore to me in his terror that he had not abused my wife, that he had only obeyed the orders of his *patrón*."

"I know, my son. I do not think any man I know could have held his hand from his sword when he discovered what you did. Even though our God says, 'Thou shalt not kill,' the sin of that *hacendado* was detestable. But turn your mind from that now, Carlos. You have the children, and Catarina is tending them so very well. Promise me, my son, that you will pray earnestly for guidance and strength. He will grant it to you, He who judges sinners and saints alike."

"I know that, Padre Moraga." Carlos crossed himself as he rose with a weary sigh. "But you must give me time to think what I must do, I beg of you."

"It is your life, my son, and I am only a humble servant of *el Señor Dios*. You must search within your heart and mind to decide how you will resume your life. I know that what you decide upon will be honorable and purposeful. And now young Pastronaz will come to me, and in this chapel I will ordain him as acolyte of this *hacienda* with its loyal families and its God-fearing people. After that, my son, I shall go to her grave and there, in front of all assembled, perform the service."

"I'll never forget how kind you've been. Thank you, Padre Moraga." Carlos kissed the old priest's hand, then genuflected before the altar, turned, and left the chapel.

A few moments later the young Mexican *trabajador* entered, knelt down at once, and bowed his head to the altar, crossing himself. The frail old priest smiled and held out his arms: "Come, my son. Don Diego has told me of your devotion and your reverence to our blessed Savior. And I know how you comforted poor Carlos. Approach me and tell me of your background and how it was that you felt you had this calling."

"Thank you, Padre Moraga." The pleasant-featured young Mexican rose and, kneeling before the priest at the altar, told him how he had sworn to dedicate his life to the

service of the Lord. "But," the young man went on, "I do not
have the education to be a priest—"

"But you have the calling, you have the gift, you have
the heart," the frail old man smilingly interrupted as he laid
his hands on Jorge Pastronaz's head. "That counts far more
than learning. The prophets of the Old Testament were not
always scholarly men, but their hearts were filled with the
greatness of their love for God and their earnestness to
communicate that to their fellow men. I feel this in you, my
son. And perhaps it was with a kind of sense of anticipation,
when I made my pilgrimage here for the memorial service for
Weesayo, that I brought with me an old, worn volume of
masses. It will be my gift to you. Study them, absorb them,
and it does not matter if you miss a word here or there, so
long as the spirit moves you to comprehend how easy it is for
man to express his desire to follow in our Lord's footsteps.
Here especially, in this verdant land, where one sees the
handiwork of *el Señor Dios,* it is much easier to feel at peace
with him and His miracles."

"This is what I feel, also, Padre Moraga. They have been
very kind to me here. If in some small way I can return their
kindness by pronouncing these blessed words, I will be happy
that I have done an act of thanksgiving."

Then without further ado, old Padre Moraga ordained
Jorge Pastronaz as an acolyte, as a lay friar. At the conclu-
sion of the ordination both men said amen and crossed
themselves; then as Jorge rose, the priest took him by the
shoulders and kissed him on each cheek, his eyes wet with
tears. "And now you will assist me in the memorial service
for the beloved wife of Carlos de Escobar," he softly said.

All of the *trabajadores* and their families, Don Diego
and Doña Inez, John Cooper and Catarina, and Carlos,
attended the moving memorial service that old Padre Moraga
held at the grave of Weesayo. Esteban Morales had carved a
magnificent cross, painting it with a varnish made of oil and
resin to resist the erosion of weather and time. He had nailed
on the cross arm a metal plaque onto which he had engraved
"Weesayo, Beloved of Carlos," with the year of her birth and
the date of her death in figures below.

Throughout the ceremony Don Diego anxiously glanced
at his son and saw how anguish gnawed at the handsome
young Spaniard. Standing stiffly erect, his fists clenched at his
sides, he seemed to watch and yet not to see, as if an inner
drama were taking place within his mind's eye and as if he no

longer belonged to this locale and its denizens. At a pause in the ceremony, Don Diego turned to whisper to Doña Inez, "I'm greatly worried, my dear Inez. I fear that he will do something rash—though I understand it only too well. What terrible torture for such a fine young man to have to suffer." He shook his head: "I can only pray with Padre Moraga that time will heal Carlos's wound, as it is prescribed to heal those of all who have suffered anguish through the centuries before him."

After the ceremony Padre Moraga was a dinner guest at the table of Don Diego. The enormous mahogony dining room table, which had been handcrafted in Spain and which the *trabajadores* had crated and brought from Taos, was the focal point of the room, and tonight it was set with the finest Toledo silver and Madrid crystal.

The families took their places at the supper table, and there, answering questions put to him by both Don Diego and John Cooper, Padre Moraga told them what had been happening in Taos. Don Sancho de Pladero tried to rule with justice for all as intendant, while Don Esteban de Rivarola sought to gain more and more affluence and power. It was the latter, the old priest said, who eagerly hoped that severing ties with Spain would lead to a readjustment of the highest echelon of native-born Spanish officials. "You see, his sins are those of greed and envy, two of the worst of the seven deadly sins, Don Diego," Padre Moraga explained.

"And you're certain that Don Sancho has never let Don Esteban know where my father-in-law is living?" John Cooper pursued, reaching out for Catarina's hand, to squeeze it, and then, as his father-in-law whimsically smiled at him, to put it to his lips and kiss it, as might have done the most gallant Spanish cavalier.

"I'm certain that Don Sancho would never betray a confidence or a friendship, John Cooper, my son," Padre Moraga replied. "But what troubles me is that the old scoundrel Barnaba Canepa is still skulking about Taos and trying to ingratiate himself with *ricos* like Don Esteban. He is a gossip by nature, and he also does much harm. This, we of the *Penitentes* learned, as you all remember." He frowned, and his lips tightened as he remembered how *Los Penitentes*—the order of Penitent brothers, of which Padre Moraga was head—had in the past visited the shop of Canepa and had threatened the old man with the scourge if he continued to cause trouble in Taos. "I also know that this rogue at times bribes the *indios* of the pueblo, and also the poorest *peones,* to spy for him and to learn secrets that will be to his own profit."

"Then it's possible, Padre Moraga," John Cooper spoke up, "that Canepa might hire some fellow to watch Don Sancho and even follow the courier he sends here from time to time?"

"That is true, my son. That is what I fear. Indeed, when Kinotatay, chief of the Jicarilla, sent his messenger to me to tell me of Weesayo's death, I urged the messenger to instruct the escort they would send with me to take a kind of circuitous route, to throw any pursuer off the track. I think we were successful—I can only pray we were." He crossed himself. "I do not trust Don Esteban de Rivarola; I consider him a corrupt man who should be banned by Mother Church and even stripped of his title and power, for he is not worthy in his heart or soul. I can tell you many episodes of his treatment of the poor *indios,* of his lechery with his servant-girls and those others whom he covets and has brought to him. It is the curse of our world that gold and silver are able to be exchanged for human life."

"Padre Moraga, you as head of the *Penitentes* have done your best to drive these infidels from the temple," Don Diego praised the old priest.

But the latter shook his head sadly and, with humble mien, demurred, "No, no, my son, that is praise beyond my humble stature. It was the Son of our dear Lord who did that. Indeed, we of the *Penitentes* are unable to intimidate men like Don Esteban, and so he continues with his excesses. No, I am only a weather vane in Taos, and I am growing older and weaker with each new month."

During all this conversation, Carlos sat at his place, his eyes fixed on his plate, picking at his food. John Cooper nudged Catarina, who tried to engage her brother in casual conversation, but he returned only monosyllabic replies, till at last Don Diego, with a poignant look at old Padre Moraga, shook his head to tell Catarina not to pursue the attempt.

With dessert, port wine and brandy, as well as Madeira, were served. Then Carlos suddenly rose to his feet and stammered, his voice low and unsteady, "I beg to excuse myself. I'm not good company for anyone. Please forgive me." And with this he turned on his heel and left the dining room.

"Do you see what I mean, Padre Moraga?" Don Diego

wearily sighed. "It has been like this for more than a month. I
know that you have talked with him, but the memorial service
that you held undoubtedly plunged him into another fit of
despair. He is usually so resilient, so optimistic and vigorous—which shows all the more how much in love he was with
poor Weesayo. I don't know how much more I can do, but
believe me, *mi padre,* it begins to torture us as much as it
does him, and I do not know the solution."

"We must be very patient with him. He has had a
grievous hurt, and he understands the wastefulness of it—it is
very difficult to cope. Sometimes even prayers do not suffice,"
Padre Moraga said ruefully. Then, clasping his hands and
bowing his head, he said softly, "I will pray constantly for the
restoration of your son's will to live."

Five

The day after the memorial service, the *trabajadores* in
the fields observed a bearded man driving a wagon attached
to three sturdy geldings. He was dressed in buckskins, like
John Cooper Baines, not quite forty, with a thick, bristly,
graying beard and heavy sideburns, a bulbous nose, but a
genial mouth and sparkling eyes. Carlos and Catarina, who
stood close to her brother and had linked her arm with his,
watched as the wagon driver approached the spacious vesti-
bule of the *hacienda*. Don Diego and Doña Inez, having
heard of the arrival of the stranger, had come out to welcome
him. And John Cooper, with Lobo at his side, watched from
the doorway of the *hacienda*.

The bearded man descended from his wagon and uttered
a hearty laugh, "By all that's holy, it's taken me long weeks to
get here. Is there a John Cooper Baines here?"

"I'm the one you're looking for, stranger. Who are you?"
the young man demanded as he strode forward.

The bearded wagon driver stared him up and down, then
burst into an uproarious laugh. "You're just as old Matt

Robisard described you, damned if you're not. Maybe a little leaner in the hip, but that's because you're ranching out here in this godforsaken territory."

"I wouldn't agree to that. We've had a good life out here, away from Spanish oppression. Who might you be?" John Cooper repeated.

"I might be the emperor of Mexico, only I'm not. Name's Joel Verdon. I'm a trader out of St. Louis. There's my squaw, Oteenoway, in the back. No papooses yet, but I suspect she'll throw one before I'm done with this trip." He grinned from ear to ear and extended his hand to the young mountain man, who energetically shook it with a responsive grin.

"You say you're from St. Louis? Why did you come all this way to look for me?" John Cooper's curiosity was aroused.

"Because Matt Robisard's beholden to you, that's why, John Cooper Baines. And fry my liver in alkali if I didn't have to traipse all the way out of Taos till I could find out from the intendant they got there where you was now located."

"I remember Matt Robisard well, he and Ernest Henson," John Cooper said. "How is Matt?"

"Well, sir, he's found himself a nice, sprightly lass, name of Irma Vodak. She's a year old than he is, but he's smitten, for fair. And I suppose that when Ernie Henson brought back a pretty Mexican maid as his wife, Matt got a bit techy and felt how lonely he was, so he up and hitched himself to Irma. They've got two boys already, the spitting image of old Matt."

"I'm glad they both got back and are living happily in St. Louis. They couldn't have had that sort of life out here—or rather, back in Taos, not with all the Spanish restrictions on trade and the like," John Cooper said. "But you still haven't told me why you made this long trip all the way out to Taos and then back around here to seek me out."

"Well, sir, I owed Matt a couple of favors, so when he asked me to bring you two Irish wolfhound puppies, and since my trading goes on all year long, and I cover all the way from St. Louis out through Texas and even this place you call Taos and some of the borderline there, I figured I'd pay my debt to him. Yes, John Cooper Baines, about four months ago, when I started out, he gave me these two puppies and said he'd got them from a fancier who had quite a kennel near St. Louis. He felt he owed you them because of what he'd heard your dog Lije did, and then how his whelp, Lobo, took over. Is that Lobo beside you now?"

"Yes, it is. He's getting a little old in the tooth, just about nine, I figure. But he's still spry."

"I can see that," Joel Verdon said, warily eyeing the wolf-dog. "That's why I didn't make any sudden moves in getting down from my wagon. Now there, Oteenoway"—he turned back to the wagon to hail his plump, grinning wife—"you just hustle yourself out here with those puppies, mind you!" And then turning back to his amused audience, he scratched his forehead and avowed, "I'll be getting back to St. Louis, now that I've kept my word to Matt. Here's your puppies. Matt says they're real pedigreed. I don't know how that Lobo of yours is going to take to them, though."

"That'll be my worry, Mr. Verdon," John Cooper said, smiling. "I'm mighty grateful to you. And when you see Matt and Ernie, you give them all our best."

"I'll do just that. I'd be mighty obliged if you'd let me water my horse and buy some vittles from you to take back on my way to St. Louis," the trader said.

"You'll stay the night with us and rest up. There are rooms enough in this *hacienda* for you and your wife. And you won't have to pay for provisions. It's little enough I can do to thank you for bringing me these puppies," John Cooper asserted. The plump squaw, who spoke enough English to understand what her husband wanted, had emerged from the back of the wagon holding two slings, in each of which was a gangling young Irish wolfhound puppy. John Cooper lifted down the slings, holding both puppies in his arms and laughing aloud as each tried to nip his nose. "Darned if that doesn't remind me of old Lije!" he chuckled good-naturedly. "We'll make do just fine with them. Now you and your wife come in and freshen up before we have our meal."

"That's mighty kind of you, John Cooper Baines. Your Lobo doesn't seem to be too jealous," Joel Verdon added.

"It's taken a while to train him, but he knows better than to show he doesn't like anybody. He gets a good cuff across the chops when he does that. Anyway, I'll put them in one of our little sheds and look after them until they get big enough to shift for themselves. No, don't you worry, Lobo won't bother them any. Oh, he'll be eager enough to see what they're like and what they do, and I hope that he'll take to them. Now let's go have something to eat."

Joel Verdon was obviously delighted to be treated as a guest of honor at the spacious dining room table in the Hacienda del Halcón. He glanced at his Indian wife from time to time and chuckled as he watched her trying to eat her food with the ivory-handled knife and fork that had been provided. Finally, shaking his head, he guffawed, "It's no use to try to civilize Oteenoway, folks. I met her out in Iowa territory just about a year back, and we took to each other like ducks to water."

"She's an Ayuhwa, then?" John Cooper inquired.

Verdon emphatically nodded. "That she is, John Cooper Baines."

"I know them well. I lived with them for a few years, you see. They're very peaceful."

"That's true enough. Only right now they're in the same boat most Indians are in these parts—the government getting edgy about the trouble they're causing white settlers, and their own gosh-darned rules about what they can eat and what they can't, and not to be beholden to the white man. Beats me for fair, except when I get into their villages and start showing the trinkets and the beads and the shawls and all the things they'd want for their squaws, they're as pleasant a tribe as you could come by."

John Cooper made a sign to Verdon to desist, for he could see that Carlos was growing more and more ill at ease. This talk of Indians inescapably reminded them all of Carlos's agonizing loss. Don Diego quickly changed the subject by lifting his glass of port and exclaiming, "A toast to Señor Verdon! Let us drink to the day when all Americans feel welcome in Texas."

John Cooper was obviously pleased at this reception of the rough-and-ready mountain man, and after the toast he exchanged a few words with the man's wife, whose language he had learned so many years earlier when he had lived among her people.

John Cooper was delighted with the two Irish wolfhound puppies and promptly called them Hosea and Jude, taking these names from the Bible, from which his faithful Lije had also been named. Although Lobo, now nine years old and discernibly not as quick as he had been in past years, had become accepted by everyone at the Double H Ranch, the young mountain man thought it best to defer the confrontation between the two male puppies and the wolf-dog. He wasn't quite sure how he would bring that about because it had been a known fact, since before he was born, that male dogs never took to one another at first, unless they were out of the same litter. But one thing was certain: Lobo was going to have to adapt himself to the newcomers.

Matthew Robisard's letter, which Joel Verdon had brought along, extended grateful thanks to both John Cooper and Don Diego for their part in getting him and his comrade Ernest Henson out of serious trouble in Santa Fe, when they had been arrested as suspected spies for an alleged American army of occupation in New Mexico. And the St. Louis trader had added, "I hope these puppies will grow up to be a help to your ranch, just like your wonderful Lobo. I remember what you told me, John Cooper, about Lobo's being sired by that heroic Lije, who saved your life and gave his up for you. Well, the man I bought them from had brought them from Ireland, just as you told me your father had brought Lije, so they should be of top pedigree. I hope you'll never have to use them to defend yourself against enemies, but I'm also sure that, if that should happen, you'll know just how to train them. I might tell you that I bought one myself, and although my lovely wife is a little apprehensive, I've convinced her that, if I take him for a run and train him, she won't have any extra chores or need to fear the dog. God bless you again for all you've done, you and Don Diego, and my warmest wishes for a long, happy life to every member of your family, and that means your workers and their families, too."

John Cooper had shown this letter to Padre Moraga, in the course of a walk the two men had taken the day after the memorial service for Weesayo. For one thing, the young mountain man wanted to discuss the hidden silver mine and the disposition of the fabulous treasure still concealed within it. For another thing, he wanted to have a more intimate discussion with the old priest on what might be done to restore Carlos to a sanguine outlook.

Padre Moraga chuckled softly after he had read Matthew Robisard's letter, and remarked with a wry smile, "You remember your Bible pretty well, John Cooper. Perhaps you'll recall that moral which says that when one casts one's bread upon the water, it is always returned a hundred and even a thousandfold. I have a feeling that these two puppies will play an important role in the well-being of this peaceful *hacienda*."

"Well, Padre Moraga, the first worry I have is how Lobo

is going to take to them. He's had the run of the roost, just about, all these years, and I'm not sure he's going to take kindly to finding two males disputing his right to all the attention. You know, I was thinking that I might give one as a pet to Carlos. Maybe that would help distract him a little."

"It's a good thought, my son." The old priest slowly shook his head and sighed. "Actually, he must work out his own destiny, for that is the only way he will be content. No, Carlos is a strong young man, with a very fierce will of his own. His happiness has been so great, so unexpected, with that unfortunate young woman, that it will be a long time before he can forget what he believes to be the injustice of her having been taken from him." Padre Moraga looked up at the sky and crossed himself. "But in the last resort, He will send Carlos the sign that will turn him back to taking up his life. For you and me, it remains only to be kind to him, to be indulgent and not to prod him too much. He's very proud."

"Yes, he certainly is that," John Cooper agreed. Then, glancing around to make certain that no one was within hearing, he said in a low voice, "I heard what you said about Don Esteban de Rivarola, *mi padre.* I gather, from that news of yours, that the poor people are suffering even more than they did when I was living back in Taos."

"You are right, my son. The *ricos,* in spite of all the humanitarian action which Don Sancho de Pladero has taken in his post of *intendente,* seem to be fighting among themselves to see who will become the strongest, the richest, the most powerful. With that, comes corruption of the soul, and I am afraid that Don Esteban is well on his way to being beyond the redemption of the confessional. Not a week goes by, but I do not hear news of one or another of his cruelties. I have tried my best to remonstrate with him, but he sneers at me and tells me that my sermons are for the poor and for the stupid, not for a nobleman like himself."

"What I'm getting at, Padre Moraga, is that I plan, as soon as I see that Carlos is getting back his good spirits, to pay a visit to that mine and to bring you one of the ingots. You'll distribute the money to the poor, as you've done before. That old shopkeeper back in Taos, he's still reliable and would melt down the ingot and exchange it for food and clothing?"

"Heitor Nuñez died, my son, shortly after your last visit to Taos. But Ignazio Peramonte, also a shopkeeper and also one of the Penitent Brothers, is a trustworthy man. He melted down the last ingots you brought to me, and he, like Heitor Nuñez, has never yet betrayed the confidence I've shown in him. But I warn you, since all of us are mortal and since I am not long until the end of my days, you must give some thought to what you will do with that mine if another priest should replace me."

"You shouldn't talk like that, Padre Moraga. Taos needs a man like you, and I'm sure that God will give you many more years."

"No man has a covenant with God, my son. I would be a fool and guilty of the same selfish pride of which Don Esteban has far too much, if I were to believe myself indispensable. Yes, you must think of the future, John Cooper. I shall go back to Taos tomorrow, for if my absence is prolonged, a man like Don Esteban, and certainly that conniving old gossip of a Barnaba Canepa, will begin to suspect my absence and may try to spy on my coming and going."

"I will tell the braves who escort you to Taos to also take a message to Kinotatay, when they return to their stronghold. I want him to know that none of us has forgotten the help he gave us in moving here to our new *hacienda*. And I want to tell him again that, as his blood brother, I stand ready at his summons to come to his aid if ever he is attacked by enemies."

"You are a good man, my son. May the Lord smile upon you and Catarina and your children, and on all of those here who keep His holy commandments."

"Amen," John Cooper murmured under his breath.

The next morning, the frail old priest took his leave with his four Apache escorts. He looked back to beam and wave at them, and John Cooper saw Carlos turn away and wearily walk toward the *hacienda*. He murmured to Catarina, "I'm really worried about your brother, *querida*. I know that Padre Moraga had a private talk with him, but it doesn't seem to have done much good. We're just going to have to be patient with him and hope that he gets things sorted out so he can take up his life again."

"I pray for that with all my heart, dear Coop," she said, covering her face with her hands and stifling her sobs as John Cooper tenderly put his arm around her and drew her to him, looking after the receding figure of Carlos and dolefully shaking his head.

Six

A few days after Padre Moraga's departure, plump, middle-aged Teofilo Rosas was just coming out of the bunkhouse as he spied Carlos and hailed him. This very morning, his lovely young wife, Leonora, had shyly told him that they were going to have another child, and his joy was complete. He remembered how, when Miguel Sandarbal had engaged him in Chihuahua to come to work as a sheepherder for Don Diego in Taos, he had ingenuously asked for Miguel's help in finding him a *mujer*. And the plump sheepherder remembered also how Miguel had disabused him of that notion and sharply told him that such a matter was up to Rosas himself. Well, how fortunate he was: Leonora was the best of wives, attentive, tender, and at night no man could want a more passionate sweetheart. And besides that, he had children who bore his name—indeed, the good *Señor Dios* had smiled upon him.

The December morning was radiant, with scarcely a cloud in the sky, and the brightness of the day made Teofilo feel his good fortune even more. Seeing Carlos ahead of him, the young Spaniard's face somber with his unshakable grief, he naively accosted him with a wave of his hand and a shout, "Señor Carlos, a word with you!"

Carlos stopped, slowly turned, and diffidently eyed the plump Mexican who hurried toward him. "*¿Qué pasa, hombre?*" he stonily demanded.

"Oh, come now, Señor Carlos, don't look so down in the mouth. It's such a beautiful day, and you're young, with all your life ahead of you. Look at me—when Miguel engaged my services in Chihuahua, I was the loneliest man in the world, and now look what I have to boast of. Yes, I know, it was a dreadful thing—just as every *trabajador* here, I was horrified at the news."

Carlos began to turn away, tightening his lips and

drawing a long breath, at this imposition on his tortured privacy. Teofilo, insensitive to such deep-rooted suffering, heedlessly went on: "Look, young master, as I said, you've all your life ahead of you. I know you're lonely. Well, there are plenty of young *criadas* here at the *hacienda* who would want nothing more than to have you smile at them. And they'd comfort you—at least for the time being, till you had another—"

"Swine, animal!" Carlos de Escobar hissed, his face white and taut. He drew back his fist and struck the plump sheepherder on the cheekbone, making Teofilo lose his balance and fall heavily with a groan as he rubbed his bruised cheek. Then realizing the enormity of his tactlessness, he babbled, "Forgive me—I shouldn't have—I didn't mean it that way—please, I was only trying—"

"I know. I ask your pardon, Teofilo. Just let me be, in the name of Heaven!" Carlos exclaimed, his voice trembling with resurgent grief.

Then he strode off toward the corral, where Miguel Sandarbal was standing and chatting with two of the newer *trabajadores*. "Miguel, have you a wild horse, one not yet tamed?" he hoarsely asked.

"Of a certainty, *mi compañero*." Miguel made a gesture to the two younger men to leave him as he solicitously drew closer to the young Spaniard. "There's one of about half a dozen Ramón and Luis brought in a week ago. That gray one there, with a short barrel and the mean look. But you don't want him, young master."

"Get me the reins and a bit. I don't need a saddle. And I want him. Just bring me what I asked for; I'll do the rest," Carlos curtly ordered.

Miguel eyed him wonderingly, then shrugged. "As you say, young master." He went to the stable and brought back the reins and the bridle with a bit. Carlos seized them without so much as a word of thanks and opened the gate of the corral. The wild mustang was wiry and not more than a yearling. As it saw this two-legged creature near it, it whinnied angrily, rearing up into the air and striking with its front hooves as Carlos leaped to one side. Then, infuriated that the man would not take heed of this warning, the mustang charged Carlos, who again leaped aside, as a matador might in leading a fresh bull in the arena.

"Be careful, young master, he's dangerous!" Miguel shouted, greatly alarmed at the young Spaniard's recklessness.

But Carlos, his eyes narrowed and fixed on the snorting mustang, ignored him, as with a thin-lipped smile he waited for his opportunity. Again the mustang rushed, and this section of the corral into which the wild horse had been quartered was narrow; the other captured mustangs were in a separate section off to one side, at least four times as large. Hence, Carlos's room to maneuver was limited, and this was what Miguel feared, though he knew that his young master had always shown expert horsemanship. Yet he sensed that there was a kind of desperation to this challenge of man against beast.

Teofilo Rosas realized his unpardonable tactlessness, and stood watching, openmouthed. He, too, perceived the intensity of this duel.

Carlos moved to his right, feinting his intention, and again the mustang charged at him. Swiftly, the young Spaniard leaped to the left and, in almost the same movement, leaped astride the wild horse. There was an angry whinny, and the mustang bucked and twisted itself, outraged at this intrusion on its liberty. Carlos leaned forward, his left hand clutching the thick mane, his other hand gripping the short reins to which the bridle and bit were attached, awaiting his opportunity.

Now, as if changing tactics, the gray mustang lowered its head and began to run in a circle within the narrow enclosure. Carlos held on grimly, crouching like an Indian, the fingers of his left hand tightly twisted into the thick mane. Suddenly the mustang stopped short, but Carlos had expected this maneuver and, by dint of clamping his wiry thighs against the horse's belly, managed to keep from being thrown. Miguel Sandarbal shouted encouragement: "Hold on, *mi compañero!* Show him you're a *gran vaquero!*"

The mustang now headed for the center of the enclosed section and stopped short, then reared up in the air, pawing with his front hooves. Carlos was nearly thrown but, exerting all his strength, managed to retain hold of the mane. The muscles of his thighs cruelly ached by now, and his face was taut and strained with both grim determination and fatigue.

The gray mustang suddenly twisted its head and, baring its muzzle, tried to nip at Carlos's leg with its teeth. This was what the young Spaniard had hoped for: swiftly he leaned toward the mustang's head and, with the kind of cast which a fisherman might essay with his rod, deftly placed the bit between the mustang's teeth. Then using both hands, he drew the reins up short.

There was an angry, strident whinny, from the pain caused by the bite of the metal bit. Carlos, the muscles of his forearms standing out, sweat dripping down his flushed cheeks, did not slacken the reins one whit, and feared that his unruly mount would suddenly try the ruse of threatening to lie down and roll over him and crush him with his weight.

At the same moment he shouted, "Open the gate, Miguel!" The foreman ran to it and flung it wide open while stepping back, breathlessly excited by the ferocious struggle between horse and rider.

The mustang's hooves came down hard, and Carlos was rudely jolted, but he did not lose control. Kicking his heels against the mustang's belly, he called out, "¡Adelante!" and the gray mustang, suddenly seeing that the barrier to freedom had been removed, raced toward the opening and out past Miguel and Teofilo Rosas, heading for the east and the uninhabited terrain it and its fellows had enjoyed before being captured.

"¡Bueno, Dolor!" Carlos shouted, a tight grin his only sign of triumph. He anticipated that the mustang would gallop almost to exhaustion. In its headlong flight, the gray horse stretched out its strong legs at the swiftest possible pace, and Carlos, glancing back, saw the buildings of the ranch recede behind him. He had already christened the mustang, since *dolor* meant "sorrow." This physical exertion was a kind of subconscious restoration of his vengeance on Don Pedro de Menguez; the mustang had faced him like an enemy, just as the evil *hacendado* had. Yet now he had a grudging admiration of the galloping gray horse, for its defiance and love of freedom matched his own troubled spirit.

The mustang tossed its head, fighting the bit again, and for an instant turned to look back at its persistent rider, then suddenly stopped short, almost pitching Carlos off its back. Only by an instinctive reflex of all his muscles did he manage to keep the grip of his thighs against the horse while he drew the reins up short in his right hand. Panting and gasping, his body aching with stress, he stared at the mustang, which turned its head round and again began to gallop with a kind of frenzied desperation.

"Bueno, bueno, Dolor, hate me, try to kill me, I will be

your master in spite of it," he shouted. In the silence of the broad plain around him on either side, his words reverberated. The air was mildly cool, though the sun shone brightly.

The mustang seemed to slacken its headlong gallop, and then suddenly came to a trot and then halted. Almost quizzically it turned its head to stare at him. Carlos exhaled a sigh of triumph. "Yes, now we both know, Dolor. I needed you, and you needed me, also. We have been good for each other, you and I. We are both sorrowful, but we know that there is honesty in a hatred which is not concealed, where there is no condescension or insolence. You and your strength against mine. I salute you, Dolor." With this he slackened the cruel bit, and he saw almost with a swirl of compassion that blood flecked the mustang's muzzle. Now the horse stood waiting, but its head did not droop; instead it tossed it from side to side, whinnying softly. Carlos abandoned himself, leaning forward over the horse's neck, closing his eyes, and letting exhaustion claim him. And with exhaustion came new tears, a purging kind of tears to relieve the pent-up agony that had churned and fermented in him all these dreadful weeks of realization.

"When you're rested, Dolor, we'll go back to the *hacienda*," he softly murmured as he patted the horse's neck. A soft answering whinny told him that a bond had been created between horse and man. It was a tenuous thing at best, but it was something he had managed to salvage, at a time when he had secretly feared for his own sanity. And yet the brooding torment was not entirely drained from him, and now Carlos de Escobar knew what he must do.

When Carlos returned to the *hacienda* toward the end of the afternoon, Miguel Sandarbal saw him riding astride the gray mustang and exhaled a sigh of deep relief. He beckoned to Teofilo Rosas and ordered, "Ride out to see how the sheep are faring, *hombre*. I think it's best you not be here when the young master returns."

"*Sí, sí, comprendo,*" the plump sheepherder hastily agreed. Hurrying to the stable, he let out his roan mare, already saddled, mounted it, and rode off as if for dear life.

Miguel stood with his hands on his hips, broadly grinning as he watched Carlos de Escobar ride toward him. "It was magnificent, *mi compañero,*" he exulted. But to his surprise Carlos only nodded and, without a word, rode toward the stable. He led the now-docile mustang into a stall and rubbed the animal down. Then, quickly looking about, he chose a saddle belonging to one of the elderly *trabajadores* and swiftly affixed it to the back of the horse he had named Dolor.

Carlos removed the bit and bridle and reins and hung them on a peg at the side of the stall, then went to bring back a bucket of oats and a pan of water, and set them down before the mustang. "Get your strength back; you will need it, *amigo*," he murmured, almost as if he were speaking to himself. Yet the mustang pricked up its ears and, eyeing him intently, tossed its head and nickered softly before attacking the generous provender.

Carlos wanly smiled, put out his hand, and with his knuckles rubbed the top of Dolor's head, as he always did with Lobo, the way John Cooper had taught him. The mustang stopped eating, lifted its head erect, and again stared intently at the young Spaniard. "Yes, Dolor, we understand each other. You will be my consolation. Eat well now, for we shall go off as soon as you've rested, to be by ourselves and think of the sorrow and of what is to come after it," Carlos murmured as he turned on his heel and left the stable.

Seven

Shortly before noon the next day, Esteban Morales rode in from the fields to excitedly announce that a gray-haired man was coming on horseback toward the *hacienda*, accompanied by one of the *trabajadores*. The stranger was a *gringo*, according to the assistant foreman, and Don Diego turned to Doña Inez, with whom he was sharing a light lunch, and eagerly exclaimed, "It is Señor Austin—he has decided to accept my invitation! Yes, my dearest Inez, if God wills it, the project of this farsighted *gringo* will make it possible for Carlos to distract himself over the loss he so keenly suffers. Finish your lunch, my dear one; I shall go welcome him. I shall also tell Tía Margarita to prepare more *almuerzo* for an unexpected guest."

Rising, Don Diego bent to kiss his wife's forehead as they exchanged a smile of complete understanding. Hurrying to the kitchen, he instructed the genial cook to lay out another plate for lunch and to bring some of his best Madeira out of the cellar. Then, flanked by the attentive Esteban, he left the *hacienda* and went outside to greet his distinguished guest.

Moses Austin was weather-scarred, with a high forehead and thick, graying hair, but his features were as alert as a young man's, particularly the keen, intent gaze of his gray-blue eyes. His straight nose, his firm mouth, his determined jaw marked him at once as a man of character and resolution, a man who would do everything in his power to carry out his dream of bringing settlers into Spanish-held Texas. Don Diego knew well that, to date, only a few Americans had made their way into this vast territory. After James Long's expedition, when an army of Americans had invaded and captured Nacogdoches, most of the settlers had been driven out by Spanish authorities. Don Diego realized that the Spanish complacently looked upon Texas as autocratically belonging to them, with only roving bands of Indians to be fended off. It was, indeed, the same complacency which had existed in Mexico City for so long and extended itself to the provinces and to Nuevo México, restricting trade, imposing penalties, barring communication, and hampering the growth of communities. Now Don Diego could see all this clearly: when he had first come to Taos, weighted down by the sorrow over his dead wife and his banishment from Madrid, he had unquestioningly accepted all that Spanish rule implied.

"Welcome to our *hacienda,* Señor Austin," Don Diego enthusiastically called out in excellent English as the frontiersman dismounted from his gray stallion. The *trabajador* who accompanied him at once took the reins of the horse and led it to the stable as Don Diego shook hands with his guest.

"It's a pleasure to meet you, Don Diego. Your workman found me as soon as I arrived in San Antonio, and as Governor Martínez will not be meeting with me for a few days yet, I decided to take you up on your invitation," Moses Austin declared in a strong baritone voice. "Ernest Henson in St. Louis told me all about you and how you believe in opening up this wonderful country to American settlements and trade."

"I do indeed. I supervised the annual fairs in Taos, Señor Austin, and long ago I was disgusted at the greediness and connivances of the merchants who had a monopoly granted them by our viceroy in far-off Mexico City."

"Henson informed me how you had helped American traders who otherwise would have been imprisoned, perhaps even shot," Austin declared as he followed his host into the *hacienda*.

Soon, a most convivial and appetizing lunch was served by Tía Margarita, and Moses Austin lifted his glass of Madeira and toasted Doña Inez and then Don Diego: "Long life and good health and happiness to you both, and my warmest thanks for this hospitality."

"You do us honor by visiting us," Don Diego courteously replied. "Tell me of your proposal to the governor. I, for one, believe that the only future of this country will be in opening it up to the *gringo*, the American. When there is competition in trade goods, prices can be regulated, and we shall no longer be at the mercy of the greedy Mexican dealers who charge us a high price for what we buy and give us a correspondingly low one for what we try to sell them or trade them."

"Exactly, Don Diego." Austin set down his glass and leaned back in his chair. "Briefly, I intend to see Governor Martínez and suggest to him that I'm not exactly a *gringo*, since at one time when I lived in Spanish Louisiana, I was a subject of the king of Spain. Now I wish to return to my earlier allegiance, and yet by way of amalgamation, as you might say, I'm going to ask his permission to settle three hundred American families in this territory of Texas. They will be peaceful families, intent only upon farming, perhaps raising cattle, making themselves useful to the community and helping it grow. They will offer no military threat whatsoever—I must make that very clear to His Excellency. And the only arms my settlers will carry will be sidearms and perhaps a few rifles needed to defend themselves against hostile Indians, or to hunt what may be in the area we are permitted to settle."

"It seems most sensible. But I must warn you, Señor Austin, that Spanish officials are—or at least thus far they have been—insensitive, even to the requests of their subjects to allow free trade. The reason is very obvious, as I am sure you know. If only Spanish or Mexican goods are brought into Texas, or New Mexico, any price which the viceroy desires to set can be imposed upon us. If we want the goods, we must pay the high tariff—it is as simple as that."

"I understand that perfectly. But I propose to show Governor Martínez, if I'm given the chance, that if we take part as peaceful subjects under Spanish rule in Texas, we will allay his fears about any military occupation, and at the same time create a need for greater supplies and, thus, more of a market. And we'd have open competition and increase the demand which these new settlers will supply. I'm sure he can see the practical wisdom of increasing his revenue."

"If logic were an inevitable effect of consideration, Señor Austin, then I should say that the governor would readily accept your proposal and welcome you with open arms. But I personally am somewhat doubtful. Moreover, there are not many Spanish or Mexican families in Texas at this moment; only San Antonio has any sort of colonization. And thus far, the inhabitants of that city depend, without exception, on what goods are sent across the Rio Grande. You see, I was formerly intendant of Taos in Nuevo México, a post which I relinquished in favor of my good friend, Don Sancho de Pladero, and there we were almost entirely cut off from trade. The Santa Fe Trail, which first enters Taos and then takes goods on to the capital of New Mexico, is still forbidden to American traders, and this will be the case as long as the province is dominated by the viceroy and his officials. Yet I can see very clearly that if Governor Martínez grants your petition, the foundation will be laid for the eventual entry of American traders into Nuevo México. Then perhaps the control of the Santa Fe Trail will not be so rigid, and we can have a commercial thoroughfare all the way from the Missouri settlements to Santa Fe itself. I shall certainly favor it."

"You're most kind. You hearten me in my resolve. If, of course, Governor Martínez rejects my proposal, I must see what I can do in finding a sympathetic champion to phrase my paltry ideas and my American speech into the flowery language of the Spanish tongue, which may convince His Excellency that it would be a very good idea and most profitable to his government."

"I would be happy to write such a letter, if the need arises, Señor Austin," Don Diego said warmly, then added, "You mentioned that you lived in Spanish Louisiana."

"Yes, in 1797, I inspected lead mines near St. Louis in that territory, was given a grant in the mining region, and a year later moved my family westward to a new home under the Spanish flag. This is the basis of my introduction to Governor Martínez, that in a sense I am not so much a *gringo* as a loyal Spanish subject, willing to accept his regulations and to cooperate in the most amicable fashion."

"You will have a good deal in your favor. But come now, do not let your lunch get cold. Tía Margarita prides herself on the way she prepares chicken with green peppers and almonds: it is a dish you might find in the elegant Creole restaurants of New Orleans, but seldom in this comparatively uninhabited country."

"Indeed you're right; it's most tasty. My compliments to your cook." Moses Austin smiled and then began to eat his lunch. Don Diego frowned, leaned over toward Doña Inez, and whispered, "What is keeping Carlos? He was not at breakfast this morning, and no one has said a word to me about what he is doing. Can he possibly be out riding his horse, still despondent?"

"Be patient, dear Diego. I am sure he will be in directly. If you would like, I'll go out to the kitchen and ask one of the *criadas* to call him in, if he is anywhere in the *hacienda*."

"I wish you would, dear Inez," Don Diego murmured, then turned back with a warm smile to his guest. "My son, Carlos, will be extremely interested in your proposal, Señor Austin. Thanks to the help of my son-in-law, John Cooper Baines, a *gringo* of great courage, I believe that all of us here have learned that it is high time we offered the hand in friendship to those who wish to extend the frontier and to live with us in friendship and peace and in good commerce."

"That has always been my feeling. My son, Stephen, shares my beliefs, and in the event that I should fail, I am certain that he will carry on in my stead with greater youth and strength and resolve."

"I believe, Señor Austin, that your proposal will be crowned with success, judging by your own energy. To me you seem a youthful man, but it is undoubtedly the vigor of your idea which gives the lie to your mature years," Don Diego smilingly responded.

Doña Inez came back into the dining room, and Moses Austin courteously rose to acknowledge her presence. There was a worried look on her handsome face as she said somewhat nervously, "Diego my dear, Marquita told me in the kitchen that she had not seen Carlos all day long, and she herself went to the bunkhouse to ask Miguel Sandarbal. He has not seen him, either. And worst of all, when I went to his room, I saw that his bed had not been slept in all night."

"What could have happened to him?" Don Diego half rose from his chair. Then shaking his head in self-reproof, he explained, "You will forgive me, Señor Austin, my son recently lost his wife, and he was deeply in love with her. He has been beside himself, understandably. That was why I had hoped he would be here, to listen to you talk about American settlements. I even hoped that perhaps he might volunteer to be of some aid to you if he could."

"My condolences, Don Diego. What a tragic thing for a young man to lose his wife. But please don't upset yourself. Moreover, I shan't abuse your hospitality—I'd like to leave for San Antonio in a few hours, after I've rested. It was very difficult to secure an interview with Governor Martínez, and I want to be sure I'm back in plenty of time for our appointment. The sooner I can get my proposal before Governor Martínez, the sooner I'll be able to learn what chance of success I have and, if he should reject it, to consider another way that might achieve the end I've in view."

Trying to hide his great concern over his son's mysterious absence, Don Diego nonetheless saw to it that his guest was granted every comfort. The hidalgo himself led the frontiersman to a comfortable guest room with a spacious bed and invited him to rest, then said, "I shall assign another of my *trabajadores* to accompany you to San Antonio, Señor Austin, so that he can report back to me of the success of your mission. As you can see, in this late fall season our herdsmen, for both sheep and cattle, do not have too much to do. We can occupy them with errands such as this, as well as with building and remodeling as needed."

"I hope that the Spanish will not look unkindly upon your extensive landholdings, Don Diego," Moses Austin replied. "I see here the opportunity for building one of the largest ranches in all of the Texas country. Everywhere there seems to be fine grazing land, and you've certainly plenty of water with that river nearby."

"What I am thinking, Señor Austin, is that if Governor Martínez grants your petition, I for one should be very happy to welcome some of the settlers here. You see, they could find occupation with us, take part in our community, and adapt themselves so that we can become a kind of small, well-run, and prosperous city."

"That's most kind of you, Don Diego. I'll remember

that. Well, thanks to you, I can enjoy a few hours out of the saddle. I'll confess I've been riding hard the last several weeks."

"Rest well, Señor Austin, and do not be in a hurry to waken. If you and my workman leave by late afternoon, you should arrive in San Antonio the day after tomorrow."

"You're most gracious, and I'm grateful to you and to your lovely wife for all your help and kindness. In your own words, ¡hasta la vista!"

Moses Austin had three hours of refreshing sleep and then, after thanking his host and hostess for their warm hospitality, went out to the stables, where a young, sturdy trabajador, Ernesto Cribaro, was already waiting with his gray horse. "Señor, I will have the privilege of riding with you to San Antonio," the trabajador said, respectfully inclining his head. "I've saddled your horse, and I've got provisions from the kitchen, so that we'll not have to stop for food on our way. There is water between here and San Antonio; that is no problem at all."

"Gracias, amigo," Austin replied, smiling and clapping the trabajador on the back. "I feel very rested and very optimistic about my mission. Let us go, then."

"Agreed, Señor Austin. Like Luis, the trabajador who brought you here, I have been to San Antonio a few times before. I have ridden with some of the herds which our assistant capataz, Esteban Morales, has driven across the border, and I will take the shortest route so that you may be there in plenty of time for your appointment. My patrón, Don Diego, has told me how eager you are to reach the governor."

"I must say, I never expected to find such cooperation from a Spaniard," Moses Austin exclaimed. But maybe this is a good augury. I'm with you, amigo. Lead the way!"

Meanwhile, Catarina wanted to have a moment alone with her brother, Carlos, and could find no trace of him. After she had gone out to question Miguel Sandarbal and Teofilo Rosas, she became greatly concerned. Finally, she went to her husband, who was in the corral, talking with some of the trabajadores about his plans for enlarging the enclosure. Taking him aside, Catarina stared earnestly into his bearded face and murmured, "Please, Coop, I'm so worried about Carlos. No one has seen him for a long time now, and his bed wasn't slept in, you know that yourself. All

Miguel could tell me was that he took the wildest mustang and broke him in and then rode off, and neither Miguel nor Teofilo Rosas has seen him since then."

"Easy now, Catarina honey," John Cooper soothed her, kissing her forehead and putting his arms around her shoulders. "I've an idea where he's gone."

"But without telling us, Coop—he knows how we love him—" Catarina impulsively began.

"Hush, *querida*," John Cooper softly intervened. "Sometimes, when a man is hurting, it puts acid in the wound if anybody feels sorry for him and says so. Right now, I'm figuring that Carlos doesn't want any more pity or sweet words about how sorry everybody is over what happened to poor Weesayo. But I think I can find him."

"Will you do that for me, Coop? And Father and Doña Inez are worried so very much about him," Catarina implored, tears welling in her lovely, dark eyes.

"Don't you fret, Catarina. Lobo and I will go after him. All he wants to do is be by himself and take stock of things and figure out what he's going to do next. But he can take care of himself; he's not in any danger, I'm sure of that. I'll pack some provender and go saddle Fuego right now, and I promise I'll find him for you."

"You're so good, Coop. The whole *hacienda* grows because of you and your strength. And I can never stop telling you how much I love you."

"Nor I you, *querida*." John Cooper sighed contentedly as he enfolded her in his arms and kissed her upturned face, first at the tip of her nose, at which she giggled, and then her eyes, and finally, a long, satisfying kiss on her soft mouth. Then he disengaged himself from her embrace and said, "Let me go do now what has to be done. I tell you, don't worry; I'll find Carlos and bring him back."

Dressed in his buckskins, John Cooper packed jerky, some flour, salt, and a small skillet, as well as his tinderbox into his saddlebag. As in the old days, John Cooper took along "Long Girl," the Lancaster rifle that had belonged to his father and that had been his means of defense when he had crossed the American continent so many years ago. He also wore around his neck, as was his custom during outings such as this, the rawhide thong that held his slim knife of Spanish steel.

The superb white palomino, Fuego, eagerly nickered

when his master entered the stable and came directly to his stall, and John Cooper chuckled and rubbed the stallion's head with his knuckles, just as he did with Lobo, saying, "Yes, Fuego, we're going for a little outing now. You'll have your freedom, and so will Lobo. We're going to find Carlos, the three of us."

As he led the palomino out of the stable, he encountered Miguel Sandarbal, who hesitantly approached him, saying, "Maybe I should send some of the workers with you, *mi compañero.*"

"No, I'd best do it by myself. You've seen enough of Carlos to know what he's feeling. It would be like a posse if I had men with me out looking for him. I'm just going there man-to-man and try to talk him into coming back."

"Perhaps you're right, *mi compañero.*" Miguel sighed and shook his head. "Everyone is sad here to see how the young master is taking it. He just can't go on grieving for her forever. I know what Teofilo said to anger him so, but just between the two of us, I'm thinking the same thing myself—it would be best if he found a sweet girl to soothe his hurt."

"No, I think you're wrong, at least for right now, Miguel. It will take time for his wounds to heal. Now tell me one thing. Carlos didn't take his palomino or Valor, did he?"

"No, *mi compañero.* He went off with that mustang he tamed. *Dios,* if you could only have seen him master that devil. I really thought at one time he'd do Carlos in, but he rode him like a *gran vaquero.*"

"Then he's taken the horse with him, and I'm pretty sure I know exactly where he went. One of the mountains off to the northwest, just before—" John Cooper stopped in time, for he had been about to recall the landmark of the mysterious mountain near whose summit the secret silver mine was located. "Yes," he hurriedly added, "it'll take more than a week of good, hard riding. It'll get some of the fat off me, too. Now I'll take Lobo along, and you let Hosea and Jude out to romp all they want. One of these days, Lobo is going to have to get used to them."

"I'll do that. God go with you, *mi compañero.*"

"And with you, also, Miguel. *¡Hasta la vista!*" John Cooper strode to the shed to take a last look at the Irish wolfhound puppies, who immediately whined and tried to get out. Laughingly entering, he played with them a few moments, then chided them and bade them be patient. Then he whistled, and Lobo bounded from around the back of the bunkhouse where he had been sunning himself.

The wolf-dog had gained weight, and though his eyes were as keen as ever, John Cooper perceived that his reflexes were not quite so quick as they had been in earlier years. Taming Lobo as he had, he admitted to himself, had helped calm the half-savage whelp of Lije, and yet he was certain that in the event of danger, Lobo could still defend them both.

"Yes, Lobo, this time you're going to get all the exercise you've wanted." He squatted down and rubbed the knuckles of both his hands over the wolf-dog's head. Lobo whined, then emitted the curious purring sound he always made whenever his beloved master showed him this kind of affectionate caress.

At the same moment there was a shrill cawing, and the black raven, Fortuna, flew down from the top of the bunkhouse, where it had been calmly surveying the proceedings, and perched on the top of the wolf-dog's head. Carlos had tamed the raven many years earlier, after finding the bird in the woods and healing its broken wing, and now Fortuna's presence on the ranch was accepted as much as Lobo's. "Well, you want to go, too? So much the better! You can peck at Lobo and keep him alert," John Cooper joked as he put out his left hand. Fortuna boldly leaped onto the young man's palm, cocking his head and eyeing John Cooper with a kind of condescending defiance, knowing only too well with what favor he was held at this *hacienda*.

"Go along with Lobo, then, you rascal," John Cooper chuckled as he mounted Fuego. The raven promptly flew back to his post atop Lobo's head and there, flapping his wings, uttered his shrill caw to denote his entire satisfaction over the outing.

Eight

John Cooper rode all afternoon until sundown, and then made camp on a high slope near a small creek whose water was pleasingly fresh. He had let Fuego choose his own gait, not wanting to tire the magnificent palomino. Moreover, since he was almost certain where Carlos had gone, he appreciated this time by himself to think over the meaning of Moses Austin's visit and its implications for the future. Thus far, in the placid years since they had moved from Taos, since the nightmare of Catarina's violation by the bandit Santomaro and the evil *capataz* Ramirez and the abduction of her firstborn, life had been wonderfully rewarding. He and Catarina had been drawn closer together than ever, partly because of the ordeal she had sustained and her courageous reaction to it. That alone had told him that his once-pampered, autocratic young wife had learned to adapt herself to the elemental law of survival. And as a consequence, he loved her as he had not believed he could ever love any human being after that unforgettable and terrible late afternoon when he had watched his family being murdered by the renegade Shawnee just as he had returned from a futile hunting trip with faithful Lije.

He thought to himself that if Moses Austin succeeded in convincing Governor Martínez to allow American settlers in the still-Spanish-held territory of Texas, the opportunities for growth were vitally boundless. Once free trade was offered through Texas, which would inevitably come once American families were permitted to settle, the next step would be the liberation of Taos and Santa Fe, which would allow people of modest incomes to buy goods at fair prices, without the present prohibitive tariffs imposed by the viceroy.

Moreover, the several sales of cattle which had gone as far as New Orleans and fed, as well, many inhabitants of San Antonio, convinced him that someday the Double H Ranch would be the greatest ranch in the Southwest. The communal efforts of the loyal workers and their families, who knew that in Don Diego they had a benevolent and indulgent *patrón*, together with Miguel's expert guidance and enthusiastic devotion, would make this isolated ranch one of the most prosperous in all of the Texas territory. The American settlers whom Moses Austin hoped to bring in would create an enlarged community, almost like a little town, independent unto itself.

The growth and the strength of such a community, he was certain, would make the *hacienda* almost impregnable, so far as Indian attack and even interference from occasional Mexican troops or officials were concerned. Besides, Esteban Morales, as soon as he had returned at the beginning of October from driving three hundred head of cattle to San Antonio, had told him and Don Diego that the talk of liberation and independence of Mexico from a nearly bankrupt and faltering Spain was imminent. Once that was accomplished—and he hoped it would be done by popular decision rather than by any kind of bloody revolution or power coups by rival factions—there would no longer be any danger of dictatorial interference by pompous officials. Then the ranch could really flourish.

When he made camp, he fitted a bag of oats to Fuego's muzzle, after first letting the palomino drink its fill from the creek. Then he made a fire and prepared some biscuits to go with the jerky. Lobo kept nuzzling him throughout the duration of the meal, his bright yellow eyes first fixing on his young master's face, then on the skillet. Amusedly, John Cooper broke off one of the biscuits after it had cooled and held it out to Lobo, who instantly bolted it down and thrust out his pink tongue to indicate that more would be quite in order.

An hour away from the *hacienda,* John Cooper had been considerably heartened to see the unshod hoof prints of a lone horse and, some three miles beyond that, comparatively fresh droppings. This had made him certain that his hunch as to the direction of Carlos's flight was correct. Through all these years in first Taos and now Texas, he had never forgotten what he had learned as a boy in the Indian villages, how his friends among the Ayuhwa Sioux had taught him to read signs from a broken twig crushed into the earth, or the bent bough of a young sapling, or the droppings of man or beast, or how to calculate the length of time that had expired since a small, sheltered campfire had been extinguished. Indeed, though this was a sorrowful errand, he was glad for the opportunity to refresh his knowledge from that past time when observing and understanding such signs had been the difference between life and death.

After their brief supper he indulged Lobo in a recreational game of fetching a stick. This he had taught the wolf-dog last year to round out the latter's complete adaptability to the placid life of the Texas *hacienda*. He had always been secretly afraid that one day Lobo's savage nature might come to the fore, and out of some misunderstanding or thoughtless provocation—on the part, most likely, of a child who could hardly be expected to know the danger—the wolf-dog might show his innate ferocity. By domesticating Lobo he had made certain that the wolf-dog would be a kind of mascot for everyone; and till now it had worked out exactly that way. Moreover, apart from that one desultory raid by the renegade Comanche band, there had been absolutely no danger to the ranch all these years since they had left Taos.

And yet it was essential that Lobo should not entirely lose his powers, for in defending against an enemy attack or in attacking when it was necessary, the unexpected presence of this wolf-dog, powerfully strong, with bared, strong fangs and gleaming yellow eyes, was a distinct advantage and would take the enemy by total surprise. It had proved so with the Comanche; it had proven as much with Santomaro and his bandits, as well as with the arrogant Don Felipe.

John Cooper tossed a dried branch as far as he could, ordering Lobo to bring it back and rewarding the wolf-dog with an extra bit of jerky. Meanwhile, he was thinking carefully of the future, weighing in the balance all those factors that might change their lives as had the sudden greediness of the *ricos* and the Mexican officials in those years in Taos.

He thought that Padre Moraga had looked frail and very weak; that never before had he seen the gentle priest look his true age, and it was inevitable to think of what would happen when Padre Moraga died. Undoubtedly, since Taos was a large parish, the ecclesiastical authorities would replace him. If that were the case, what kind of man would they send? Would it be someone in whom John Cooper could confide as readily as he had always been able to do with Padre Moraga? And then there was the secret of the treasure.

This last thought roused him to action again. He was determined to shorten this journey as much as he could to ease the worry of Catarina, as well as that of Don Diego and Doña Inez. He rose, extinguished his campfire, untethered Fuego, and whistling to Lobo to follow him, rode off toward the northwest.

Urging Fuego on, John Cooper rode into the darkening night, with Lobo racing along, his pink tongue lolling out of his mouth, glancing upward at the soaring black raven who, out of sheer whimsy, would dart down from time to time to peck at his lupine playmate. Lobo, aware that John Cooper was watching him, made a great pretense of whirling round and trying to snap at the raven, but never quite catching him, while Fortuna, with a mocking caw, would soar high overhead, only to plummet down with its beak open to nip at Lobo's tail or hindquarters. Despite his concern over Carlos and his grief for Weesayo, the young American could not help laughing at this interplay between beast and bird. How open it was, how free of guile and deceptiveness. If only human beings could be this way, how much better off the world would be.

At midnight, fatigue claimed him, and he made camp again and flung himself down on his blanket, with Lobo guarding him. Fortuna took refuge at the top of the tallest mesquite in a thick clump, and the silence of the night claimed all of them.

Most of the journey passed uneventfully, and Carlos's trail continued to lead to the northwest. More than a week later, the peaks east of Taos loomed ahead, and the mountain man and his three animal friends made camp at night near a clear-running stream.

With the first rays of dawn, John Cooper sprang to his feet, attuned to instant waking by his years on the plains with Indian tribes, and made a swift breakfast. Once the fire was out, he mounted Fuego again and set out in the same direction.

He was convinced that Carlos had taken refuge in one of the mountains to the southeast of the mysterious peak that had always intrigued him and where he had found the silver hoard. It was of easy access, and if Carlos had really gone there, as he thought, he would have had to climb several hundred feet. He could have ridden his mustang on the winding, narrow trail almost halfway up. However, he doubted very much that his brother-in-law would have taxed the mustang to that extent; more than likely, the young Spaniard had left the mustang to its own resources and found himself some cave where he would contemplate and examine his conscience. That would be well in keeping with the character that marriage to Weesayo had inspired in him, John Cooper was certain.

Just before sunset, John Cooper reined in the white palomino with a satisfied smile. The hoofprints of the solitary horse he had been following turned slightly southward, as he had expected, a few hundred yards in front of the summit of a small, jagged peak. As he sat in his saddle looking upward, he could vaguely make out irregular ledges, thickly covered by wild foliage and scrub trees here and there. Very likely there were caves along these ledges. The mountain itself was no more than two thousand feet high, he quickly estimated, contrasting it with the mountains where the Jicarilla Apache had their stronghold in the northernmost portion of the Sangre de Cristo range.

He rode Fuego until the first winding turned into a path that narrowed enough to allow a single horse to ascend. As he halted and dismounted, wanting to look back over the way he had come, he uttered a cry of delight: a gray mustang was placidly grazing to the south of him and below, at about the level that he and Fuego had taken for the first ascension. There could be no doubt about it, judging from the saddle and the reins: this was the mustang that Carlos de Escobar had tamed in his frenzied grief. He tethered his palomino to a heavy log lying in the path that wound slowly upward around the low mountain.

Inhaling, his eyes squinting to detect what he could in the failing light before nightfall, he suddenly smelled a faint odor of burning wood. Carlos was evidently making a fire. He looked up again and saw a thin wisp of smoke rise into the air far above him, at least two hundred feet.

He would leave Fuego, for the narrow trail was rather treacherous, and there was no need to endanger the palomino. Carlos would not escape, and he could go on foot for the next quarter of an hour and be certain of finding his brother-in-law.

As he took the narrow trail, leaning forward to ease the weight and to make climbing more effortless, he smelled the characteristic odor of a rabbit being cooked over hot coals, perhaps even held in an improvised spit over the fire. It was a smell that drew back memories of his boyhood years in

Shawneetown when his mother had made rabbit stew, and of his years living in the wilderness, foraging for himself.

He quickened his footsteps, and the tasty aroma of cooking rabbit grew stronger. Lobo was with him and now impatiently forged ahead of him with an anxious little yipe. "I know what you're after, boy," John Cooper good-naturedly told him and grinned.

"Who's there?" Suddenly he heard Carlos's hoarse voice, and a moment later the young Spaniard emerged, pushing aside the heavy growth of ferns and moss that hung from the top of the ledge and obscured the opening of the cave in which he had sequestered himself. If John Cooper had not recognized Carlos's voice, he might have paused a moment before he recognized his brother-in-law: Carlos's short Van-dyke beard was untrimmed, his hair was unkempt, and the way he gripped his Belgian rifle in both hands indicated that he expected intrusion by an enemy rather than by a longtime friend.

"Don't get yourself in an uproar, *amigo*," John Cooper called out. "It's John Cooper, and Lobo and Fortuna are here to say hello to you. Is it all right if I climb on up?"

"Wait—yes—no—I—mean—how did you find me?"

"Now that's a stupid question, Carlos. Are you forget-ting that I lived with Indians so many years? And Pa taught me how to track long before I had to go live with them, if you'll remember. Enough of that nonsense—why are you hiding away from the world like this? You've made your father and Doña Inez very unhappy and restless. And then there's your sister. She's also worried about you, *amigo*. So am I, to tell you the truth."

"All right, John Cooper, I recognize you. Come on up—unless you've got the *trabajadores* with you. I won't let them take me back—"

"Now you've really got the wind up, Carlos! What's got into you, for the Lord's sake?" John Cooper scratched his head and grinned as he kept climbing. And then he found himself on the thickly verdant ledge, wide enough to give him secure footing, and there was Carlos, wearing the costume of a *peón*. Only the gold ring that his father had bought for him to celebrate his acceptance into the ranks of men at the age of twenty-one betrayed the young Spaniard's attempt to pretend that nothing had happened and to seek to keep from John Cooper the real intensity of his emotions.

"Now I'd have to be a real fool, wouldn't I, Carlos, to

try to trap you that way. All I've got with me is Lobo, and you can see him now. And there's Fortuna—look, he's flying up to perch on Lobo's head."

Carlos emitted a doleful sigh and then, despite himself, turned to watch the wolf-dog and the raven, the latter contentedly perching atop Lobo's head and facing him with intent, beady eyes.

"He doesn't seem to recognize me, that raven of yours," he laughingly remarked to the young American.

"Don't call him my raven," John Cooper protested. "He's yours. Don't you remember that time when you went hunting and found the lame raven, and how Weesayo was afraid that it was an evil omen, but you talked her out of it?"

"Yes, I do—and then—oh, *Dios,* why did you have to speak her name, John Cooper?" For just an instant Carlos's face had softened. He had lowered his rifle and stared out along the plain below. Now, his lips were tightly compressed and he gripped the rifle at the ready, and John Cooper sensed that he was almost at the breaking point. It had, indeed, been an unfortunate allusion.

Seeking to make amends for this show of tactlessness, John Cooper shrugged and said gently, "I'm sorry for talking that way, Carlos. But I am going to take you back, and I don't need any *trabajadores* to do it for me, if you resist me."

Carlos dropped the rifle to the ground, his face pale. "*Amigo,* I don't want to hurt you, and I won't strike you— but I don't want to go back to the *hacienda,* believe me," Carlos earnestly declared, now gripping his brother-in-law's shoulders with his hands until John Cooper could feel the fingernails dig into his flesh.

"Hey now, take it easy, I'm on your side, remember?" John Cooper said, pulling away from Carlos. Then looking straight into the other man's burning gaze, he said, "You must really hate us all, and we never guessed it."

Suddenly Carlos's eyes filled with tears as he leaned forward and exclaimed, "But what are you saying to me, John Cooper! Of course I don't have any hatred for any of you. It's only that I didn't want to inflict myself and my sorrow on the *hacienda.* You see, I remember the Apache ways in the stronghold. I have been fasting here, living on herbs and bits of bark and water from my canteen. I've wanted to feel, as much as I could, like a man who was at one with the elements. Only I got so hungry this afternoon that I went out and shot a rabbit. I guess I'm not suited for a life of fasting and meditation."

"You're going to come back and be with us, Carlos, where you are suited. We'll talk about it on the way back, and by the time we reach the *hacienda,* maybe I'll have some suggestions for you. I know that you want to start a new way of life and that you have to turn your face from poor Weesayo. But she'll always live in your heart and mine, too."

"Don't, Coop! In God's own name, don't speak her name again. Remember what the Apache do once someone is dead: they never again repeat that name in public. That's what I'm going to have to do myself with the girl I loved, not ever say her name aloud from now on."

"I understand what you've been through, Carlos."

"That's why I came here, to fast and to think, just as braves who wanted to be consecrated to battle for the first time did in the stronghold. It shouldn't be strange to you— you were the very one who told me of their custom the first time I visited the stronghold," Carlos almost plaintively pointed out.

"Yes, I know. All right then. Will you go back with me?"

Carlos hesitated a moment, then said, "I know what you're trying to do for me, and I'm very grateful, *mi compañero.* Yes," he added, shrugging, and his voice had absolutely no animation to it, "I'll go back with you. But in all honesty, I have to admit to you that I have figured things out for myself. I think I know what I'm going to do, and I don't want to be hemmed in. I know that Don Diego and Doña Inez will scold me and then watch over me the way a mother hen watches over her chickens—and that I don't want at all, any more than I do if the *trabajadores* show me that they're feeling sorry for me. Or you, either, Coop, do you understand?" His eyes blazed fiercely, and he clenched one fist as he took a step toward John Cooper. Lobo uttered a low growl by way of warning, not expecting the young Spaniard to advance against his master.

"Careful, now, Carlos, he's getting a bit old, and he knows just so much. If you try to hit me, I couldn't really guarantee that Lobo wouldn't go for your throat, even though he knows you're my best friend—"

"Of course. Forgive me, Coop." Carlos shrugged again.

"As it happens, I haven't eaten any of the rabbit yet. Perhaps you and Lobo would like to share it with me, before we go back?"

"I'd like to, and I'm sure Lobo would, too." John Cooper smiled as he followed Carlos back into the cave without further comment.

Half an hour later, holding his rifle in both hands, Carlos went ahead of John Cooper and Lobo, calling out to Dolor, who, recognizing the sound of his master's voice, whinnied loudly and began to trot toward the base of the low mountain.

"He's a fine horse, Coop. And I didn't kill his spirit when I broke him in. He still has plenty. Well, I don't think I'll feel much like sleeping, so why don't we ride all through the night to get back the faster? The sooner I'm at the *hacienda,* the sooner I'll be able to put my plans in order." Carlos turned to look almost yearningly at the young mountain man.

John Cooper said nothing, but gave his brother-in-law an understanding nod. Then, snapping his fingers, he bade Lobo follow them down to where Dolor and Fuego waited.

The young man tried to appear casual, for he could see that Carlos looked lean and drawn, not only because of his fasting. He knew exactly what the young Spaniard had done, for he himself, before he had met the personable young man who was destined to become his brother-in-law, had heard Descontarti tell of how a warrior who was despondent over his failure in an important battle against tribal enemies had retreated to one of the bleakest ledges of the mountain which housed the Apache stronghold. There he had gone without food except for a few bits of bark and herbs and only a mouthful of water three times each day, for a full ten days, communing with the Great Spirit, till he felt himself purged of his loss and sense of defeat. And in the very next battle that had been a test of strength, the warrior had saved Descontarti's life—at the cost of his own.

At the same time John Cooper hoped that the recollection was, in no way, a fateful omen: the tragedy that had scarred Carlos's life seemed monumental now. Yet surely if the energetic son of Don Diego plunged himself into arduous, purposeful work, there would certainly be compensation to ease the agonizing loss of beautiful, gentle Weesayo.

Tonight there was a full moon, but the sky was ominously dark, and hurrying gray clouds frequently obscured the luminous rays. John Cooper led the way back down the trail, finding that his memory amply sufficed to give him secure footing. Lobo, as was his wont, loped ahead, Fortuna soaring high above him and uttering from time to time his playful caw.

Carlos had shouldered a backpack and held onto it with both hands as he doggedly descended, his face stern and taut. In his dark eyes was a look of indifference and resignation, and he was silent as they took the winding way down to where the palomino and the mustang waited.

Suddenly there was a dry rattling sound, and John Cooper could read the wolf-dog's meaning in that yelp and throat dry. But ahead of him, Lobo, with an angry snarl, had darted to the right and was shaking something between his strong jaws.

"¡Madre de Dios!" Carlos ejaculated, crossing himself. "It very nearly bit you, my brother-in-law."

"Whew, that was a close call! But Lobo's taken charge of things. All right, good boy, drop it. It's dead now."

Lobo backed away, still gripping the convulsively wriggling body of a gray diamondback, his yellow eyes gleaming with exultance at having made the kill. When John Cooper repeated the order, he opened his jaws and backed away again, then growled angrily at the rattlesnake. It was at least four feet long, with seven distinct rattles. Now its feeble squirmings ceased, and it lay lifeless on the dusty, claylike earth a few feet ahead of, and to the right of, John Cooper.

"It was an old one and very deadly," John Cooper declared. "I thought Lobo was getting old, but he has better eyesight in the dark than I do. You saved my life, Lobo." He squatted down and fondly scratched the wolf-dog's head with his knuckles. Then he remembered that he had several bits of jerky in the pocket of his buckskin breeches, and now, delving into one, held out his palm. Lobo uttered a pleased little bark and, wagging his tail, accepted the reward, then backed away and barked again, his front paws shifting nervously and impatiently. It was obvious he was eager to be off, believing he had done his duty and that all danger to his beloved master was now completely averted.

John Cooper chuckled, reached down, and patted Lobo on the rump. "That's a very good dog. When we get back home, you'll get a special treat. Jerky isn't reward enough, not for saving my life, it isn't."

This good-natured sally drew a faint laugh from Carlos, and John Cooper, who had walked slightly ahead of his brother-in-law on the winding trail downward, frowned to himself. At least, that was a good sign. If Carlos could still laugh, then there was hope he'd eventually get out of these awful doldrums. For the life of him, though, John Cooper didn't know what kind of medicine could possibly cure Carlos's tragedy. He remembered—how strange it was that, at this very moment, back through those distant, fading years, the plight of his brother-in-law should recall this to him—how his mother had read to him by the dying light from the fireplace about the tribulations of Job. The devil had bargained with God for Job's soul and had slyly proposed that if he were to visit this faithful servant, he would turn on the Lord God Almighty, and curse Him and be content to die to escape his torments. God had told the devil to go ahead, and Job had suffered more misfortunes than anyone he, John Cooper, had ever heard about before or after, and yet he'd remained faithful and loyal. And then God had rewarded him. Well, maybe this was God's way of testing Carlos. You couldn't be sure about such things, but somehow, deep down inside him, just like when he was a boy, the young mountain man felt that there'd been a reason for all this, and that one day, maybe not right away, they'd all find out and things would go well for Carlos again. He certainly prayed that would be the case.

They reached their horses, and at Carlos's vigorous whistle, the now-thoroughly docile gray mustang came trotting up. It moved close to the young Spaniard, nuzzling its muzzle against his shoulder and neck, and Carlos smiled wanly despite himself and reached up to rub the mustang's ears and neck. Lobo had paused, turned back to look, and let out a soft yelp, as much as to say, "Why should that horse get all the attention, when I just killed a big rattler?" John Cooper could read the wolf-dog's meaning in that yelp and burst out laughing. It relieved the tension. Now he felt free and knew it would be easier to talk to Carlos on the way back home.

Nonetheless, he waited until they had both mounted and let Lobo take the lead again. Almost triumphantly, the graying wolf-dog set out in a quick lope, while Fortuna soared above the scrub trees, flattening his wings and emitting his familiar taunting caw from time to time.

They rode on for a few miles in silence, and then John Cooper casually remarked, "You know, Carlos, what I'm really sorry about is that you missed the visit of Moses Austin."

"Did my father say he would help him?"

"Indeed he did, Carlos. He offered to write a letter recommending the colonization project to the governor, whom he met in San Antonio a while back. For myself, I think the project would be a great idea. We could even have some of the families settle on our ranch—it's certainly big enough, and it's going to get bigger in the years to come. We could have almost a kind of little town at the *hacienda* if that happened. We could even have stores, a blacksmith, maybe even a hospital and a bigger church—I know Padre Moraga would like that fine."

"That's very ambitious, John Cooper. Yes, I'm sorry I didn't have a chance to meet this man. But you understand—"

"Yes, of course, you don't have to tell me." Then after a pause, John Cooper asked, "What will you do now, Carlos?"

"I've been fasting up here and praying to find out the answer myself, *amigo*," was the young Spaniard's forthright reply. He looked up at the sky and drew a long breath. "I don't seem to want to go on at the ranch, I'll tell you that much."

"You don't mean you'd go away and take the children and live by yourself, Carlos?" John Cooper said with some alarm in his voice.

"No, not that. Catarina was wonderful to take charge of my little ones. I have great admiration for her. She has become a true woman, and she'll be loyal to you and love you all the rest of your days, John Cooper."

"I feel the same way about her. She loves children. Yes, she'd look after them for you—but the way you talk, you make me think that you plan to go away for a good long time."

"I can be frank with you. You saved my life, you brought me to happiness—" For a moment Carlos was silent, compressing his lips and closing his eyes and letting the mustang move along without any guidance from his slack hands at the reins. At last he resumed, "Yes, I can't lie to you, John Cooper. I have to do something, something that has meaning. I'm trying to say, as best I can, that—well, I don't know if you ever read Cervantes's *Don Quixote?*"

"No, but I remember that my mother told me about him—I mean, Don Quixote was the knight Cervantes wrote about, who fought for lost causes, wasn't he?"

"Exactly. I don't want to fight for a lost cause; I want to

fight for a good one. I believe that old Spain and Nueva España are about to go their separate ways—and to me, that's all to the good. I've been thinking a good deal while I was up in that cave in the mountain there, John Cooper. I've always loved the outdoor life, and I've had a little taste of soldiering, at least when I helped defend my father, Catarina, and Doña Inez against that Indian attack when we were on our way to Taos from Mexico City. So I've been thinking that I might enlist in the Mexican army, to be on the side of the poor people, the *peones,* all those who've been swindled and brutalized by their rich masters. I saw enough of them in Taos, I can tell you that. I know who my father's enemies still are, and those are the sort of people I'd like to fight against. That's what I've been thinking, if you must know, John Cooper."

"I go along with you on that, Carlos, all the way." John Cooper tried to propitiate his brother-in-law, sensing the underlying tone of distraught indecision which sounded in Carlos's voice. "I never cared for people who thought they were better than everybody else just because they had some money or an important position. The way my mother taught me, God made us all equal."

"I believe that, even if I was born the son of a hidalgo." Carlos was silent a moment, then said, "John Cooper, let's just ride. I want to think this out for myself—I just have to. But whatever I do, I hope you'll stand by me."

"You can be sure of that, *mi amigo,* just as I'm sure that whatever you do, it'll be the right thing."

Nine

Don Diego de Escobar paced the floor of his study, while Doña Inez stood watching him, a look of great concern on her lovely face. "I only hope John Cooper has been successful in finding my son, dearest Inez," he said as he at last turned to her, his arms held out in a gesture of frustration. "But then I think to myself, if he runs away because of a terrible sorrow he has experienced, will he stay here? Will he be content—and, further, what distractions can we offer him here on this peaceful ranch that will make him pursue some sort of disciplined life that will ease his suffering?"

"You must let him make his own decision, dear Diego," she said softly as she came to him and put her arm around his shoulders. "He is spirited, and you have never had any reason to doubt his courage. It will see him though these terrible days. But if we try in any way to constrain him and to keep him here, he will only end up resenting it, perhaps even us. That must not happen."

"If only he had waited until Moses Austin came," Don Diego snapped. "His proposal for American settlement in Texas will change history, and would be a grand project for my son to involve himself in, a project that would consume his time and energies and waking thoughts, so that the loss of Weesayo would gradually lessen in its intensity. You know yourself that my *gringo* son-in-law, John Cooper, had a similar tragedy befall him when his family was killed by Indians so many years ago—and think in some ways how much more dreadful it must have been for him, a mere boy, with only that heroic wolfhound as his companion, through blizzards and Indian camps and the chance meetings with rogues and renegades and bushwhackers who could easily have killed him, if he had not been tested to survive, and by his wits done so."

"It was destiny that brought him to us," Doña Inez murmured as she kissed his cheek.

He nodded, took her in his arms, and stared deeply into her eyes. "It was his coming and his saving Carlos from the mountain lion that changed all our lives, my darling one. It was his courage, his very youth, his endurance, that showed me what an old fool I had been in clinging to the customs of the past, gave me wisdom enough at last—and thank *el Señor Dios* that it was not too late!—to ask you to share my life with me."

"How willingly I would have done that long ago, dear Diego," she whispered.

"I know that now. And sometimes I say to myself that I was a fool not to have seen it long ago. Think of the added years we could have had—yes, even more children."

At this, Doña Inez blushed, for it was her fervent wish to have another child. But for now she was content to nestle in his arms and to kiss him again. Then finally she murmured, "We must just be patient. And whatever Carlos decides to do, we must support him and show him that we have complete trust and confidence in him."

"Yes, you are right, my darling. And now let us go out to the kitchen and tell Tía Margarita to prepare something special. By my calculations, if John Cooper has found Carlos, he should be home anytime now, maybe today."

Tía Margarita bustled about the long dining room table, serving a festive dinner with the aid of two of the maids of the household. The old cook was beaming with happiness to see the young master once again reunited with his father and handsome stepmother, with Catarina sitting at his right and John Cooper beside Carlos.

Don Diego raised his glass of vintage Madeira and rose, his face radiant with happiness: "To my son, to many long years, and to his success in whatever he endeavors!"

"I drink to that!" Smiling radiantly, Catarina lifted her glass, as did John Cooper.

"Yes, Carlos," Doña Inez softly interposed, "it is cause for rejoicing for us all that you have come back where you belong. We respect your grief, and we promise not to intrude upon it. Only know this: we are very happy to have you back."

Carlos halfheartedly lifted his glass to respond to this effusive toast. Then, with downcast eyes and in a noncommittal tone, he replied, "You do me too much honor, my respected stepmother. And you, too, my father. While I was out meditating in that cave, I came to a decision about my life. And I beg your indulgence, because I'm sure that you will be surprised when you learn what I have decided. Knowingly, I'd never want to hurt any of you—you have been my very life to me. And you, Father, with your courage in changing your entire way of life and looking forward with a vigor and youthfulness that I deeply respect, in no way would I wish to make you grieve for me. But my mind is made up, and I leave tomorrow for Mexico."

Don Diego tried to adopt a casual air. "Oh? And what do you propose to do there, my son?"

"I want to enlist in the Mexican army to fight against the autocratic leaders and the *ricos* who abuse the Mexican people and the Indians, my father."

"I can understand that," Don Diego began, carefully

choosing his words and glancing quickly at Doña Inez, as if seeking her moral support. "I know only too well that infernal delays and inconsequential correspondence took up so much of my time when I was *intendente* back in Taos. Conflicting orders came from everyone who fancied himself to have power, and the result was that nothing was ever done."

"Except to make the *ricos* grow smug with assurance and believe that they were the law of Nueva España, *mi padre*," was Carlos's reply. "I have talked to a few of the *trabajadores* who most recently visited Chihuahua, Durango, and some of the other provinces. They do not think that it will be too much longer until Mexico breaks away from Spain, and they all hope that there will be a leveling of the upper classes who have been brutalizing them for many long years. I wish to ally myself on the side of the *peones,* those who have nothing, not even a clean *camisa* to wear to mass. They have a cause that deserves fighting for. If, as I've heard, Ferdinand VII will soon be forced to give up his throne and allow a separation between this new, still-untried world and decadent Spain, I want to feel myself part of the fight for liberty and freedom for all."

"My son, when I was your age, I was as confirmed an idealist as you. It is true that Spain flourished then, and there was no enmity between father and son, as between Carlos IV and his son Ferdinand VII. But my father before me was born and bred to the service of the monarchy, and that was why it was difficult for me to adjust myself when first I came to Taos. My only fear is that you may mistake the integrity of the cause. I should not like to think of you as a mere revolutionary."

Carlos leaned forward, his eyes warm with an eagerness to explain his motives, his face earnest and sober. "I don't want to be a soldier for the sake of killing, *mi padre.* But I've reason to believe that the army would support the common people. Their leaders are weary of this division between orders from Madrid which have no bearing on our present-day life, and then orders from the various provinces which eventually come into Taos and are expected to be followed with almost blind obedience. You know that yourself, *mi padre.*"

"Only too well," Don Diego confessed. "But if you are truly certain that you want to fight for justice, for an end to the brutality and selfishness of men like Don Esteban de

Rivarola, who is my sworn enemy, then I say, *bueno!* And I would be the first to give you my blessing for this new adventure. Only I wish you would be very certain, my son. I do not want to hear of you learning that the cause for which you fought was not at all the one in which you believed. "No," he said, emphatically shaking his head, "you must be certain of what you do, my dear son."

"I think I am, Father," Carlos softly rejoined as he leaned back in his chair. Catarina was frowning while trying her best to dissuade him by means of her eloquent, mute stare. But Carlos pretended not to notice his sister's grave concern as he now went on, "You know yourself, *mi padre,* that there is discontent throughout all of Nueva España. And I have known for some few months now of a man, once very loyal to the king as you were, who has become disillusioned with Ferdinand VII and has been preparing to take control of the government and to fight for independence. He has three goals, my father. First, independence from Spain, which everyone wants."

"True," Don Diego grudgingly conceded. "Old as I am, I can still recognize how important that can be. Especially if we ever hope to have free trade in these parts."

"Exactly so, *mi padre.* Then this man has promised full equality to the *peones.* And finally, since he must have his army financed by some wealthy *patrón,* he has appealed to the clergy, who have control of the wealth. He says that he will guarantee the Church's traditional rights as a state religion of Mexico. And he's already formed his own army—indeed, he has been doing this for some little time now."

"And who is this great patriot, if I may ask?" Don Diego queried.

"But you already know his name, because you heard of him when you first came to Mexico City. It is that of Colonel Agustín de Iturbide. Men flock to his army from all over Mexico, and it seems to me that a man like this, who can inspire the confidence of strangers who have come a long way to join his army, must have a doctrine worth following. And his talk of equality for the peasants pleases me most of all."

"I know that, my son. And it is true that I have heard of him. He was once very loyal to the king."

"But he has always been loyal to Mexico, my father, and that is what concerns me now. I urge you to believe me in all sincerity, my father, that I must do this for my own well-being—indeed, for my own sanity." Carlos's voice rose, and then, as if abashed at the sound, he bowed his head and leaned back in his chair.

"Well now, young man," Don Diego said, attempting to make this farewell a cause for laughter rather than brooding sorrow, "you are not giving us much time to prepare a farewell banquet for you. This evening's meal was admirable, but I should hardly say it represents Tía Margarita's best efforts."

"I don't want any farewells, *mi padre*. I plan to leave in the morning, and I'll take Dolor, the new mustang I broke in. Also my rifle and hunting knife. And if I have wages coming from the times I helped in the fields—you yourself told me that you were writing a ledger page with my name on it—"

"And so I did," Don Diego boomed. "But surely you know that when I am gone, you inherit a good part of this land, its cattle and sheep, as well as the gold and silver that I have managed to save in my post since I came here from Madrid. And I have put some away for you. I shall give you whatever you need when you are ready to leave. Only do not waste it, and promise me that you will honestly try to make things better because you are there."

Carlos gave his father a grave nod. "You have my word on that." Then turning to Catarina, he humbly asked, "Is it too much of an imposition, *querida*, to look after my little ones till I come back?"

"No, *mi hermano*. You know I love children, and it's been wonderful taking care of yours for the past several weeks. Only I beg of you, my dear brother, not to do anything rash or impulsive that you'll regret in later years."

"I give you my word that I've thought about this for some time now, and I can't see that it's anything but honorable. I'll be fighting for my country."

"But when you say you want to fight against *ricos*, Carlos," John Cooper put in, "in a sense, you'll be fighting against your own kind, like your own father. Assuredly, he's a *rico*, you can't get away from that."

Carlos bowed his head for a moment, and Don Diego quickly interposed, "Of course, you must do what you must do, *mi hijo*. But do not renounce us, as you have the autocrats—do not include us in their number. We still love you, and we shall pray daily to *el Señor Dios* to bring you back to us once more happy and determined to live a good, purposeful life."

He saw his son bite his lips, and in this time of overpowering grief, he ventured to reach Carlos as never before, "Yes, I know what you lost in Weesayo—I considered her my own daughter almost, for she was good, kind, wonderfully intelligent. But if you trust in God, He will reward your faith. He will see to it that there will be someone to bring up your little children, to heal the wounds you so unjustly sustained. Forgive me, my son, if I mention her name again—but it will always live in my heart. And she will live in yours, too, and so you see, she will not really be dead for you. You will remember always how much she brought you in love, and it has made you such a strong, courageous—"

Carlos could bear no more. Bursting into tears, he abruptly rose from the table and strode to the door. There, he turned back to say, "I know you are trying to be kind, my father. God forgive me if I've hurt you or Doña Inez, or you, my little sister Catarina, or you, John Cooper. But I shall leave. Do not think too badly of me. One day I'll be back, when I've found my own destiny."

Don Diego did not sleep that night. Rather than worry his beloved Doña Inez, he lay still and kept his breathing audible so that she would think he was asleep. But as soon as he was certain that she was deep in slumber, he rose from his bed very carefully and tiptoed to the little chapel in the *hacienda*. Kneeling, crossing himself, he bowed his head and prayed for nearly an hour, and then, somewhat eased, went out into the courtyard, wearing a heavy robe to protect him against the cool night air. Stars twinkled in the sky, there were no clouds, and he looked up and fervently prayed again that Carlos would be returned safely to him, his mind eased and his resolve for a rich, intrepid life firmly settled, without the lingering distraction of this overpowering grief.

He understood what his son was feeling. Dolores, his first wife, had died peacefully, at least, unlike poor Weesayo; and yet he had been haunted by guilt for some years after that, for she had died on the very day he had gone to the Escorial at the summons of the fussy, importunate Carlos IV. There he had learned that because his pride in the great Spain of the olden days had been expressed to a traitorous, lackey-like nobleman he had believed to be his friend, he was to be banished from his beloved Madrid and given the sop of *intendente* in a sleepy little village far across the ocean, far from the intrigues and the ceremonials, the dances and the colorful life of his birthplace. He had seen in this punitive demotion a kind of spiritual retribution for whatever sins he might have committed, but he had never believed that Dolores would be taken from him. He had come to associate her death with his own failure, and that was why it had taken him so long to adjust to the life of Taos and its humdrum demands upon his skill and vigor.

All this ran through his mind, though he had not been able to see it in those distant years; and now he understood how much he had missed of life by putting that burden of guilt upon himself. Otherwise, he would not have waited so long to have married Inez, so loyal, devoted, and faithful, hiding her love so carefully and yet always being there to proffer it.

He felt that Carlos was even now reproaching himself for not having ridden with Weesayo, torturing himself—as any sensitive man who loves someone and loses her must inevitably do—for not having been there to defend her against the brutal *hacendado* who had abducted her and driven her to suicide. He did not know what this decision of Carlos's would entail, other than courage against physical danger—and courage, he thought to himself with a certain stiffening of his shoulders in paternal pride, Carlos had never lacked. Yes, there would be danger. Yet perhaps danger would provide the very distraction which alone could obliterate—if only temporarily—the brooding, stifling, choking torment of remembrance, of self-accusation, and of agonized doubts. How many times during the centuries since *el Señor Dios* created the world had men looked up at the sky as he was looking now and said, "What if I had done this or that? What if I had not done this or that? Would she still be alive, or did I fail her? And if I did, what was there in me that made me do it?"

He wept now in the darkness, in the silent night, weeping mostly for Carlos and only a little for himself and the wasted years which had followed Dolores's death. How stubbornly he had fought the transition from Spain to this strange new world, only to find that, here at last, was true happiness. Carlos must find that, too. And because he was young and more resilient, his chances were greater, and perhaps becoming a soldier was the answer.

Somewhat comforted, he went back to bed, vowing not to fall asleep. He wished to say farewell to Carlos and to give him a bag of money that would provide for his wants. At least he could buy a commission, for certainly a fine, sturdy man like Carlos did not deserve to be a lowly private or corporal. He smiled with his pride in Carlos, and he remembered how valiant the youth had been in defending him and Inez and Catarina when the Toboso Indians had attacked the carriage in which they rode to Taos. He remembered, also, how Carlos had climbed up the mast of the Spanish ship, as if he were a seaman of long standing, without the slightest fear. And this comforted him, too. Such courage, such strength, and with the golden years ahead, surely would mean there would be peace and happiness again for his beloved son.

Thus it was that when Carlos left the house at dawn and went out to the stable to saddle the mustang Dolor, Don Diego was waiting for him near the stall, seated on a footstool—a concession he had grudgingly made to his advancing years and his comparative lack of energy after such a sleepless night. Carlos wore his rapier, and carried his new Belgian rifle with him, as well as a pair of *pistolas* holstered at his belt, but when he saw his father, he dropped the rifle and uttered a startled gasp, "¡*Mi padre!* Why are you here—you should be sleeping—"

"Do you think I would sleep on the day you leave this *hacienda, mi hijo?*" the white-haired hidalgo fiercely declared as he rose to his feet, trying not to grimace from the stiffness of his joints. "A father does not say farewell to his son every day, you know. I wanted to see you off properly, and I wanted to give you this. There are plenty of silver *pesos* and a little gold, as well. It will keep you during these first hard times. I was thinking, also, that they may not recognize your excellent lineage and offer you a lowly soldier's rank, instead of an officer's brevet."

"I will ask for no favors, *mi padre*. But I'll admit that I want to lead and not follow in this fight for freedom."

"Then take the *dinero* and use it shrewdly, my son. I know that it will be a long time before we have letters from you—the mails from Mexico City to Taos are hardly reliable and often take from three to six months. But try at least to send us some news as soon as you reach your destination, how it goes with you, and about this army of freedom that you seek to join. I only hope you are not disillusioned in the man Iturbide. From what I have heard of him, he is an opportunist."

"Some of the world's greatest leaders have been just that, *mi padre*," Carlos said, smiling warmly. He tried to hide the tears in his eyes as he faced his father, taking the bag of money and putting it behind his back in his left hand, holding out his right to his father. "You aren't angry with me?"

"No, I could never be angry with you, Carlos. You were my firstborn. You carry the family name, just remember that." Don Diego's voice became suspiciously gruff. "A curse on you if you get yourself killed in some silly duel or some fight in an alleyway. I expect you to come back to me, and by then I shall be ready to turn the ranch over to you. You and John Cooper will run it; you will make it one of the greatest in this territory of Texas. And if you win your fight for freedom, there will be far less oppression for the settlers who will come after you have gone and try to make a new life here. I only hope that this struggle for independence from Spain does not lead to interminable revolutions in which one selfish man tries to hoist himself above his fellows. No one ever wins in a case like that, my son."

"I'll be careful, Father. You'll tell Doña Inez how much I'll miss her."

"You great oaf, you might have told her that yourself last night instead of stamping off in a fine huff," Don Diego exclaimed. Then, because he could no longer control his tears, he put both his arms around Carlos and embraced him. "*Vaya con Dios,* for all of your days. Know that you have my prayers and Inez's and your sister's, too. And remember, your children will be well taken care of in your absence. Only try to come back before you no longer recognize them, and that is an order from a father, my son."

"I will do my best, Father. Say a prayer for me. And if you send word to Taos or John Cooper does, ask Padre Moraga to pray both for my wife and myself. *Adiós.*"

Don Diego nodded and then strode out of the stable, trying not to look back, tears flowing down his cheeks. Carlos watched after him and then with a sigh turned back to the stall and saddled Dolor.

He put the bag of money into his saddlebag, tossed the Belgian rifle into its sheath, mounted the mustang, and wheeled its head sharply to the south.

Ten

Two days before Christmas in the year of 1820, Moses Austin was finally granted his audience before Governor Antonio de Martínez after having been escorted to San Antonio by the young *trabajador* whom Don Diego de Escobar had placed at his disposal. Because of numerous postponements and delays, he had to wait an entire week after his arrival in San Antonio before this meeting was granted. Consequently, the valiant, aging frontiersman had misgivings as to the success of his project.

At last he was ushered into the governor's office by an ostentatious majordomo, resplendent in red livery with gold buttons and polished shoes with silver buckles.

"It's gracious of you, Your Excellency, to receive me," Austin said in fluent Spanish to the governor, a rather florid-faced, stout little man with an enormous waxed mustache.

"Ah, you speak our tongue well, Señor Austin!" the governor complimented him, and at the same time waved his visitor to a chair before his ornate, beautifully hand-carved desk. Then, as if to demonstrate his familiarity with his visitor's project, he airily added, "Of course, knowing that you were in Missouri and, therefore, under Spanish rule, it is not surprising. I have before me your written proposal, Señor Austin. I have read it very carefully."

Moses Austin, though his face was impassive, felt a flicker of excitement surge through him, and he leaned forward, his gnarled hands gripping the arms of the chair. "And what does Your Excellency think about my proposal? I hope I have expressed myself fluently enough to show you what great advantages would be gained by opening the frontier to American settlers, as well as to traders. It would, you see, Governor Martínez, bring much more revenue into your own coffers."

The little man eyed him with cautious scrutiny. "I am

well aware of the possibilities, Señor Austin. You must not think for a moment that I, who serve to carry out His Majesty's orders as relayed to me by the viceroy of our Nueva España, do not realize that we are almost surrounded by Americans. And for many years they have been seeking to cross our boundaries and to establish trade routes and stations. Imperial Spain has forbidden this by passing prohibitive tariffs and restrictive laws which could forbid American settlers to enter as they pleased and to sell and trade as they wished."

Anticipating the governor's irritation, Austin diplomatically interposed with a propitiating smile, "What you say is certainly true, Your Excellency. And that's exactly why I'm anxious to have your support. Once word comes from the governor of Texas, it will be established law. Thereafter, only what your law permits will take place, and this will keep out the unscrupulous adventurer, the lawless ruffians, the mercenaries who seek a fight on any battlefield—for I well know that you fear these intruders. And I fully support your feelings in that matter; the settlers I have had in my own company in Missouri were righteous men, family men, Your Excellency, who toiled and tilled the soil for the welfare of the community, who caused no trouble, and who were devout Christians."

"You argue your cause well, Señor Austin." Governor Martínez abruptly rose and paced the floor, his hands clasped behind his back, his lips pursed in deep thought. Suddenly he turned and, pointing an accusing forefinger at the frontiersman, almost angrily declared, "But you have not forgotten the Long expedition, I trust? It is still fresh in my mind, Señor Austin, and that is why I must not only reject your proposal, but also order you to leave this province as soon as possible."

"But, Your Excellency—" Moses Austin stared uncomprehendingly at the officious little man.

"Let me refresh your memory, Señor Austin," Governor Martínez irascibly began. "A good many of your countrymen believe Texas is part of Louisiana and do not care for the treaty signed by Spain and the United States last year, delineating the western boundary of the Louisiana Purchase. Some of them showed their resentment by deciding upon an invasion of this territory, which I am empowered to govern by the will of the viceroy and of His Most Catholic Majesty

Ferdinand VII. From the report that I had, Señor Austin, Dr. James Long was chosen the leader at a meeting held in Natchez, and by June of last year he had occupied Nacogdoches with some three hundred men. Also, he was named resident of this would-be republic of"—he almost spat out the word—"Texas."

"Yes, but Your Excellency—" Austin tried to interpose.

"A moment, *por favor,* Señor Austin!" the governor interrupted, imperiously holding up his hand. "Then this James Long went to Galveston to meet the pirate, Lafitte, whom he had named as governor of Galveston under this so-named republic of Long's. However, even that misguided pirate was wise enough this time not to join Long in an expedition against our forces in this territory. And the rest is left to history. We routed these would-be invaders of Spanish soil. Now you see why I am suspicious—not of you personally, for I know that you have loyalties to Spain—but of what might befall this territory if I grant your request. There will certainly be ambitious men, many of them thieves and murderers, who will come in with your settlers and pose as upright citizens. No, señor, I regret that I must cause you disappointment, for I personally hold you in high esteem. But I am also the servant of His Majesty, and I am responsible to the viceroy, Juan Ruiz de Apodaca. I should be remiss in my duties if I were to grant this proposal."

Moses Austin rose despondently, his eyes dull and his lips tightened in a look of dejection. "I deeply regret, also, that Your Excellency does not understand that if I were in charge of this colonization, I should personally hold myself responsible to you, as well as to the viceroy and the king, for the security you wish to retain. I should see to it myself that no man or woman who was suspect, should be allowed to join our group. They would be very carefully selected as to background, aims, and desires, and without any connections of political or military influence—of that I could certainly assure you!"

"Please, do not distress yourself." Now Governor Martínez was smiling effusively, as if to console his visitor for the disappointment he caused. "Believe me when I say that I would accept your word. And when I tell you that you must leave this province, it is only because I am following orders that are strict and allow of no deviation. I personally should be glad to keep you at my own private quarters as my guest, but—"

"I understand, Your Excellency. I thank you, Your Excellency. And now I have the honor to wish Your Excellency a good day." Moses Austin inclined his head and, his face somber, his shoulders slumping, walked slowly from the audience chamber.

As he walked down the busy main street of San Antonio to the little inn where he had taken a room which he shared with the young *trabajador*, Austin felt the full weight of his fifty-nine years. The governor's attitude had distressed him, though he understood the protocol imposed by autocratic, unfeeling Spanish *juntas* which invariably set aside not only all personal friendships, but even the most common of courtesies. He admitted to himself that it had been gracious of Governor Martínez to say that he would have been welcome to stay at his elegant house, if his superiors hadn't ordered the American to leave the province. Yet words cost the governor nothing, and as for Moses Austin himself, he would have to turn elsewhere. Perhaps the place to go now was the Double H Ranch, where he would enlist Don Diego's aid for his cause, as the former intendant had promised.

Suddenly he was hailed by a familiar voice. "Señor Austin, *por todos los santos!* What brings you here to San Antonio?"

Looking up with a start, he uttered a joyous cry: "Baron de Bastrop, my old friend from Spanish Louisiana! How good it is to see you, and how welcome a sight you are at this black moment in my life!"

Baron F.E.N. de Bastrop was an elegant figure of a man, a few years younger than Moses Austin, dressed like an aristocrat and with a fine rapier with a silver basket hilt at his side. He enthusiastically shook hands with the frontiersman and then anxiously queried, "But why do you say this is a black day, *amigo?*"

"I've just come from Governor Martínez with a proposal to bring American settlers here into Texas, Baron. Not only has he rejected it, but he's ordered me to leave the province at once."

"Well, perhaps I am not without some influence with His Excellency," the baron said, chuckling. "Tonight, you shall dine at my house, and meanwhile, while you go back to your inn and refresh yourself—I see you are weary—let me see what I can do to forward your petition. You know, the final say in such a matter would not be by the governor, but rather by the commandant general, Joaquín de Arrendondo, the hero of the Battle of Medina."

Austin was overjoyed at this unexpected intervention on his behalf. By the same token, he was diplomatic enough to realize that to disagree with his friend's enthusiastic acclaim of the commandant general ((whom he personally considered a butcher) would be totally out of place. Instead he said, "I'd be most grateful to you, Baron. His Excellency seems to fear that if I bring American settlers into this area, there will be a military force. Please assure him that it is not my intention in the least, and I should screen all applicants who wish to settle and be very certain of them before I permitted them to accompany me."

"I know you well, and I know what you have done in Missouri. Have no fear. Now take my advice and rest. I'll send my servant for you this evening, and we'll dine. As it happens, I have a good deal of influence in San Antonio, and Governor Martínez listens to my recommendations with great concern."

"You're truly a friend, Baron." Austin exhaled a sigh of relief and extended his hand, which the nobleman again enthusiastically shook. "I'll go back to my room, then, and rest—and also pray for your success. God bless you!"

Moses Austin was fatigued, not only from all his recent traveling, but also from the emotional stress of the unfavorable audience, and the sudden unexpected hope which this chance meeting with his old friend had evoked. He was alone when he entered his room, Don Diego's workman having gone out for the afternoon, and he flung himself down on his bed and soon was fast asleep.

He was wakened some two hours later by the innkeeper, who first respectfully knocked at the door and then, alarmed that his guest did not promptly answer, began to hammer with his fist and call out, "Señor Austin, *por amor de Dios, respóndame,* I beg of you!"

Groggily, Austin got to his feet and opened the door as the innkeeper stammered, "Thank heavens—I had imagined—well, I will not offend you by saying what I imagined— this is only to tell you that the carriage of the Baron de Bastrop awaits your good pleasure, Señor Austin!"

The elderly frontiersman started with surprise, and then,

remembering, exclaimed, "Please be good enough to tell th
baron's servant that I need a few moments to make mysel
presentable, and I'll be with him directly."

The innkeeper, bowing and scraping, was obviousl
impressed that this somewhat shabbily dressed man was a
personal friend of one of the most influential noblemen in th
town. After he left, Austin quickly turned to the basin o
water that had been provided earlier that day and made
hasty toilette. Mopping his face with a clean towel that hun
from a wooden peg, he smoothed his sparse gray hair wit
both of his slim, nervous hands, adjusted his waistcoat an
britches so that they did not look too badly wrinkled, an
then, with a self-disparaging sigh, left his room to be ushere
with great ceremony by the baron's valet into the carriage
which was driven by an elegantly liveried coachman. En rout
to the baron's mansion, the personable, middle-aged vale
gossipingly provided Austin with the latest news of what wa
taking place in sleepy San Antonio, not without adroitl
insinuating a few praises of his master so that if the latter'
guest were to discuss the escort provided to his domicile, hi
guest's report would be as favorable as possible.

Moses Austin was driven to the section of San Antoni
known as the Villa of San Fernando, and the carriage drew
up before a distinctive, sprawling house built with a patio an
sheltered corridors, not unlike the Spanish architecture o
early New Orleans. The valet obsequiously got out of th
carriage and held the door open for the frontiersman, bowin
low as if to a nobleman equal to his own master's status, an
at once the door was flung open and the genial baron himsel
appeared with outstretched arms: "*Amigo*, tonight we feast
and I have good news for you! I have convinced *su excelenci*
that your proposal is honorable and with no deception to it. I
told him that I have known you for years, that never did yo
aim at any military coup which would endanger the Spanis
overlords, and as a result, I am happy to tell you that he ha
agreed to forward your proposal to Monterrey, where a boar
of superior officers, whom we call the provincial deputation
will rule upon it."

"This is wonderful news indeed, Baron!" Austin grate
fully exclaimed. "I can't begin to tell you how indebted I am
to you for your help! A few hours ago I was beside myself
feeling myself almost a criminal as a result of what Governo
Martínez told me."

The mustachioed nobleman shrugged and spread out hi

hands in a gesture of complicity. "Well now, *amigo,* he was merely following orders. He did not know you too well, but he defers to me in matters of importance. So it was a lucky thing that I was here to meet you when you came from his chambers. Now then, you are going to be my guest until such time as we have news from Monterrey."

"But surely, Baron, it would inconvenience you too much—"

"Not another word, *amigo!* You are going to stay here until we hear the good news, which is already assured. It will, of course, take a certain amount of time for a courier to ride to Monterrey with your proposal, but Governor Martínez has already endorsed it and approved it, thanks to my recommendation. I should think that, by the middle of next month, you would have a favorable decision."

"It's incredible!" The gray-haired colonizer shook his head, an incredulous smile on his thin lips. "Truly *el Señor Dios* answered my prayer to bring you here at this exact hour when I had given up all hope."

"I am happy to be able to render you such a service. You and I have had many a glass of wine together, and we have talked of the future. You see, I am not far from your age, and I know that things are changing. Spain—let us be honest with each other, since there is no one to eavesdrop on our conversation—Spain, as we once knew it, is dying. Ferdinand VII believed that he had shown great valor in deposing his father, but the truth was that his father was a weakling. A weakling, mind you, dominated by his dissolute wife and the prime minister, Godoy, who virtually delivered all of Spain to Napoleon and his hordes. But when this filial usurper occupied the throne, he showed himself to be inept, and thus he is beginning to lose all of Spain's possessions in this new world of ours."

"You are right."

"I know that. You see, I'm a realist. I may be of the autocracy and my blood is as pure as that of any *rico* or *hidalgo,* but I am also aware that, today, the *peones* can look to the future with more hope than our own class." The baron dolefully shook his head. "Come now, my cook has prepared a feast to celebrate this happy occasion. We can philosophize at our leisure over some excellent terrapin, and he has made a Creole gumbo which is as good as any you would find in New Orleans, believe me. I have opened some of my best Burgundy, so that we may toast each other, *amigo.*"

* * * * * *

On January 17, 1821, Moses Austin's petition that would allow him to bring three hundred settlers into the Spanish-dominated territory of Texas was formally approved, and the signature that authorized this approval was none other than that of the commandant general, Joaquín de Arredondo, who had put down one of the earliest revolutionary outbreaks against New Spain, at the Battle of Medina.

Joyously, Austin expressed his gratitude to the Baron de Bastrop and took leave of the young *trabajador* who had served as his companion through all this arduous waiting. The *trabajador* would return to the Double H Ranch with the news of Moses Autsin's success, as well as with the American's repeated thanks for Don Diego's kindness and support.

Austin insisted on riding back to Missouri alone, and the baron saw to it that he rode a gelded yearling whose vitality and strength would be better suited to the long journey back home than the weary horse that Austin had ridden in his travels to San Antonio.

It would be a long, dreary journey, a solitary one, but the frontiersman did not mind this in the least. His eyes were bright with hope, and his lips were smiling as he headed the yearling toward the northeast. For all these weeks, as a guest of the house of the influential nobleman, he had seen what the *ricos* enjoyed: paintings, a desk covered with Cordoba leather, another desk decorated with tortoiseshell and silver, a writing desk inlaid with ivory, with many luxurious rugs and cushions. In the dining room, where he ate exotic foods and drank rare wines that he had never before tasted in his colony in Missouri, there were services of ancient silver and many exquisite pieces of china and crystal decorated with solid gold. He thought to himself that the wealth of the baron's mansion, if melted down into silver or gold and sold on the open market, would be enough to pay for the transportation of his three hundred settlers and to ensure them a comfortable life for the next two or three years.

And as he rode toward the northeast, his shoulders straight, the years seemed to fall away from him, and he felt again as he had when he first proposed the colony in Missouri. He had the dream of an idealist, as well as a practical man, who saw that the only hope for the expansion of a new country and the establishment of peace between an old country and a new was through the interchange of peoples, of honest communication, and of free trade. The wearisome journey he had taken meant nothing now. He rode back to his son, Stephen, with the anticipation and eagerness of a young man who has seen a dream finally come almost into being.

Eleven

Life had been rewarding for Don Sancho de Pladero during the six years since the de Escobars had moved to Texas and Don Diego had abandoned the post of *intendente* to his good friend. Though he was now in his early sixties and nearly bald, as well as even more corpulent than he had been when Don Diego had first been welcomed by him in Taos, Don Sancho had more animation and amiability than he had enjoyed since leaving Spain with his once-shrewish wife, Doña Elena.

For one thing, he had finally asserted his conjugal mastery over Doña Elena following her censure of young Conchita Seragos, to whom their son Tomás had been pledged and eventually married. He had taken his wife by the hand and led her like an errant schoolgirl into his bedroom, and there he had proceeded to administer a long-overdue spanking. The passionate reconciliation that had followed had transformed his nagging wife—who had never failed to remind him of what she had abandoned in her beloved Madrid in order to follow him to the desolate little town of Taos— into a warm, attentive, and thoroughly devoted spouse. Moreover, he was ecstatic over the happiness that his son and Conchita had garnered from their marriage. He could now boast of being a grandfather of two little boys and an adorable little girl whom he had diplomatically induced Tomás to name after his wife. And besides, the firstborn, as son, was named after him, Sancho.

The flocks of sheep on the estate now numbered well over five thousand, and the revenue from their wool had almost doubled since Don Diego had left Taos. With paternal pride, Don Sancho would tell anyone who was interested at

banquets or festive dinners that all of this was due to the
industry and skill of his fine son, Tomás. Thus, in the twilight
of his years, he was enjoying life as he had never done before
and even Doña Elena, now in her mid-fifties with her black
hair turned entirely gray, seemed almost beautiful to him.
The primness and disapproving countenance that she had
invariably bestowed upon him in earlier years had been
replaced by an ever-present smile, and her gray-green eyes
were warm and tender when she looked at him. Best of all,
they were still lovers. There were times, when he knelt in the
little chapel to give his thanks to *el Señor Dios* for all his
blessings, when he was irreverent enough to chuckle.

Yet, as to his official duties as intendant, he was not
quite so serene as in his domestic life. The unrest that was
now sweeping Mexico was felt in Taos as well as in Santa Fe.
Facundo Melgares was now governor of Nuevo México,
having replaced Pedro María de Allande. Don Sancho considered Melgares a fussy, importunate, rather indecisive man
who veered like a weather vane from week to week, depend-
ing on the strength of the rumors brought by courier or
military troops from Mexico City or Chihuahua. Don Sancho's own authority had been greatly curtailed, mainly because of the viceroy's concern over the growing revolutionary
movement that surrounded the capital of Nueva España.
Viceroy Apodaca had only recently sent an order to all
intendants to stash away, in a secret hiding place, the tithes
due the crown until such time as order could be restored to
the ruling Mexican government. Every now and then, merchants or friendly Indians or visitors from some of the
provinces to the south came into Santa Fe and then Taos.
They returned with reports of sporadic outbreaks of banditry,
lawlessness, and even revolt among groups of *peones* who
chafed under the tyrannical yoke of *hacendados* who ignored
the rumors of an independence movement. It was, in a word,
a time of grave and almost sinister unrest.

But this, however, was not what cast the shadow over
the serene horizon of Don Sancho de Pladero. It was rather
his growing dislike of Don Esteban de Rivarola, who had
taken over Don Sancho's former post of *alcalde mayor,* and
exercised his powers like a feudal lord. Over the past two
years, particularly, there had been complaints to Don Sancho
himself from the impoverished *indios* of the pueblo that
flanked the sleepy town of Taos about the brazen lechery, the
cruel insolence, and the flagrant exploitation of not only Don

Esteban's *peones,* but also of such luckless *indios* whose services he arrogantly commandeered whenever it suited his fancy.

And so it was with a scowl on his face that he watched Don Esteban de Rivarola leave a shop on the outskirts of the plaza and walk toward the building in which were housed the two official chambers of the *intendente* and the *alcalde mayor.* Don Sancho drew aside the shutters that kept the hot, late-morning sun from filtering into his office, and then sighed aloud, wishing that he could consign his assistant to the most distant province in all of Nueva España—or, better still, back to Barcelona whence he had originally come.

He knew exactly how Don Esteban would harass him this mid-January morning. Yesterday he had attended the courtroom where Don Esteban presided and had cast the deciding vote in favor of a Pueblo *indio* who had brought a claim for damages to his humble *jacal.* Two of Don Esteban's servants, riding on horseback in pursuit of a fleeing *criada* who had escaped from Don Esteban's *hacienda* fearing a whipping, had believed they had seen her go into the Indian's hut and, in their quest, had let their horses trample the old man's garden, while they helped themselves to a jug of tequila and two handwoven blankets, which the Indian's wife had woven for the comfort of the *jacal.*

Don Esteban had been openly contemptuous of the old man's complaint, and had harangued him from his seat on the dais in the narrow but long room which served as the court of Taos. He had been ready to dismiss the case, when Don Sancho, who had been seated at the back attentively listening to the testimony of the two servants and of the old Indian himself, had risen and placatingly suggested that the treasury of Taos itself pay the claim for damages. He had cleverly argued, with a mocking sarcasm that had not escaped the fuming Don Esteban, that one could not hold servants accountable for what their animals did, and so, therefore, one should regard the damages as both impersonal and accidental, and the town should make restitution. There had been a murmur of laughter as well as applause from the spectators who had come to the courtroom, most of them neighbors of the old *indio.* And Don Esteban had grudgingly agreed to pay the old man twenty silver *pesos* out of the town's treasury.

Don Sancho turned back to his desk so that he could not be caught spying on his judicial associate, just as Don Esteban de Rivarola entered his office. The *hacendado* owned

some five thousand sheep, and his ranch and elegantly decorated *hacienda* were located about three miles west of the site
of Don Diego de Escobar's former home in Taos. He was a
little man, five feet four inches in height, with crafty, narrow-
ly set brown eyes and a peaked little nose, his mouth fleshy
and small and constantly set in a petulant expression. Ever
since he had been appointed *alcalde mayor*, he had bedecked
himself in the gaudiest raiment of a *caballero* that he could
find, with a gold chain around his neck as a symbol of office.
And since he had been nearly bald since his twenties, because
of an attack of fever, he wore a curly wig that made him look
almost grotesque. He was a bachelor and presently fifty-six
years of age.

"Good day to you, Don Sancho," he began in a voice
with an ingratiating whine to it, which Don Sancho knew was
meant to sound respectful but which, in reality, contained all
the malice of which this little man was capable.

"And to you as well, Don Esteban. May God's grace
shine upon you," the *intendente* blandly riposted.

"Thank you, Don Sancho," the little man said, drawing
himself up stiffly. "I have been thinking about the decision
you made yesterday, and I have my belief that it is illegal."

"Pray do not concern yourself, Don Esteban. I myself
have paid the silver *pesos* back into the treasury of Taos, out
of my own pocket," was Don Sancho de Pladero's smiling
reply.

The pompous little *hacendado* drew himself up, thrusting out his chest like a pouter pigeon, his face darkening with
anger: "You make a mockery of our justice here in Taos,
Don Sancho! But then, it doesn't surprise me in the least.
You've always been too lenient with *peones* and *indios*. And
that, too, is to be expected, seeing that you were always on
such intimate terms with that traitorous Don Diego de Escobar. Do you know, Don Sancho, it has long been in my
thoughts that you and he were confederates together, disloyal
to the crown."

Don Sancho de Pladero banged his fist down on the table
as he rose from his chair to reply to this infamous accusation.
"If I were younger, Don Esteban, I would challenge you to a
duel to demand satisfaction for so malicious a remark. Know
it now and for all time, that Don Diego and I were friends,
nothing more. We worked well together, and there was no
friction between us in our offices, as there is between you and
myself."

"Oh, I don't doubt that," the little *hacendado* sneered, self-consciously reaching up to adjust his wig. "My friends and I believe that you were in sympathy with Don Diego's welcoming the *americano* traitors, even though our laws prohibit such intrusion by *gringos*. As for friction between ourselves, I am sworn as *alcalde mayor* to officiate at trials, at complaints by these lowly, worthless people who are good only for the most menial of labor, who are illiterate and dirty, little more than savages. And the *indios* in the pueblo are constrained only by the knowledge that we could use military force against them, else they would rise and revolt against their rightful masters."

"There was once such an uprising, when a gallant Indian named Popé rose up against tyrannical overlords. We do not learn very much from history, Don Esteban, in my opinion. I personally prefer a more benign treatment; they were here before us, and, indeed, in some instances, it may be said that they outnumber us. But tyranny and brutality, and the usage of the medieval law that the master has the first corporal rights over any female *peón* in his household, can only antagonize these docile people."

"I do not like your insinuations, Don Sancho. Merely because you are an old man and have a wife, you think to lecture me on morality. I have never married, and if I choose to amuse myself with my willing *criadas*, it is surely no concern of yours," was Don Esteban de Rivarola's answer as he glared at the elderly intendant.

Don Sancho shrugged and sat back down again, wishing that this irascible little man would take himself off to his own office. But at this last jibe he could not resist countering with, "You said they are willing, Don Esteban. From the case of yesterday, it would appear that your *criada* Luz was not quite so willing, or she would not have fled from your *hacienda* and hidden."

"That is entirely my affair! I was told she took sanctuary in the church and that old fool Padre Moraga helped her get away. And that is another thing, Don Sancho. He meddles too much in our affairs. Let him stay in his church and preach his sermons and hold his masses; that is the work for which he was ordained, not to dictate how the privileged and the *ricos* should live their lives," the *alcalde mayor* snapped. Then at last, turning on his heel, he stomped out of Don Sancho's office and went to his own.

Don Sancho de Pladero sighed and shook his head. He

began very industriously to examine a sheaf of papers before him, wishing to distract himself from the disturbing interview. What perturbed him most was the vindictive comment about his friendship with Don Diego. Thus far, neither Don Esteban nor his crony Luis Saltareno had succeeded in discovering the whereabouts of the former intendant, although Don Sancho was convinced that both of them had sought to find that information out by devious means.

However, he could not help smiling to himself because, before coming to his office this morning, he had gone directly to the church to see Padre Moraga, and had arranged for the frightened young Luz to be sneaked out of the church in a *carreta*, concealed in a blanket and with bales of hay piled around her, and driven by one of his own *trabajadores* out of Taos to the little village of Clarindo some twenty-five miles to the northeast, where her aunt and uncle lived. And he had given her forty silver *pesos* out of his own purse as a kind of dowry, wishing her well and telling her never again to set foot in Taos. Padre Moraga had blessed him for his humanitarian deed, and Don Sancho felt a comforting warmth as he began to undertake the routine work of this January day.

There were only two cases on the docket late this morning before the *alcalde mayor* and the *intendente*, and they were simple matters readily disposed of, to which Don Sancho found no objection in agreeing with Don Esteban's decision. He, for one, was glad that the day would be short, for he was eager to get back to his *hacienda* and confer with his son, Tomás. The latter had asked him last night for permission to spend several hundred *pesos* in constructing wooden troughs, and for the purchase of a strong medicinal oil to kill ticks in the summer. Last year, Don Sancho recalled, the yield on wool was not quite so profitable as that of the previous year because the sheep had been stricken with ticks that had ruined the wool and had killed at least fifteen ewes before Tomás had shrewdly instructed his *trabajadores* to keep the healthy flock at a distance from the diseased ones. Also, Tomás, with some embarrassment, had asked his father if they might not have a fiesta to celebrate his wedding anniversary. Don Sancho was in hearty agreement with this idea, except that he did not deem it advisable to make the fiesta open to all of the *ricos* in Taos, particularly men like Don Esteban and Luis Saltareno. By now he understood quite well that these two men were his avowed enemies, as they were of his old and beloved friend, Don

Diego de Escobar. And their presence in his house would be unseemly and intolerable, as they would no doubt ridicule and abuse the young *criadas* and other servants, as Don Sancho had seen them do at other gatherings.

But the prospect of paying tribute to his son and to Conchita, as well as to his adored grandchildren who he could enjoy in his old age, filled him with great joy, and he smiled to himself as he signed the papers that required his official signature as *intendente*. Then, making certain that there were no further irksome details to occupy him for the rest of the day, he left his office and, mounting his piebald mare Rosita, rode happily back to his *hacienda*.

As he passed the church, he crossed himself and thanked *el Señor Dios* for giving him a man of faith and contrition like Padre Moraga. He had not, however, liked how the old priest looked when he had seen him this morning. Padre Moraga looked haggard and he was certain that the old man was not at all well. No doubt the long journey to the *hacienda* of Don Diego and then back to Taos, had sorely taxed Padre Moraga, and Don Sancho told himself he should have a word with the priest's housekeeper, old Soledad Tordisa, and urge her to consult a *médico* to examine the old man. It would be a calamity for all of Taos if so wise and benevolent a spiritual leader as Padre Juan Moraga were to be summoned to his Maker; it would allow such unscrupulous and scurrilous men like Luis Saltareno and Don Esteban de Rivarola to unleash all their licentious and corrupt whims upon the impoverished *indios* and *peones,* over whom they held such arrogant and ruthless sway.

Twelve

On the evening of the same day that the *alcalde mayor* had confronted Don Sancho de Pladero and all but accused him of traitorous collaboration with Don Diego de Escobar, the merchant, Luis Saltareno, was a guest at dinner in the

elegant mansion of Don Esteban de Rivarola. These two men
had been drawn together over the years by their envy and
hatred of Don Diego de Escobar, and they were now strength-
ened in this alliance because they had discovered that his
successor, Don Sancho, had proven to be as incorruptible as
his predecessor. As such, he was an obstacle to their own
selfish plans for greater power over the province of Taos.

Luis Saltareno was now fifty-one, of medium height,
with stooped shoulders, and a considerable paunch as the
result of overindulgence in food and drink. He wore a
Vandyke beard, curly and luxuriant, which he fastidiously
trimmed each day, and his insolent upper lip was decorated
by a carefully thinned mustache. His brown eyes were set
close together between the bridge of a broad Roman nose,
and his lips were large and ripe, the mouth of a sensualist and
a sadist. An only son, he had come to Taos in the year of
1803, shortly after the death of his ailing mother in Chihuahua. His father, who had preceded her in death by a dozen
years, had established a thriving shop and often visited Taos
for the annual fair. The wealth he had inherited from his
father had been supplemented by his own shrewdness as a
merchant, and although it had never been proved, he had
been suspected of selling guns and *aguardiente* to Indians.

He had never married, which had distressed his father,
who had prayed for grandchildren. Luis had incurred an
almost fatal accident in his early twenties, when he had been
hunting the wild *jabalí* with a group of friends. His horse had
thrown him to the ground when a huge wild boar charged out
of a mesquite thicket. Luis's companions had heard his
screams for help and had ridden up in time to kill the boar,
but not before it had gored the young Saltareno in the groin.
As a consequence, he had been rendered not only sterile, but
also virtually impotent—though this loss in no way impeded
his licentious nature. Soon after he had come to Taos, he had
hired an elderly Pueblo Indian named Castamaguey to carve
a religious statue for his chapel. He had forcibly appropriated
the old man's daughter and made her his housekeeper. When
Don Diego had come to Taos as intendant and sat in
judgment on Saltareno's case against the old Indian, who had
been denied payment for his statue on the grounds that the
Cristo resembled an Indian and not a Spaniard, Don Diego
had ruled in favor of Castamaguey and bought the statue
himself. By so doing, he had made friends among the Pueblo
Indians of Taos, and a mortal enemy of the merchant.

The young Indian girl had died two years ago, as a result of frequent brutal floggings and incarceration in an airless, narrow dungeon in the cellar of Saltareno's house. She had been replaced by two other girls in their early teens, one an orphaned Mexican girl, the other an Indian. Padre Moraga had often sought, during the confessional, to urge the arrogant merchant to set them free, but Luis Saltareno had speciously declared that he was indeed acting as a benevolent humanitarian by giving these orphans a proper home, with good food and clothing and an opportunity to educate themselves. Such cynicism had outraged the ailing Padre Moraga, but Saltareno ignored the old priest's warnings that such conduct might bring with it excommunication.

This evening, he sat across the table from his good friend Don Esteban de Rivarola, and was served by a comely Indian girl who herself was not more than fifteen, and whose gentle, timid demeanor excited his sadistic nature. As for Don Esteban, he shared Saltareno's penchant for cruelty and perversity toward helpless young girls, but in his case his own impotence was due to many years of flagrant dissoluteness. Now he derived his principal erotic pleasure from witnessing the degradation and chastisement of servant-girls at the hands of his exotic and equally perverse mistress, Noracia.

Noracia, born to a now dead *hacendado* and a Pueblo Indian mother, was twenty-two and had become Don Esteban's mistress two years ago. The deceased *hacendado* had been miserly and given Noracia's mother very little money for his daughter's support. Upon his death the mother tearfully told her daughter that because of this liaison, Noracia was regarded as an outcast by her own tribe. Ailing, and with the realization that she did not have long to live, she urged her attractive daughter to seek out the protection of some *rico* who would care for her and doubtless treat her well because Noracia had the advantage of Spanish blood in her veins. She was slim, with long black hair that fell nearly to her hips, her face oval, with high-set cheekbones, a small, insolent mouth, dainty nose, and large, wide brown eyes. Her body was lithe and exquisitely sculptured, with long legs and high, firm breasts, and her warm tawny skin excited Don Esteban.

On their first night together, when he had failed to achieve fruition with her despite all her wiles, he had cruelly thrashed her. But Noracia had had sufficient insight into his carnal nature to extricate herself most cunningly from further suffering: on the next occasion when he had summoned her to his bedchamber, she had slyly insinuated, "Perhaps the *patrón* would like to watch me give the whip to the naughty *criadas* of his household. I, being a woman, can cause them more pain and shame than you as a man, *excelencia!*"

The idea had amused Don Esteban de Rivarola, and that very night he had had two of his brutish *peones* bring in a timid *criada* of sixteen, accusing her of breaking one of his fine teacups. The charge, of course, was trumped-up, but it provided an excuse for his sadistic pleasure. Noracia had purringly declared, "The little *puta* is lying, *excelencia*. I will make her confess and then repent, *con su permiso*."

The men had taken her to a windowless chamber built at the side of his elegant *hacienda*, and there, at Noracia's bidding, she was tied to a post in the middle of the room. While Don Esteban, wearing only his red-brocaded dressing gown and slippers, had watched with growing excitement, Noracia seized a three-thonged leather whip and proceeded to flog the unfortunate girl until she was nearly fainting and ready to confess that she had committed every mortal sin in the lexicon of man and devil alike.

Don Esteban had thoroughly enjoyed this cruel voyeurism. Grateful to Noracia for thus providing him with so refinedly perverse a spectacle, he had henceforth treated her almost with the respect he might have shown a wife. Her tenure was certain, her powers accepted by all the *peones*, all of whom secretly coveted her without hope and had to content themselves instead with the unfortunate *criadas* who became her frequent victims. Meanwhile, thanks to her cleverness and inventiveness in providing him with sadistic spectacles to whet his thwarted lusts, Don Esteban rewarded his mistress with clothes and jewels. To be sure, because of his own despotic nature, he would occasionally relegate her to the status of one of those *criadas* when he felt that she waxed overconfident in her self-assurance in his household, and then again she knew the ignominy of the lash and torture. But she was not violated by the *peones*, a relative mercy for which she was grateful and which, indeed, spurred her on to new flights of invention.

This evening, seated at his right, Noracia wore a stunning blue silk gown cut low enough to show the cleft between her proud, firm breasts, and there were gold bracelets on her wrists and a necklace of topaz around her slim throat. Luis Saltareno covetously eyed her and lifted his goblet of Madeira in tribute to her beauty. "I drink to your health and long life, señorita," he praised her.

Noracia demurely lowered her eyes and softly thanked him, while Don Esteban, twisting the tips of his finely waxed mustache, chuckled, well understanding how his less wealthy though influential ally longed to possess a concubine of such enticements and abilities. "Noracia thanks you, Luis," he guffawed, patting his moist lips with a lace-trimmed napkin and reaching for his goblet, which he drained nearly at a gulp. "It is pleasant in this dying little town, so far from the court of the viceroy, and even farther from that of the Escorial, to live at one's ease like this, Luis. And, to be sure, to have so beautiful a companion beside me." In his turn he lifted his goblet toward Noracia, who again inclined her head in an attitude of total humility and gratitude.

"Ah, Don Esteban," the merchant enviously exhaled, "you live the sort of life one can only dream of. Here we are marooned in a dying little town overrun with those accursed, lazy Pueblo *indios*, hundreds of miles away from the palace of the viceroy, obliged to wait long months before the slightest news comes from him—and all the time we hear rumors that Nueva España is on the point of breaking off all relations and ties with the Escorial. Is it any wonder that I envy you, for you have found your own little paradise here within these walls."

"Paradise is for any man who can afford it, Luis," the *hacendado* chuckled, reaching out to stroke the cheek of his handsome half-breed concubine. Then, frowning, he went on, "But there are still clouds upon the horizon of this paradise you so envy, Luis. One of them, to be sure, and one on which we both agree, is none other than our present *intendente*. It's true that I succeeded to his post when he in turn replaced the long-absent Don Diego de Escobar. I confess to you, Luis, that over the past few years I have made some attempts to track down this man whom I regard as a traitor, though I have no real proof. All of us who are of the aristocracy and who took land from the king or the viceroy have reason to detest Don Diego de Escobar. He set himself up as a kind of humanitarian, showing the stupid *indios* that he alone of all of us was willing to give them what they believed to be justice." His lips spat out the very last word, and he sneered as he reached for his goblet of wine, which his concubine had thoughtfully refilled. After a hearty draught, he continued, "I have tried to examine what I should do if I had been in Don

Diego's place, Luis. Evidently, the charges which the governor at Santa Fe levied against him that time, you recall, when he was accused of complicity in aiding *americano* traders, did not have sufficient weight to destroy him, as all of us hoped they would. But undoubtedly he understood that we—and the governor himself—were not content with that verdict, and that sooner or later he would have to pay for his disloyalty and obduracy."

"I am trying to follow your logic, Don Esteban, but I confess that I do not yet see—" Luis Saltareno apologetically began as he helped himself to more wine.

"Well then, to make a long story short, my own belief has been for some little time that he and his family and that accursed *gringo* who married his pampered daughter, Catarina, took themselves off to California. We know there are Spanish missions at Monterey and in the valleys where grapes are grown. He could have easily taken up a bucolic life there, for Spanish rule is now tenuous at best, and with the long distances between Mexico City and Monterey, for example, it would be well-nigh impossible for the viceroy to find him. Besides, there is internal unrest, as well, throughout all of Nueva España, so that His Excellency the viceroy has far more important matters to deal with immediately than to worry about an absentee traitor."

"Then you think he is in California?"

"I do. I will tell you, also, that about two years ago, being of a curious nature, I sent one of my *trabajadores* to follow a rider who had come to see Don Sancho de Pladero at his *hacienda*. My suspicion was that it might have been a courier from Don Diego. And my man reported to me that this courier had stayed the night and then ridden off at dawn, but in a westerly direction. That would suppose California to be his destination."

"I see." Saltareno frowned and considered what he had just heard. "But you have no objection, Don Esteban, if I do a little investigation of my own? I have in mind a certain scoundrel who runs an apothecary shop, Barnaba Canepa. You know his background only too well, I'm sure. He peddles love potions to the stupid little *criadas* who mourn for a lover, and he has been known to dispense poison—"

Don Esteban held up a hand as he smilingly interrupted the merchant. "I do not wish to hear that in my official capacity, even though we are friends at table. And it would be just as well, Luis, if it were not generally known that you and I have any sort of association other than being mere acquaintances. You gather my meaning, I'm certain. There is another meddlesome old fool in this town, by the name of Padre Juan Moraga, the leader of the *Penitentes*. Let him wield the lash of the *sangrador* over the superstitious and the *peones* and the *indios*—he'd best keep out of my business and yours, as well as that of some of my influential friends. Mind you, I am a devout churchgoer, I confess my sins to him; but when he begins to mix politics with his religion, then I say to myself, I owe him no allegiance. What we need in Taos is a young, aggressive priest who understands on what side his bread is buttered, and who caters to the *ricos* who furnish the tithes that run his church. The house of God, never forget it for a moment, Luis, is mortgaged by man. Well now, will you have more wine? I'd offer you a girl for the evening, but I have some important business." Here Don Esteban de Rivarola significantly glanced at his concubine, who covered her mouth with her napkin to hide the conspiratorial smile she would otherwise have shown him.

"Very well, perhaps another time. I thank you for an excellent dinner and the good wine. I'll drink to your health with the dregs in my glass." Luis Saltareno rose, lifted his nearly empty goblet, and drained it, then set it down with a clatter. "To the damnation and confusion of those who would stand in our way for the progress of Taos!"

"A sentiment I'm in full accord with, Luis. Now my charming hostess will see you to the door. I have some business, as I told you, and must confer with my servants."

Half an hour later, after Luis Saltareno had been driven home in his carriage by his coachman and two obsequious servants, Don Esteban de Rivarola left the dining room and went out to the bunkhouse several hundred yards to the south of his elegant mansion. Entering it without knocking, he stared at the startled faces of his men, some twenty of them in various stages of undress, and his eyes fell on the two men who had let young Luz escape. "You," he pointed to each in turn, "shall have no pleasure with my *criadas* for a month, to teach you to be more alert when I send you after a runaway *puta!*"

"But, *patrón*," Hernando protested, "we learned that she took sanctuary in the church. We cannot go there; it is a great sin."

"Had you been smarter and quicker, she would not have got there. Well, I see old Padre Moraga is meddling again in my affairs. But so much for that. You, Jaime, and you, Bernardo, I have an errand for you. And if you are more successful than your two stupid *compañeros,* you shall each have one of my young *criadas* and enjoy her in one of the cottages at the edge of my estate—a reward I grant only to my most faithful and diligent *trabajadores.* Come outside with me, *hombres,* and I'll tell you what I want you to do."

The two *trabajadores,* both short, squat men in their mid-thirties, swaggeringly left their bunks, turning back to smirk at their crestfallen associates, and followed the *hacendado* out into the night. There he confronted them, jabbing each man in the chest with his pudgy forefinger to emphasize the secrecy and urgency of the errand with which he was commissioning them: "You know the old *indio,* Marga, who lives in that small *jacal* and raises some melons in his garden?"

"*Sí, patrón,*" Jaime spoke up, eager to show his master that he was attentive to the latter's desires and hoping to win the reward, which would be the choice of the prettier of the two unfortunate maids.

"*Bueno.* You, and you, too, Bernardo, will go to this Marga. He owes me some work. You remember that, a week ago, he came out here to show some of you how he plants his melons and gets the biggest ones in all Taos. Very well. He has a daughter, a tall black-haired *puta* whom I would accept in place of that stupid runaway Luz. I want both of you to find her and bring her to me. Because her father has not yet done his work I shall hold the girl as a hostage, until he completes the task to my satisfaction. *¿Comprenden?*"

"Oh, yes, *patrón,* at once." Bernardo was first to reply, with a salacious grin and wink. "We'll bring her back to you *muy pronto,* you will see."

Marga, crippled and illiterate and in his early fifties, had actually completed his task by showing the *trabajadores* in charge of the produce garden of the *hacendado* exactly how it was that he planted and cared for and fertilized the melons to grow them to an extraordinarily large size. But Don Esteban had cunningly harangued him to such an extent that he was totally confused and understandably fearful of this *rico* whose ruling could affect his life and those of his friends in the little village. What was more, the old man's health was very poor, and in the last few days he had grown so weak that he was confined to his bed, totally helpless.

Thus even as Don Esteban was ordering his two henchmen to kidnap Marga's daughter, the old man himself was almost tearfully pleading with the girl, Listanzia: "My daughter, I am old and weak, and I cannot read or write. You went to the *padre*'s school, and you can talk to the *alcalde mayor*. He has said that I have not done the work, but I do not understand this. I thought it was necessary only for me to instruct the *trabajadores* in the way that I planted the melons, but he insists that I still owe him work. What it is I cannot understand—will you not go to him and explain to him that I do not wish to offend him, that I'm willing to do whatever he wishes, if he will only make it clear to me so that I understand what is expected."

"Of course I will, *mi padre*," Listanzia smilingly replied as she knelt before him on his straw pallet and held a bowl of nourishing broth to his trembling lips. She was nineteen, lithe, her black hair plaited in a single thick braid almost to her waist. She had soft brown skin and an intelligent, sensitive face whose high-set cheekbones and bright, widely spaced, inquisitive brown eyes denoted a gentleness and naive courage. Marga's wife had died two years ago of fever, and although Listanzia had then been betrothed to Taguro, a twenty-three-year-old pueblo artisan, who was skilled with tools and whose talents were occasionally utilized by Padre Moraga, she had firmly refused to marry him until she could be sure that her father's health was improved and his welfare assured. Taguro helped support not only his mother and father with his skill, but also two young cousins and a sister of twelve, and there was no room in their already overcrowded adobe dwelling for a wife.

"I shall go in the morning, after I have been to mass and seen Padre Moraga," Listanzia declared after her father had nodded that he had had enough of the broth. "I will tell him that I do not think it is right for Don Esteban to say that you still owe him work."

"Please, *querida*," the old man pleaded, "you must not anger this *rico*. He is *alcalde mayor* of Taos. If he wished, he could drive me from this *jacal* and force you to work as a *criada* to pay off the debts he would say I owed him. I should rather die than see you enter that evil house—all Taos knows that he hungers for innocent young girls and lives in shame with that *mestiza*, who betrays her very own people, and sins against the *Cristo* by surrendering herself to his evil desires."

"Hush, *mi padre*," Listanzia gently murmured as sh
stroked the old man's head. "You must sleep now. Do no
think of such things. I tell you, I will talk with Padre Moraga
he will understand what I must do. And you must not fea
Don Esteban. The Church has power even over him, so long
as Padre Moraga tells us that the *Cristo* looks over all o
us."

"It is all very well for you to say this, my daughter,'
Marga querulously protested as he closed his eyes and eased
himself into a more comfortable position on the pallet. "Bu
we *indios* have known little justice from the *ricos* of Taos
Only a man like the *intendente* and the one who was her
before him—I do not remember his name—"

"I do, *mi padre*, it was Don Diego de Escobar. It is sai
that he left Taos forever, and that he did not like the law
that were given him to enforce and sent from Mexico City,'
Listanzia interrupted. "But now you must sleep."

"You are a good girl. I wish your mother were still alive
to comfort you—I am old and sick, and I have not many
years ahead of me; I wish you had married Taguro. He is a
fine young *indio*, and he would be good to you."

"But he has no room at his *jacal*, *mi padre*. We have
spoken of this many a time. And now I shall leave and no
talk to you anymore, so that you may sleep. And in the
morning I will bring you the *desayuno* before I go to see
Padre Moraga." Listanzia leaned over to kiss her father's
forehead, and then she went out of the *jacal* into the peaceful
night.

Taguro, whose *jacal* was over a quarter of a mile to the
east of Listanzia's, had eaten his supper quickly, seeing to it
that his parents were comfortable, and then had offered the
excuse that he wished to walk to the old church to study the
design on the door, since he was thinking of making a wood
carving for a *rico*. There was, to be sure, no such pending
commission for the gifted young Indian artisan, but he wished
to escape the confines of the overcrowded hut, to drink in the
evening air, and to think of his comely sweetheart. He was
downcast, realizing that her fealty to her ailing father had
already kept the two of them apart for longer than he wished,
and that it might well go on for even another year or more.
But until such time as some compassionate *hacendado* made a
contract with him for long-term services, he could never hope
to be free at last of his crowded living quarters.

As he walked out of his *jacal*, he raised his head to the

serene sky, its blue a dusky, darkening canvas on which only an isolated star faintly twinkled, and prayed to the Great Spirit to let Listanzia and himself come together as surely it was meant to be, in their own little hut, where they might rear a family and she would help him with his craft. "I will promise You, Keeper of the Sky," he said half aloud, "a painting on the adobe wall of the *jacal* in which Listanzia and I shall dwell together, if You permit it. It will thank You, and it will show Your wonders in giving life and breath to this world."

He was tall, wiry, and handsome, and other young *indias* who lived nearby would silently tell him with their eyes that they would not reject him if he were to drop an arrow outside their *jacal.* They would then return it with the point thrust down into the earth, as a symbol that they would accept his suit. But Taguro had no thought for anyone but his tall, gentle Listanzia.

The loneliness, the despair, the awareness of the contemptuous rejection by the *gringos* and the *ricos,* not only of him but also of his people, made him turn his footsteps toward Listanzia's little hut. Perhaps he could steal a word with her if her father were asleep. They had had so little time together these last few weeks, and he knew that he loved her beyond all hope. Indeed, if the Great Spirit had appeared to him suddenly in a flash of lightning and with a thunderous voice declared that He would permit the union of these two *indio* mortals only if Taguro agreed to forfeit all his craftsmanship and skill and be content to be the lowliest of *peones,* drawing water or currying the mules in the stable of the cruelest *hacendado* in all of Taos—and that, of course, would be Don Esteban de Rivarola—he, Taguro, would unflinchingly and unhesitatingly agree.

He smiled to himself, for he meant to tell this to Listanzia. Surely, she would care more for him because he was so devoted to her.

By now Jaime and Bernardo had gone to the stable, chosen horses, saddled them, and ridden out of the gates of their *patrón's* estate toward the pueblo section of the drowsing town of Taos. Armed with sheathed daggers and old Belgian pistols, they had no fear of the docile, long-subjugated *indios* of the pueblo, for it was wellknown that these nameless dogs had no weapons and were afraid of their own shadows. As they rode toward Marga's *jacal,* they ribaldly exchanged expressions of vicious anticipation of the rewards

Don Esteban would bestow upon them for this night's work.
It was Jaime who shrugged and drawled, "From all I've
heard, Marga's whelp is almost as handsome a *puta* as our
patrón's Noracia."

"Are you mad, *amigo?*" Bernardo gasped. "Truly you
must be, to say such things about that one. If Don Esteban
had heard you just now, he'd have you flayed alive and your
raw flesh staked out on an anthill. And besides, why do you
give such praise to a dirty little *india puta?* There are a
hundred like her in Taos, *hombre.* And if we bring her back
to our *patrón,* he'll let us choose the prettiest of his *criadas,*
and I tell you truly I'd rather bed with them than any dirty
india girl."

"Say what you like, Bernardo, a man has a right to
express his own opinion. Yes, even in the face of the *patrón*
we work for. He hasn't heard us, unless you blab to him—"

"Now there you misjudge me, *amigo,*" Bernardo complained as he spurred his horse down the dusty narrow road
that led to the Indian section of Taos. "I for one would rather
have the slut he beds each night, that Noracia. But that's my
feeling, and I've a right to it, as much as you have to yours.
But we are agreed on one thing: we'll bring the bitch back,
and our master will reward us well. That you can say about
him, though he's mean as a miserly old dog when it comes to
the rest of the time we serve him. I swear to you, when he
dies, he will have all his gold and silver placed in the coffin,
which the *padre* will lower into the good earth. But till then,
we must serve him with tribute and great praise and perhaps
he will throw us a *peso* or a *real* or two."

They had reached the outskirts of the pueblo section,
and they continued to ride slowly so that they would attract
no attention. Night had fallen over Taos, the moon was
obscured, and the dark cloud that covered it portended a
rainstorm. But it pleased the men, for there was so little light
that they would have more of an opportunity to carry off the
abduction.

Taguro had begun to run, each step bringing him nearer
to the lovely face and form of the girl whose mate he longed
to be. All this last week, desultory thoughts had crowded his
mind on ways that he might earn *dinero* enough to have a
jacal all to himself and for Listanzia. He knew very well that
Padre Moraga would marry them in the church, and he knew,
also, that her old father could not object too much, though he
was a descendant of the old strain of *indios pueblos,* who had

come to this Nuevo México more years ago than could be counted on one's fingers and toes. It was comforting to think of how he would stand holding Listanzia's hand before the good *padre* and hear those words whcih made them one. They would then have the ceremony of the *indios* after that, to be sure; his parents, as well as old Marga, would insist upon it: the cutting of the wrists, the mixing of the blood, the tying of the wrists together to symbolize the cohesion of oneness which was marriage to the end of one's days.

Heartened, he quickened his footsteps, until he had come within a hundred yards of the dilapidated little *jacal*, and he uttered a stifled gasp of delight to see the silhouette of tall, supple Listanzia in the yard. Rapt, her eyes uplifted to the sky, her hands clasped, she, too, was praying—was it for the same reason?

And then suddenly he stepped back with a gasp of alarm to see two horsemen riding toward the little *jacal*. Dismounting, they leaped from their horses and one of them peered into the hut, while the other moved quickly round to the side of it and toward the little garden. Putting his fingers to his mouth, the second man emitted a low whistle, and at once his confederate hurried out of the hut and came up beside him. With a gesture, the second man pointed to Taguro's intended, and both of them vaulted the rickety wooden fence which set off the garden from the hut, then seized her. Before she could cry out, one of them had thrown his poncho over her head, muffling her outcries, pinning her and immobilizing her, while the other lifted her by the lower thighs as the two of them swiftly carried her away back to their waiting horses.

Taguro uttered a cry and ran with all his might to intervene. The second *peón*, Bernardo, was in the act of binding Listanzia's wrists behind her back with a rawhide thong when he heard Taguro's cry, and he muttered something to his crony. Jaime, drawing his pistol, leveled it at the onrushing young *indio* and warned in a hoarse voice, "Stay back, ordure of a nameless dog! I'll kill you, if you try to interfere, *¿comprendes?*"

But Taguro, blind to all else save his overwhelming love for Listanzia and his horror at this intended abduction, disregarded the threat of death from the hollow muzzle of the pistol aimed at him and rushed forward, crying out, "No, no, you shall not take her!"

Setting his teeth, Bernardo squeezed the trigger, and the ball grazed Taguro's shoulder. He spun around, clapping a hand to the wound, and Jaime, thus having gained time, hurried back to help his companion hoist the still-struggling, bound captive onto Bernardo's horse.

A moment later they were riding off, and as Taguro staggered to his feet, blood seeping through the fingers which he had clamped over the superficial wound, he saw them head off to the west and then disappear entirely from sight.

Stanching the blood from his wound with a piece of his torn shirt, Taguro peered into Marga's hut, but the old man's snores told him that there was no point in wakening him. The young Pueblo Indian brave ground his teeth and compressed his lips, telling himself that he must go at once to Padre Moraga. He had not recognized the men who had kidnapped Listanzia, but they must be the servants of some *gringo rico*. Padre Moraga would know.

The wound soon stopped bleeding, and Taguro made his way, a little unsteadily, toward the old church.

The two *peones* carried Listanzia's poncho-wrapped body in through the main entrance of Don Esteban's *hacienda* and found him in his study. He was writing a letter to the viceroy to complain of the high-handed behavior of the *intendente*, Don Sancho de Pladero. Things had come to a pretty pass, he declared, when the chief official of the Spanish-held town would flout so important an official as the *alcalde mayor*. And then this nonsense of intervening his own aid and rendering judgment, finally to pay the tariff out of his own pocket. It was as audacious, as much an affront to traditional protocol, as anything the former *intendente*, Don Diego de Escobar, had ever done.

Feeling properly righteous, Don Estaban greeted the two rogues who had abducted the attractive pueblo girl, and his face at once brightened. *"Amigos,* you have done your work well. I'm very pleased with you. Now take her to the prison room where we interrogate undisciplined *muchachas."*

"Bueno, patrón." Jaime grinned salaciously. "You will keep the promise to us? It has been a long time since we have enjoyed a pretty *criada."*

"May all the devils in hell warm your testicles," Don Esteban snarled. "I keep my promises, and once I have questioned this Indian slut, I will see that you are rewarded. Now tie her up, and then go to your beds. I have no further work for you this evening."

Reluctantly, they exchanged a lingering glance and then carried Listanzia's writhing body between them out to the annex of the mansion, which had been turned into a torture chamber.

Stripping Listanzia stark naked, without regard for her pleas and cries, her earnest and often-repeated prayers to see Don Esteban and to explain why her father, Marga, was still puzzled over what was required of him, the two *peones* tied her to the center post, then blindfolded her.

A few moments later Don Esteban entered the wide, windowless room, followed by his concubine, Noracia, whose eyes sparkled with sadistic anticipation as they fixed on the shuddering, naked body of the attractive Listanzia.

She whispered into Don Esteban's ear, and he grinned delightedly and nodded. Then he moved off to a comfortable low armchair opposite the bound woman so that he could watch what would take place. Noracia went to a taboret to fill a glass with a fine old red Bordeaux and brought it to her master, then slowly approached the helpless, naked Indian girl, and for a long moment contemplated her.

Noracia had already been informed as to her master's hypocritical reason for abducting Listanzia. Without further ado, therefore, she leaned toward her and mockingly declared, "Now then, you *india puta*, let me tell you why you are here. Your stupid old father still owes my master and his a good deal of work. He refuses to present himself, and so my master has no recourse but to bring you here to teach you a lesson. And after you have had it, perhaps he will be more sensible. When he sees how we shall punish you in his stead, he will surely appear at once to pay his debt to Don Esteban."

"But I was coming to see His Excellency of my own will," Listanzia tearfully pleaded with her perverse, beautiful torturess. "My father is willing to work; it is only that he does not understand what is required of him. He thought that he had already done what was asked—"

"You Indians are all alike—stupid, acting without humility before your betters," Don Esteban snapped as he made himself comfortable in his chair and poured himself another generous glass of the Bordeaux. Noracia looked back at him and smiled provocatively, understanding precisely what would both please and inflame him.

She began by using a thin mesquite switch on the Indian girl's hips and thighs, while Listanzia gritted her teeth to suppress her outcries. By the time the half-breed concubine had finished, there were darkening, crisscrossing welts on the girl's soft brown flesh, and here and there beads of blood ooozed from intersecting cuts of the switch.

Not content with this, Noracia now poured some *aguardiente* over these cuts, and Listanzia uttered cry upon cry of dire suffering.

Observing how Don Esteban's eyes glittered, Noracia pursued the torture. With a long darning needle, she prodded the sobbing, writhing naked victim from the nape of her neck to her ankles, till there was not an untouched area of skin which did not bear the darkening little mark of the sharp bone needle. Then as she groaned aloud in her despair and shame, Listanzia was told that she would be put to further and more severe tortures until her father came to the *hacienda* and fulfilled his debt.

Thirteen

When Taguro arrived at the church, he went around to the back where the little rectory was located. Padre Juan Moraga lived there with his old, very devout housekeeper, Soledad Tordisa. She was deaf and nearly blind, and had served the priest for almost forty years, despite her infirmities. The *indios* of the pueblo looked upon her as they would a shaman, and she was known for her good deeds. Often Soledad would bring baskets of food and bundles of clothing to be distributed among the very poorest of the priest's parish.

Hesitating a moment before the door of the rectory, Taguro at last picked up the brass knocker, shaped like a cross, and rapped three times. He regretted that he had to waken the old priest, but he knew of no one else he could turn to in his anguish over Listanzia's abduction. There was no sound from the rectory and no sign of light, either, so again he rapped the knocker three times, this time as loudly as he could. Straining his ears, it seemed to him that he could at last hear footsteps. And then slowly the door opened, and holding a candle in one hand, frail old Padre Moraga stood before him in his nightshirt. "Can I be of help, *mi hijo?*" he solicitously asked. "Come in, the night is dark, and I can already feel the cold air."

"*Gracias, mi padre.*" Taguro swiftly entered and at once felt sorry again that he had wakened the old priest. He had never seen Padre Moraga look so frail and emaciated and so weary. His eyes were lusterless, and his shoulders seemed to be more stooped than ever. "I didn't mean to wake you, truly I didn't, *mi padre,*" he apologetically faltered.

"My son," Padre Moraga gently chided him, "I am the shepherd of this flock, and of what use is a shepherd if he will not seek one of the stray lambs, no matter what hour of day or night it should be? Now tell me why you have come to see me. But you're wounded, my son!" His eyes widened as he saw the raw splotch on Taguro's shoulder, the blood having already coagulated.

"It's about that I came to see you, *mi padre,*" Taguro anxiously exclaimed. "Listanzia has been carried off by two *peones!*"

"Who were these men?"

"I don't know that, *mi padre.* Just as I reached her little *jacal,* these men saw me and one of them fired a *pistola* at me. That is how I came by this wound—but it is nothing. I could do nothing, and I saw them seize her and ride off with her."

"Her father is Marga, isn't that so, Taguro?"

"*Sí, mi padre.*"

"Then I know for whom those *peones* work. There are perhaps two men here in Taos who would do so dastardly a thing. And one of them—and the perpetrator of this abduction, as I now believe—is Don Esteban de Rivarola. You see, my son, last week after the mass, old Marga had a few words with me, and said that he was doing some work, planting some melons or some such thing, for Don Esteban. Yes, I'm convinced it was the men of that unscrupulous *hacendado* who carried off your Listanzia." Padre Moraga shook his head. "He is a godless man, and I have warned him many times before, that one day his offenses will stink in the nostrils of heaven. And this time he has gone too far. That pure, decent girl who cares for you and wishes to be your wife and to bear your children—in the hands of so conscienceless an evildoer! I will go to him myself, now, Taguro, and I will demand in the name of Mother Church that he free Listanzia."

"But it's late, *mi padre,* and you don't look well. I'll go with you—"

"No, my son. This is the business of the church, and it is for me to demand of this *hacendado* that since he also comes to my church as a supposedly good *católico,* he not commit this dreadful sin which will blight his immortal soul forever. Do not worry about how I look. I know full well that I am old, and the journey I made—" He halted himself there, for he did not wish the young *indio* to know that he had gone to the Hacienda del Halcón. "Well, it does not matter. I have journeyed to see those who need me, and God will give me the strength I need to condemn this man who would flout His holy laws and ordinances. Do go back to your *jacal* and get your sleep, my son."

"Thank you, *mi padre.* But if I may, I'd like to wait for you at Listanzia's house. And I will pray for her and for you." Taguro inclined his head and made the sign of the cross. There was a beatific smile on the old priest's face as he put his hand on the young Indian's head and made the sign of the cross above it. "One thing you can do for me, and that is saddle my old horse in the stable."

"But, of course, *mi padre!* I'll do it at once and bring it out to the yard for you," Taguro offered.

When he had saddled the docile horse on which Padre Juan Moraga had ridden to conduct the memorial service for Weesayo, he assisted the frail old man to mount it and held the reins until Padre Moraga could take firm hold of them. "*Vaya con Dios,* and I will pray that no harm has come to her, *mi padre,*" he said as he slapped the horse's rump. With a protesting whinny, Padre Moraga's mount trotted forward as Taguro stared after him in the darkness, sighing with anxiety and then slowly tracing his footsteps back to Listanzia and Marga's *jacal.*

Nearly an hour later, fighting the fatigue that threatened to break off his vital errand, Padre Moraga arrived at the gates of Don Esteban's estate. The *peones* who would usually guard the entrance to the *hacienda* were playing cards and drinking in their bunkhouse, and several of them were amusing themselves with two maids whom Don Esteban had turned over to them as a kind of bounty to assure himself of their loyalty and readiness to execute any commission, no matter how heinous.

Dismounting with an effort, Padre Moraga advanced to the door of the elegant mansion and, disregarding the knocker, balled his hand into a fist and hammered on the door as he called out sternly, "Come forth, Don Esteban de Rivarola! I, Padre Moraga, command you to come forth!"

Earlier that evening, the *hacendado*, wildly excited by the voyeuristic pleasure which his concubine had given him by administering torture to the valiant young Indian girl, had one of his *peones*, a tall, hairy, and burly Mexican named Grigorio, come to the adjunct of his *hacienda* that was used as a torture chamber, and had ordered him to violate Listanzia.

Grigorio and his older brother, Manuel Servacios, were proscribed outlaws. They had murdered a sexton in San Luis Potosí, and although they had been under a sentence of death, they managed to escape from prison by overcoming a guard and compelling him to procure horses for them. They had managed to come to Taos, and in a little *posada* on the edge of town had met the two rogues who had carried off Listanzia, Jaime and Bernardo, who thought their ruthless master might well have need for the services of such outlaws, and shrewdly invited them to return to the *hacienda* of their *patrón*. Don Esteban had interviewed them, learning that they were under sentence of death and had been formally excommunicated by the priest of that church whose sexton they had murdered. He had said to them, "A word from me to the authorities, and you will be garroted as a public show. If you serve me well and always remember that I can return you to San Luis Potosí for a very painful and very slow death, I will give you sanctuary here. You must both swear that one day when I will call upon you to fulfill your debt to me, you will both then unhesitatingly do whatever I ask."

The brothers had eyed each other, shrugged their shoulders, and Grigorio had replied, "*Sí patrón*, it's all the same to us whether we serve you or the devil himself. We're done for otherwise. We'll do what you want. All we ask is food, a hut to sleep in, and if you don't mind now and again, a *muchacha* to share our pallet."

"You'll have all the women you want if you serve me well. I have many *criadas* who at times need discipline." Don Esteban had chuckled. "You both look like murderers and hairy apes, and I'm sure that it would be punishment enough for a pretty young *puta* to have to bed with you—I think she'd rather have the whip if she had her choice. Very well, we will bargain then."

And so while Noracia came to Don Esteban's side, he had shuddered with an unholy lust as he watched the brutal Grigorio approach the half-fainting Indian girl, untie her from the post, and savagely deflower her, till she fainted in her shame and suffering.

Grigorio had then been dismissed by a peremptory wave of Don Esteban's languid hand, and Noracia had turned her head in the direction of the adjacent *hacienda*. "*Patrón*, I hear someone calling out for you," she murmured, half afraid with a kind of superstitious premonition.

"At this hour? Who dares to disturb me? Oh, very well, very well. Leave the bitch here, and we'll go back into the *hacienda* through the secret passage. Now who the devil could it be at this hour?" he grumbled.

Belting his robe securely and continuing to grumble, Don Esteban approached the farthest wall, pressed his thumb against a scarcely visible indentation, and the panel slid back, opening into a small, elegantly decorated salon. Noracia followed him, while the unfortunate, unconscious Listanzia lay in the other room, huddled on the floor.

Once again Padre Juan Moraga banged on the door with his fist and called out with all his strength, "Don Esteban, unless you are a coward and care nothing for your immortal soul, come forth; appear before me! It is I, Padre Moraga!"

"The meddling old fool!" the *hacendado* hissed, as he turned to his concubine. "Go back to your room; he is not to see you. I want no sermons on morality at this hour, not in my own *hacienda*. By what right does he presume to interfere with my life? Be off with you, girl!"

"But what about her, *patrón?*" Noracia timidly hinted.

"That is my business," Don Esteban snapped, and cuffed her across the cheek. "Now do what I tell you to!"

She cast him a look of venomous contempt, which he did not see, and then hurried off to her room. Don Esteban, still muttering to himself about the temerity of this village priest who would dare accost him in his own domain, at last unbolted the door.

"Why have you come all the way from Taos to hammer at my door late at night, Padre Moraga? I did not send for you," he said sourly.

"I am sure you did not, Don Esteban. But I have come

to demand from you the release of the girl Listanzia, whom your men abducted from her father's *jacal* and brought here for your sinful pleasures."

"Come now, Padre Moraga, you go too far this time!" The *hacendado* feigned righteous indignation. "Why do you accuse me of having her brought here? I resent your importunity, disturbing me so late at night when I am enjoying the companionship of my charming housekeeper."

"As to that, examine your own conscience, Don Esteban," was the old priest's reply. "You ask me how I know? Because the father of this girl, the old Marga, talked to me not long ago and told me that he had been summoned to do work for you. He was concerned because you did not seem to wish to pay him, and also you left him feeling that the work was not well done, though he did it to the very best of his knowledge. No, Don Esteban, do not try to deceive me. *El Señor Dios* looks down and judges us both, and He knows when you lie."

"I do not like your tone, Padre Moraga. I tell you, the girl is not here!"

"Don Esteban, if this were the first time that I had learned that you had attractive Indian girls carried off to your house so that you could have your way with them, I might be more inclined to believe your protestation that Listanzia is not here. But over the years that I have been a humble priest serving the ministry of our dear Lord, your offenses against the poor and the helpless *indios* and *peones* are innumerable. You are a man who believes that mortal power gives you all of the rights of law and morality to act as you choose, but I, Padre Moraga, tell you that you have sinned so grievously— and in this act of yours most of all! —that I am prepared here and now, upon your very threshold, to pronounce the ban of excommunication against you."

"Now wait, Padre Moraga! You go too far this time!" Again still playing his role of incredulous innocent, the *hacendado* spluttered and made gestures, as if to indicate that he was cruelly wronged by such a judgment.

"No, you will listen to me for once in your life," the priest interrupted, his eyes stern, his lips compressed. "If you do not have this girl brought to me now so that I may take her back to the pueblo and to her father, I will invoke excommunication against you. And all your *peones* who come each Sunday to hear the mass and who come at other times to make their confessions, they will no longer be loyal to you, once they learn that Mother Church has cast you off as an incorrigible and unrepentant sinner! Now then, bring Listanzia here and have one of your men bring a horse so that she may ride back with me."

For a moment Don Esteban hesitated, still wishing to rid himself of the cantankerous old priest by lying to him. But the threat of excommunication was something he had not envisaged: he knew, just as the priest had intimated, that if his *trabajadores* learned of this banishment from the church, they would leave him at once and seek another *patrón*. All the while he meditated, he saw the priest eye him with such contempt that hatred for the old man very nearly burst within him. At last, clenching his fists and in a cold voice, he capitulated: "Very well, then. If you must know, Padre Moraga, old Marga did his work badly, and he is still in debt to me. I wished to have the girl brought to me so that I might have her explain to her stupid old father why I am displeased with him. Perhaps when she speaks to him in their native tongue, he will have better comprehension, for he does not appear to understand Spanish."

"I am not concerned with your explanation. Have the girl brought here. And I hope that I will find her in good health and not subjected to the depraved violence of which I know you to be capable, Don Esteban," was the priest's stern answer.

Don Esteban clenched his fists, goaded almost beyond the limit of his patience. He was about to speak, then thought better of it. Finally he snarled, "Come in and stand here. I will have her brought to you. And I will have one of my men get her a horse. I do not understand why you concern yourself so much about these stupid *indios*. They are good-for-nothing, they lie and cheat and steal, and they are lazy, as well."

"I am waiting," was the priest's only answer.

"Very well," Don Esteban almost shouted, stamping his foot in petulant rage. "I warn you, I do not take kindly to your flouting me as if I were a schoolboy. You do not understand that here in Taos I am the *alcalde mayor*, and that I have the ear of the viceroy himself!"

"I understand only that you are very near to not having the ear of God if you do not bring Listanzia here to me without more of this needless discussion."

Don Esteban shrugged, and strode down the hallway. Sleeping in a chair near his bedroom was a majordomo, wearing a black blouse and breeches, booted, his sombrero on his lap, a pistol holstered at his side. Don Esteban bent over to the man and rudely shook him by the shoulder: "Wake up, you lazy dog. Is this the way you look after me? Go find Jaime and Bernardo, do you undertsand? Have them saddle a horse, and then get Listanzia. They will give her new clothes—you know where you can find them."

While he waited for his two henchmen to rouse the unconscious girl, give her brandy, clothe her, and bring her out to the stony-faced old priest, Don Esteban inwardly cursed the old man. It had been his plan to keep Listanzia a prisoner until he tired of her, compelling her father to indenture himself in order to save her. At the same time, he cursed the stupidity of his *peones* whom he had sent to abduct Listanzia for allowing themselves to be seen. But most of all, Padre Moraga's remark that he knew of many of the *hacendado's* sins against the defenseless and the poor of Taos rankled, and so Don Esteban's rage was well-nigh murderous. It came to him, also, that when the Indian girl rode back with the priest and told him, as she surely would, what had been done to her, there was no guarantee that Padre Moraga would not pronounce the ban of excommunication against him. And that must not happen. It would discredit him within Taos, limit his authority, and, particularly with Don Sancho de Pladero, utterly discredit him.

He paced back and forth, trying to ignore the silent old man who stood like a condemning angel at the door waiting, until he at last heard footsteps. The two *peones* had roused Listanzia with salacious pinches, forced her to drink down a full glass of strong *aguardiente*, and then she was lifted from the floor, tottering with exhaustion and shame. Bernardo tugged a shapeless cotton dress over her lissome body and, grinning with lewd malice, knelt down to thrust her bare feet into sandals. "See, *puta?*" he had mocked her, "how kind we are, acting like the *criados* of a true *rica?* Now then, you'll accompany us. Someone will take you back to your miserable little hole—but be warned, girl, best nót say a word about what has happened to you, or we might come back for you again and this time you won't get off so lightly, ¿*comprendes?*"

She had been mute, her face scarlet with shame, her head bowed, trying to stifle the sobs of the wretched degradation she had endured. Only vaguely did she understand that she was free at last, and she could not comprehend who

might have performed the miracle to free her from this
torture chamber and from the depravity of Don Esteban de
Rivarola.

When they led her toward the foyer of the *hacienda*
where the *hacendado* and the priest waited, she stiffened and
uttered a pitious little cry, "Padre Moraga—oh, no, ¡que
vergüenza!"

"Be careful, *puta*," Bernardo hissed. "Remember what I
told you!"

"My child, I have come to take you back to your
father," the old priest gently told her as he held out his arms
to her. This kindly gesture unleashed Listanzia's agonized
stoicism. She burst into hysterical sobs and flung herself into
the priest's arms, disconsolately weeping.

His eyes glittered with anger as he stared at the smirking
hacendado. "Is the horse ready for her? Saddled and ready? I
am taking her from this evil *hacienda* as swiftly as I can. And
I can see already that she has not been treated with the
respect one owes to one of God's children. You will answer
to Him for this, Don Esteban de Rivarola, you and your
trabajadores."

"Come now, Padre Moraga, there is no need for slander.
The girl is frightened, that is all. These stupid Indians do not
understand the way we think. You should know that, after all
your years with them," the *hacendado* sneered. "Of course,
the horse is there—isn't it, Jaime?"

"Of a certainty, *patrón!* A very gentle mare, with a soft
saddle for the girl."

"I keep my promise, Padre Moraga. Take her, then. But
make certain she tells her father that I am still not pleased
with his work and that I wish him to come to see me to
conclude this annoying matter."

"You will doubtless hear from me on another subject,
Don Esteban," was all that Padre Moraga permitted himself
to say, as gently, an arm around Listanzia's quivering shoulders, he led her outside, to where one of the *trabajadores*
from the bunkhouse stood yawning, holding the reins of a
brown mare.

"Come, my daughter, I'll take you home. Are you strong
enough to ride, Listanzia?" Padre Moraga gently demanded.

The Indian girl slowly raised her tear-stained face and
nodded, striving to compose herself. Straightening, she turned
and walked very slowly, haltingly, toward the horse being
held for her, as the old priest turned back to look at the

hacendado and then said in a low voice, "If this girl has been harmed, if I learn from her that you have wrought your filthiness as you have done on others, God will turn His countenance away from you, for this I shall pray."

Then he went out into the starry night, helping her to mount the mare, and then laboriously mounted his own horse and turned its head back toward Taos.

From time to time he glanced at her and saw that, with the most indomitable courage, she was holding back grimaces of pain. These were evident in the tightening of her lips and in the sudden deep breaths she took as she held tightly to the reins.

"Listanzia, confide in me. I am your priest. Tell me, was your innocence taken? But no, my daughter, it was none of your doing and you committed no sin. Those who did this to you were the sinners, and God will make them pay. In Taguro's eyes you are still unblemished, as you are in mine and in His also." He looked up at the starlit sky and crossed himself.

"*Sí, mi padre.*" Her voice was low, and she did not look at him. "It was not Don Esteban, but one of his men. He had a woman with him, and it was she who tormented me."

"Detestable lechery, unholy wantonness!" Padre Moraga gasped, his eyes burning with anger. "Remember, you have done no sin; you are still a virgin. And I will see to it that you and Taguro are wed."

"But how can you, *mi padre?*" Incredulous, she turned back to stare at him with widening eyes still swollen from her tears.

"Because, my daughter, a kind, good man contributed a gift of much silver to our poor church. He asked that it be given to aid the needy. And before I take you home to Marga, we shall stop at the church—that is, if you feel yourself strong enough—and I shall get for you two hundred silver *pesos*. It will be more than enough to build a *jacal* which you and Taguro can have to yourselves, and it will help him with his work. Besides, there is work that should be done in the church over which I preside—and I shall commission him to do it and pay him for it."

"Padre Moraga, you are good, I believe in your *Dios*, and so does Taguro," she eloquently burst out. Then she bowed her head and began to weep again, a controlled and soft weeping that tore at his heart more than her previous anguished sobs. "I wish it had not happened to me— I wanted to come to him untouched—I love him, Padre Moraga."

"Of course, my child, my daughter. But I told you, He who rules us from above knows that you are still virgin in your soul and your heart. Taguro will know this, also. And I will marry you quickly, before that evil one can take any steps to prevent it."

"We shall pray for you all our lives, Padre Moraga."

"Yes, my daughter, that will be the only reward I seek. I am old, and I feel myself weak from my journey. And when I face that man who has done so many evil deeds that have gone unpunished in Taos all these years, I feel myself still weaker. Wait—I have an idea that will take you and Taguro away from his power."

"How can that be, Padre Moraga?" she exclaimed.

"I spoke to you of a kind, good man, who had given the church many gifts. He is not in Taos, my daughter. He and his wife and her father and their workers live many miles from Nuevo México. But I was thinking that they could use a craftsman as skillful as Taguro, and that you would find work there, also, for you sew well, I know this—"

"Yes, my mother taught me when I was a little girl, Padre Moraga," Listanzia said proudly.

"So much the better, then. Listen, my daughter. I will come to your *jacal*, and I will marry you and Taguro. Then I will tell you both how you will get to this place—but you must promise to tell no one else in Taos where you are going. The man to whose *hacienda* you will go has reason to hate Don Esteban de Rivarola. And Don Esteban, if he could learn where this man is, would attempt acts of cruel vengeance against him for an imagined wrong."

"But my father—"

"He is ailing now, I know, my daughter. I have been thinking about this. If Taguro goes, could your father not move into the *jacal* with Taguro's people? And I would see that he had nourishing food and warm blankets and medicine—there is an old *médico* whom I would send to care for him."

"Oh, that would be wonderful, Padre Moraga! Taguro and I will never be able to repay you—"

"Don't concern yourself, my daughter," the old priest interrupted. "And now, let us ride to Taos, for I am eager to have this done and, also"—his face hardened—"to denounce Don Esteban de Rivarola from my pulpit and to declare him banished from Mother Church."

It was well after midnight when Listanzia and Padre

Moraga reached the little church. Bidding her to wait outside, the old priest entered the rectory and went to a chest of drawers in the bottom of which, tucked away in the folds of a chasuble, he had hidden many silver *pesos* obtained from the ingots John Cooper Baines had given him for the poor of Taos. Ignazio Peramonte had melted down these ingots and had fashioned beautiful trinkets, which were exchanged for the *pesos* that bought the clothes and food for the needy and the downtrodden of the village.

Padre Moraga counted out two hundred pesos into a little rawhide sack, drew the strings tightly, and then went back to the girl. "Now we'll ride to your father's *jacal*, my daughter," he assured her.

When they came to Marga's little *jacal*, Listanzia uttered a joyous, startled cry: "It's Taguro—he's waiting here for us!" Then, hiding her discomfort from the torture she had sustained, she got down from her mare and embraced the sturdy, handsome young *indio*. "I am safe, my beloved one. Padre Moraga brought me away from Don Esteban's dreadful house," she tearfully declared.

"I can never thank you enough. I shall work for you for the rest of my days and for the church, *mi padre*," Taguro said as he turned to the priest, his face shining.

"No, my son. I have a better plan. Listen carefully, for I must speak in haste, and I wish this done before dawn breaks. I shall marry you both here and now, and God will forgive my not publishing the banns, as is customary in our faith. And then, Taguro, you will take Listanzia away with you to a *hacienda* far from here, where you both will begin your new lives." Padre Moraga hastily explained what he had in mind, and then he instructed the amazed young Indian couple to join hands and repeat the matrimonial vows.

In a few moments he had conducted the beautiful wedding service as he might have done before a large audience in the church in the public square. And when Taguro took Listanzia into his arms and kissed her with reverence and joy, Padre Moraga at last smiled, knowing that he had not wrongly appraised the stalwart honesty of this talented *indio* artisan.

Listanzia now saw the wound in Taguro's shoulder and whispered, "But you're hurt, my dear one."

"It's nothing. Come, we mustn't delay," he eagerly assured her.

The old priest made the sign of the cross over each of

them. "And now, my children, Taguro must carry Marga to his *jacal*. If he wakens, you will tell him the joyous news, and you will tell him that he will be cared for by your people and by the *médico* I will send in the morning."

Taguro nodded, brushed Listanzia's cheek with his lips, and then hurried into the little *jacal*. Very carefully, he lifted up the old man's emaciated body, and carried him out of the hut.

"Take my horse, Taguro, and carry Marga to your *jacal*. There you will tell your people what has happened and that they are to take care of Marga. And then you will come back here, and I will tell you how to go where you will be safe."

Half an hour later, Taguro rode back to Padre Moraga and Listanzia, who were both kneeling in prayer. Taguro dismounted and came to the old man, lifting him to his feet with an awkward reverence. "It's done, *mi padre*. Marga wakened, and I told him that I would care for his daughter to the end of my days. He is happy in the news. But he asks how he can repay you and whether he must still work for Don Esteban?"

"The *médico* will tell him that he owes Don Esteban nothing. Now, my son, here is the sack of *dinero* I promised Listanzia. If you wish, one day you will be able to buy your own land, perhaps to have your own farm or cattle. And now here is what you are to do. Do you know the mountain of the stronghold of the Jicarilla Apache?"

"I do, *mi padre*," Taguro said quickly.

"*Bueno*. Ride there with Listanzia. Ask for the *jefe* who is Kinotatay. Tell him what has happened, that I have married you, and that I wish one of his braves to guide you to the Hacienda del Halcón. It is a far journey from here, my son, but you will not mind it once you are there. A new life will begin for you both."

Then he turned to the girl, who was now radiant and who had forgotten her suffering and degradation. He put his hands on her forehead and prayed aloud. And then he said. "I will walk back to the church and pray for both of you that your journey will be safe. Think of me in your prayers."

"*Mi padre*, I—I can't find words to thank you—but I swear by the Blessed Virgin that if we have a child and it is a son, we shall name him after you, *mi padre*." Taguro's voice was choked with emotion. Then he took hold of the priest and embraced him. And helping the young woman astride her mare, he mounted the priest's horse and the two rode off toward the Jicarilla Mountains.

Padre Moraga stood alone before the deserted *jacal.* Once again he raised his eyes to the starry sky and, clasping his hands, fervently declared, "Oh, blessed *Dios,* whose light of stars and sun and moon illumines the darkness of this world, shine the light down upon these two, who are worthy of Thy compassion and goodness. Grant me strength enough to speak with all my voice against the evil man who would have besmirched their lives and for whom Your gift of life is as nothing with his greed and his possessions and his ignoble lusts. I feel myself failing, but You are my strength, and I pray unto You to give me time for what must yet be done."

Bowing his head, he made the sign of the cross and then turned to walk back to the little church in the square.

Fourteen

Don Esteban de Rivarola spent a sleepless night. The threat of excommunication would be of no importance if it only meant he would spare that stupid old priest's interminable sermons and boring homilies. For himself, if he never set foot inside the church again, the time thus conserved could be put to far better use. Yet if there was public knowledge of his excommunication, it would be damaging not only to his reputation but to his power over the Christianized *indios* and the stupid, untaught *trabajadores* who were in his employ. They were blindly devout, he knew only too well, because it was the only sop they had, being poor.

It was nearly dawn when he flung himself out of bed and stalked to a sideboard, where he poured himself a full goblet of a fine imported French wine and practically gulped half of it down. Scowling, he tried to think what must be done. The damned old fool had a loyal following in Taos, there was no doubt of that. Yet he must be silenced at any cost. And

silenced in such a way that it could not be traced back to
him—that would be a mortal sin which the people of Taos
would be certain to hold against him. No, nothing must go
wrong in planning the removal of this meddling fool. It must
be made to look as if some hostile Indian— That was it! If he
should be killed by marauding Indians, or even better, by one
of the *indios pueblos*—

And then a crafty smile curved his fleshy lips as he
finished his wine. There were two men on his estate who
owed their lives to him and who were already banned from
the church. They would be the ones to do the deed. And
after it had been done, they could be easily disposed of.

Thus fortified, he flung himself back down on his bed
and was soon fast asleep, smiling as he dreamed of dragging
Listanzia back to the torture chamber, this time in chains and
with no one to intercede for her.

As he was breakfasting, served by his faithful concubine,
Noracia, he looked up and ordered, "Go fetch Grigorio and
Manuel Servacios and be quick about it!"

"As you wish, *patrón*." She could not help shivering.
"They're dreadful men; I don't trust them, *patrón*."

"Did I ask for your opinion, you *mestiza* bitch? If you
irritate me, Noracia, I can send you to a bordello in Cuernavaca or Durango, there to spend the rest of your days taking
on any *peón* who has a few *centavos* to pay for an hour's
pleasure with you. Would you like that?"

"Oh, no, *mi patrón*, please, you know I want to serve
only you and please you!" she tearfully exclaimed as she flung
herself down on her knees and wound her satiny arms around
his waist, entreatingly looking up at him.

He grinned lewdly, stroking her hair, and then boldly
putting his hand down inside the bodice of her shift beneath
the robe to cup one of her ripe breasts. Gently, he kneaded
the warm, tempting flesh and insinuatingly declared, "You
must never question me again, my dove. You see, I can be
very kind when a *puta* does what I wish. Or again, I can
punish—" And with this, he tightened his fingers against her
breast till Noracia uttered a plaintive cry and writhed on her
knees, tears starting to her dilated eyes.

"I perceive that you understand me. *Bueno*. Now go
fetch those rogues and don't delay me any longer!" he
grumbled.

In a few minutes the two outlaws entered the room and
curtly inclined their heads as a grudging token of respect to

the wealthy *hacendado*. Don Esteban turned to Noracia and dismissed her with a wave of his bejeweled hand. "Leave us and don't come back till I send for you," he warned.

With a frightened gasp Noracia hurried out of the room, closing the door behind her. Don Esteban reached for a lighted taper and carefully lit the fine Cuban cigar which was part of a shipment of luxuries that had been brought to him from Mexico City a month ago. The two brothers eyed each other wonderingly, then shrugged and awaited their master's orders. Don Esteban amused himself by keeping them waiting, blowing smoke rings and watching their slow ascension toward the ceiling.

Then at last he leaned forward, scowling, his eyes narrowed, and in a low voice declared, "You'll recall that I have saved your lives thus far, and that so long as you obey me, you are safe. I've kept my word to you both, haven't I? You have had food, wine, clothes, horses, and at times some of the young *criadas*. And you, Grigorio"—this with a lascivious wink and chuckle—"most recently you enjoyed the favors of that long-legged Indian bitch, did you not?"

"It's true, *patrón*. She was a tasty one, she was." Grigorio smacked his lips in nostalgic recollection. "I'd not mind being alone with her again tonight."

"If you do what I tell you to, you and your brother Manuel, it is very likely that you shall have her for as long as you both wish. But you must be most careful, and if you dare utter a word of what I am about to tell you, you will be dead men before anyone has a chance to believe you, *¿comprenden?*"

"Of course, *patrón*. We know how to be grateful, when it's a matter of our lives," Manuel spoke up.

"Now you are being a sensible man, *amigo*," Don Esteban chuckled, and poured himself some wine. "You were both excommunicated from the church, as I recall. *¿Es verdad?*"

"*Sí, patrón*," Grigorio growled, with an uneasy look at his brother.

"Then you are beyond the damnation of Mother Church wherever you may go, and your lives are forfeit, if I should ever decide to let the authorities know where you have taken refuge. That is also true?"

"You know it is, *patrón*. What are you getting at, what do you want of us?" Manuel irritatedly exclaimed.

"There is a meddlesome priest in Taos. His name is Juan

Moraga. His church is in the village square, with a little rectory behind it. He dares to go beyond his station to attack the *ricos* and the *hacendados* who are the very lifeblood of Taos. It was he who came here and demanded that I return that *india puta* you enjoyed, Grigorio. And I heard you say you would like her back. Well then, this man must be removed. Besides, he is old and weak, and he doesn't have many more days. Once you dispose of him, you have both fulfilled your debt to me, and you will have my word that I shall never notify the authorities of your whereabouts. And besides, I shall know how to be grateful for such a favor, which will ease my own arrangements considerably."

"You want us to kill this priest, *patrón?*" Manuel gasped, scratching his head and eyeing his brother, as if awaiting confirmation.

"Exactly. But in a way that won't be traced, either to you or to myself. I have in mind that Taos is still, from time to time, beset by hostile Indians. Now it is also possible that this Padre Moraga may have made some enemies in the pueblo. If an arrow were to strike him down in the dark of night, who is to say that it was not one of those accursed Indians who pretends to be converted to Christianity? Or again, some renegade band of Comanche. Of course, you will have to use arrows. No knives, either of you—I know you are expert with them, but I want to be sure there is no doubt in anyone's mind as to who is responsible for this murder. Well then?"

"Let me understand you, *patrón*," Grigorio began slowly, scowling at his brother, who had taken a step backward and put a hand to his mouth, as if not quite certain as to the wisdom of this unholy enterprise. "You want us to kill this priest, and with arrows, to make it look like *indios*."

"Precisely."

"And then we're to come back here and report to you when it's done? But how will you have proof? We can't very well bring you the body—"

"Of course you can't, you imbecile!" Don Esteban rose and slammed his palm down on the table. "*Diablo,* I thought you both had some intelligence. We will all know it soon enough. You're forgetting that I am the *alcalde mayor*, and that I go into town almost every morning to confer with the *intendente*. I am sure to be told the dreadful news when our beloved priest has gone to meet his Maker. That will be sufficient proof. You will come back here as swiftly as you have done the deed, and you will stay isolated on this *hacienda*. When the proper time comes, I will make other arrangements for you, as well as give you your reward." Then as he saw Grigorio frown and glance again at Manuel, he slyly added, "Don't tell me you have become a coward since your easy life here on this *hacienda, amigo*."

"I don't take kindly to such talk, even from a *patrón*," Grigorio snarled, putting a hand to the knife thrust through his belt.

"Gently, gently, I was only testing you. Of course, you are no coward, neither one of you. Let it be tomorrow night. As I recall, this stupid old priest takes the air during the late evening out in the garden near the little rectory. And he has a housekeeper who is deaf and almost blind, I am told, although I have never seen her. Darkness will conceal everything. Just make sure your aim is true. I do not want him wounded; I want him out of the way forever, *¿comprenden?*"

"Very well, *patrón*. It will be as you say. When I was a kid, I used to be a pretty good shot with a bow and arrow, so I'm not worried about that. And the arrows will be easy enough to steal off some stupid *indio* in the pueblo. But you'd best reward us well. Even though we're outside the church, this isn't the sort of thing one does every day. It's not like carrying off an *india puta*," Grigorio said in a surly tone. Then, shrugging, he took Manuel by the arm and led him out of the room. Don Esteban smiled to himself and poured out another glass of wine. Lifting it high, he murmured to himself, "At last, I will have the power I have always wanted in Taos. The next step will be to get rid of that much too benevolent Don Sancho. And that could be done by discrediting him." So saying, he drained the glass and then flung it against the wall, grinning evilly to see the shards fly about. "And that will be the end of a meddlesome fool, if ever there was one!" he added.

Padre Juan Moraga had said mass for the last time on this Saturday, the day after he rescued Listanzia. There had been only a few parishioners and only a single confession, that of a pueblo basket weaver who had avowed that he had coveted the comely wife of the *indio* whose *jacal* was next to his. Padre Moraga had smiled to himself as he bade the contrite supplicant to say a dozen Ave Marias and to think of the lesson of the Holy Commandments. Also, out of a shrewd practical wisdom, he had counseled, "It would be easier for you to move to another *jacal*, Nouranto. In that way, temptation will not cross your path. For verily the sin of lust grows greater if it is nurtured in the mind, and you must learn how to purge yourself of it. Even the greatest of men are often subject to such unhallowed thoughts, and God understands this well. Now that you are repentant, He will show you the way."

Yes, the old priest reflected to himself, as he ate his frugal supper, some *frijoles* and only a tiny bit of meat, a small *tortilla* and water as drink, *the problems of the poor are always the same and eternal; it is only those of the rich that grow complex and cause trouble in the world.* And as he said his prayers of thanksgiving for the abundant food that was privileged to him, he looked up at the wooden crucifix nailed to the wall of his little room, crossed himself, and prayed again. On the morrow, Sunday, at high mass, he would denounce Don Esteban de Rivarola as a forsaken lamb of the flock, an outcast hence from the fold, forbidden the sanctuary of the sanctity of Mother Church. He did not fear the consequences. Had not *Jesu Cristo* driven the moneylenders out of the temple of our dear Lord? And He had known that He would die on the cross for the remission of man's sins. Alas, that these sins were still committed and this glorious sacrifice had seemingly been in vain.

How weary he was tonight. It seemed to him that all the rumors of the separation of Nueva España from Spain herself were as nothing compared with the weariness and defeatism that seemed to encompass the people of Taos. It was as if they were all in a kind of lethargic sleep, which no news could penetrate, neither good nor evil. And only Don Sancho de Pladero, the worthy successor of Don Diego de Escobar, maintained justice and honor and decency, as our dear Lord intended men to live by in His holy name.

Perhaps it would be the *americanos* who would one day come to Taos and to Santa Fe with their trade, vigorous young men, untainted by the superstitions and bigotry and hatred of the Old World, which he could now see so plainly was dying. The oblivion in which Taos remained was a kind of symbol of what was happening to all of Spain. And if this independence came about, there was certain to be bloodshed. There would be greedy, ambitious men, many like Don Esteban de Rivarola, who would wage war on their fellows with the aim of becoming the leader of a revolution solely for the sake of power. And the poor, the neglected, the outcasts, like the *indios* of the pueblo, would go on with no betterment of their condition, still exploited and tyrannized, the way Don Esteban desired.

It was a kind of Gethsemane—though in no way would he think himself, a humble little priest in a sleepy, dying town, even so much as the symbol of the Blessed Son—for tonight there would be agony for him as he wrestled with the problem he must solve on the morrow. Don Esteban had powerful friends, and even though they might not strike at him for the excommunication of the *alcalde mayor,* they might take their reprisals on the *indios.* There would be more girls carried off and abused, as Listanzia had been. There would be more feeble old men forced to work for a pittance and then denied even that on some trumped-up charge or other, as had been done to Marga.

He smiled, remembering that he had sent Taguro and Listanzia off into a new life. Of that, at least, he could not be ashamed, and he did not think that John Cooper would reproach him for having given the young artisan two hundred of the precious silver *pesos.* They would buy the redemption of two worthy, good people, who would be fruitful and multiply, as our Lord commanded at the dawn of time.

He must sleep, for his bones ached with weariness. That journey to the Hacienda del Halcón had been more than he should have undertaken, and yet it had been his duty. He said a prayer for Carlos and again for Weesayo, and then walked out into the night.

The old housekeeper had tried to plant a little garden. There were only a few withered flowers there now, for it was not the season. But at least it was the thought of beauty, and this pleased him. And in the spring it would again be verdant. Perhaps someone from Chihuahua would bring good seeds, and then there would be flowers. Flowers he could lay upon the altar to exult the majesty of our blessed Savior.

He walked slowly toward the little plot, and the moon, hidden behind a cloud, suddenly emerged to bathe his face with a gentle glow. He was smiling as he stooped to touch one of the withered blossoms.

There was a sudden whir in the air, and Padre Juan Moraga stiffened, his eyes widening, and then another whir, and this time he was plummeted onto his back and lay with his arms in a cross. Two arrows had transfixed his heart.

From their place of hiding behind a crumbling low adobe wall near the little garden, Grigorio and Manuel cautiously straightened. And it was Manuel who, though an outlaw and excommunicated like his brother, made the sign of the cross with a shaking hand. "¡Vámanos! We'd best get back to the *patrón*. I don't like this business, Grigorio, I tell you."

"Keep your mouth shut, you fool. Our horses are over there. Let's go, then, since you're so afraid. He's an old man; he was going to die anyway; you heard the *patrón* say that. And think of our reward. We'll be safe at last and not have to worry about the garrote. And think of the women. Come on, you imbecile!" Grigorio urged.

When they returned to the *hacienda*, Don Esteban beamed at the two renegades. "You have done well indeed, and it's well that you did it quickly. I have the feeling that tomorrow, at mass, that old fool would have pronounced the formula of excommunication. Yes, you have done very well. Now listen, just in the event that anyone saw you—"

"But no one did, *patrón*, we're sure of that," Manuel protested.

"All the same, best not to take any chances. I have a cousin twenty miles southwest of here. I'll send a message by Jaime and Bernardo, and he will put you up for a week or two, until this blows over. Oh, yes, here's something on account." He opened the door of his desk and took out two little sacks of coins, one of which he tossed at Grigorio and the other at Manuel. "Be off with you, then. And one thing more—my cousin has lots of pretty *criadas*, and I'll tell him in the note to see that you, too, have your choice."

"Well, in that case," Manuel hesitantly agreed, "we'd as well get started, then."

"Excellent! Send Jaime and Bernardo in, when you go to the bunkhouse to pack your saddlebags."

A few minutes later, the two men who had abducted Listanzia entered Don Esteban's study. He spoke in a low voice and to each of them he tossed a sack of coins. They nodded without a word and left the *hacienda*.

Two other *peones* rode with Jaime and Bernardo to escort the Servacios brothers toward the nonexistent ranch of the "cousin." Once they had left the main highway, at Jaime's glib explanation that the shortest road was through this little copse of scrub trees, the four *peones* drew their pistols and shot Grigorio and Manuel down. Then dismounting, they dug graves and, before burying the two outlaws, retrieved the money sacks from the corpses of the murderers of Padre

Juan Moraga, after which they rode back to the *hacienda* of
Don Esteban de Rivarola.

Fifteen

On this same Saturday, Frank Corland had kept his little
shop in Taos open longer than he had originally intended.
Amy had been nursing their two-month-old daughter, Jocelyn, and Frank had hoped that he could close his shop by
four this afternoon. But a florid-faced, quite gregarious merchant had ridden in from Santa Fe. He had disposed of only
part of his trade goods from Chihuahua at the capital, and
had therefore decided to push on to Taos so as to give the
citizens there an equal opportunity to sample his exceptional
wares. He had walked into Frank's shop, which was located
near Padre Moraga's church, about half an hour before
Frank had planned to close, and had been so full of anecdotes
and so reluctant to get down to specific business that the
genial young man had not had the heart to chase him out.

Moreover, some of the merchandise was indeed exceptional, particularly the elegantly decorated bric-a-brac which
had come from an antique dealer in New Orleans, been
carried by ship to Veracruz, and thence overland to Mexico
City. Also, there were dress materials and gaudy ribbons,
even some exotic leather shoes that the wives of the *ricos* of
Taos would be sure to want.

More than six years earlier, Frank Corland had been a
prosperous trapper and trader along the Mississippi, and
trying his luck, he had ventured into the Spanish territories of
Texas and New Mexico. But in those days he had no idea of
the severity of the Spanish treatment of *gringo* traders, and
only the intervention of John Cooper Baines and Don Diego
had prevented the young man from being thrown into a
Spanish prison or, worse, facing a Spanish firing squad.
Thanks to Don Diego's cleverness and full use of his authority as *intendente,* Frank had been adopted by Don José de

Bernados, an elderly widower who had sought someone to be his assistant in the thriving Taos shop. Last year Don José had died peacefully in his sleep, and his will, duly registered by the current *intendente*, Don Sancho de Pladero, had named Frank Corland as his heir.

Frank had married Amy Prentice, who, with her brother, Tom, had been captured by a Ute chief. John Cooper had exchanged weapons and presents for the release of the two captives, who had then come to live on the *hacienda*. Young Tom had gone to work with Miguel Sandarbal and the *trabajadores* and had moved with them to the new ranch in Texas, but Amy remained in Taos with Frank. They had been blessed with two boys and, most recently, a little girl who had her mother's heart-shaped face and light brown hair, and they were prosperous.

Frank had thoroughly adapted himself to his new life as the adopted son of the old shopkeeper. And now that he owned the shop, because of his hospitality and genial demeanor, together with Amy's charming attentiveness when she assisted him behind the counter, he was well accepted in Taos. Traders and merchants had learned that although he was a *gringo* and, still worse, an *americano*, he spoke Spanish as fluently as they did, did not try to cheat them, and made them feel thoroughly at home.

When the Mexican trader had finally left the store, Frank had acquired an exquisite piece of native craftsmanship, a crucifix made out of garnets onto which the Toboso artisan had inlaid the figure of Christ in onyx. The work had been breathtakingly detailed, and Frank did all he could to keep his amazement from the trader, who was already asking a far higher price than was customary. At last they had come to terms, and Frank had decided to make a present of this beautiful crucifix to Padre Moraga, because the old priest had married him and Amy and christened each of their children.

Eager to show his wife his acquisition, he closed the shop and hurried into the back rooms that several years ago he and four young *indios* from the pueblo had constructed to serve as comfortable living quarters.

"See what I bought from Señor Farago," he exclaimed as he showed Amy the cross.

"Oh, Frank, it's very beautiful! How did he come by it, did he tell you?"

"From some Indian in Mexico. From a tribe that has

done a lot of rebelling against the authorities, too, he told me. Only, I guess this one went to a mission school, or something like that. But whoever he is, he created a work of genius. Look at the detail of the limbs and the face of Christ inlaid over the garnet!" Frank exclaimed with the appreciation of a connoisseur.

"Oh, yes, it's just wonderful"

"I'm going to give it to Padre Moraga by way of saying thank you for all he's done for us, Amy dear."

"That's a wonderful idea. Frank, I do love you so very much."

They kissed, then Frank said, "Would you mind if I invited Casaguey to eat with us? He put in a lot of hard work today, and he's a fine fellow."

"Of course I don't mind. He's helped us a lot, and I'm already making a large stew with the lamb you bought yesterday from one of the Indians." Amy rose, and Frank took from her young Jocelyn, whom she had finished nursing. Then, with the baby in his arms, he followed his wife into the kitchen.

"You know," he began, "I've been thinking. You haven't seen your brother in a long time. We've often talked about closing the shop for a few weeks and paying him and John Cooper and Don Diego a visit. But from all I've heard about the coming revolution that's going to split Mexico away from Spain, my feeling is that we ought to start moving out of Taos. It might have less business than ever, after the revolution. Then again, if American settlers can ever get into Texas and here, things could change. But I'm betting on Texas getting there first. There's so much land out there, the Spaniards wouldn't have a chance to patrol for all the settlers who might want to come in."

"I would like to see Tom again, I'll confess it, honey. But things are going so nicely for us here in Taos. Of course, you're the businessman of the family. Whatever you do, I'll follow you, you know that by now." Amy smiled up at him and earned another kiss for her pledge of loving fidelity.

Frank again went into the front of the store, where Casaguey, a young Pueblo Indian, was busy sweeping the floor. Frank had hired Casaguey as an assistant so that Amy could be free to nurse and care for their most recent child. The Christianized and exceptionally devout Pueblo Indian had proven to be a most conscientious and loyal worker. Inviting the young man for supper, Frank then hurried back to the kitchen, where Amy was tasting the lamb stew she had prepared.

When it was ready, he set places on the dinner table for the three of them, by which time Amy had taken little Jocelyn from him and put her to sleep in the bassinet that Frank had carved a month before her birth. The two young boys had already been put to bed, and as soon as the tall young Indian had seated himself, Frank said grace.

During the supper, Frank showed Casaguey the exquisite cross and indicated that he planned to take it to Padre Moraga as soon as supper was over.

"It is a wonderful gift, Señor Corland," Casaguey grave-ly averred. "We of the pueblo love him, for he is kind, and he speaks out against the *ricos* who hate us and abuse our women and our old ones. I know myself of one man who does not follow the teachings of *Jesu Cristo*. He has already caused the father of my cousin's *novia* much sorrow."

"Oh?" Frank asked. "Tell me about it, Casaguey."

"My cousin is Taguro, and he and I support the rest of our large family. Taguro is talented, and one day I think he will make a cross as beautiful as this. But Taguro's *novia* has a father, Marga, who has done some work for the *alcalde mayor,* only the *alcalde mayor* will not pay Marga and says that he still owes him work. He is a cruel man, and last night he did something despicable."

"Tell me."

"Two *peones* from the *hacienda del alcalde mayor* came to Marga's *jacal,* and they took Listanzia away. Taguro told me this, and when he called out and tried to stop them, one of the *peones* shot at him but did not hurt him badly. Then Padre Moraga rode to the *hacienda* of the *alcalde mayor* and demanded that he give back the girl. And then he married my cousin to Listanzia and sent them off to the mountains before dawn. I know this, because Taguro told me just before he left with her."

"I've heard from others like yourself, Casaguey, that the *alcalde mayor* takes his pick of the young women of the pueblo. I wonder why Padre Moraga does not turn him out of the church for his sins," Frank declared with a glint of anger in his usually mild blue eyes.

"I think he will. Taguro said to me that the *padre* was very angry with what Don Esteban and his *peones* had done to poor Listanzia, and he will not stand for it."

"I'm glad for that. Yes, he's certainly a wonderful,

compassionate man. I'm sorry to see him grow so old and weak—I've noticed it lately, more than ever. I don't know what Taos would do without him," Frank solemnly declared.

"Taguro said that when old Marga is better, they will send for him to live at their new home. It will be far from Taos, where the *alcalde mayor* cannot find them," Casaguey said. Then he shook his head and admiringly said, "Señora Corland, you cook as well as my own *madre*, may she rest in peace."

"That's a very nice compliment, Casaguey," Amy said, smiling.

They finished their meal in amiable silence, and then Frank said, "Come on, Casaguey, you can help me clean up the dishes. Then, if you like, we'll both go over to see Padre Moraga and give him this cross."

"I should like that very much, Señor Corland."

Amy sent a grateful look at her husband as she went to check on her sleeping children. The thought of possibly seeing her brother, Tom, again in the near future delighted her immeasurably.

Just as Frank and Casaguey were preparing to leave for the church, they were interrupted by a knock on the front door. When Frank opened it, he discovered that there was a fussy little *hacendado*, Don Nacio de Miromar, who had belatedly remembered that tomorrow, Sunday, was his twentieth wedding anniversary, and he had just discovered that he had no gift for his beloved wife. Frank was secretly amused, for everyone in Taos knew that Hortensia de Miromar was an ill-tempered shrew. Nonetheless, he could hardly turn down such a good sale, and spent half an hour with the little man before the latter decided upon an exquisite cameo brooch with a gold chain and the most delicate links.

Finally, the shop was locked for the last time, and after taking an affectionate leave of Amy and smiling down at his sleeping children, Frank Corland left home in the company of Casaguey and headed toward the church.

The streets were dark, the moon hidden behind a cloud, and from a distance there was the faint rumble of thunder that heralded an oncoming storm. As the two men moved toward the rectory, they heard a wild scream of terror, and then the sound of an old woman's voice babbling, "Oh, *mi Dios*, oh, may all the saints have mercy upon us—they've killed Padre Moraga!"

"My God!" Frank ejaculated as he began to run, the

young Indian alongside him. They came upon the old housekeeper, Soledad, who, her trembling hands pressed to her
wrinkled cheeks, was swaying back and forth in abject grief.
Before her was the lifeless body of the old priest, who lay on
his back with his arms outstretched in a cross, his sightless
eyes wide and staring up at the somber sky.

"Arrows!" Casaguey exclaimed as he knelt down and
examined the two feathered shafts that had pierced the old
man's heart. "But this cannot be! No *indio* of the pueblo
would do such a thing—and see, Señor Corland, they have
the tribal markings of our people. Yet it is well-known that,
for many years, we have never done harm to any *hacendado*
or *mejicano,* and surely not such a man as this!"

"I agree with you, Casaguey. Soledad, please, don't weep
so, try to control yourself. What can you tell us about this?"
Frank turned and spoke gently in Spanish to the hysterical,
deaf old housekeeper.

She could read his lips, he knew, but her immediate grief
had stunned her so that she did not comprehend his meaning;
he had to take her gently by the shoulders and shake her and
slowly move his lips to form the Spanish words: "Please,
Soledad, we can catch his murderers, if you will only tell
us what you know. When did you find him? Did you see
anyone nearby?"

At last, controlling her sobs, and with a last look at the
inert body at which she crossed herself, the old housekeeper
tried her best to recollect her thoughts. No, she had seen
nothing. Padre Moraga had gone out into the garden, as he
often liked to do before he retired for the night. She had seen
nothing, but since he had stayed so long and the night was
growing chilly, and knowing that he was still exhausted from
the long trip he had made, she had taken it on herself to go
out to fetch him back to bed. That was how she found him.

"Who could have done this horrible thing?" Frank
hoarsely demanded.

"An enemy," Casaguey replied simply. "Do you not
remember what I told you about old Marga's daughter? And
how Padre Moraga went to the *hacienda* of Don Esteban de
Rivarola to bring her back to Taos? It could well have been
that man—or his *trabajadores* who are bound to him and
loyal to the death."

"But we couldn't prove that, Casaguey. And now the
town of Taos has no priest. This is a terrible blow for all of
us. To be murdered in this way!"

"They would use arrows, Señor Corland, to blame it on our people."

"I understand, Casaguey." Then he turned, because the old housekeeper had prodded his shoulder with her bony forefinger and, bobbing her head up and down, began to speak. Because of her deafness, her voice was strident and she spoke louder than was necessary. She said she wanted to show them something Padre Moraga had written. Maybe it would tell them what they had to know about the man who either did this, or had it done for him.

They both followed Soledad, who led them into Padre Moraga's plainly furnished room. And there on the writing desk to one side of the door lay a sheet of manuscript paper on which, in an unsteady hand, Padre Moraga had written the beginning of a document.

Frank picked it up and read it aloud:

"I, Padre Juan Moraga, as priest of the Mother Church in Taos, have a duty to save sinners, to help those who are contrite and seek repentance. Yet tomorrow, at mass, I must fulfill another function. It is that of pronouncing the ban of excommunication upon the *alcalde mayor* of Taos. I denounce him as a lecher, a usurper, a man who is dissolute and corrupt and who believes that the power of his office and of his wealth entitles him to break not only man's law, but God's as well.

"I know there will be an uproar in Taos when I pronounce the words, and that he will probably have his spies in the church to try to stop me. Nonetheless, I could not be faithful to my oath as a priest if I refused to do my duty. He would use Mother Church to his own selfish ends."

"Then it is true, as I feared," the young Indian slowly said. "When our people know, they will rise up against Don Esteban de Rivarola!"

"No, Casaguey, that would not be wise. If they did, the authorities in Santa Fe might send troops and many innocent people would be wounded or killed. No, I think I know someone who can avenge Padre Moraga's death. I will go to the stronghold of the Jicarilla Apache and tell them what has happened. Then they will locate this man."

"Let me go with you, Señor Corland!"

"No, Casaguey. I cannot tell you who the man is, for it is a secret. I'll go back to the shop with you, to tell Amy where I'm going. You must go back to your village. And pray for Padre Moraga's great soul."

"Yes, Señor Corland, you are right. But when I tell my people in the pueblo, all of them will want to avenge the murder of this kind, good shaman, for that is how we thought of him. And more than that, as a good friend, who loved us and did not look down upon us because we are poor and despised."

Sixteen

The February afternoon was mild and sunny, a good time for young children to play. That was why John Cooper was making Lobo show off his tricks, as well as giving the gangling young Irish wolfhound puppies, Jude and Hosea, a chance to gambol and play with the tamed wolf-dog. By now the young mountain man had taught both puppies how to fetch a short stick, after which he would rub their heads with his knuckles and give them a bit of jerky or fresh mutton as a reward. They had become most adept at this sport, and by now were competing valiantly with Lobo, who was not to be done out of his own share—the lion's share.

Lobo had displayed incredible patience these past few months as he had submitted to the rather bustling and unceremonious manner of brash introduction on the part of the puppies. Perhaps something stirred within him that made him realize that they were of the same breed as his famous, heroic sire; but for whatever reason, he pleased John Cooper.

Now this afternoon the wolf-dog, his tongue lolling out of his mouth, gave an impatient little yipe when Jude ambled up to his young master, stood on his hind legs, and pawed at John Cooper, while nudging the stick gripped between his sharp young teeth as close as he could to the young mountain man's face.

Even grave little Francesca de Escobar clapped her hands and gleefully laughed at this show of canine histrionics, and both Andrew and Charles Baines simultaneously called out, "Daddy, can we throw the stick next, can we?"

Catarina was seated in a chair that her husband had brought out for her, while Doña Inez sat beside her, industriously knitting a scarf for her beloved daughter. Francesca liked green, and green it would be. Ruth, the last-born to Catarina and John Cooper, was in her mother's arms, an arm around Catarina's neck, watching and giggling with delight as the puppies challenged Lobo in retrieving the short branch.

Don Diego, enjoying the sun and the warm blue sky, stood behind Doña Inez's chair, and from time to time, as he watched with a twinkle in his eyes, he would stroke her hair and lean over to whisper an endearment.

Carlos's son, Diego, already showed signs of being his own man, just as his absent father was. He stood off to one side, arms folded across his chest, haughtily surveying the competition between the puppies and Lobo. Little Inez de Escobar was seated on the grass, clapping her hands and trying to talk to the baby, Dawn, who, well dressed to prevent any danger of chill, sat beside her on a blanket, watching delightedly as the puppies and the wolf-dog engaged in their amicable rivalry.

Bess Sandarbal had joined them with her children, too, for Don Diego, from the very first days at the Hacienda del Halcón, had made it clear to everyone that he considered his *capataz* more a friend than a *trabajador*. Miguel's lovely blond wife and their children were more than welcome to take part in the family entertainment that occurred in this, their new home. Don Diego was well aware that if it had not been for Miguel's stewardship from those first days when they had landed at Veracruz and gone in carriages to report to the viceroy in Mexico City, he could never have prospered in Taos and then so eagerly accepted a new life in this bounteous valley near the river, with its relative isolation from onerous Spanish authority.

Miguel laughed aloud at the antics of Lobo and the puppies, glancing from time to time at Bess, his face softening and his eyes warm with love. She had made him a changed man, no longer glum and dour for long intervals, but almost as buoyant as an adolescent. There was only one weighty matter: the absence of his beloved young *compañero*,

Carlos de Escobar. To date, no message had come from Carlos. Don Diego had made light of this, explaining that his son would doubtlessly survey the terrain and take a leisurely journey down to join the forces of Iturbide. He was certain that his son would appraise not only the political situation, but also the actual living conditions of the helpless *peones* in the neighboring provinces. And until he had found his post and living quarters, Carlos would hardly be likely to stop off at some little hamlet and trust a letter to the unreliable courier service.

Nonetheless, his heart was heavy as he watched the children, outwardly smiling with the pleasure of knowing that here they had found a kind of commune where everyone was equal, where everyone worked together for the general good of all. When he thought of his life back at the Escorial, which was rarely now, he was both amused and amazed at the absolute turnabout in outlook that had taken place within him. That was due to his fine young *gringo* son-in-law, and then, of course, his beloved Doña Inez.

For John Cooper, too, it was a period of readjustment since he was affected by Carlos's absence. The young Spaniard had become far more than a brother-in-law to him ever since the two young men had been holed up in a cave during a blizzard over the Jicarilla Mountains, where Carlos had recovered from a badly sprained leg. His horse had shied and thrown him because of its terror at the scream of a mountain lion, and John Cooper had expertly felled the lion with a single shot from "Long Girl."

At the moment, John Cooper was enjoying his leisure that came after the cattle roundup and before he made his next trading trip to San Antonio, when he would look for new strains of cattle and supervise the purchase of supplies for the ranch. He had also taken advantage of his free time to train Lobo to accept the two Irish wolfhound puppies, and to do what he could to comfort his family over Carlos's leavetaking. That was why today he had decided to devote the afternoon to a kind of public show.

Don Diego laughed softly when he heard the eager, impatient voices of the children mingling in both pleas and orders to have the puppies and Lobo run after the stick again. As he caught the eye of Bess Sandarbal, he graciously inclined his head by way of greeting and called to her, "It is like the Tower of Babel, isn't it, Señora Sandarbal? Do you know, I was just thinking to myself, what a fine idea it would be to have a little school for all these children—as well as those of the *trabajadores*. And if, as I believe certain, the *americanos* are going to come to Texas in the next few years, it will be a very good thing to teach them all English."

"I'd be very glad to volunteer, Don Diego," Bess smilingly called back. "And I agree with you. It would be wonderful if some of the settlers whom that Mr. Austin proposes to bring into this territory could live near us and share the protection we'd have to give them. And, also, perhaps some of our relatives—" She caught herself short, flushing as she recalled that this was selfish. Nonetheless, she hoped that she would see her dead husband's brother one day. She had not known him very well, although when she had seen him last, just before her husband was killed, he had said that he thought Edward had made a wonderful choice in asking her to be his wife. But now that she had found her own home, she couldn't help wondering how this one surviving member of her family had fared all these years since she had first arrived in Taos as a slave, and then had been given this new chance at a wonderful life with a devoted, kindly husband like Miguel.

"Why not, indeed?" Don Diego boomed, feeling very expansive and very patriarchal. Doña Inez, meanwhile, had become caught up in thoughts of her own, and bit her lips with a sudden wave of sadness. She had prayed in the chapel that they be granted just one more child, but now she had resigned herself to barrenness at her age. Yet they had beautiful Francesca, so well behaved and so mature already in her outlook, yet at times capable of a mischievous streak which endeared her all the more to everyone. She murmured a prayer under her breath, lest the Holy Virgin misinterpret her momentary disappointment and think her not grateful for the blessings already bestowed upon her and Don Diego.

John Cooper had decided to conclude the competition. By now, Jude and Hosea were so brash and so certain that they had the run of the place that they pushed Lobo out of the way. He gave a plaintive little growl, and John Cooper understood that there was more chagrin than enmity in it. He laughed softly as he put his hand into the back pocket of his britches and found a large piece of jerky, which gratified the wolf-dog and made him wag his tail, as if to say, "The two of you are new and strange, and maybe that's why my master

likes you right now—but don't you forget that I am still his
favorite, and I have been here a lot longer than you, and I
know more, too."

Indeed, it seemed that the only joys these days at the
Hacienda del Halcón for Don Diego and his wife, and for
John Cooper and Catarina, were in watching the children
play and smiling at the sight of the powerful but aging
wolf-dog Lobo being perplexedly besèt by the two exuberant,
completely uninhibited Irish wolfhound puppies. In a sense, it
was a merciful anodyne to the pain that they suppressed
within themselves, a pain shared by all the *trabajadores* over
the absence of Carlos de Escobar. And beyond them, far to
the south, the cause for which Carlos had declared himself
was being fomented from theory into rabble-rousing rhetoric,
and soon, inexorably, into revolution, blood, and death.

Already, Facundo Melgares, the new governor of New
Mexico who had replaced Pedro María de Allande three
years ago, felt like an official stripped of power in his
resplendent office in Santa Fe. He had only a small contingent
of troops, and most of their time was spent patrolling to make
certain there were no disturbances by drunken or quarrel-
some *indios* from the pueblo, or quarrels in the *posada*, where
knives might be drawn and harsh words spoken. Over the
past few months an occasional courier had ridden in from
Chihuahua or Durango with reports that all governors and
intendentes should be on their guard against the possibility of
local outbreaks, which might signal a widespread revolution.
And in addition to these couriers, messengers from the
viceroy himself came even less frequently, urging those in the
highest echelon of administrative rank to hide all tithes in a
safe place until a stable government could be guaranteed in
Nueva España.

In these troubled times, the *alcaldes* or the *intendentes*
rarely concerned themselves with the possibility that *americanos* might slip across the Spanish borders in Texas and
Nuevo México to engage in the prohibited trading which had,
in the past, caused so much punitive reprisal, and even the
hint of a breaking off of diplomatic relations with the Estados
Unidos. Now the most pressing issue was whether rebel
forces of the Mexican Army would rise up in force against
troops loyal to the Spanish crown. Even the viceroy himself,
Juan Ruiz de Apodaca, had been most recently, around the
Christmas holidays, questioning his most loyal officers to

determine what strength he could count on, in the event the rebels should try to overthrow the royalists.

What irked Governor Melgares most of all was that last year, according to the latest census, Nuevo México was said not to have the ten thousand inhabitants necessary to qualify for a deputy under the Constitution. Hence, the reforms which Governor Melgares hoped to see put into effect to alleviate the poverty of his constituency would not, and could not, come to pass simply because no representative could appear in the courts of Madrid to demand recognition. And this, too, was a sign that the last tenuous hold of Spain of the Escorial and of the great Philip was dissolving.

What he did do was farsighted and imaginative, considering the restrictive laws by which the Spanish had sought to govern their conquered subjects, the *indios*. He announced that the minority status of the *indios* was ended, and that henceforth they would be regarded as "Spaniards in all things, exercising especially their rights to vote and to stand as candidates for office." It was this farsighted act which doubtlessly prevented battles and bloodshed north of the Rio Grande, for they were assuredly about to begin to the south.

And now, just at about the time that the de Escobars and the Baineses were enjoying their children's games, the man for whose cause Carlos de Escobar had declared himself had just published his three-point revolutionary credo. Having secretly been building up a corps of troops loyal to himself instead of to the monarchy, he understood perhaps better than anyone else in all of Mexico the reason for rebelling against Spanish rule—particularly when a king as weak as Ferdinand VII sat on that once all-powerful throne.

The native-born Mexican upper classes, which included military leaders, high clergymen, and landed aristocrats, had for over three hundred years been disqualified from holding the top posts in their own government. They had become little more than frustrated underlings subject to arrogant and too often inept royal officials sent over from Madrid with long lists of picayune regulations that ignored the temperament of the people of Nueva España. These officials also made the mistake of equating both the political and geographic climate of Spain with that of Mexico itself. Yes, the time was ripe for an opportunist, and Iturbide knew it.

His program was indeed what Carlos de Escobar himself had told his father prior to his departure from the Hacienda del Halcón: first of all, total independence from Spain; secondly, full equality for the peasantry; and thirdly, the guarantee of the traditional rights of the Catholic Church as a state religion in Mexico.

By means of pamphlets, by word of mouth, by galloping riders on foam-lathered horses throughout the provinces, Iturbide spread the news. And he organized a patriot force for which he had already coined a grandiose name: "The Army of the Three Guarantees."

It was toward the headquarters of Colonel Agustín de Iturbide that Carlos slowly rode his mustang Dolor, journeying through the provinces, seeing for himself what was taking place. And everywhere he saw the oppression of the peasantry, by the *ricos* and by the influential, as well as the literate—for most of the *peones* could neither read nor write. Always an idealist, and now needing to be one more than ever because of the grief that consumed him like a gnawing cancer, he felt himself more and more justified the farther he rode southward to join that idealistically named army.

What neither Carlos nor history had any way of knowing was that there was a still more ambitious opportunist who had begun his career as a lieutenant, and was now a captain at the age of twenty-seven. His name was Antonio López de Santa Anna Pérez de Librón, and he was destined to transform an idealistic cause into bloodthirsty militarism that one day would make all of Mexico mourn.

Seventeen

In this last week of February, John Cooper Baines, despite his outward show of buoyancy and enthusiasm, was seized with a curious malaise. For the past several days he had found himself distracted, and even Catarina had complained of his brusque behavior. In the darkness of the night, ruefully contrite, he had made love to his beautiful Spanish wife, who was now more mature and sensitive than she had ever been, and thus comprehended his aloofness, as he clung to her with a kind of ardent need, feeling the inexplicable loss of the vital force which had been Carlos de Escobar.

Shortly before dawn, she had turned to him and seen him sleeping, his face taut, his jaw compressed, as he lived out the dream that secretly burned his innermost thoughts. Sitting up, she stroked his cheek with her fingers, and tears glistened in her eyes as she sensed his distance. She understood, and she knew that he was grieving just as she was, for the exuberant, forthright personality that had made their life here on the Hacienda del Halcón even more satisfying and fruitful: her brother, Carlos.

She had stared at him for a long time and murmured, half to herself, "Oh, Coop, ¿que te pasa?" And since she knew he could not answer and would not answer, and perhaps even if he were conscious could not totally define the subtle difference that had arisen between them, she turned on her side and went back to sleep, frowning and concerned for her young husband.

When he woke that morning, he found the bed empty. The sheets were redolent with her perfume, and he sighed deeply and put out his hand where her head had been on the pillow, touching the hollow which that lovely black-haired head had shaped. Then he straightened and uttered another sigh, that paralleled her own, though he could not know it. He had strange dreams this night. He had dreamed that he had ridden back to Taos, invisible to all save those who knew him well, clouded and protected by a mist, and there Kinotatay had told him news that made him tremble. And yet he had only the vaguest recollection of his dream, except that its presentiments lingered even in the bright sunlight of this late February morning. And because he could not understand his dream, he dressed himself in his buckskins, and once again he seemed to be the *wasichu* who had lived with Indians for so many years, sharing their life, their hopes and dreams, identifying himself with their well-being, even if it only half fulfilled the strange, and then not yet fully revealed, destiny to which he was impelled.

Perhaps it was because of this inexplicable anxiety, that was so unlike his candid nature, that he went at once into the chapel, knelt down, and prayed. He prayed for his wife and his children, and then he prayed for Carlos de Escobar, urging that this intrepid, courageous young man who was his peer, and perhaps his own Spanish counterpart, should be returned safely to the Hacienda del Halcón. Yet even as he prayed, he sensed that if Carlos did return, it would be with a meaningful difference, and that with the return, there would be changes in their carefree life that they hoped would be in no way hampered or shadowed by the dying atmosphere of old Spain.

Never before had he thought so much about the struggling new country: the United States. So little of it was as yet chartered and set forth in authentic, credible maps. And yet he believed in it and in its future. And he also believed that one day the future of this impetuous, hopeful young country would be fulfilled in the land which was now called the Texas territory. A land not yet free from the oligarchy and the traditional ceremonials that had marked the pompous and colorful regimens of that Spain whose days of power and glory were over.

He crossed himself repeatedly as he knelt with bowed head in the chapel. And when he rose, he still felt ill at ease, not quite comprehending what would happen and yet anticipating much.

That was why early in the morning, the young mountain man left the chapel and, forgoing breakfast, went at once to the stable and saddled the superb white palomino Fuègo.

As he mounted, he heard the disconcerting, impatient barkings of the two Irish wolfhound puppies, and then Lobo, barking joyously, raced past their shed and stood wagging his tail and looking up at him. His yellow eyes were wide and glowing with anticipation.

"Well then, come along, Lobo. Maybe you feel what I feel. Something's stirring today, I don't know exactly what, but it's troubled me all night long. Come on, then, and maybe Fortuna will join us. At least, we'll have a good, exhausting ride, and whatever it is in our system, we'll try to get rid of it, eh, boy?"

As if understanding his every word, the wolf-dog seemed to nod, then uttered a perfunctory bark and again wagged his tail. Then stiffening, as if eager for the hunt, Lobo started ahead without looking back a single time. And he moved at a rapid pace toward the northwest.

John Cooper watched him for a moment and then patted Fuego's back and murmured, "Let's see what he's up to, Fuego."

The palomino arched his head, tossed it, and whinnied, and then began to lope forward. Crouching low in the saddle, his eyes surveying the widespread horizon and the illumination of the sun that touched the mesquite and the grass and the trees and the flowers with a radiance that betokened the oncoming spring, he overtook Lobo and raced ahead of the wolf-dog. Crestfallen by this, Lobo barked stridently and then, lowering his muzzle, determinedly quickened his pace, till he was running abreast of the magnificent white stallion.

But John Cooper ignored him. Beyond was a tiny dot at the horizon, the vague figure of a man on horseback. Instinctively he kicked his heels against Fuego's belly, as the palomino stretched out his long, strong legs and furiously galloped forward.

Now the dot came closer, and John Cooper perceived the figure of an Indian, hunched over his mustang's neck and jerking his elbows, as if to spur his steed on to an even swifter gait.

Reining in Fuego, he waited, while Lobo turned and then trotted back to his master, quizzically looking up, then turning to eye the oncoming rider.

From every side a warm silence held the open, level landscape, almost static under the rising sun. John Cooper could hear his own heart beating, and the strange premonition of unwelcome news pricked him and made him almost impatiently urge Fuego forward to meet the oncoming rider.

Then with a surprised gasp he raised his right hand in a signal of welcome. The man who came toward him was in his early thirties, wearing the breechclout, the moccasins, and the headband of the Jicarilla Apache. And as the rider neared him, John Cooper scowled, anticipating the very worst of tidings.

"I have ridden here as fast as I could, *Halcón*," the man exclaimed as he reined in his mustang and faced John Cooper. "A *wasichu* rode from Taos to our stronghold and had words for Kinotatay, our chief, from whom I bear the greeting of one blood brother to another."

"I am honored that he remembers the bond between us. But why do you come in such haste to find me?" the young mountain man demanded.

"Once the *wasichu* had told Kinotatay what he had learned, our *jefe* bade me come to you without delay. What the *wasichu* told our jefe concerns you, as it does all of us who live in peace in our stronghold and make no war with the *gringos*."

"And what is Kinotatay's message to me?"

"It is this: the *wasichu shaman* has gone to the Great Spirit."

"Padre Moraga? Dead? Tell me how!" John Cooper hoarsely exclaimed. And as Fuego whinnied and tossed his head, the young mountain man hissed, "Stay, quiet there, *mi caballo!*" And then again to the laconic Jicarilla he urged, "Was it from the weight of his years or the wasting sickness?"

The rider shook his head. "Neither of those brought him to the sky where the Great Spirit awaited his being. He was found with the arrows of *los indios pueblos* piercing his heart."

"He was murdered, then! But there's no Indian in Taos who would lift a hand against so kind, so good a man!" John Cooper was in a rage. "Tell me all you know, quickly!" he feverishly demanded.

The Jicarilla brave carefully explained what had happened: how the young *wasichu*, Frank Corland, had come to the stronghold of the Apache to tell of the murder of Padre Moraga and how the chief, Kinotatay, bade his brave to ride out immediately to the Hacienda del Halcón to tell John Cooper the news. The brave also told the young American about Listanzia and Taguro and how Padre Moraga, before he died, had hoped John Cooper would give them shelter at the *hacienda*.

"Tell Kinotatay of course they will be welcome here," John Cooper hastily replied. "But, please, tell me what else you know about this murder."

"Only that the old woman who cared for the *wasichu shaman* had a piece of paper with the writing of the shaman that said that the *alcalde mayor* of Taos was to be cast away from the church of the white-eyes because of the evil he had done for many moons."

"Don Esteban de Rivarola—he is the *alcalde mayor*, and a very wicked man," John Cooper exclaimed, as if speaking for his own ears.

"It is said," the Jicarilla courier observed, "that a new shaman is to be sent from Santa Fe. Of this I know nothing. And Kinotatay sends you greetings and bids me to tell you that all is at peace within our stronghold. One thing more— the *gubernador* of Nuevo México has issued a proclamation in Taos that we who live high in the mountain are to be the equal of the *gringos* and the *mejicanos*, and that we may have a say at the white-eyes council. This our *jefe* believes to be a good thing."

"Yes, yes it is," John Cooper said, and though this news would have gladdened him at any other time, right now his mind was reeling with the news of Padre Moraga's murder—and his murderer. "No one has punished the *alcalde mayor?*" John Cooper demanded.

"No, *Halcón*. It is still believed in Taos that it was one of the peaceful *indios* of the pueblo who sent the arrows into the old man's heart. But our *jefe* believes otherwise, and that is why he had me hurry to you, and he said that you would know what should be done."

"How are you called?"

"My name is Benitay," the wiry Apache rejoined. "Do you ride back with me to the stronghold?"

"No. I must make plans first. Come back with me to our *hacienda*. You are exhausted, and your mustang needs rest and water, as well. After you have slept and eaten, we shall talk again. Then I will go back to talk with Kinotatay, my blood brother."

"I am to obey what orders you give me, that was told to me by the *jefe*."

"Then let us ride back now. I will think over what has been told to me, and then I shall do what must be done."

When he and Benitay arrived at the *hacienda*, John Cooper took Miguel Sandarbal aside and quickly told him the news of Padre Moraga's death. The *capataz* crossed himself and groaned aloud: "What villainy, what insanity to kill that kind old priest! And you are sure that it was Don Esteban de Rivarola?"

"From what Benitay has told me and the story that Listanzia and Taguro told Kinotatay, there can be no one else," John Cooper grimly declared.

"And what will you do, young master?"

"Padre Moraga means more to me than you can know, Miguel. And to all of us he brought kindness and the word of our Lord to comfort us in our time of need. The lowliest *trabajador* will mourn him. For Don Diego and Doña Inez, he was both their father confessor and the priest who wed them, as he was for Catarina and myself. And for Carlos and Weesayo, and for you too, Miguel."

"I know, I know." Miguel's face was twisted with anguish. "And who can replace such a man?"

"That concerns me a great deal, Miguel. With what's going on in Mexico right now, I don't know whom they'll send to replace him. Most likely the bishop at Santa Fe will appoint someone, and quickly, because it's a large parish. Now see that Benitay is given food and drink, and that he and his horse get some rest. I'm going to the house to tell Don Diego and Catarina." John Cooper seemed to ponder something as he studied the ground for a moment without speaking. Then he looked up and said to the *capataz*, "Miguel, do you remember back in September when we had that renegade Comanche attack?"

"I do indeed, young master. Yes—and the arrows marked red and yellow, that I thought meant that Sarpento had sent his braves to take my Bess away from me!"

"You put the arrows away, Miguel. Get them ready for me. I think they can be of use. And now, look after Benitay, that's a good fellow." John Cooper clapped him on the shoulder and then strode off toward the *hacienda*, leaving Miguel wondering what the young man had in mind to do.

"I cannot believe it, John Cooper," Don Diego gasped as the two men stood together in the household chapel. "I knew he hated me, but I never dreamed that he would be responsible for such a heinous crime—he will be damned to hell for all eternity!"

"That's true. But don't forget what the old housekeeper showed Frank Corland—that paper which Padre Moraga had started to write, and which began the ritual of excommunication. Don Esteban surely guessed that his goose was cooked. No. I'm certain it is Don Esteban. But what concerns me most is that there isn't any priest in Taos, unless the bishop has already appointed one. I want to go there to find out what kind of man they're going to have in Padre Moraga's place. I think it's important, not only to me, but to all of us."

"Yes, you may be right," Don Diego slowly agreed, tugging thoughtfully at his beard and scowling. "I know that when Don Sancho has from time to time sent a courier here to tell me what's going on in Taos, he has always indicated that Don Esteban lives like one of those feudal lords who believe that all the people on their land are little more than slaves and owe their very lives to them, and thus their bodies and souls, too." Again he shook his head. "But I never dreamed he could be so self-sure as to have a priest killed because the priest condemned the sinfulness of his way of life. It is as if he tried to set himself up as a kind of emperor, who believes in neither the laws of God nor man."

"That's exactly how I feel, Don Diego. I'm going to go to the stronghold and talk with Kinotatay, and see Listanzia and Taguro. Then I'll go to Taos and see that justice is done."

"But how will you do that?" Don Diego said, his eyes narrowing with concern.

"I'm not sure, *mi padre*, but I will think of something on the way, even if it means asking Kinotatay to lend me enough braves to take Don Esteban by force and bring him to the governor of Santa Fe to be tried for his crime."

"But as you well know, John Cooper, the courts are weak and corrupt and do not mete out justice where it is due. But that is not my primary concern. How do you know Don Esteban will not try to have you killed by some of his despicable henchmen?"

"I don't know that he won't, Don Diego, but you can rest assured that I'll look after myself. I won't let any of his men ambush me."

"I am sure you will not, my son. I do not believe there is anyone in the land who is as valiant and brave as you."

"When I've completed my errand and all is safe, I'll return to the stronghold and have Listanzia and Taguro come here and settle down with us. I'll tell Miguel to have a little cottage built for the two of them. Taguro is a very skilled artisan, from what I'm told—he can help Jorge Pastronaz and Esteban Morales in making paintings and statues and holy artifacts for the grand church that we'll have one day."

"Yes, I am optimistic about that. That good man, Señor Austin, showed me that here is a man of about my own age who looks forward to the future with a vitality that I envy. It has given me hope and courage for the future—at a time when I need it most, as I need not tell you." Don Diego put his hand out and gripped John Cooper's shoulder, and the two men stared knowingly for a long moment into each other's eyes.

"Well, then, I have to tell Catarina. This is the perfect time for me to go back to Taos, since our work is all caught up at the *hacienda*."

"Yes, do go. And may God go with you, my son. I call you that, and you know why—since Carlos left, you are dearer to me than ever before. You have brought much to this household, and God will reward you."

John Cooper flushed and lowered his eyes. Then he took his father-in-law's hand, shook it vigorously, and left the chapel to go find Catarina.

She was in the nursery, reading to the children, and when she saw him at the door, she called, "Come in, dear Coop. I'm just telling the children the story about Orpheus and his beautiful songs."

He smiled lovingly and closed the door behind him, sat himself in a chair beside her, and reached out to take both her hands in his. "How's my darling girl?"

"Just as you see me: very happy. It's so wonderful to have all these children around me. A woman can't ever get old when she has children like this."

"I know, *querida*. That's the thing that keeps us going. What we do now is for the future of our children, making a good life for them, an easier one than we had." With this he reached over and affectionately patted young Andrew, who was sitting near him on the floor, and winked at little Francesca, who was standing by, soberly watching the proceedings. Then John Cooper turned to his wife and said quietly, "I'd like to talk with you alone for a moment."

"Of course, dear Coop," Catarina said, eyeing him warily as she rose from her chair. "It's time the children went outside, anyway." With this she turned to the children and addressed them. "Now all of you go out and play in the courtyard. I'll join you there shortly, and then I'll finish the rest of the story about Orpheus and his beautiful music." The children scampered out obediently, and when they were alone in the nursery, Catarina, still standing, asked her husband, "What is it you have to tell me, Coop? Is it news of Carlos?" She leaned toward him, her eyes wide with expectancy.

"No, I'm sorry, but you know yourself how slow the couriers are from Mexico here. Besides, if Carlos wanted to send a message, he'd have to find someone he could trust, because we don't want all Mexico knowing exactly where we are now. Your father still has a few enemies, and there's one especially who's done something that he's going to pay for. And that's what I'm going to tell you about—I have to leave now, and I may be gone quite a few weeks."

"Why? Where are you going, darling?"

"Back to Taos, Catarina," John Cooper said, rising from his chair. "I had news from Kinotatay today. He sent one of his braves here to tell me that Padre Moraga was murdered."

"Oh, *Dios!* No, that can't be true—that good, kind old man—oh, Coop!" Tears glistened in her eyes, and she locked her arms around him and pressed her face against his chest.

Affectionately he stroked her hair. "Yes, I'm afraid it is true. His old housekeeper found him lying on the ground with two Indian arrows in his heart."

"Indians? But why would they kill him? And not in Taos, surely not the *indios pueblos?*"

"No, I'm sure it wasn't. They're at peace there. And it was Padre Moraga who made them that way, and saw to it that they weren't treated too badly by the *ricos*. Only there's somebody who thought he was above the law and decided to get rid of Padre Moraga."

"Oh, no, Coop! But who would want to do such a horrible thing? And to kill a priest—that's the worst kind of sin—that's damnation to hell—"

"Yes, it is, and the man who killed Padre Moraga is going to pay for his crime. It was done by Don Esteban de Rivarola, and I am going to see that he's brought to justice. You need not concern yourself with how I'll do it, *querida;* just trust me. I'm going back to see Kinotatay first, and I'm going to leave very soon now. I also want to know whom they sent in Padre Moraga's place. It's very important for all of us."

"I know, and I do trust you, Coop. Just don't get into any danger, and come back to me as quickly as you can. Your children need you, and so do I."

He kissed her and then, not wanting to prolong their leave-taking, abruptly left the room.

John Cooper went directly to the stable to saddle a brown palomino stallion, not quite two years old, which he had named Pingo. This Spanish word meant both saddle horse and, with a Mexican connotation, devil. John Cooper had whimsically given the stallion this name because he was still unpredictably skittish, playful at times when hard riding was demanded. This journey to Taos and back, the young mountain man was certain, would stabilize the stallion's temperament and make certain once and for all that his breeding would be borne out by the arduous test of performance.

Fuego whinnied at him from a neighboring stall, and John Cooper chuckled, then fed his favorite white palomino two carrots that Tía Margarita gave him from the kitchen. "That's all right, old boy, you'll stay here and rest this time.

I'm not slighting you, it's just that Pingo has to carry his weight around here, or he'll never be any good. And don't forget, it was you who sired him. You want to make sure your son amounts to something, don't you?" And when the white stallion, his brown eyes fixed intently on the young mountain man's face, tossed his head and nickered, John Cooper burst into laughter and rubbed the palomino's forehead and ears. "That's just what I thought. I'll see you when I get back."

He then went to Pingo's stall and saddled the brown palomino, who tossed his head and eyed his sire as if to say, "You see, it's me he's choosing this time, not you. Don't give yourself airs, because I'm younger."

The levity that John Cooper derived from this encounter with the horses was heartening because of the secret anxieties which consumed him. First, because of the shattering news that Padre Moraga had been assassinated; secondly, because he himself was beginning to be somewhat worried about the lack of any communication from his brother-in-law.

And, too, he was thinking about the secret silver mine. Whom could he trust, now that Padre Moraga was dead, to keep this secret? True enough, as an act of trust he had told Catarina that the treasure was somewhere on the mountain they had visited before going back to Taos after their second honeymoon. But now, only he knew its real whereabouts. There was untold wealth there, yet it was not really for himself. It must be used to help the poor, the oppressed, the needy, as well as to help the community on the Hacienda del Halcón. It might also be used to help Americans settle in Texas, and now, with a revolution imminent, some of it could be used perhaps even to prevent bloodshed. He could only pray that the other *ricos* in Taos would not emulate Don Esteban de Rivarola's example and try to take the law into their own hands simply because the rigorous ties with the capital of Nueva España seemed now to be broken off. It was a time that would try the souls of men and determine swiftly how honest or how corrupt they truly were.

He packed his saddlebag carefully, with enough provisions to reach the stronghold of Kinotatay. He intended to travel alone, leaving Benitay behind at the *hacienda*, until the Apache and his horse had thoroughly rested from their taxing journey.

John Cooper did not want to be recognized as the son-in-law of the missing former *intendente*, so he also shaved before he left. He meant to pose as an Indian on entering Taos, and Indians were not hirsute. He thus packed his razor so that he could shave again before entering Taos. Also, he had taken some vegetable dyes and greased soot with which he intended to stain his face and hands and hair to complete the disguise.

Before the sun set on this day, he mounted Pingo and rode off to the northwest. Don Diego had shaken hands with him just before his departure and had assured him that he would look after Catarina in John Cooper's absence. He had not questioned why his son-in-law had shaved his beard; he was able to guess that John Cooper would not want to be recognized in Taos as he made sure that Don Esteban was brought to justice.

This time John Cooper did not take Lobo. The wolf-dog raced up to him, his tongue lolling out of his mouth, staring up at his young master with eager yellow eyes, wagging his tail, importunately begging John Cooper to take him along. But the young mountain man shook his head: "No, Lobo. Stay. Stay and look after the *hacienda*. And try to be friends with Jude and Hosea. We'll have our romp when I get back. You be good now. I'm relying on you to look after everything. And Fortuna will make sure that you behave yourself—there he is now, coming down to peck you, see?"

As he spoke, the black raven swooped down with a strident caw and nipped at Lobo's tail. There was a soft growl as Lobo whirled and snapped at the playful raven, but Fortuna had already soared high into the air and perched on the top of the stables, from which vantage point he mockingly taunted his lupine companion.

"Just as I told you. Fortuna, you keep Lobo on the straight and narrow, mind you. I'll be back when you see me, both of you. *Adiós!*" John Cooper called, lifting his hand in salute as he kicked his heels against Pingo's belly.

In his saddlebags were the two arrows with their red and yellow markings, the spent arrows that the renegade Comanche had launched against the *trabajadores* in their brief and unsuccessful attack against the ranch last September. Once he reached the stronghold, John Cooper would borrow a strong bow from his blood brother Kinotatay, *jefe* of the Jicarilla Apache. If he had to use them to defend himself, those arrows would not incriminate any of the Indians in Taos.

Clean shaven, in his buckskins and moccasins, he looked

as young as he had been when he had entered the village of the Sioux as a captive, even after rescuing the chief's daughter, Damasha. But his eyes were hard and cold, and he was no longer the naive and trusting youth he had been then. It was not the frontier that had toughened him, but the discovery of evil men who would betray and cheat and steal and even murder, for material gain. The renegades who had killed his family had done it because they were greedy for whiskey. But Don Esteban de Rivarola's sin was far more grievous. He had destroyed a man who had been born and dedicated to helping those who were held in scorn because their skins were coppery, because they had been the first upon the land before the *hacendados* came to wrest away their birthright.

Eighteen

John Cooper felt his heartbeat quicken as he rode the winding, narrow road up to the stronghold of the Jicarilla Apache. It was cold in the mountains, and the air was redolent with the scent of the fir trees that thickly lined the narrow, overgrown trail. John Cooper trained his eyes on the markings that seemed to fall back into place in his memory as if he had been there only yesterday, and he urged the brown palomino onward.

Pingo had proved himself with a steadfast master holding the reins and punishing his mischievous attempts at dallying by applying pressure on the bit. The breeding was good, John Cooper knew, and the test of endurance had been exactly what this young stallion had needed.

It was true that his first reaction to Benitay's news of the assassination of Padre Juan Moraga had been one of fierce hatred that had irrationally driven out all thoughts save that of vengeance. Now he was coldly calculating what must be done, and knew that Don Esteban de Rivarola must be brought to justice. He realized that, in some ways, he was setting himself up above the law, but this was necessary in a land where that law was often abused. It was his intention to sneak into the *hacienda* of Don Esteban de Rivarola and to order him to accompany the disguised John Cooper to the governor of Santa Fe, to whom the wicked *hacendado* would confess his crimes. Even in a lawless and corrupt land, John Cooper believed, the governor would have to arrest Don Esteban after such a confession and try him for murder.

John Cooper had no illusions about the dangers of such an endeavor, but he wanted to confront the *hacendado* man to man. However, if Don Esteban was unwilling to go to Santa Fe and make his confession, or if his *hacienda* was so well protected that John Cooper could not gain entry, then the American would return to the Jicarilla stronghold and ask Kinotatay for ten of his braves to go with him to apprehend Don Esteban.

Yet even bringing the evil *alcalde mayor* to justice would not expiate the death of Padre Moraga. In his relationship with the priest, John Cooper had almost felt that here was the man who had, after his long wanderings through a desolate and lonely adolescence, supplanted his murdered father and had become his spiritual advisor. Now that all that kindness, that dispensation of mercy, that levelheadedness was buried, there was no spiritual guide in Taos. Nor could John Cooper know what kind of priest the bishop of Santa Fe would appoint, and if he would be able to share with him the secret of the lost silver mine, whose limitless treasures must be conserved to help the needy and the downtrodden.

These thoughts crowded his mind, and he marveled at them, for during his years with the Indian tribes he had thought of little except his own survival. Yet now he could reason and think and remember the lessons that his father and mother had tried to inculcate within him. He knew he was not so much a patriot, but a man who believed that it really didn't matter who a man's ancestors were, so long as he was good and just, and so long as he did not covet his neighbor's possessions.

Realizing this, he could clearly understand why he had adapted himself so well to life with the Ayuhwa, the Pawnee, the Sioux, and the Jicarilla. If the whites had not tried to cheat and lie and kill to grasp that land that had been their birthright, the Indians, who were considered savages, might have lived in peace and made a greater nation out of this young country.

Now he heard the sound of a crow, and then the screech of

a mountain lion—the signals given by the sentries hidden in the rocks and narrow caves along the path that he took to the stronghold. They were telling those back in the camp of Kinotatay that *El Halcón* was riding to them.

He rode onto the level of the wickiups of the chief and the elders, and Kinotatay stood waiting to greet him, his eyes bright with recognition and a warm smile on his lips. Beside him stood a handsome young woman, almost as tall as Kinotatay, in her late twenties, and in a buckskin sling on her back she bore a papoose. She glanced at Kinotatay with admiration, and then with equal pleasure at the sight of the young mountain man who dismounted from his palomino and led it forward till he stood face-to-face with the stalwart chief of the Jicarilla. "It is good to see you, my brother," he said.

"And for me, too, it is good. This is Corigay, my squaw, and our firstborn, Nemigda. She is the daughter of the chief of the Mescalero, and I took her into my wickiup as my squaw twelve moons ago as a pact of peace between our tribes," Kinotatay smilingly informed him.

"Long life to you and your squaw." John Cooper inclined his head toward the handsome young Mescalero woman whose smile broadened. She had the candor and forthrightness of a warrior, he thought to himself, and it was good that Kinotatay had eased his own grief at the loss of his son, Pirontikay, by taking this new squaw and renewing the cycle of life.

"You have heard the news that I sent by Benitay," Kinotatay observed. "It is a bad thing, and we here in the mountains know it was the *alcalde mayor* who brought it to pass, though he sought to blame it upon *los indios pueblos*. But now the people of Taos are also beginning to see the truth, and there are those now who openly say it was not the *indios*, but the *alcalde mayor*."

"Tell me this, have the white-eyes replaced our murdered friend? Have you heard word yet, Kinotatay?" John Cooper asked.

"I am told that it is not yet done, but that it will be soon. Listanzia and her mate, Taguro, are still with us. I did not have one of our braves escort them to your *hacienda* because I knew you would be coming here when you learned of the death of the *wasichu shaman*."

"Yes, and I will take them to the Hacienda del Halcón when I have done what I have come to do, Kinotatay," John Cooper said, "and I hope I have your support." He went on to explain his plan, and the Apache *jefe* listened gravely, his eyes searching the young American's face.

When John Cooper finished, Kinotatay spoke: "You shall have ten braves if you need them, *Halcón*. I know what the old shaman meant to you, and to all of us. Even though we live here in our stronghold many miles from the church, we knew of his kindness, and his belief that we who have *indio* blood within us are as well beloved by his Great Spirit as by our own."

"This is the lesson that all men have not yet learned, Kinotatay."

"Yes, my brother. And my heart is sad within me for the news of our Beloved Woman, who was the squaw of the young Spaniard whose sister is now your mate, *Halcón*."

"He has ridden across the Rio Grande to fight for the revolution that will give the *mejicanos* freedom from their Spanish *jefes*, Kinotatay," John Cooper told him. "We have not had word of him, and I know why he does this. It is out of grief for her memory, and because he hates the *ricos* and the *hacendados*, for it was they who looked down upon her because she had the blood of the great chief in her veins, and they could not accept her marrying the son of a hidalgo."

"The Great Spirit, who you have often told me is the same for your white-eyes people as for mine, cannot understand why there is so much hatred over the difference in blood and skin and in customs," Kinotatay solemnly observed. He turned to the lovely, smiling Corigay, and in a gesture of companionship, unusual to the Apache, put his arm round her shoulders. "She is Mescalero, and for many moons longer than I can remember, and even before I was born, I learned that the Mescalero and the Jicarilla were at war with each other. But there is no war between Corigay and me. We respect each other, and we accept each other's differences. This to my mind is what was meant to be between all people."

"You are right, Kinotatay. You are wiser than many a *hacendado* or even the great *jefe* of a *ciudad* whose people number ten or even twenty times those braves now in your stronghold," John Cooper told him.

"We shall prepare food for you, my brother. And you will meet Listanzia and Taguro. They have waited eagerly for your coming. But at least they are safe from the *alcalde mayor* of Taos. Come now, I will take you to a wickiup where you will rest and prepare for the feast tonight."

"I am indebted to you, my brother. Life is good for you. That is what I had hoped it would be."

"And you, with the sister of the Spaniard who is also our blood brother?" Kinotatay asked, his eyes quizzical.

"It is good with us. She loves the *niños*, not only those she gave me, but those of Carlos, of Doña Inez, and of Miguel Sandarbal, who married the Texas girl who was captured by Sarpento, *jefe* of the Comanche."

"That one!" Kinotatay grimaced with disgust. "He is an outlaw, and he is greedy. He would make traffic with the *mejicanos*. He would sell his own mother on the auction block for *dinero*. We know that the Comanche call themselves the People, and they are proud, and they have reason. But not Sarpento. His soul is small, shriveled, like a long-dried acorn, and he will betray whomever it suits him for his purpose. Already his braves rebel against him, and it is only because he has much power and much *dinero* that he holds them together."

"I know this. And now, I will leave my palomino, and I will refresh myself in the wickiup until it is time for the feast. I give you thanks, Kinotatay, for remembering me, your blood brother, and lending me your support. I will have much to tell you when I return from Taos."

John Cooper entered the wickiup that Kinotatay had pointed out to him, and he lay on a mat on the earthen floor to rest for a few hours. He felt great contentment, and it seemed to him that he had never been absent from the stronghold. The years had fallen away, he was young and free again, and he thought of Lije, the great-hearted Irish wolfhound who had given his life to save his young master. It was only yesterday, John Cooper thought to himself, that he stolidly carried the heavy body of the dead wolfhound in his arms down the winding road, with the silent riders flanking him, impressed by his grief and not importuning him, only watching to see what he would do. He had buried Lije on a ledge, and then he had gone silently with the Jicarilla Apache to the stronghold and lived with them and shared their lives, their sorrows, their hatreds, and their yearning for freedom.

Moved by this memory, he slept for some time. When he awoke, he was refreshed, and in his buckskins he went out where the braves and the maidens danced, a distance from the wickiups. There he danced the ritualistic dance of one who has been long absent but returns in fervor and amity, acknowledging his allegiance to the Jicarilla in their proud, high stronghold at the top of the mountains. And there was silence as the Apache, young and old, watched this *wasichu* brother, who had exchanged the sacred bond of blood between, first, the chief Descontarti, who had died six years ago, and then his successor, Kinotatay.

When it was done, Kinotatay beckoned to him and led him to a smaller wickiup about a hundred yards away, where there stood the tall, lithe pueblo girl Listanzia and her husband, Taguro.

"That is a good thing, seeing them together," John Cooper gravely averred. "I will talk to them now, and I am grateful that you have given them the hospitality of your stronghold."

"They are good people. They are devoted to each other, in spite of their suffering, and that will make for a long, happy life." Kinotatay smilingly took John Cooper by the hand and led him toward the wickiup. As they approached it, the young Pueblo Indian, Taguro, came toward the *jefe* of the Jicarilla. "Is this the man for whom we wait, Kinotatay?"

"It is he, *El Halcón*. He once lived in Taos, and he is our blood brother. You can speak to him with a straight tongue, and he will answer in kind. His heart is good, and there is no difference between us, though his skin be that of a white-eyes," Kinotatay declared.

"Tell me, Taguro, is it true that Don Esteban de Rivarola had your squaw taken to his *hacienda*?" John Cooper asked.

"I swear it by the Great Spirit," Taguro exclaimed, and he looked at Listanzia tenderly and took her hand.

"Well, Taguro, when I return from Taos, I will come back here for both of you. You will return with me to the *hacienda* that I have in Texas. There are no *gringos* or *hacendados* to interfere with us. We shall have freedom. I am told that you are a clever artisan, and we think of building a church to the glory of *el Señor Dios*. You can help us with this."

"I will do it with love and with thanks in my heart, *wasichu*." Taguro extended his hand, and John Cooper heartily shook it.

Tears glistened in Listanzia's eyes as she bowed her head in thanks, and John Cooper greatly moved, turned back to Kinotatay. "You must lend me your strongest bow. I go into Taos on the morrow."

"I will pray to the Great Spirit to watch over you always," Kinotatay gravely declared.

Well before sundown on the next day, John Cooper mounted Pingo and, saluting Kinotatay with his right hand, rode back down the trail, which wound along the side of the Sangre de Cristo Mountains toward Taos. Freshly shaven, dressed in his buckskins and wearing moccasins, he had strapped over his shoulder the long bow of the Jicarilla Apache, and a quiver, thonged loosely round his neck, contained the two arrows marked with the red and yellow signs of the Comanche. Also, strapped to his saddle, in its special sheath, was "Long Girl," primed and readied with a ball already in the barrel and adequate powder. He hoped these weapons would be enough to intimidate the evil *hacendado* and persuade him to turn himself in.

Two or three miles past the stronghold, he veered off the trail down a narrowed path known only to himself, a shortcut toward the village of Taos. First he wanted to stop at the *hacienda* of Don Sancho de Pladero, not so much to divulge his mission in Taos, but to see the man who had carried out Don Diego's humanitarian policies toward the lowly Pueblo Indians.

The journey took more than two days, and it was nightfall when John Cooper rode along the level path that broke off from the mountain trail and headed toward the southwestern sector of this Spanish-held village. In the distance, in the dusky moonlight, he could see the sprawling *hacienda* of Don Sancho de Pladero and, far beyond it, what had once been the *hacienda* of Catarina's father. No one occupied it now; it had been deserted ever since Don Diego had taken his retinue and his household to Texas. John Cooper smiled knowingly to himself. Truly, Don Sancho had been a trustworthy friend, but John Cooper knew also that Don Sancho was powerless to avenge Padre Juan Moraga. All of the people of Taos were fearful of the evil *hacendado,* or else they believed that justice was an impossibility in this decadent land.

Staining his face and hands with the vegetable dyes and carefully combing the blackened grease into his hair, John Cooper let Pingo graze a bit, then slowly headed the palomino toward the *hacienda*. He could now see the lights of oil lamps.

He wasn't challenged by any sentries as he rode his horse

up to the patio and there tied Pingo's reins to a hitching post. He strode to the doorway and struck thrice upon the heavy door of Don Sancho's *hacienda*.

A suave, gray-haired majordomo whom he did not recognize opened the door and querulously demanded, "Who calls at the house of the *intendente* of Taos at so late an hour?"

"Tell your master that it is *El Halcón,* who asks for private audience with him," John Cooper replied.

The majordomo stared at him, alarmed at seeing a fierce-looking, buckskin-clad Indian at the door. He quickly went inside to tell Don Sancho, but five minutes later when he returned, it was with a great sense of relief. Inclining his head low, he ingratiatingly declared, "My master bids you come in at once. I will take you to him, señor."

Without a word, John Cooper followed the majordomo down a narrow corridor toward the study of Don Sancho de Pladero, where the majordomo bent and thrust out his arms as if to intimate that this visitor was eagerly awaited, then turned on his heel and disappeared. John Cooper put his hand to the doorknob and turned it and entered. Don Sancho, more portly than he had remembered him, clad in a black velvet robe and slippers, stood there, astonished. "*¡Madre de Dios!* Señor John Cooper! It is you, isn't it?" he exclaimed, then seeing the familiar smile, he held out his hand in welcome. "I did not think that you would come to Taos now, when there is such unrest here. I suppose that disguise is so your enemies will not know you are here."

"You're right about the disguise, Don Sancho—But what do you mean, unrest? Because of the death of Padre Moraga?"

"Yes, that, too. But mostly because we have news each new day of uprisings throughout the provinces of Nueva España. And each of the *ricos* here is greedy and impatient for the time when it will be possible for him to proclaim his own superiority and take possession of Taos. All of them forget that I am still *intendente*, until my power is dissolved by the *junta*," Don Sancho proudly declared.

"And among these *ricos*, I am told that the worst of them is the *alcalde mayor* of Taos, Don Esteban de Rivarola," John Cooper hazarded, watching the swiftly impressionable features of the *intendente*, which told him at once, by the sudden shadow crossing his face, that Don Sancho knew the *alcalde mayor* was guilty of murder.

"Yes, John Cooper, he is an evil one," Don Sancho

began slowly. "And there are those in Taos who say it was h
who arranged the murder of Padre Moraga. But he is a ve
powerful man, and we in Taos who believe he is guilty a
helpless."

"That's what I thought, Don Sancho. You've been a ve
loyal friend. In all these years, my father-in-law feels great
friendship for you than he knew when he was living nearb
You haven't betrayed us."

"There have been those who have asked me pointed
where Don Diego went, and I have shrugged and said that
was told in the dead of night that he had suddenly decided
quit his job because of reasons of health and take his fami
elsewhere. It was an answer that cost me nothing, and whic
forced those who were really curious for motives of their ow
to do their own ferreting out," Don Sancho smilingly replie
"Will you share a glass of Madeira with me?"

"Gladly. I'll drink to your health, and Don Diego invit
you, when you can, to bring Tomás and his wife, as well
your own Doña Elena to visit us."

"I hope to do that soon. Indeed, I have begun to thi
more and more of following my old friend's footsteps, a
moving to Texas myself. Ayúdame, if you only knew t
frustrations of my post!" Don Sancho groaned and roll
his eyes. "We are not only cut off from trade, but we a
separated by the many leagues between Taos and Mexi
City. Besides which, the viceroy is trying to gather his ow
forces to repel the expected insurgency, and so he has
time for us outside the boundaries. I think you have hea
that it was necessary to group the citizens of Taos with tho
of Chihuahua in order to give us a representative vote. A
fortunately, our wise gobernador decided to take the irc
from the fire when it was hot, and offer equality in t
vote to all the indios of the pueblo. Yes, that was a good thing

"It was indeed. It will at least keep them from joining
rebellion and attacking the innocent people here, who are n
the allies of the ricos and the strong," John Cooper avowe
"Well, you have probably guessed that I am here to pay ba
the debt I owe Padre Moraga, but I will say no more in ord
not to incriminate you in any way, except to say that I w
do everything I can to see that justice is done. But tell me,
there no new priest yet to replace the padre?"

"Not yet. I expect, however, that very soon the bishc
of Santa Fe will appoint a man of his own choice, and I ca
only hope that he has the same feeling for our parishione

hat Padre Moraga had. Yet that is too much to hope for, in a situation like this."

"And Luis Saltareno, whom I know to be another enemy of yours, Don Sancho, is he as greedy as Don Esteban?"

"He is a scoundrel, but he doesn't have the noble blood of a hidalgo such as Don Esteban professes to have," Don Sancho contemptuously declared, dismissing the thought of the rich merchant by opening a teakwood box and thrusting a pinch of snuff into each of his nostrils with a decisive gesture of his thumb pad. "The trouble is, I think he has nearly as much money as Don Esteban, and for that reason he is dangerous because he is willing to spend it to get more power. Oh, yes, he would love to be *intendente* or *alcalde mayor,* but these two posts are still held by men who live."

John Cooper eyed his host, then nodded. "I'll take my leave of you. But remember Don Diego's invitation. Whenever you and your family are ready, we'd like to welcome you at the Hacienda del Halcón. One thing more, Don Sancho. Not long ago, an *americano* named Moses Austin came to visit my father-in-law. He was on his way to see Governor Martínez in San Antonio to ask permission to bring about three hundred settlers into Texas. He hopes that perhaps when there is friendship between Mexico and the United States, the door will be open to free trade and enterprise."

"By all the saints, that would certainly help Taos, and we have needed somebody like that for years," Don Sancho broke out. "Well, I'll be interested in hearing how successful Señor Austin will be with his proposal. Governor Martínez acts on protocol and orders, and I do not think he has too much imagination of his own. But then," he philosophically shrugged, "who is to say what can happen to a man when a revolution is taking place? He can change overnight. And now I think I know where you are going from here, Señor John Cooper, so I won't keep you any longer."

"I'll send word to you through one of the Apache in the stronghold, and you'll know what is the outcome in good time."

"*Vaya con Dios, amigo.*" Don Sancho offered his hand, and John Cooper shook it, then took his leave. Mounting Pingo, he rode through the dark, still night toward the estate of the *alcalde mayor,* where he would sneak into the house and confront Don Esteban de Rivarola.

About half a mile from the ornate *hacienda,* he tethered the palomino out of sight in a copse of scrub trees and,

remembering how he had hunted the killer bear in the land
the Ayuhwa, crouched low to minimize the chance of h
being seen by any sentry. Swiftly and noiselessly, moving
an Indian might on the toes of the moccasins so as to lea
the smallest trail possible, John Cooper edged toward t
adjunct of the *hacienda,* that edifice which served as t
torture chamber of the *alcalde mayor,* in which the sto
Listanzia had endured her ordeal.

Agilely, he shinnied up one of the vertical woode
beams to reach the low roof, and there lay conceale
Beyond, in the bunkhouse, he saw the light of oil lamps ar
heard the bawdy laughter and the buzz of the voices of t
trabajadores who, at their ease, were drinking tequila ar
recounting boastful stories of their own erotic prowess wi
the *criadas*.

Then suddenly he heard a shrill cry, a girl's cry, follow
by uproarious bursts of laughter and then the sound
leather on flesh and more pitiful cries till at last they cease
And then, suddenly, a naked girl came running out of t
bunkhouse, wildly sobbing as a *trabajador,* laughing u
roariously, pursued her.

Now John Cooper saw Don Esteban de Rivarola himse
hurry out of the bunkhouse toward the smirking *trabajad*
who forced the helpless, naked girl down on her back ar
turned his head to call out to his *patrón,* "Manuela w
not cooperate with us, *patrón.* She will not be obedient to us

The *alcalde mayor* frowned. He wore a yellow silk tun
and drawers of the same costly material, and his robe w
loosely belted. He was barefooted, his wig was askew, his fa
was flushed, and his eyes bright from lechery and tequila.
he came closer, Manuela uttered a frightened cry, whimpe
ing, "No, no, *señor patrón,* let me go—it hurts me so fro
the wh—whipping—have pity—haven't I been punish
enough—not anymore, please, I hurt so!"

"I'll give you a few minutes to regain your composu
my little good-for-nothing," Don Esteban taunted her in
soft, insinuating voice. "But if you do not cooperate, I w
have to punish you—severely. But maybe you should take
lesson from my favorite *puta,* Noracia. Then, while t
still-trembling, weeping girl stared uncomprehendingly up
his leering face, the *alcalde mayor* turned toward the bun
house, cupped his hands, and bawled at the top of his voi
"*Hombres,* bring out Noracia. I want her to show t

ungrateful lump of flesh how to satisfy a man. Now *pronto, ahora mismo!*"

John Cooper could not believe what he now beheld. From the door of the bunkhouse, three swaggering, half-drunken, laughing *trabajadores* shoved a handsome young woman. She wore a red silk shift, which had been tattered and hung by only a single strap from her shoulder, baring one of her breasts. There were welts on her arms, shoulders, and thighs as the three men forced her forward toward the *hacienda,* mocking her with lewd promises as to her fate.

"Yes, put her down beside Manuela, so she can instruct the little *puta* how to be a good whore," Don Esteban excitedly cried as he made an imperious gesture with his right hand. "Here under the stars, on the ground, let her know what it's like to feel strong *cojones!* And then, after you've had Noracia, you may have your fill of Manuela, too."

"Oh, no, *señor patrón, por piedad,* no!" Manuela fever-ishly sobbed as she tried to rise from the ground. But the brutal *peón,* Jaime, who held her down, cuffed her playfully across the mouth and hissed, "Don't interrupt the master, you little slut! He's already—be good, and he may let you share my bed in the bunkhouse. Why, it will be almost as if you were my wife, don't you see? And if you're kind to me, and you do all the tricks I want a little whore like you to do, I promise I shan't beat you too often!"

Noracia was struggling, and now she lifted her head and cried out, in a strong voice, "Don Esteban, in the name of mercy, why do you do this to me? Haven't I always pleased you? Didn't I give you pleasure when I punished that *puta* from the pueblo of Taos, that Listanzia? You said after that, when we were in bed together, that never before had a woman given you such pleasure—now why do you have me dragged out here and given to these vile dogs?"

"Because you give yourself too many airs, Noracia," Don Esteban jeered at her. "And you're a *mestiza,* thinking that because you have a little Spanish blood in you, you are as good as I am. No girl, you'll learn your lesson tonight, and so will Manuela. Now then, *amigos,* down on the ground with her, rip that shift away, and let's see how she takes to you. Make it last; it will excite me the more, and I'll give you *mucho dinero* for it!"

As the three men ripped at Noracia's shift and held her down, the wildly frightened younger girl began to shriek.

"*Silencio, puta,*" Don Esteban hissed, and when she did not desist, he kicked her and shouted again, "*¡Silencio!*"

John Cooper ground his teeth, his eyes narrowed and cold. Then what he saw horrified him. Don Esteban had taken out a small pistol and was aiming it at the girl named Manuela. "Since you will not stop screaming I will have to fire this bullet into your head," the *hacendado* roared, and as he cocked his pistol, John Cooper wasted no time. He put an arrow in his bow, drew his arm back to the maximum, and let the arrow fly.

It struck Don Esteban in the throat, and he uttered a gurgling screech, which was cut off by the rush of blood. He dropped the gun as his pudgy hands tried to tear at the piercing shaft, and then his eyes rolled upward, and he crumpled to the ground.

"*¡Madre de Dios, indios! ¡Protéjanse, protéjanse, amigos!*" Jaime cried out as he sprang up, forgetting Manuela in his terror at seeing his *patrón* struck down before his very eyes.

"But this *puta*—" one of the three half-drunken Mexicans ruefully interposed.

"You imbecile, you want us all to be shot down? I don't know whether these are Comanche or Toboso, but you saw what they did to Don Esteban! To the bunkhouse and get your weapons—leave the *putas*. Let the *indios* carry them off if they like. Maybe they won't attack us then! See, the *patrón* is dead. He doesn't move—it's every man for himself now!" Jaime cried as he began to run toward the bunkhouse. The three men who had brought Noracia out for her violation looked at one another, then took flight, outdistancing Jaime as they ran back to the bunkhouse to get their *pistolas* and muskets.

Noracia, finding herself freed, turned on her side toward the terrified Manuela and panted, "They're going away now we'll go into the *hacienda*—we'll save ourselves—oh, thank the Blessed Mother that they didn't do any more to either of us!"

But then Jaime seemed to realize that all the treasures of the *hacienda*, together with the *criadas* and Noracia, were at the disposal of whoever was shrewd and opportunistic enough to take advantage of this bounty. He turned back, a wide lecherous grin on his bearded face, and then hurried toward the two young women. By now, Manuela, despite her weak ness from the flogging, had managed to get to her feet as she held on to Noracia's arm.

"Not so fast, *lindas!*" Jaime called, drawing a knife from the belt of his britches. "The *patrón* is gone to meet his Maker, so now I'll take charge. Just stay where you are, *muchachitas*—I'll protect you both, if you're good to me, *¿comprenden?* Otherwise, you'll be back in the bunkhouse with all the *compañeros*, and you'll be busier than you would in the crib in Chihuahua!"

Noracia gasped when she saw her former benefactor lying dead on the ground, his hands still gripped around the fatal arrow in his throat. Then she shrank back, trying to cover herself with her hands, as Jaime, his eyes glittering and his knife held like a dagger, craftily approached her and the still-whimpering Manuela.

John Cooper straightened, drew the second arrow from the quiver, fitted it to the bowstring, and sped the shaft. Jaime uttered a strangled cry, the knife dropping from his nerveless hand, then spun around and fell on his side, away from the two naked women, with a last convulsive thrashing of his legs. Then he was still.

John Cooper cupped his hands to his mouth and called in a husky voice, "Save yourselves, *mujeres!* Go back to the house, clothe yourselves, then go out to the corral in back of the *hacienda*. Take horses and go from this accursed place. Otherwise those *trabajadores* will use you worse than ever Don Esteban did!"

"Who speaks? Is it an angel or a devil?" Noracia crossed herself, as the younger Manuela huddled protectively against her. But John Cooper's advice had penetrated her dazed mind, and she whispered, "Hurry, Manuela, let's do what he says—let's get away from here, before those men take us again—I've had my fill of men, believe me. I've a cousin near Nuevo Laredo. We'll ride there if we can find horses. Hurry, let's get some clothes and see if there's any *dinero* the *patrón* left lying around—then we'll leave here forever!"

John Cooper, still crouching so as to present no target for any of the men if they should emerge from the bunk-house, ran swiftly to the other end of the *hacienda*. Then he shinnied down the beam and ran swiftly toward the sheltered copse where he had left Pingo. Leaping astride the horse, he took a last glance back at the estate of Don Esteban de Rivarola. And then, crossing himself, he urged the palomino back toward Taos and to the Sangre de Cristo trail, which would lead him to the Apache stronghold.

As he sped away, John Cooper let out a sigh of relief. Don Esteban was dead, and the debt to Padre Moraga had been paid in a totally unexpected way. Justice had been done.

Nineteen

John Cooper Baines rode back to the Jicarilla stronghold and shut himself up in the wickiup of Kinotatay for some time, explaining to the chief the strange turn of events in Taos, and the death of Don Esteban de Rivarola and one of his cruel *trabajadores*. "I feel Padre Moraga has been avenged," John Cooper told his blood brother, "and I am greatly relieved that the evil of this *hacendado* has come to an end. Affairs in Taos will still be unsettled until there is a new priest and a new *alcalde mayor*, but it's good to know that at least none of the innocent *indios pueblos* will be called to account for the death of Don Esteban de Rivarola. If anything, it will look like an attack by the Comanche."

"You have done well, my brother," Kinotatay said. "Those two unfortunate females whom you rescued will be free to go about unmolested, and the people of Taos will see how evil men like this Don Esteban pay for their crimes."

After this meeting with Kinotatay, John Cooper went to the new wickiup that the friendly villagers had built for Listanzia and her husband, Taguro. The artisan's face glowed with gratitude and pleasure at the sight of the young mountain man, and he began at once to praise John Cooper effusively. "You don't have to thank me, Taguro," John Cooper somewhat embarrassedly declared, "just say some extra prayers every so often for a great man who died before his time, Padre Moraga. Now then, I'd suggest you and Listanzia start packing for the trip back with me. I'd like to leave at sundown, after I've had a few hours to rest. Also, it's harder to trail at night than during the day, and we don't want anyone to follow us to the ranch."

"*Comprendo*, Señor John Cooper. And again, *gracias por mi vida.*"

When the sky was dark that evening, Listanzia and Taguro mounted the saddled mustangs that Kinotatay had given to them, the blankets and saddlebags filled with provisions for the journey. And John Cooper raised his hand in the sign of brotherhood to the chief of the Jicarilla, with the promise that he would return again.

They took a leisurely journey back to the *Hacienda del Halcón.* As they neared the ranch, they saw in the distance the large *hacienda* and the clusters of outbuildings surrounding it, with the grazing lands spread out as far as the eye could see. The cattle looked like little specks, and the *vaqueros,* mounted on horseback, looked no bigger than insects.

When they arrived, John Cooper at once introduced Taguro to Miguel Sandarbal, who found him an admirable worker. Within a week, Listanzia and Taguro had their own little cottage not far from Miguel's, and on that first night in their new house, they paid a visit to the chapel where Jorge Pastronaz presided as acolyte priest, there to give their grateful thanks to a benevolent Creator and to the laconic, candid young mountain man.

Nor did Taguro forget the promise he had made to the Keeper of the Sky to paint a mural on the wall of his house, giving thanks to the Great Spirit and showing the wonders of His creation. The young *indio* went out and extracted from plants and rocks all the dyes and pigments he needed. Taguro worked on the massive painting whenever he wasn't busy crafting little icons for the chapel or working with the *trabajadores* on new buildings for the ranch. Listanzia helped him, extracting the pigments and dyes, making brushes for him, even helping him apply the colors. The members of the community on the Hacienda del Halcón visited Taguro and Listanzia's cottage and stared in awe as they watched the young Indian create his masterpiece.

Meanwhile, John Cooper had been happily reunited with his family, and Tía Margarita had prepared a grand feast in honor of his homecoming. At the dinner table there was much cheer and animated conversation. John Cooper smiled as he held Catarina's hand beneath the dining room table and listened to Miguel Sandarbal, who with his lovely Bess had been invited to dinner that evening, in honor of the young

American's return. The dignified foreman related a humorous account of an incident that had occurred that morning. A fierce young bull on the ranch had gotten its head stuck in an oak drinking bucket and had run about its enclosure wildly, bucking and banging its head against the ground. Several of the *trabajadores* had gone to the bull's aid, but they were unable to restrain the beast and remove the bucket. Indeed, the workmen had become engaged in a kind of bullfight, as they used blankets and staves in an attempt to quell the maddened animal. Young Tom Prentice had saved the day by leaping on the animal and riding bareback, finally subduing the beast. Coming to a halt, the animal was surrounded by the *trabajadores*, who at once removed the bucket, and the bull was none the worse for wear.

Everyone at the dinner table laughed, none more so than Don Diego, who was delighted to have his family and friends in such grand high spirits. If he was thinking tonight about his absent son, Carlos, he did not reveal it, and his pride in his son-in-law did much to allay any sadness the older man might feel. John Cooper had told him earlier what he had accomplished in Taos, and Don Diego was grateful that justice had been served.

Now Catarina spoke up, and with a glance across the table at Bess Sandarbal, addressed the others. "I have something I wish to propose," the beautiful and poised young woman began. "Or I should say, there is something Bess Sandarbal and I wish to propose."

"What is it, my dear one?" aksed Doña Inez, who was seated next to Bess. "We all want to hear."

"Bess and I are going to open a school on the ranch, just as we all once discussed. We have so many children here, and until now they have had to be content with the occasional lessons Doña Inez or I taught them. But now we're going to have a real school, with lessons every day.

"That's a wonderful idea, *mi* Catarina," Doña Inez said, and taking Bess's hand she said to both of the young women, "I think you will make wonderful teachers."

"Catarina and I have already devised a curriculum," Bess now put in. "We decided she should teach literature and history, since she is so knowledgeable in those subjects, and I would teach the children English and mathematics."

"I can attest to your superb mathematical ability, Bess," Don Diego exclaimed. "In the years that you have been keeping the books for the *hacienda*, I have been constantly amazed at your ability with figures."

"We will begin giving lessons on a regular basis starting next week," Catarina enthusiastically went on. "We will use the nursery for our schoolroom."

"Until we build you a new schoolhouse on the grounds of the ranch," Miguel added.

"We look forward to that day, Miguel," Catarina said, and then turning to her husband, she added, "And Coop, I'm hoping when you and the *trabajadores* make your trip to San Antonio for the ranch, you will be able to order some books for Bess and me."

"You can count on it, *mi corazón*," John Cooper said, beaming. It had long been a dream of his to have a school on the *hacienda*. And his pleasure and happiness were increased greatly when later that night, after he and Catarina had gone for an after-dinner stroll on the grounds of the ranch, Catarina put her hand in his and whispered, "*Querido* Coop, I'd love to have another child with you."

He took her in his arms, and as they embraced, he was serene at heart, knowing that all he had longed for was happening. In this new life there was great joy for every single member of their community, and in the years to come there would be many new children to share that joy.

Yellow-haired Bess had been twenty-six when she had come to the *hacienda* in Taos, and Miguel's shy courtship had been furthered by none other than John Cooper himself, who had told Bess of Miguel's valor and decency and his secret yearning to marry her. Now they had a five-year-old son, whom she had named Timothy after her late husband's brother, and a three-year-old daughter, Julia, who had her mother's yellow hair and soft blue eyes and delicate pink skin.

Bess Callendar and her husband, Edward, had originally come from Virginia, where she had been a schoolteacher; they then traveled to San Antonio to visit Timothy Callendar, his wife, and two small sons. A few weeks later Bess and Edward had gone further north, in the hope of settling on a small piece of land, where Edward would resume the farming and ranching he had done back in Virginia. Then it was that a renegade band of Comanche, led by the treacherous Sarpento, had attacked the wagon train, Sarpento himself killing Edward Callendar and forcing Bess to work for him as a slave until she would agree to marry him. Her consistent refusals cost her many beatings, and Sarpento had angrily dragged her off in fetters to the fair, to be sold to anyone who would pay his price.

Don Diego and Miguel had arranged for Bess's release; she then occupied a privileged place on the great Texas ranch, married to the accomplished foreman and hired to keep the ranch's ledgers. Her future looked all the brighter now that she and Catarina would be starting their school in the next few days.

Seeing that her son and daughter were well occupied with some of the toys Esteban Morales had made for them, Bess now went outside her cottage to breathe in the surprisingly mild air, and to revel in the magnificent vista of sky and valley and river that stretched all around the ranch.

At the same time, Doña Inez came out of the *hacienda*, her eyes twinkling with conjugal pleasure. She had persuaded her husband to sleep as long as he wished, since there was really nothing to demand his attention before midday. She then went out to the kitchen to chat amicably with plump Margarita Ortiz, whom everyone called Tía Margarita, to help prepare her husband's breakfast, and to then serve it to him on a tray. She blushed delightedly, remembering his reaction: he had sat up in his nightshirt, his eyes wide with amazement at the sight of her performing the role of a maid, and then, with a hearty laugh, after she had set down the tray very carefully on the table beside the bed, he had drawn her down into his arms and resoundingly kissed her. He had whispered, "My sweet Inez, how young you make me feel!" And his hands had caressed her lovingly yet intimately, till she had to reprove him in a tone that quite belied her real emotions.

She felt such indescribable happiness, having such a loving husband and such an adorable Francesca, who gave every promise of being a mature little woman, even at her tender age. It was true that she played with the other children, but even though she was younger than some of them, she insisted that games be played by fair rules, and she never teased her companions.

She saw Bess Sandarbal standing looking out at the sumptuous, sun-bathed landscape and hurried toward her. This morning she felt she had to talk to someone with whom she could exchange confidences and little bits of gossip. She needed a woman-friend—and she had always felt the greatest sympathy for Bess, knowing how dearly Miguel loved her and how happy she had made this mature, once-somber man, who was now as youthful in attitude as her own beloved Diego.

"A good day to you, Señora Sandarbal," Doña Inez smilingly exclaimed as she approached the attractive blond woman.

"And the same to you, Doña Inez. My, isn't it a lovely day!" Bess looked around, her eyes rapt with the verdant colors of the landscape beyond her and the serene blue sky which, in this month of March, reminded her of the winters she had known back in Virginia with her first husband.

"Yes, certainly. It is a joy to be alive, with everyone here at the *hacienda* so happy and content." Then her face sobered, remembering Carlos's departure. "If only all that happiness could have prevented poor Carlos from leaving us to join the army in Mexico—I say prayers daily, and so does Don Diego."

"I, too, Doña Inez. But Miguel assures me that Carlos is so young and strong and brave, he'll come back, you'll see."

"To hear you say that comforts me," Doña Inez confessed. "Meanwhile, life must go on."

"Yes," Bess said, then impulsively clutching Doña Inez's hand, she whispered, "And there's something I'd like to share with you. Miguel and I are trying to have another child. This time, perhaps it will be another strong son. He's so proud, and he loves me so much—I thank God for him whenever I go to the chapel."

"Oh, my dear, I am overjoyed to hear you say this." Doña Inez squeezed Bess's hand and then kissed her on the cheek. "May I tell Don Diego? You see, inwardly, he is grieving for Carlos, and it is almost as if he were in mourning. To hear that his good friend and loyal companion Miguel might be a father again will be a kind of inspiration—it will prove that life does go on, and that the good *Señor Dios* watches over us if we believe in Him and are faithful to His commandments."

"I feel that way, too," Bess confided. "My parents died when I was about sixteen, and although my mother was Catholic, my father was a Methodist. Yet they got along wonderfully. After all, there is only one God for all of us—" Bess uttered a nervous little laugh and her cheeks flamed. "My gracious, I'm chattering away here like a parrot. Won't you come in, and I'll make you a cup of chocolate? And please, you must call me Bess."

"I would love some chocolate. And you must call ▮
Inez, dear Bess. There is no need for titles between us. Y▮
are a very lovely, thoughtful young woman, and I can s▮
why Miguel loves you so very much." Doña Inez paused ▮
moment, then continued, somewhat shyly, "You don't kn▮
how I envy you, Bess, to be able to have another child. Af▮
Francesca, I thought my happiness was complete, but I lo▮
Don Diego so, I wanted to give him still another—but that ▮
in His hands, and I must not complain. I have been blessed ▮
it is."

Bess Sandarbal put her arm around Doña Inez's wai▮
and the two women, drawn together by this sympathe▮
bond, entered the pleasant little cottage.

An hour later, when Doña Inez emerged, it was almo▮
as if she had known Bess since they were children. It w▮
delightful to have a friend and confidante, all the more ▮
since Bess's husband, Miguel, was the good friend of D▮
Diego. As she hurried back to the *hacienda,* she look▮
forward to telling her husband about the bond that she a▮
Bess had established, and she hoped her enthusiasm wou▮
take Diego's mind off what they both now never spoke of: t▮
self-imposed absence of Don Diego's beloved only son.

Twenty

Noracia, the half-breed mistress of Don Esteban ▮
Rivarola, and the young servant-girl, Manuela, had fled fro▮
the estate of their *patrón* on the night when John Cooper h▮
avenged the assassination of old Padre Moraga. When t▮
young mountain man had called down to the *mestiza* to sa▮
herself, she had regained her wits. She and Manuela h▮
hurried into Don Esteban's lavishly furnished house, quick▮
procured dresses to cover their nudity, and Noracia h▮
remembered that the debauched *hacendado* kept large su▮
of money in leather sacks secreted in the false bottom of ▮
chest in his bedroom. Once, when he had been particula▮

eased with her perverse skill in punishing one of his errant
adas, before compelling her to minister to his carnal needs,
opened the chest, took out a small sack, and tossed it to
r, saying, "This is for the pleasure you've given me tonight,
oracia. Continue thus, and you'll be able one day to buy
ourself a husband when I'm tired of you!"

Manuela had timidly protested that this was theft, but
oracia had boldly acclaimed, *"Estúpida,* he's dead now, and
we don't take it, the *peones* will! I'll take two sacks, and
ou take another. Perhaps the rest will go for the poor if the
aurch seizes his property—may it happen thus!" and she had
ossed herself, as much from a sense of new-found piety as a
arowback to her earlier religious training.

Although John Cooper had suggested that the two young
omen take horses from the stable and ride off to freedom,
Noracia was again quick-witted enough to realize that with
ae furor created by her master's death, all his *trabajadores*
ould be gathering near the bunkhouse and the stable and the
orral and she would very easily be detected. So she decided
ot to go to her cousin near Nuevo Laredo. "We'll go on
oot," she told Manuela. "We'll slip out of the back of the
acienda and go to Taos."

Manuela tearfully wrung her hands. "But my parents
ren't there; besides, only my mother's alive and she's very
ick—and she lives in Calderón, that's fifty miles from here—
he doesn't ever expect to see me again."

Noracia's lips tightened, and she slapped the young
riada. "Stupid one, who said we were going to see your
nother or anyone else? I know someone who will take us in,
es, and be glad of it."

"And who could that be?" Manuela sobbed. "I'm so
rightened, may the Holy Virgin save us—they whipped
ne—and they were going to do awful things to me—"

"I'll slap you again and harder if you keep up your
vhining, *puta!*" Noracia hissed, as she smoothed the folds of
he elegant silk dress she had found in a closet adjacent to
Don Esteban's bedroom. It had, indeed, been a dress im-
orted from New Orleans, and he had intended to give it to
ner as a special favor. It was a bit large in the hips, but it was
o elegant and beautiful that she was certain that, when she
appeared in it, the man whom she had chosen to be her
orotector would be dazzled. Besides, she sewed well enough
o be able to take it in so that it would fit properly. "And
hat's enough sniveling, do you hear me, Manuela? Let's

hurry, before they come to the house and think of the sa
thing we've just done. Some of them know how much *din*
Don Esteban kept, and they'll be looking for it. And if we
still here when they find us, it'll be far worse than what v
going to happen to us just now, *¿comprendes?"*

Manuela was finally convinced and, suppressing
sobs, had followed the beautiful half-breed out of the back
the house. There was the rumble of a coming storm—the s
was dark, and the moon was obscured by racing clouds. Th
it had been an easy matter for Noracia and Manuela to ma
their way out of the estate and to head for the town
Taos.

As Noracia had suspected, the *trabajadores*, after milli
around and excitedly discussing the death of their *patr*
began to enjoy their first taste of freedom. Almost to a m
they hurried into the house and began to ransack it. In d
time they found the false bottom of the chest and the rest
Don Esteban's money. Then there was quarreling, kniv
were drawn, and by the time the men who had slaved for t
hacendado had made their final disposition, three of them
dead on the floor of Don Esteban's bedroom. Many of t
men decided to remain on the estate, which they would ha
all to themselves. The rest of them, fearful of more viole
quarrels, headed for the stable, took the best horses, saddl
them, and rode toward the Rio Grande. With the *dinero* th
had taken, they would be rich enough to buy a piece of la
in the province of Durango, Chihuahua, or San Luis Poto
perhaps even a *mujer linda*, and settle down like *hacendad*
themselves.

Dawn was breaking when Noracio and Manuela, dishe
eled and breathless, reached the elegant mansion of Lt
Saltareno on the western outskirts of Taos and far remov
from the pueblo village. There had been no pursuit, a
Noracia was already congratulating herself on the success
her stratagem, though the young *criada* was timidly dubiou
"May the holy saints protect us, Noracia! I'm so afraid
what if he turns us away? What if he tells the authorities v
belong to Don Esteban and that we've run away?"

"If you'll keep your mouth shut, Manuela, I'll get you
fine new situation. First off, I'm going to get myself or
You'll see. Just watch, listen, and keep your mouth shut. N
to waken Señor Saltareno," Noracia boasted as she strode
the door and, making a fist like a man, struck upon it as ha
as she could. Manuela watched her, shrinking back, b

rown eyes wide and still glistening with tears. It had been a ectic night, beginning with the threat of repeated violations y the brutal *trabajadores* for the voyeuristic amusement of on Esteban. Then had followed this long walk through the arkness, in which she had envisioned many terrible wraiths nd brigands lurking behind the trees and the mesquite clumps.

There was no answer, so Noracia struck the door again several times and called out, "Señor Saltareno, Señor Saltareno, it's important!"

At last a light flickered through the partly drawn shutters of a window near the door, and then it was opened, and a stooped, gray-haired servant, the majordomo, angrily demanded, "Who dares to wake Señor Saltareno at an hour which is neither fit for beast nor for man?"

"Tell your master that it's Noracia and that I have important news for him. Tell him that Don Esteban de Rivarola is dead."

"*¡Jesu Cristo!*" the old man gasped, as he crossed himself, then turned and hurried back to the merchant's bedchamber.

A few minutes later, grumbling at being wakened from a sound sleep, Luis Saltareno appeared, a dressing gown hastily drawn over his nightshirt. "What the devil are you doing here, Noracia, when the world's not yet awake?" he scowlingly demanded.

"It's as I told your man here, Señor Saltareno, Don Esteban de Rivarola is dead."

"Yes, I heard that, but I was still half asleep—are you certain? But it can't be—who could have done such a thing?"

"It was an *indio*, Señor Saltareno. He shot Don Esteban with an arrow. I saw it, and it was dreadful—I shall never forget such a horrid sight—" The *mestiza* dramatically put a hand over her eyes and uttered a feigned sob. Manuela incredulously shook her head and crossed herself, glancing up at the sky, as if to beg divine forgiveness for participating in such a charade. At the same time she expressed her eternal gratitude at being saved from the ravaging *trabajadores* to whom Don Esteban had wished to consign her for his own lustful gratification.

"By the bones of the saints! This is serious indeed— come in, girl, come in—who's that with you?" the merchant irritatedly demanded as he caught sight of Manuela shrinking back to efface herself.

"It—it's my maid, Señor Saltareno, it's Manuela. Com
here, girl, nothing to be afraid of now. The good Señ
Saltareno will look after us." And then, wheedling, Norac
added, "I think I can be of value to you, Señor Saltaren
Now that Don Esteban is dead, who will be the *alcalde maye*
of Taos? It should truly be you, you are so well-known, s
distinguished—and what a fine figure of a man!"

Despite his irritation at being wakened so early, Lu
Saltareno gave Noracia a fatuous smile as he floridly ge
tured, "Come in, girl. I'll have Maximilian prepare *desayun*
for you and your *criada*. Better still, I'll share it with yo
though it's much earlier than I usually breakfast." With thi
turning on his heel, he bruskly ordered the gray-haire
majordomo to have the cook prepare breakfast for three an
to bring it to his bedroom. Meanwhile, another serva
brought him his morning chocolate.

"Now then, Noracia," Saltareno directed as he took
hearty swig of his chocolate and smacked his lips with gust
"Are you certain that Don Esteban is dead?"

"Oh, yes, Señor Saltareno, I saw it myself—there wa
someone on the roof of the *hacienda*, and when Don Esteba
came out of the bunkhouse with his men because he wante
to watch—"

"I can imagine what he wanted to watch, *querida*," th
merchant sniggered, leering at pretty little Manuela, wh
blushed and hung her head. "I know something of his foible
But do you mean that you were included? I mean, he gave m
to understand that you sometimes helped him—you unde
stand—"

"Of course, Señor Saltareno," Noracia said, calmly mee
ing his lecherous stare. "But this time, I was being punishe
you see. He thought I gave myself airs beyond my statio
and so he wanted to watch the *trabajadores* take me. He als
wanted to teach my—ah—little maid here, Manuela, a lesso
and he was even going to shoot her. And it was then an arro
was shot into him, and he fell dead. I swear it on my hope
salvation, Señor Saltareno."

"Hmm! This is very serious. An Indian, you say? B
you didn't see him?"

"It was very dark—he called to Manuela and me fro
the roof and told us to get away. And of course—you can s
how frightened we both were, and we thought his men wou
take us as their own, now that he was gone—"

"Of course, of course. So you made your way her

eeking my help and advice. You do me an honor, Noracia."
The merchant took another swig of his chocolate, leaned
back, and let his robe loosen at the belt. "I don't mind telling
you, when I had dinner with your late master that evening, I
was much taken by you. And I envied him. But now that he's
gone, you'll want someone else to look after you, won't
you?"

"That's true, Señor Saltareno. And I know that you're
the wisest man in Taos."

"Do you now?" He chuckled, highly pleased at this
obsequious flattery.

"And besides"—she chose her words carefully, as she
levelly eyed him—"they'll be needing a new *alcalde mayor* in
Taos. Now, if you were to send someone to the governor in
Santa Fe and tell him about Don Esteban, and that someone
were to recommend your name to succeed poor Don Esteban—"

Luis Saltareno slapped his thigh. "You're a marvel of
wisdom as well as beauty, Noracia! I forgive you for waking
me at such an ungodly hour. You and I have much in
common, and we'll discuss it a little later in the day. Now
finish your breakfast, that's a good girl, and then you both
will have a room where you can sleep. At noon, after I
have—ah—recovered myself sufficiently over my grief, we'll
take up this matter in detail."

Saltareno, as soon as he had given orders that Noracia
and Manuela be given one of the most ornate guest rooms in
his *hacienda*, summoned Pedro Nuñez, whom he had entrusted as an assistant to him in the shop which he maintained
in Taos. When the obsequiously bowing, stocky, bearded
clerk entered, Saltareno exclaimed, "I'm sending a letter to
Governor Melgares. You will take it directly after I've finished with it. Make certain that it gets into His Excellency's
hands and, if he should happen to question you, explain that
you've worked for me these last ten years and can read and
write, as well as supervise a shop. And it wouldn't do any
harm, Pedro, if you were to volunteer a word of praise on my
behalf, do you catch my meaning? You see, Don Esteban de
Rivarola died last night, from an Indian arrow."

"May the saints protect all of us" the stocky little man
gasped as he crossed himself and stared at his master with
horrified eyes. "Indians here in Taos? Surely not the *indios* of
the pueblo, *patrón?* But there hasn't been an uprising here for
many a year—"

"Well, it hasn't been proved yet who actually killed Don Esteban, but the important thing to remember is that he's dead and that the office of *alcalde mayor* is now vacant. And if you do your part in helping the governor select me as the worthiest of all the replacements in Taos, Pedro, I shall reward you handsomely. Now be off with you—there is the letter with my personal seal so that His Excellency will recognize it."

And so it came to pass that, with the death of one of Don Diego de Escobar's enemies, a second and even more virulent one was appointed by Governor Facundo Melgares to take his place. Only a week after the formal announcement of the assassination of Don Esteban de Rivarola, word had come from Santa Fe that Luis Saltareno was herewith appointed *alcalde mayor* of Taos, with all the privileges and authority pertaining to that title.

Twenty-one

Carlos de Escobar had ridden slowly southward, avoiding the main roads and the highways, a lone figure under burning skies on his mustang, Dolor. All around him, the rocky Mexican landscape was withered and barren.

Still brooding over his loss, he burned with the desire to lose himself in an idealistic cause that would champion the oppressed and bring justice at last against the handful of arrogant *ricos* who believed it was their supreme right to govern and to rule in tyranny. There were many nights when he had made only a small campfire and ate paltry rations so that he might feel as humble as any *soldado* recruited from the lowliest of the *peones* in this coming fight for the independence of Mexico. And there were many hours along this circuitous and ambling route in which he found himself weeping for having thus purposely estranged himself from his beloved father and from Doña Inez, whom he had come to respect and to love almost as much as he had his own mother.

Although his father would be termed a *hacendado* and a *rico*, Carlos knew very well that it was only against the blindly ambitious men of that breed with whom his quarrel truly was. And that was why his journey to Mexico City, whose purpose was eventually to join up with Iturbide's army of liberation, was punctuated constantly by excursions into the obscure little hamlets and towns, rather than on a direct route that would lead him to the capital.

He ate and drank at the humblest *posadas*, listening to the talk that went on there; he often stopped to water Dolor at some small well at the outskirts of a dusty little town miles away from El Camino Real. And when old men or women, struck by his youthfulness and the spiritedness of his horse, talked with him out of curiosity, he asked them what they knew of the revolution, and what was happening to them in this far-flung village.

And the answers were always the same: rumor, fear, and uncertainty, and all of this compounded by sporadic raids by troops of royalist soldiers who often proved to be as cruel and rapacious as the thieves and murderers they were sent to punish as they took advantage of the upheaval to rape and pillage and to murder when it suited their fancy.

In many a town he saw pigs rooting in the trampled gardens, half-starved dogs snuffling at some pile of garbage or a scrap of stale bread or a dry bone, mothers in rags weeping, as they cradled babies to their emaciated bosoms and looked up at him and begged for a *centavo*—or, what sickened him still more, coyly offered themselves for a meal or perhaps a jug of milk for their little ones.

He passed by the estates of the *hacendados*, who ignored all this misery and who lived in luxury and comfort, barricaded within the security of their walls, with their armed *trabajadores* constant sentries against the bands of looters. And the serfdom of the *peón* and of his sister or young wife or daughter continued.

The old order was changing, but those who had been tyrants under the placid, ancient system of the Old World had not changed their ways. As he rode through the town of Celaya in the province of San Luis Potosí, he came upon a platoon of royalist soldiers in their green and red uniforms, breaking into a large *jacal* and emerging with young and middle-aged women, whom they were dragging by the wrist, or by the hair. Their commanding officer and the rest of the troops had ridden on to the north, so that these eight men were virtually deserters.

Furious at what he saw, Carlos de Escobar rode straight toward them, calling upon them to release the women, as he drew a loaded pistol from the holster at his belt and pointed it at the head of the burly sergeant who had gripped the wrist of a mature, handsome woman with one hand and, with the other, was dragging her thirteen-year-old daughter by the hair.

"*Amigo*, would you aim your weapon at a soldier who only does his duty?" the sergeant guffawed. "These people are known to favor the usurper Iturbide."

"Your company has ridden to the north; what do you do in this village? And the women have no voice in a revolution—you care only about their bodies. I order you to let them go, or I'll pull this trigger," Carlos angrily exclaimed.

One of the privates who was struggling with a slim, teenage girl whose skirt and blouse he had nearly ripped off, released her now and, with an oath, dipped his hand toward his holstered pistol. Carlos saw the movement, turned in his saddle, and fired; the private sprawled face-down on the ground, and the girl cried out and crossed herself. In almost the same movement, Carlos put his left hand to the other pistol and aimed it at the sergeant again. "Now will you believe me, you filthy dog? You disgrace the uniform of the crown by what you do here! To your horses and to your company, at once!"

"All right, all right," the sergeant growled. He released the two women, spat on the ground, and then angrily beckoned to his men to follow. Carlos had unsheathed his Belgian rifle and was cocking it. But there was no fight left in the others, not after having seen one of their comrades killed by this fierce stranger.

And when they had mounted their horses and ridden off in a cloud of dust to the north, the women knelt down and sobbingly blessed Carlos de Escobar. His eyes were filled with tears as he opened his saddlebag and took out a handful of the silver *pesos* his father had given him for the purchase of a commission. "Here is *dinero* for milk for your babies and food for yourselves. Stay inside your *jacales*. Have you no men in this village to defend you?"

"No, señor, most of them have run away. The *bandido* came through here a week ago and took away with them six of the women and killed some of the old men," the girl whose assailant Carlos had shot down tearfully declared.

"Pray in the church, then, and perhaps our merciful *Señor Dios* will spare you. I ride on to Mexico City to join in the fight for freedom. And I swear to you, all of you who hear the sound of my voice, that I will fight to prevent such sights as I have just witnessed here. If Mexico is to be free, if the Nueva España is to separate itself for all time from Spain, then people like you in the smallest villages must be able to live in peace and without fear of murderers and abusers of the helpless." Crossing himself, Carlos rode off amid the grateful prayers of the women he had saved.

Now more than ever, he felt his cause just, and for the time, what he had done allayed the throbbing, relentless torment of his irrevocable loss. For a moment there, the face of one of those women whom the soldiers had wanted to violate had reminded him of the sweet visage of Weesayo, but he knew that this had been only an illusion born out of his nightmarish dreams and his nostalgic recollections of the exquisite days and nights they had known before the tragedy. Now he rode on, his face grim, determined to reach Iturbide and to enlist, even as the lowliest of privates. Idealistic as he was, he had not conceived that such evil would follow the stirring of revolt; he had believed that the oppressed *peones* would wrest arms away from the soldiers and liberate themselves, or even, if the soldiers understood how they themselves were tyrannized by their loyal masters, they might lay down their arms of their own accord and join the *peones* in an eager army of total liberation. Now he saw that this, too, had only been a dream.

Carlos de Escobar reached the headquarters of Colonel Agustín de Iturbide late in the winter of 1821, and after an interview with the revolutionary leader, was appointed lieutenant. What pleased Don Diego's dedicated son was that Iturbide proposed this commission after interrogating Carlos not only on his political, but also his philosophical views of life, and there was not the slightest hint that the commission was being offered because Carlos was the son of a former hidalgo and, therefore, affluent enough to purchase that commission.

Indeed, Iturbide rather grandiosely declared, "Mexico has need of intelligent young men like you, Señor de Escobar, men who put aside even the comfortable and placid life of an aristocrat in favor of the stern discipline which our revolution insists upon if we are to gain total freedom from the autocracy of Spain. You see, *mi teniente,* it is necessary to gain the support of the clergy in this revolution, which makes it very different from what might have taken place in Spain itself. The clergy resents certain policies of the *Cortes,* which were set forth when the weakling king, Ferdinand VII, was compelled to restore the liberal Constitution of 1812." He embraced Carlos, saying, "You will be like a brother to me. You combine the intelligence of the aristocrats and the clergy, indeed, yet you also have the fiery ardor of a young *peón* who defies the centuries of oppression and tyranny which the *hacendados* and the *ricos* have imposed upon this Nueva España, which will soon become a Mexico for all who feel themselves brothers!"

In the capital the daily growing strength of this liberalistic revolution had made Viceroy Apodaca resign, and in his place the timid Don Francisco Novela had been appointed viceroy by a hastily summoned *junta.* His role would be to temporize and to prevent any bloodshed until the struggle for power could be, it was hoped, peacefully resolved.

There were other leaders in Mexico who furthered this final separation from the Spain of the Old World, men like José Mariá Morelos and Vicente Guerrero. These men, along with Iturbide, had proposed such a revolution two years ago, but at that time the royalists had been certain that they could entirely suppress the rebels. Indeed, the viceroy had reported to Ferdinand VII that no additional royalist troops were necessary. But in these intervening years, the privileged classes had been antagonized by the restoration of the very Constitution of which Iturbide had spoken to Carlos de Escobar, and thus it was that the aristocracy itself was in favor of the revolution. They, leaders of wealth and power in Mexico, made it clear to Viceroy Novela that they would go over to the side of the rebels; thus frustrated and realizing that the cause was lost, he left his office.

And this same winter young Lieutenant Carlos de Escobar was one of the officers who marched under Iturbide's command of twenty-five hundred troops toward the camp of the liberal leader, Vicente Guerrero, not to fight, but to negotiate. Iturbide and Guerrero came to an agreement known as the Plan of Iguala, which declared that New Spain was an independent, moderate, constitutional monarchy, guaranteed the Catholic religion, and proclaimed racial equal ity. This doubled the strength of Iturbide's idealistic platform and solidified the patriotic force that he had already called "The Army of the Three Guarantees." Shrewdly, he had sought the favor of the clergy because he knew that their wealth surpassed that of the selfish *hacendados,* who would prefer to keep the status quo so long as they might maintain the feudal power of life and death over their *peones.*

News of this uprising, thus far bloodless, reached Vera Cruz, where the royal commandant of the province gave orders to a highly gifted young officer, Lieutenant Antonio López de Santa Anna Pérez de Librón.

Santa Anna had begun his guest for an illustrious destiny at the age of sixteen, when he had protested against the decision of his father, a modest mortgage broker, to apprentice him to a merchant in their hometown in the province of Vera Cruz. His eloquence had been so persuasive, and his depiction of the service he could render his country in the army so forceful, that both his father and mother had allowed him to join the army, since it offered young men from undistinguished families their only chance to elevate themselves in Mexican society. The revolution against Nueva España, led by the gentle priest Miguel Hidalgo, had erupted while Santa Anna was taking his cadet training. But the young man had been graduated in time for the Texas expedition at the Battle of Medina, where a bloody outbreak against New Spain had taken place in 1813. And it was there, inexperienced as he was, that he displayed both the qualities of leadership and of cynical amorality that were to mark him as a chameleonlike opportunist, who would always favor the stronger side.

Although General Joaquín de Arrendondo had publicly praised him for his vigor and courage, Santa Anna had shown a dangerous weakness for snap judgments, and in later years he would pay dearly for his belief that regular army troops could never be defeated by irregulars. Yet, he was thoroughly familiar with the great military campaigns of the past, and he had the personal magnetism and eloquence of a great orator, so that he could make his defeats seem like personal triumphs. Five feet ten inches in height, clean-shaven—a rarity in that era—his poise and good looks had already made him intensely attractive to the opposite sex, an endowment that he would use unscrupulously for his own pleasure, sometimes even at the cost of delaying a military decision.

His uncanny good luck was demonstrated even at the

outset of his military career. He had already discovered the lure of cards and dice and was saddled with gambling debts just before the Battle of Medina. To pay them off, he had forged General de Arrendondo's name to a draft on the company funds. This flagrant error was swiftly discovered, and his uniforms and cavalry saber had been sold to replace the purloined cash. But he felt no shame, and he learned nothing from the experience—particularly after his commanding officer, very much as an indulgent father might do to a prodigal son, lauded him for his heroism in helping crush the rebellious Texans.

Now, sworn to uphold the royalist cause, the commandant at Vera Cruz ordered the handsome young lieutenant to move his troops into position to punish rebels in the town of Orizaba. At four in the morning of March 28, 1821, Santa Anna launched a surprise attack and was victorious. Five hours later, however, the rebels received reinforcements, and Santa Anna, who had shortly before received his promotion to a captaincy, now reconsidered the situation.

Accordingly, under the terms of a truce, he entered the rebel camp and conferred with his military opponents. And at the end of an hour of discussion, he offered his hand and said, "I wish to aid in the great work of our political regeneration." He had very callously and shrewdly switched sides, but not without personal gain: he had been promised a colonelcy for joining the ranks of those who wished to free Mexico from tyranny and from the dying traditions of the Old World. Santa Anna would bring to Mexico the stamp of his own peculiar personality, the imposition of which would change history in an unexpected manner.

Twenty-two

Moses Austin had been overjoyed by the knowledge that thanks to his friend, the Baron de Bastrop, his petition for the settlement of American families in Texas had been approved.

He wanted to return to Missouri to tell his son, Stephen, the good news and to plan what would be the monumental beginning of American settlement in hitherto Spanish territory. It would bring peace and trade and, best of all, a warm friendship and understanding between the peoples south and north of the Rio Grande.

But his long journey to Texas had weakened him; he had overestimated his stamina. He became ill with pneumonia, and in the spring of 1821, Moses Austin died. His last words were, "I have seen my dream realized, but I have not lived to see it built and flourishing." He indeed had been the person who envisioned an Anglo-American population for Texas; destiny had already chosen his son, Stephen Fuller Austin, as the man who would make this long-held dream come true.

But in Nueva España the implications of General Joaquín de Arrendondo's formal approval to the Austin petition and the death of its original protagonist went unnoticed. For now the break with Spain had come. Don Francisco Novela had fearfully resigned his temporary post as viceroy in Mexico City and had been replaced by General Juan O'Donoju. This stalwart man, who had commanded troops and knew what fighting in the field was, was also a realist. It did not take him long to realize that Mexico was lost and that the royalist armies could not hold out against the combined forces of Iturbide, Santa Anna, and Guerrero. Moreover, the rich *hacendados* and the wealthy clergy were clamoring for the declaration of independence from royalist Spain. And thus, on June 30, 1821, General O'Donoju signed the peace treaty with Iturbide, officially recognizing the independence of Mexico. It was the dashing Colonel Santa Anna who arranged for the last Spanish viceroy to confer on the subject of peace with Iturbide, and after that conference O'Donoju remarked, "This young man, Santa Anna, will cause all Mexico to weep."

There were celebrations in all the provinces as each departing Spanish governor relinquished his authority. In Texas, however, Governor Martínez remained in office. He had realized after Moses Austin's visit that conditions in Nueva España were changing, and that it was necessary in these uncertain times to be more open-minded and tolerant. Thus, Governor Martínez was one of the civic and military leaders who assembled in San Antonio to swear allegiance to the new republican government.

It was a bloodless revolution, a victory for independence. And young Carlos de Escobar, who wore his lieutenant's uniform smartly, had already distinguished himself from the many newly created officers who had flocked to the armies of Iturbide and Santa Anna. Carlos was commended for his poise, his knowledge of military protocol, and his ability to transmit orders from his superiors to his men and hold their respect, despite his aristocratic breeding.

In this first flush of the bloodless victory, of a triumph of the oppressed—so Carlos still fervently believed—the sorrowing son of Don Diego de Escobar felt that he had at last found a cause worthy to champion, one to which he could dedicate his life until there was peace and prosperity and the time for military intervention would end.

It was a thought that comforted him at a time when he needed it most. And, flatteringly, he found himself singled out by none other than Colonel Santa Anna himself. Indeed, Santa Anna had asked Iturbide to transfer Carlos de Escobar to his own regiment, and Iturbide, glowing with his triumph, indulgently agreed.

On the night that the treaty was signed, Colonel Santa Anna bade Carlos attend him as an official aide. "We shall enjoy the fiesta, *mi teniente*," he chuckled as he clapped Carlos on the back. "I've had my eye on you for some time now. Everyone comes forward to join the army of the victorious, so that he may claim for his heirs the lion's share of the glory of Mexican independence. But in you I recognize a genuine patriot, the more surprising because you are the son of a *hacendado*. One would have expected you to take an opposing side, with the royalists."

"No, *mi coronel*," Carlos earnestly protested, "I have never felt that the accident of birth gives one special privileges over one's fellow man."

"There, you see, Santoriaga?" Santa Anna turned to a tall, pleasant-faced, twenty-nine-year-old colonel, who had been thus commissioned by Iturbide himself and had been sent by the latter to act as a liaison officer between the two leaders. "I told you that Teniente de Escobar was a genuine patriot; he's had it in his soul since brith. And mark you, he was born in Spain, and his father was a grandee. This shows what sound thinking and loyalty to one's new land can bring about. I tell you, gentlemen, Mexico will soon outstrip Spain and be so rich and prosperous that none of you would ever care to go to the Old World. It will be Mexico for the

Mexicans. This is the cause for which I fight, and I trust that you both share my views."

"Assuredly, *mi coronel*." Carlos de Escobar inclined his head toward Santa Anna, and Ramón Santoriaga, whose wife, Mercedes, and their two girls lived in a fashionable suburb of Mexico City, smiled at Carlos. The two men already had many chats, and Carlos had found himself revealing much of his background to the affable young colonel. The latter never stood on ceremony and did not show rank over Carlos but accepted him as an equal. And thus a warm bond of friendship had begun between these two men.

But for many, the open profession of allegiance to Mexico's independence was only lip service. In Taos, in Santa Fe, nothing had really changed. Indeed, there was only a sense of futility and isolation. The conquering armies of Iturbide and Santa Anna and Guerrero had so diverted the hastily temporizing officials that few orders could be sensibly relayed to the distant provinces, and particularly toward Nuevo México. As for the territory of Texas, still less had changed. The province which included San Antonio was still beset by Indian raiders and Amercian squatters from Louisiana. The citizens there could only hope that their homegrown leaders would do more than the Spaniards to relieve their plight. And in San Antonio itself, the demarcation between the *ricos* and the *pobres* was still more intensified.

But perhaps there was a basis for the hatred of the Spaniards and Mexicans toward the Texans. It went back to the secret Treaty of 1800, when Spain ceded Louisiana back to France, with the stipulation that the territory would never be allowed to come into the possession of an English-speaking government. But the Corsican usurper, Napoleon, needing funds for his campaign to conquer Europe, reneged, and three years later sold Louisiana to the United States for fifteen million dollars.

When that took place, the *americanos* flocked to this huge territory, and Texas seemed to lure the dregs of society: deserters from the United States Army, runaway slaves, and debtors. By 1805, the chaotic conditions along the Texas border caused both Spanish and American authorities to attempt to bring about order. A so-called "neutral ground," situated between the Sabine River in the west, and the Arroyo Hondo, a Red River tributary, in the east, barred citizens of both nations. Yet since the Spanish could not police this vast buffer zone, and the Americans did not choose to do so, the area continued to be a haven for outlaws and a site of great conflict. Out of this came the participation of many decent, Texas-born citizens in Padre Hidalgo's ill-fated revolution, and finally their merciless massacre at the Battle of Medina.

Old hatreds and prejudices, momentarily forgotten when Mexico had at last declared independence from Spain, were still remembered. An opportunist like Santa Anna, who had learned the history of his country all too well, intended to profit from the volatile conditions that had been brought about by American migration into what, even with independence, the Mexican government considered the property of Mexico.

On those occasional forays that had taken place during Santa Anna's apprenticeship into the military, this wily colonel, who secretly meant to rule all his countrymen, had observed that Texans were untrained as soldiers, but by compensation, they were superb frontiersmen, who thought nothing of living outdoors and feeding themselves with what game they could bring down with their rifles. General de Arrendondo, his commanding officer years earlier, had called them with a grudging sarcasm *"soldados goddames"* because of their language habits and, when he had had Texas prisoners brought before him, often addressed each individual as "Señor Goddamn." He had observed to his young lieutenant, "How strange it is to see men like this, ragged beggars, made into moving armories. Some of them wear two, three, and even four braces of *pistolas*, a cloth bag filled wth bullets, a powder horn, a saber or knife, besides a rifle, musket, or carbine. They do not have our colorful uniforms, they do not march in formation, but they know how to kill. Therefore, we must kill them first and more of them than they can manage to kill among our ranks, or assuredly we shall have trouble with these *tejanos*."

So while Agustín de Iturbide prepared to enter Mexico City in triumph to proclaim himself as head of the new liberal government, Colonel Santa Anna rode at the head of two hundred fifty men toward the Rio Grande. With him were Lieutenant Carlos de Escobar and the latter's close friend, Colonel Ramón Santoriaga, who had been ordered by Iturbide to continue as liaison officer between himself and his foremost military commander, Santa Anna.

Much to Carlos's distress, Santa Anna crossed into Texas near Eagle Pass and headed for the little village of El

dio, less than a hundred miles from the Hacienda del
alcón.

"*Amigo*," Don Diego's son uneasily said to Colonel
antoriaga, "I don't understand why we come all the way to
exas."

"Our commander feels that the Americans, particularly
te Texans, are a threat to an independent Mexco," was the
ffable officer's reply. "After all, he remembers the precedent
e learned from our great General de Arrendondo at the
attle of Medina, which, as you will recall, is where Santa
nna first won his military laurels."

"But there are only a handful of settlers in this southern
ortion of Texas, Ramón," Carlos demurred. By now the two
oung men had become such close friends that when they
vere by themselves they called each other by their first
ames, though to be sure, both were punctilious to a fault
vhile riding with their commander to observe Ramón San-
oriaga's more imposing military status.

"That may be true, but the Spanish authorities have long
elt that even a handful of *gringos* can be a kind of outpost
y which weapons and supplies can come from Louisiana and
Missouri, and perhaps foment a revolution. The authorities
ave always feared that the United States would one day seek
o take Texas away from our control," Ramón explained.

"Well, I daresay it's a good possibility. But to use
vell-armed troops, and as many as we have, on a small
village—that seems barbarous," Carlos declared.

"You must understand something about Santa Anna,
amigo," the colonel explained. "He's a superb opportunist, as
vas shown when he resigned his captaincy on the royalist side
and went over to Iturbide. He knows that he's personable and
attractive to women, and he's also eager to make enough
dinero to be sure that he can maintain control of his troops.
Alas, bribery is an art which not only the French perfected;
our own Spanish authorities could give the French lessons on
how to hold mercenaries loyal by dangling *pesos* and *reales* in
front of them as they march." He shrugged. "What would
you, *hombre*? Thus far, at least, you'll have to agree, Carlos,
Mexico has achieved independence with very little loss of
life."

"Yes, that's true enough," Carlos mused. "Still in all, I'd
have thought Santa Anna would head for Mexico City, so as
to be certain to hold it for Iturbide."

"Mexico City is no problem, now that the last viceroy

surrendered to peace terms, Carlos," the colonel again patiently explained. "For that matter, Iturbide himself counseled me to suggest to Santa Anna that he patrol in the north, just to be sure that there would be no uprisings at the time our revolution was taking place. In a sense, therefore, he's only following the orders of his chief. You cannot fault him for that."

"No, perhaps not. Still, last week, when he took the village of Nagara, not far from Quemado, our commander had two Texans shot."

"That was because they would not give up their arms, and they refused to swear allegiance to our new government. That made them enemies, capable of insurrection. I myself did not think them very dangerous men, but I am only a liaison officer here, and I cannot countermand the orders of Santa Anna to his men, only advise."

"But one of these men had a sister, Ramón, and Santa Anna had her sent to his tent and there conferred with her for a long time. And after that he had a priest marry them."

Ramón Santoriaga frowned and looked away for a moment. Then he said slowly, "I know that our commander is tempted by the lusts of the flesh. He had been a bachelor all this time, and he has ridden hundreds of miles with troops to put down insurrection. At least the señorita did not find him objectionable. She still travels with him, as you know, and shares his tent."

"I did not know we had a priest accompanying our troops, Ramón."

Again the colonel frowned and looked away for a moment. "I am not especially proud of that deception by our commanding officer," he at last admitted. "You are right, we have no priest. The man you saw acting as a priest is Sergeant Juan Proberón. A good many years ago, he was an altar boy in Durango. He knows the rituals, and so he put on the garb of a priest to officiate at this marriage."

"¡Dios mío!" Carlos de Escobar exclaimed, "are you telling me the truth, Ramón? Why, that's scandalous, villainous—"

"Hush, amigo." Ramón drew up his reins and glanced nervously around to make certain that none of the nearby soldiers overheard their conversation. "Keep your voice down. I agree, it's not anything I intend to tell Iturbide. And know this: Santa Anna could have had the young woman shot because weapons were found in the jacal where she ed, the one next to her brother. So you must regard what did as merciful by comparison."

"I see." Carlos tightened his lips and shook his head. "I onder if our commander is truly destined to be the savior of exico. When I joined the forces of Colonel Iturbide and as transferred at Santa Anna's request to this regiment, I as proud that I had been so chosen. Now I'm not so sure. I gin to wonder if the grief over the loss of my beloved wife ouded my wisdom at the time."

"Grief drives a man to extremities, it's true, Carlos. But n't reproach yourself. I should have done the same thing in our place," Ramón consolingly replied.

Carlos drew a deep breath. "I must remember that I am soldier and that I obey orders. Thank you for reminding me f my duty, my *coronel*."

Twenty-three

San Antonio boasted a population of nearly four thou-and, and the Spaniards had maintained a small military stablishment there, known as a *presidio,* consisting of several tone and adobe buildings surrounded by a stockade or wall. he Spanish architect, Aguyo, had designed the San Antonio *residio* as a square with each side being about two hundred eet long, with a bastion at each corner and the original arrison made up of fifty-four soldiers. These bastions were o serve as their defense against marauding Indians, for the rea around San Antonio was plagued by the Karankawa, who lived near Matagorda Bay. They neither rode horses nor ared about trade, but stole for food and raided for pleasure, nd many of the colonists believed them to be cannibals as vell. There were also the Tonkawa, who spent most of their ime stealing horses. In addition, there were roving bands of Apache and Comanche, who boasted that the Spaniards were heir horse raisers.

Though the well-to-do people of San Antonio had their

homes in the Villa of San Fernando, built with patios and sheltered corridors, the poor people lived across the river near Mission San Antonio Dolero in an area which came to be known as La Villita. These were adobe houses with hand-carved mesquite doors, their floors made of dirt, kept hard by sprinkling and sweeping. There were no connecting doors, so one had to go outside in order to get from one room to another. The doorsills were often a foot high, the window sills often three feet wide, and the walls about three feet thick. Some of the traders and smugglers who came in from Louisiana and obscured themselves among the impoverished section of the populace lived in houses of stone or mud with a *jacal* of woven twigs and grass serving as a kitchen. The price paid for such a house was four mules and six docile horses.

To San Antonio, nearly five years ago, six *americanos*, originally Texans, had come to settle. They were the brothers John and Henry Ames, born of a light-haired Mexican woman from Nacogdoches and of a yellow-haired English seaman father, who had gotten off his merchant ship at Corpus Christi and impulsively decided to try his hand at farming near the Nueces River, just inside the province of Texas. These two brothers retained a fierce love for the vast country of Texas, and they had fought at the Battle of Medina. Two others were Edward Molson and his cousin, Ben Forrester, who had lived in the little Texas village of Sonora. They, too, had survived the Battle of Medina, and they had very special reasons for hating the royalist soldiers of Mexico City. For while Edward Molson and Ben Forrester were out hunting, their young wives, each barely twenty, had been abducted from the little farmhouses by a platoon of royalist troops, first brutally ravished and then bayoneted.

And finally there were Malcolm Pauley and Jack Williams, men now just past forty, who had been trappers along the wide Missouri River and had come to Texas to seek their fortunes. They had gone into partnership in a small ranch near San Antonio, spoke Spanish fluently, even made friends with the Comanche and sold beef to those wanderers of the plains. But royalist troops had seized their herd, threatened them with death if they dared protest, and so they, too, had fought at the Battle of Medina.

All six men had a communal bond: after they had escaped from the royalist army during the Battle of Medina, they had been pursued by the glory-seeking, sadistic Lieutenant Jaime Dondero, and after John Cooper Baines and his

carilla friends had killed their pursuers, they were brought
Don Diego's *hacienda* in Taos. There they had gained back
their strength, and John Cooper had given them horses and
silver in order to go back to Missouri, if they so chose, for
they had originally professed a desire to take up trapping or
farming.

But these six Texans had, long before the Austin colonization project, decided to build their own little commune
about eighteen miles southeast of San Antonio, along a
freshwater creek and about a mile from the placidly me-
andering San Antonio River. There was a broad strip of
bountiful green grass for the grazing of the two hundred head
of cattle they owned, and three of the wives had started truck
farming on a modest scale, sufficient not only to furnish all
the families the fruit and vegetables they enjoyed as a staple
part of their diet, but also enough to sell at a good profit in
San Antonio when their men rode in for supplies. Edward
Molson and Ben Forrester, as well as Malcolm Pauley, could
boast of being expert carpenters, as well as traders and
trappers from their earlier enterprises, and they had built a
sizable barn for the cows, as well as a stable for the horses.
There was also a pigpen with two hogs and six sows. Their
adobe and timber houses had been erected in a kind of circle
and situated on a high knoll near a small copse of oak trees,
so that the occupants could see any attackers from a distance
and be ready for them.

These six men had met their wives either in San Antonio
or Nuevo Laredo, and their happiness at starting new families
comparatively late in life came as a grateful boon to them,
especially to Molson and his cousin, who had experienced
such tragedy years earlier when their wives had been murdered. Edward Molson had married the spirited eighteen-
year-old Margarita Sanchez, only daughter of a San Antonio
harness maker, and she had given him two sons. Ben Forrester had married the twenty-two-year-old Carolina Rivera,
who had been widowed two years earlier when her young
vaquero husband had been gored by a stampeding bull.
Carolina had given him twin daughters and, just a month
ago, borne him a son.

John and Henry Ames had for a short time courted the
same girl, twenty-one-year-old Magdalena Suarez, who had
preferred Henry. Nothing loath, John had courted her widowed twenty-five-year-old sister, Eleanora, who had a three-
year-old son by her storekeeper husband, a Mexican who had

been shot down by a band of thieving Karankawa Indian
She had borne John a daughter and a son, and Magdalen
also had given Henry a son.

Malcolm Pauley and Jack Williams had watched the
friends marry young girls and resolved that at their age th
responsibility of young children would be much too taxing i
view of the difficulties they would be sure to encounter i
establishing their little colony and assuring its survival. Ac
cordingly, each married a woman nearly his own age
Pauley's choice was a handsome, barren woman of thirty-five
Florencia Medantes, who ran her dead husband's *posada*
Williams chose Juana Cardozo, a year older, her husband an
two little girls having died of fever a decade earlier, afte
which she had gone to work as a housekeeper for Governo
Martínez.

To Jack's mingled consternation and sheepish pride
Juana had just blushingly whispered to him as they sat at th
rough-hewn table in their small kitchen, "*Querido*, I did no
think it would happen, but the Blessed Mary has answeree
my secret prayer. I am with child by you, my adored *es*
poso."

"My God!" Jack gasped, turning red in the face. Then
recovering, he got up, went round to take his wife in hi
arms, and blurted, "Juana, I'll try to be the best damned
father in Texas, I swear I will!"

Yet the hatred for the Texans among many Mexican
officials and officers—an unreasoning and groundless hatred
that would, not quite a generation hence, result in war and
make Texas at last part of the United States—created many
problems for the stalwart Americans who had come in ad
vance of Moses Austin. For now, just one week after Jack
Williams learned he was going to be a father, a detail of a
dozen Mexican soldiers, part of Santa Anna's patrolling force
under the command of an ambitious *subtiente*, raided a small
village composed entirely of Mexicans who had come into
Texas after nearly a generation of peonage. Under the pre-
text that there were *americanos* there, they killed the elderly
alcalde when he mildly protested the raid, raped three of the
women, confiscated what food and *aguardiente* they could
find and, aflame with their shabby "victory," headed north.

By chance they came upon the little commune, and the
subteniente, a cousin of the same Jaime Dondero who had
tried to ride down the six Texans who had later returned to
build this commune, ordered an attack. Edward Molson, who

was in the barn tending a heifer about to foal, heard the rattle of musketry and emerged with his long rifle that he had bought from a Kentucky trapper shortly before coming back to Texas. His first shot brought down the *subteniente;* without a leader, the soldiers panicked, but before they retreated two of them fired muskets into Jack Williams's house. One of the balls, ricocheting and almost spent, struck Juana in the belly. Thanks to the aid tendered her by Margarita Molson and Carolina Forrester, Juana's life was saved, but at the cost of her child.

After the soldiers had galloped off, Jack Williams, his face pale and grim, declared to Edward Molson, "By God, Ed, I've just about had it. These damned greasers still want to cut our guts out, the way they did at the Medina fracas. We'd best think about moving somewhere in this big Texas territory where we don't have to fret about Mex patrols—no, nor those pesky Karankawa either."

"You may be right," Molson said slowly. "And I'm going to do some asking around from now on. Maybe we'll run across some Texan like ourselves, or just a plain American who's found himself a place where he can breathe without wondering if some ornery Mex or injun's going to measure him fer six feet under."

Stephen Fuller Austin mourned his father, but told one of his close friends after he had learned of his father's death by courier sent to find him in Louisiana, "The best way to mourn him is to carry on the dream he had, and I propose to do that. I'd not be worthy of being his son if I didn't. I'm younger, stronger, and with God's help, perhaps I can make his dream the reality he always longed for."

Although he was only twenty-seven, he was already a man of vast experience. He had been ably educated, served five years in the legislature of the Missouri Territory, and had been appointed district judge in the territory of Arkansas. Moreover, he had engaged in various business undertakings in Missouri, Arkansas, and Louisiana. By nature, he was patient, methodical, energetic, and fair-spoken. And still more important, so far as the success of this grandiose undertaking was concerned, was the fact that he had been acquainted from childhood with the characteristic social types who mingled on the southwestern border. Not only did he speak Spanish fluently, but he could converse with, and sympathize with, the most eloquent *caballero,* as knowledgeably as he could with a *peón* who tilled the soil on a small farm.

Taking several of his closest associates, he left Louisiana shortly after his father's death and went directly to Governor Martinéz in San Antonio. There, on August 11, 1821, he was received cordially and was recognized as the heir to his father's commission; the governor authorized him to explore the country and make other arrangements for the proposed colony.

From San Antonio, Stephen Austin went to Goliad, and from there turned eastward to choose a fitting site for the colony. He carefully explored the lower courses of the San Antonio, Guadalupe, Colorado, and Brazos rivers. The lower valleys of the Brazos and the Colorado and the lands lying between these two rivers were finally decided upon as the most desirable location for the colony, though a much larger area was requested.

In Stephen Fuller Austin's plan, each settler would be granted a section of land, plus half a section for a wife, a quarter of a section for each child, and eighty acres for each slave. There would be additional grants offered for the erection of mills or other establishments of value to the community. Austin pledged himself to obtain titles and to have the land surveyed, in return for which the settlers were to pay him twelve and a half cents per acre.

Twenty-four

As it chanced, Stephen Austin left San Antonio two days before the arrival of John Cooper and Miguel Sandarbal, who had ridden there with three of the *trabajadores* to discuss cattle breeding with a prosperous *hacendado* and to buy supplies for the Hacienda del Halcón. John Cooper also wished to purchase more rifles to defend the Texas estate, in the event of any hostile Indian attack. The two men, longtime friends, had achieved an even closer bond when they both learned before leaving the ranch that they were to be fathers, sometime next spring.

On the trail to San Antonio the young American confided in the loyal *capataz* about how the death of Padre Moraga had been avenged. "The murderer of Padre Moraga has been brought to justice. He will no longer oppress the weak and the poor and the Indians of the pueblo, nor will he ever again harass my father-in-law. This is between us, Miguel. It is not to be discussed with anyone else." And Miguel Sandarbal had understandingly inclined his head.

The three *trabajadores* had leisurely driven the supply wagon along the trail from the Hacienda del Halcón to San Antonio, and John Cooper had intently studied the territory between his new home and the sprawling town where Governor Martínez presided. For many miles in every direction there was only verdant plain and, here and there, stretches of arid land where only scrub trees and cacti grew. Now and again the two men saw the vague outline of a little farm, and John Cooper said to Miguel as they neared their destination, "It takes courage to live out here all alone, Miguel. I've had the advantage of living with Indians who will accept me as a friend, but these settlers, especially if they're *americano,* are sitting ducks for any hunting parties who might take a notion to steal horses or cattle or whatever else they think these intruders have."

"I agree with you, *mi compañero.* That's why I'm thinking that, the larger we make our ranch, the more settlers we can attract to have a kind of homemade army always ready, in case anybody wants to attack us."

"Exactly. And that's why I'm very interested in the grant that the governor gave to Moses Austin. If the government recognizes it, especially now that the Spaniards have been overthrown and the Mexicans have taken over, it'll mean settlers will be crowding into Texas. And there won't be enough soldiers in the country to bother them. And once they see that the people of my race come in here just wanting to make a new life and plant crops or raise cattle and families, there won't be any need of talking about war. Nobody ever wins one, that's for certain. I learned that much when I was studying my books back in Shawneetown. My pa used to say, 'John Cooper, all you have to do when you study the history of a war is to find out who really stood to gain the most profit, and that'll tell you maybe why the war was begun in the first place.' The more I think about it, the more I know he was right."

The *capataz* nodded. "Yes, *amigo*. When I went to school in Madrid, I learned about the *Conquistadores* and the great galleons that sailed to the New World and brought back gold and silver, spices and slaves. But now Spain is dying, the Spain I knew and was taught to think was the strongest power in all the world. And my *patrón* found that out, too, when he came to Taos. In fact, he already knew it years ago back in the old country when he made that remark to that nobleman he thought was his friend, saying it was too bad that Spain couldn't be ruled by a king as strong as the great Philip who launched the Armada."

As they approached San Antonio, with its imposing *presidio* and its dusty main street lined with shops, John Cooper pulled in his reins and said to the *capataz*, "Well, Miguel, we'll let the *trabajabores* have a day in town to reward them for the dreary work they've had driving the wagon. It can't be too much fun for them. Besides, I want to talk to Joaquín Cobrara. The last time I visited San Antonio, he was telling me about short-horned cattle from the east and said that if we could breed a good bull with some of the long-horned heifers we've got roaming around near our ranch, we could have a better grade of beef. I'll tell you one thing, if the Austin plan goes through and settlers come in here, as they're bound to, there'll be a demand for beef. Not all of them are going to be cattlemen. There are some from places like Missouri and even my own Illinois and Ohio and Indiana and Kentucky who'll want to have a little dirt farm, maybe raise fruits and vegetables, maybe keep some chickens. It's a good life where land is cheap, with plenty of water and grass and a good sun to nourish what you plant, if you know your trade."

"You're beginning to talk like a farmer yourself, John Cooper," Miguel humorously retorted with a twinkle in his eyes. "I don't recognize you at all in what you've just said from the fierce buckskin-dressed young savage who arrived in Taos for the first time, after you saved young Carlos's life." A shadow crossed his face, and he swore under his breath. "Well, all of us have changed these last few years. The young master most of all, and it wasn't his doing, God give peace to his troubled soul."

"Amen to that, Miguel. Now let's see, while I'm talking

to Joaquín, do you want to go with Benito, Felipe, and Sebastian and make certain they don't forget the supplies they're supposed to pick up? Then maybe we'll go pay our respects to Governor Martínez after we freshen up a mite, and maybe we'll find out just how the Austin grant is coming."

"A very good idea, *mi compañero*."

The young American tethered his horse to a hitching post outside the trading post where Miguel and the three *trabajadores* would purchase the supplies for the *hacienda*. He had also given Miguel a list of the books Catarina and Bess would use in their new school, but he realized that many of the books would have to be shipped from Mexico City and New Orleans. The English books, in particular, would be hard to come by, and it would take many months before Bess Sandarbal would have sufficient texts with which to instruct her pupils.

Taking his leave, John Cooper walked down the dusty street till he came to the adobe and wood-constructed edifice where the cattle breeder held sway. Joaquín Cobrara was a short, thickly bearded, genial little man in his late forties, invariably enthusiastic and gracious almost to a fault, as well as scrupulously honest. Through factors in New Orleans, Galveston, and even as far east as St. Louis, he was able to import well-bred bulls and heifers at a time when this venture of crossbreeding was virtually unknown. He had originally come from Pamplona, where cattle raising had already become a science in the Old World. He himself had operated a small ranch near San Marcos, and his brother-in-law now ran it for him. There, experimenting with the huge, shaggy longhorns that ran wild throughout the southeastern and southwestern part of Texas territory, he had found that, while they were plentiful, they did not furnish the most edible beef.

As John Cooper entered, Joaquín Cobrara was busily talking to a tall, short-bearded blond man in his early forties, and the young mountain man waved a greeting to his friend and then waited his turn. Suddenly, he heard the cattle breeder say, "I think I know what you need, Señor Callendar, and my factor in New Orleans is expecting a shipment of three bulls and five fine short-horned heifers from St. Louis within the next fortnight. I can't guarantee the price yet, but I do not think it will be much above what we discussed the last time you were in last year."

John Cooper moved forward, his eyes aglow with interest. "Excuse me. Did I hear you say 'Señor Callendar'?"

"Yes, sir, that's my name, Timothy Callendar, at your service. Who might you be?"

"My name's John Cooper Baines, Mr. Callendar. You've a sister-in-law, Bess Callendar, I believe?"

"Yes, sir—that is, I don't know what happened to her. You see, my brother, Edward, married her, and they visited my family and me some years ago, and then were on their way north to try to get some land for their little farm. I learned later the awful news that they were attacked by Comanche and that my brother was killed. I never heard about Bess, but I assume that she was killed, also."

"Then this is really a miracle, Mr. Callendar. You see, I come from the Hacienda del Halcón, which we call the Double H Ranch, for short, and my *capataz* is named Miguel Sandarbal. He and three of his men are over at the trading post right now. And he married your sister-in-law."

"The devil you say! You mean that Bess is alive?" The tall man came forward and gripped John Cooper's shoulder.

"Fact is, when you finish your business with Señor Cobrara, I'd like you to come by and say hello to Miguel. And I know that Bess would be very happy to be in touch with you. What happened was, the Comanche chief who killed your brother took her as a slave and tried to make her marry him."

"I'd heard of things like that—and I thought to myself at the time it would be far better if she died in mercy rather than to have to be an Indian's slave," Timothy Callendar said in a low, unsteady voice.

"Well, Sarpento—he was the chief who killed your brother and took Bess as a slave—he certainly tried to get her to marry him, but she wouldn't have any part of him. Finally, he gave up and brought her to the annual fair in Taos. He was about to sell her off to some rich old *hacendado*, when my father-in-law, Don Diego de Escobar, stepped in and bid higher for her, so he could free her. And Miguel fell in love with her, and now they've a couple of kids."

"That's excellent news! I didn't know Bess real well, but I liked her when I met her, and I thought my brother was lucky in finding her—yes, I'd like to meet your *capataz*."

"Well, when you've finished your business and I've had a quick chat here, we'll go to a *posada* and all have a drink

And maybe you could come visit us and see Bess—she'd love that."

"It's just lucky that I happened to come in today, because, you see, I've a small ranch about twelve miles northwest of here. My wife and three kids are there, and I've got a foreman who knows a good deal about cattle, and who came out here from Ohio looking for a brother who got scalped by a hunting party. He more or less settled down here, and we got to be friends, and he's taking care of things for me. My God, it's really wonderful to learn that a relation of mine is living not too far away." Timothy Callendar vigorously shook hands with John Cooper. "Anyhow, I've just about finished my business with Señor Cobrara." He turned back to the cattle breeder. "You go ahead and see what price you can get me; I'll take all you've got. Now then, Mr. Baines, it's your turn."

While Timothy Callendar waited outside, John Cooper and Señor Cobrara discussed the prospects of breeding the merchant's special short-horned bulls and heifers with the American's longhorns. John Cooper arranged with the trader to get a message to his factors so that he would be able to quote a price on the bulls and heifers when John Cooper next visited to San Antonio. Then, concluding his business with Señor Cobrara, John Cooper rejoined Timothy Callendar.

"Where's your ranch, Mr. Baines?" Callendar asked as they walked up the street in the hot sunshine.

"Just about eighty miles west of here, Mr. Callendar. You know, it would be fine if you and your wife and kids would come out and spend some time with us as our guests. Bess would love to see you."

"Well now, I'd like to do just that, if you're sure it's no imposition on your hospitality—"

"We've a big ranch, plenty of rooms, and as for food, we've got plenty of beef and lamb running around loose," John Cooper Baines humorously retorted as he led the way to the trading post.

Miguel Sandarbal was at the moment in charge of loading supplies into the wagon, and he stopped short when he saw the tall man beside John Cooper, his eyes at once quizzical and curious.

"What's that saying they have about a small world, Miguel? I want you to meet Mr. Timothy Callendar; he's Bess's dead husband's brother."

"Señor Callendar, this is a wonderful surprise! Bess will be delighted—in fact, only a short time ago she was mentioning that she hoped that you and your family were still in Texas and doing well."

"We are, and I'd sure like to see Bess and your *hacienda*." Callendar vigorously shook hands with the mature *capataz*. "You've made me feel a lot better, just by meeting you. And I can tell from the way Mr. Baines here talks about you—just as I can see for myself at first look—that you've made my former sister-in-law very happy. God bless you for that."

"He has blessed me, Señor Callendar. And much more than I deserve, believe me! Do make your visit soon, because, when I go back with Señor John Cooper here, I'm going to tell Bess that I met you, and that you will pay us a visit."

"Mr. Callendar," John Cooper put in, "all of us would welcome you and your family, and we'd like to show you real hospitality. In fact, once you get out there and see what we have to offer, you might just think of moving your family out to our ranch and helping us establish an American settlement. You've probably heard about Moses Austin and the land grant the Spaniards said they'd give him?"

"Yes I have. Only we've just learned that old Austin died. Word has it that his son, Stephen, is going to take over the project."

"We hadn't heard about any of this," John Cooper said. "It's a real shame about Moses Austin." He shook his head sadly, then said, "I'm glad his son intends to take over."

"The only trouble," Timothy Callendar explained, "is that the Spaniards are being ousted by the Mexicans all over the provinces, so I can only hope that Governor Martínez is allowed to keep his promise. But don't you worry, Mr. Baines, and you, Señor Sandarbal. I'm going to take you up on your invitation just as soon as I can take some time off from my ranch. I'm planning to sell about three hundred head of cattle over the border in about two months, to some of the troops stationed there. After that, I'd like nothing better than to come see this place you have. It sounds big."

"It is, and that's why we can stand lots of good friends and neighbors all around us, so we can defend ourselves, just in case there's trouble coming out of this revolution. Well then, Mr. Callendar, I'll bid you good day, and I hope it won't be too long before I have the pleasure of seeing you and your wife and children." John Cooper shook hands with the tall rancher.

Late that afternoon, as they were preparing to return to the Hacienda del Halcón, Miguel was still talking about this incredible meeting, and he was beaming. "My *querida* Bess will be so happy to know that Señor Callendar is alive and well and still thinks of her. What a surprise it will be, when they come out to visit us, *¿no es verdad, amigo?*"

"It's good to have relatives and family come together," John Cooper soberly said. Once again a shadow of the past had crossed his mind, and he was momentarily silent. The *capataz*, sensing exactly what he was thinking, said no more.

Twenty-five

"Let's take the trail south back to Uvalde, down to the Nueces River," John Cooper proposed to Miguel Sandarbal after they had concluded their business in San Antonio. He had paid a brief visit to the governor, been cordially received, and had taken the opportunity of the meeting to ask if there was any news from Mexico City. To this Governor Martínez had sighed, shaken his head, and replied, "Nothing that is too official as yet, Señor Baines. We do know that Iturbide now ranks himself as a general and that he plans to enter Mexico City by next month, at the latest. But we must wait for orders from the capital before I can determine what changes there will be here in San Antonio."

John Cooper had nodded and then asked, "Are there any signs of Mexican troops along the Rio Grande?"

"Yes, I am afraid there have been several, Señor Baines. I am told that Colonel Santa Anna is alarmed at the number of *americanos* who have come to settle around here without official authorization. And I know that he sends troops to patrol some of the little frontier villages to flush out those who may be *soldados* for the Estados Unidos."

"I thank Your Excellency for the information and for the kindness with which you receive me and my *capataz*." John Cooper extended his hand, and the governor warmly shook it.

Somehow the young mountain man had an uneasy premonition. It had troubled him all the way to San Antonio. From what little news had trickled in from Mexico City, and from occasional riders who stopped to water their horses or to ask for provisions at the ranch, he had heard that thus far there had been little bloodshed in the revolution that was liberating Nueva España into what would now be called Mexico. Yet he knew only too well, from his days in Taos, how the Spanish authorities had seen ghosts at every turning and, fearing that their trade monopoly might be endangered, had dealt so rigorously with any enterprising American trader who dared venture into New Mexico. And he did not think that the substitution of Mexican authorities for Spanish would ease that almost obsessive fear.

That fear had begun as early as 1783, when General Felipe de Neve, the Spanish commandant responsible for Mexico's northern frontier, had employed Jean Gasiot, a French frontiersman whom he used as a liaison agent between the Spanish and the Indians. Gasiot had written to him in October of that year:

> It is necessary to keep in mind that a new independent power exists now in this continent. It has been founded by an active, industrious, aggressive people. Their development will constantly menace the dominion of Spain in America, and it would be an unpardonable error not to take all necessary steps to check their territorial advance.

Since that prophecy, the Spanish authorities had done all they could to thwart their new nemesis—the *americanos*—but there had never been enough troops to patrol the vast plains, the hills, and the mountains of Texas and New Mexico. And the roving Comanche, Kiowa, and Apache had wrought havoc among those sporadic bands of soldiers sent from time to time to patrol this vast land whose potential gold and silver and copper Spain had long coveted.

John Cooper knew only that he had seldom met Spanish officials who accepted him as a friend and neighbor rather than as a deadly enemy. One friend, he now believed, was Governor Martínez himself, and another was the farsighted Facundo Melgares, the Spanish-appointed governor of New Mexico. And to be sure, there was Don Sancho de Pladero, who had, from the very first, shown a warm friendship to both Don Diego and the young mountain man and who had kept the secret of their whereabouts for the past many years. But even now that the revolution was freeing Mexico from Spain, John Cooper did not think there would be a wholesale welcoming of the *americanos*. He himself had learned a certain amount of diplomacy and, by becoming fluent in Spanish, had become able to converse on the same level with men like Governor Martínez, as well as with *vaqueros* and *trabajadores*. And he knew that their temperament, their character, their very roots and beginnings vastly differed from his own and from the countless hundreds of adventurous men, men seeking fertile land and a chance to lead lives unhampered by punitive restrictions, oppressive taxes, and for that matter, religious or political prejudices.

As he rode southward now with Miguel beside him and the three *trabajadores* driving the supply wagon, he thought ruefully that his mother and father might have been pleased to find how much he had learned and studied since he had left Shawneetown, so as to become a "gentleman." And yet the will to survive, the shrewdness and cunning which he had learned on the boundless frontier he had crossed from Illinois through the plains, and then into Taos, still flared vigorously within his spirit and would always do so. And until there was peace between the lands north and south of the Rio Grande, he would always be vigilant.

Taking a long, circuitous route back to the Hacienda del Halcón, John Cooper, Miguel, and the three *trabajadores* in the wagon had crossed the Frio River not far from the little village of Millett, and two days later were heading toward the southwest and the winding Nueces. They were then about seventy miles north of the Rio Grande. The young mountain man studied the terrain intently, and he said to the *capataz*, "There are thousands upon thousands of acres here, Miguel, all of them fertile, and also unclaimed. It would be impossible for Mexican soldiers to patrol so wide a boundary, just as it was for the Spainards. That's why I'm glad that the Austin grant has been approved, for once we have peaceful settlers all along this stretch, they'll be able to defend themselves against hostile Indians, grow their crops, raise their cattle, and gradually convince the new Mexican government that they're after peace and not war."

"I agree with you, *mi compañero*," Miguel vigorously nodded. Then suddenly he stiffened in his saddle and, squinting, exclaimed, "May the devil take me if I don't see mounted soldiers coming toward us!"

"Off there to the south? Yes, I see them, too!" John Cooper exclaimed. He held up his hand to order the *trabajadores* to stop the wagon, and then he reached for "Long Girl" in the saddle sheath, swiftly made certain that it was primed and loaded, and instinctively touched each of the holstered pistols at his belt. "We'll just be ready, but there certainly can't be any fighting between us. There must be at least a hundred men, judging by that cloud of dust that's coming from the horses' hooves."

"But what are soldiers doing so far north?" Miguel was puzzled.

"Patrolling, I suppose. But why they'd want to come by this desolate stretch of land is more than I can figure," the young mountain man scowled, and shook his head.

It was a cavalry column of mounted troops numbering well over a hundred, as John Cooper carefully counted. And at the head, on a sturdy mustang, there rode a handsome young officer with garish epaulets on his shoulders and a metal helmet, on the side of which was a feather plume. The coat of the uniform was blue, with crisscross white straps, and he wore white trousers and shining black boots. Just behind him rode another officer, with affable features, his epaulets and shako marking him with the rank of colonel.

"It can't be!" John Cooper hoarsely ejaculated, pointing out the officer at the head of the column to Miguel. "But that's Carlos!"

"By all the saints, you're right, *mi compañero!*" Miguel cupped his hands to his mouth and shouted out, "*¡Amigo, holá, es Miguel!*"

The young officer drew his saber and lifted it in the air to halt the column. Then gently spurring his mustang, he rode forward.

"John Cooper! Miguel!" he joyously exclaimed. "It's good to see you both, so very good!"

"It's good to see you, Carlos," John Cooper said. "We'd

only had one letter brought by a courier a short time ago, saying that you'd arrived safely in Mexico City and were going to enlist in Iturbide's army."

"But what are you doing here, John Cooper? Isn't this quite a distance from the ranch?" Carlos demanded.

"We wanted to survey the terrain, Carlos. You know, we finally got word about your revolution. And we were just wondering if this area was going to be patrolled. You remember what I told you about Moses Austin and his grant that was approved? I'd hope that we'd be having settlers soon, so that Mexico and the United States can come to friendly terms."

The smile left Carlos de Escobar's face, and he forced himself to become stern. He had already formed his own private doubts about the task he was assigned to do. "I regret I cannot share your optimism, John Cooper. I have been placed in command of this small regiment to search for *americanos* who may be bearing arms and have come to Texas to cause trouble."

"You can't be serious, Carlos!" John Cooper exclaimed with an incredulous chuckle.

"But I am. It's my duty. And Colonel Santoriaga, whom you see behind me on the white horse, is the official liaison officer sent by General Iturbide to make certain that I carry out my command. It is also the wish of our foremost leader, Colonel Santa Anna."

"The man who distinguished himself at the Battle of Medina by hunting down helpless, wounded men, I'm told," John Cooper ventured.

Carlos's lips tightened. "I would not advise you to speak of Colonel Santa Anna in such terms, not where my men can hear you, John Cooper," he stiffly replied.

"Oh, come on, Carlos, for God's sake! We're not sitting here trying to plan a battle or anything. You're Carlos, my brother-in-law, and I'm your friend besides all that—or have you so easily forgotten?" the young American urged.

"You know I'll never forget you, and you know that I'm bound to you in many ways—you saved my life, John Cooper." Carlos spoke in a more conciliatory tone now. Then with a faint smile, he asked, "How are my children? And my father and Doña Inez? And my sister Catarina?"

"All well. Catarina's going to have another baby sometime next spring," John Cooper told him. "And you know, a few days ago in San Antonio, we ran across Timothy Callendar, that's Bess's brother-in-law, and we invited him and his family to visit us.".

"That's good news indeed. And you, Miguel, *mi compañero,* I can see you're a happy man. I knew that Bess would make you a wonderful wife." Carlos saluted the *capataz* by lifting his saber in the air and touching the tip to his helmet's plume.

"That she has, *amigo.* So you like army life? You look wonderful, young master!" Miguel enthusiastically declared.

"Yes, it suits me." Again Carlos's face became impassive. "This is a revolution against the enemies of Mexico. And we've already arrested a few *gringos,* confiscated their weapons, and we've had to have them shot. It's a military rule, you know. They couldn't prove they weren't bearing arms against our new government—"

"But that's ridiculous, Carlos!" John Cooper burst out. "Look, when I came to Taos I had a gun, and that was to keep Indians or bushwhackers from killing me, and it was to fetch game so I could eat. You mean to say that your regiment found some Americans with guns and shot them without even giving them a hearing? That's not you, Carlos, you always had a code of honor—"

"I must ask you not to discuss military matters, John Cooper, please." Carlos turned in his saddle and glanced nervously back at the colonel beyond him, hoping his friend or the enlisted men were not able to detect his uncertainty and lack of resolve. "And now I must go on. There are two villages we must inspect before we go back across the Rio Grande."

"My God! I'd heard that the revolution was without bloodshed, but now I'm not so sure. Carlos, reconsider. It's not right to harass peaceful settlers. Don't you think that Americans from the east want to come out here because there's so much land and they want their freedom to start a family, have a farm or a ranch, live in peace? You can't certainly think that all Americans, just because they have guns, are going to declare war against Mexico?"

"Please, I told you, I cannot discuss military matters. I myself am under orders, and Colonel Santa Anna has explained to me the need for caution at this time. It is one in which the delicate balance of power can be overcome if we, who fight for independence, allow traitors and spies and enemy soldiers to infiltrate into the country." Carlos talked so volubly that he was almost able to convince himself.

"I'm sorry for you, Carlos. Wait—don't ride off yet—isn't there a message you want me to take back to your father and Doña Inez and your sister?" John Cooper anxiously asked.

Carlos's eyes softened, and with a sigh, he nodded: "Of course. Please don't think I'm your enemy, John Cooper. I wouldn't want to be that for all the world—but I must fulfill my mission. That's why I took my commission, and I lead men now, and I'm under orders. Yes, do please tell my father and Doña Inez and Catarina that I love them, with all my heart. I'll write when I can. And kiss my children for me, and my sister, and ask her to pray for me."

"We all pray for you daily, Carlos. ¡Vaya con Dios!"

Carlos stared at his brother-in-law for a moment, then sighed again, wheeled his horse, and shouted, "¡Adelante, hombres!"

John Cooper and Miguel sat silently in their saddles as they watched the mounted column pass by. And then, when dust obscured their passing and they were lost to view, the young mountain man turned to the *capataz* and said softly, "I wanted to reason with him, Miguel. It's all wrong. If you have incidents like this and you kill innocent people just because you suspect them of being soldiers or spies, we'll never have peace between our countries. I'm beginning to think that Carlos made a terrible mistake."

"He will pray to *el Señor Dios*, who will teach him wisdom, *mi compañero*," the *capataz* gravely responded as he crossed himself. "Well, we'd best go on."

"Yes, and I've learned more than I wanted to. But at least I'm glad I saw Carlos, because I know how worried Don Diego and Doña Inez are about him, and Catarina will be happy to hear that he's strong and well—and I'm sure she'll think he's very dashing in that uniform when I describe it," John Cooper said with a wry humor. "All right, let's ride on back to the ranch."

Two hours later, as John Cooper and Miguel turned their horses toward the northwest, they saw a distant cloud of smoke. The young mountain man called back to the *trabajadores* in the wagon, "Miguel and I will ride ahead to see what the fire is, *amigos*. Join us slowly, and keep your weapons handy. It might be Comanche." Then spurring his horse, he galloped ahead, with the *capataz* closely following him.

A mile farther on, they reined in their horses and glumly stared at the sight of a small house built of hewn timber and adobe, with a stable and a barn off to one side, all three in flames.

"I didn't know there were any settlers out in this abandoned part of the territory," John Cooper said, turning to Miguel. "I can't tell who burned that ranch house, Indians or soldiers."

"I'm praying it wasn't Señor Carlos's men," Miguel solemnly observed. The two men dismounted and, drawing their pistols, cautiously advanced. As they approached the door of the burning house, Miguel crossed himself and murmured a silent prayer at the sight of a blond, heavyset man in his mid-thirties lying sprawled across the threshhold, his rifle still clutched in his lifeless hand.

"It's an *americano, mi compañero*," he murmured. "*¡Que lastima!*"

"Let's see if there's anyone alive inside, Miguel. Come on, take a deep breath, and let's see if we can get on in. Be careful now," the young mountain man urged.

John Cooper was the first to enter, carefully stepping over the lifeless defender of the little ranch. He uttered a groan when he saw a flaxen-haired woman, about ten years younger than her husband, on her knees with her head bowed on the counterpane of the crude, wooden bed, her hair sticky with the matted blood from a fatal musket ball wound.

"God rest her soul," John Cooper murmured. The acrid smoke nearly overcame him, but he forced himself to move toward the back of the wide room and suddenly heard a whimpering sound. "Miguel, there's somebody alive in here—in that chest there in the corner. Look out, the fire is getting near it, from the shutter! Let's both grab the chest and pull it out away from the fire—that's it."

He opened the chest and uttered an astonished cry. There were two little children, one a girl no more than two years old, and the other a boy baby about six months old. He and Miguel hurriedly stooped down and lifted the children into their arms and then rushed out of the burning house.

"Thank God we came in time, Miguel! Damn it all, who would want to kill a man and his wife, living out here all alone on the prairie like this?"

"It doesn't look like *indios, mi compañero*," the *capataz* muttered, shaking his head. "I'm afraid it was soldiers.

Perhaps it was some of the men from that regiment Señor Carlos commanded."

"I'm hoping that for his soul's sake and his peace of mind, it wasn't he who gave that order. If the man fired on the soldiers, well, maybe I could understand somebody firing back. But to kill the woman—it's so stupid, so needless ... Come on, Miguel, let's take these poor kids to the wagon, and Antonio can look after them till we get home safely. He's got three little ones of his own and a fourth on the way. If we hurry, we'll be home early the day after tomorrow."

John Cooper and Miguel walked slowly back to the wagon, each silent with his own dark thoughts.

It would have comforted them to know that the attack on this isolated ranch house had been directed by a Mexican captain commanding thirty men, who had ridden from Nuevo Laredo about the same time Carlos had led his men across the Rio Grande.

Twenty-six

"Oh, Coop, how terrible for these poor children—yet thank God they didn't see their parents die! And the little boy must be starving—just listen to his screaming! I'll take him into the house and see that he's fed." There were tears in Catarina's green eyes as she tenderly took the crying infant boy from John Cooper's arms and headed into the *hacienda*. Meanwhile Miguel Sandarbal cradled the little girl in his arms, smiling and crooning to her to calm her fears, since she had been whimpering and sobbing for most of the trip and had started to cry loudly when the wagon was halted in the courtyard of the Hacienda del Halcón. They had returned this bright August morning, and Bess Sandarbal had hurried out of her cottage to welcome back her husband. She stood a little to one side now, her eyes warm and tender, smiling as she saw the mature *capataz* try to comfort the still-crying little girl. Then, impulsively, she hurried forward and exclaimed, "*Querido,* maybe a woman can do it better—that's not to say that you aren't acting like a wonderful father, which you are! Give her to me, poor little girl, poor darling!"

"Of course, *mi corazón,*" Miguel genially replied as he carefully transferred the little girl into his wife's eager arms. "I have wonderful news for you, and I'll tell you once we're alone."

"I'll take the little girl back to our cottage and give her some milk. I shouldn't be surprised if apart from being scared, she's hungry." Then feigning indignation, she scolded, "I'll bet none of you men had the common sense to feed her."

"Oh, now, *querida,*" Miguel protested, a look of anguish on his strong weather-beaten face, "you know I would never be so stupid! It's true, we had no milk to feed the little boy, but the little girl ate very well. John Cooper and I probably overfed her, if anything."

"I see," Bess primly retorted. "And what did you strong, grown-up men try to feed a little girl—she's hardly old enough to walk!"

"Why," the young mountain man said, blushing as all eyes fixed on him. "I gave her some pieces of jerky that I chewed up a little so they'd be easy to swallow. And then we had some coffee—"

"Oh, yes, that's exactly what a little girl should have for supper! I thought so. Never mind, honey, I'll give you some milk, and I think there's some pudding left from last night." With this, Bess flounced off in pretended high dudgeon, and both Miguel and John Cooper looked at each other sheepishly. Doña Inez, who had come out with Don Diego to welcome back the young mountain man and the *capataz,* now spoke up: "She was only teasing, John Cooper, Miguel."

"Of course!" Don Diego exclaimed, then extending his hand to the two men, he said, "Welcome back, Miguel, John Cooper." His soft laugh eased the embarrassment of both the young mountain man and the *capataz,* who again glanced at each other, then began to laugh wholeheartedly.

Catarina returned to join them, having left the little boy in the care of one of the *trabajador's* wives, who was nursing a child of her own. She was smiling contentedly, and John Cooper put his arm around her, then addressed everybody.

"I've got some news I want to tell you all," he announced. Catarina looked up at her husband, and Don Diego and Doña Inez listened intently as he told them about the death of Moses Austin and his son's intention to continue with the colonization project.

"That is a great loss," Don Diego reflected, "but if Moses Austin's son is anything like you, John Cooper, or like my Carlos, then the success of the project is assured."

"Now I must tell you my other news," John Cooper soberly interposed. "I met Carlos on the trail."

"My son!" Don Diego anxiously exclaimed, stepping forward and gripping John Cooper's shoulder. "You say you saw him—how is he? What was he doing? Did he have any words for us?"

"Of course, Don Diego. He said he was going to write again. He's doing just fine. He looks strong and healthy. Being out in the sun on horseback has really given him a tan—he looks like a *mejicano* or an *indio,* but he couldn't be in better physical shape, from what I saw," John Cooper contributed. "And he certainly looks important in his officer's uniform."

"An officer," Don Diego said proudly, turning to Doña Inez. "I always knew my son was born to be a leader of men. What rank does he have, John Cooper?"

"That of *teniente,* Don Diego," the young mountain man smilingly replied.

"*¡Por todos los santos!*" Don Diego exploded. "By rights, he should be at least a *capitán!* With his breeding, his courage—what can they be thinking of in Mexico City?"

John Cooper could not suppress a smile at this outburst of paternal concern and esteem, but hastily proferred, "But from all we've heard, Don Diego, there really hasn't been any warfare, no battles, nothing like that. And promotion is slower when things are peaceful. I'm sure he'll be a captain before the year is over. And he said to be sure to give you and Doña Inez all his love. He promised to write, as soon as he got back from this patrol duty of his."

"Well, the scoundrel cannot be so busy, if there are not any battles to fight, that he cannot take time off to let those who love him know what has been happening to him," Don Diego fiercely declared, again glancing at Doña Inez for corroboration, and she smilingly nodded and patted his shoulder in reassurance.

"Well now, we'll just unload the supplies and then perhaps we can have lunch together," John Cooper suggested.

"Of course, of course!" Don Diego exclaimed. "I'll tell

Tía Margarita to prepare a very special lunch in celebration of your safe return and with this wonderful news from my son—our son, *querida*." He apologetically turned to Doña Inez and put his arm around her shoulders, drawing her to him as they headed to the *hacienda*.

As the men began to unload the supply wagon, Catarina put her arms around her husband and kissed him passionately. "Dear Coop, you were just wonderful to save those two children."

"Thank God we came in time so they didn't suffocate. And there's no way of knowing what their parents' names were or what they called the children."

"We'll think of names, and we'll adopt them—that is, if you don't mind, Coop?" she said, looking up at him intently.

John Cooper kissed her eyelids and then her mouth, while she happily clung to him. "You really love having a lot of children around, don't you, honey?" he softly asked her.

"I love taking care of them. And do you know, our little school is already a success. The children actually look forward to their lessons," Catarina said excitedly.

"That's wonderful. And how are Carlos's children?

"Just fine. And so is Francesca. She's so serious, such a little mother all to herself. But, with all these children around, Coop, she's beginning to be less formal with them now, and I can see she's developing some good, lasting friendships. My father and Doña Inez are so happy about that."

"And I know Carlos is grateful, too, for what you've done."

"And you're sure he's all right? You're not hiding anything from me about him, are you?" she anxiously asked. John Cooper shook his head, hoping his wife could not detect his concern.

In the cottage, Miguel was admiringly watching his beautiful wife caring for the little girl he and John Cooper had saved from the burning house. When she had finished, he said, "I met your brother-in-law, Timothy Callendar, in San Antonio. He's very well indeed, and he sends you his love. John Cooper and I invited him to bring his family out here and be our guests whenever he wanted, and he promised he would."

"Oh, Miguel, that was wonderful of you!"

"I'd feel better if your brother-in-law and his family could settle down here on all this land with us, dear Bess,"

Miguel averred, his face shadowed by the recollection of the armed Mexican patrol led by Carlos, and then the discovery of the burning house and its murdered victims. "I don't think it's going to be too safe for *americanos* in the next few months, not till there is a stable government in Mexico City. All of a sudden it seems that the military leaders of the revolution are worried that the *gringos* are planning war against them, which isn't true at all."

Bess came over to him and put her hands on his shoulders, and kissed him. "Dear, thoughtful Miguel. You've made me so happy, fulfilled, and needed. And I'm so proud and happy that I'm going to have another child."

"I'm more than that, *mi corazón*. You've made me feel young again, and I shall never think about my age so long as you continue to love me—and I'll try always to be worthy of it," Miguel said in a low, unsteady voice as he kissed her.

John Cooper Baines felt an urgent need to go off by himself with Lobo on one of their usual outings. The meeting with Carlos had both delighted and troubled him. He was happy to see how well his spirited brother-in-law had adapted himself to the rigors of military life, an ideal anodyne for his grief over the loss of Weesayo. But John Cooper was also convinced that if Iturbide authorized Santa Anna to make raids against isolated American settlers just over the Rio Grande, these episodes would inevitably lead the idealistic Carlos de Escobar into confrontations with his own compassionate ethos. It would be impossible to turn Carlos into a callous executioner, a man who would be judge, jury, and murderer. He did not want to think that the man and the woman whom he and Miguel had found shot down in their own house had been executed at the order of his brother-in-law. If what he had seen at that little house was typical of the way the government of Iturbide would seek vindictive reprisal against innocent homesteaders, then the Double H Ranch might prove the salvation for many of these powerless people.

It was unfortunate, he thought, that Carlos had not been able to find peace on the ranch. For his own part, John Cooper had discovered that by having friends, even among the lowliest of the workers, he was beginning to overcome his former, almost impatient yearning for independent existence with no one to dictate to or harass him. For the first time in his life, he could look back and realize how much he belonged to this thriving ranch with its boundless acres of fertile plain, river, rolling hills in the distance, and the indescribable blue sky that gave him each new day a cheerful optimism for the future.

He smiled as he whistled for Lobo, who answered with a joyous bark and came running up to him, his tongue lolling out, thrusting forward his head to be knuckled in token of the bond that he enjoyed with his young master.

John Cooper bent down as he spoke to the wolf-dog. "We're going off by ourselves this time, Lobo. No training, no tricks, just friends, the way you and I like it best, isn't that right?" Lobo uttered a soft little growl and licked the young mountain man's earlobe, and John Cooper burst out laughing at this unexpected mark of affection. "My, you really want this outing. I can see how you're making up to me. All right, now, just let me saddle Fuego and we'll be off. Poor old Fuego, he feels he's neglected, too, these days. So I've a debt to pay to both of you, and this afternoon's as good a time as any!"

Saddling Fuego and taking along "Long Girl" in the saddle sheath, as well as the Spanish dagger that he wore around his neck, John Cooper turned the magnificent white palomino toward the west. He was thinking of the mysterious mountain with its hidden silver mine, which now, due to the death of Padre Moraga, only he knew of. And it was too great a secret to be retained by any one man, especially in chaotic times like these. By now, he felt certain, the bishop of Santa Fe would have sent a replacement for the valiant old priest who had, despite his infirmities, been the leader of *los Penitentes* and dispensed stern justice to the miscreants who defied the laws of both God and man. Only to such a man would he divulge this secret.

The sun was hot but not unduly oppressive. Lobo raced along, wanting to show his master that despite his years, he could still keep up with the palomino. And Fortuna, the ever-faithful black raven, wheeled overhead, emitting his sometimes plaintive, sometimes taunting caws. At times, just to remind Lobo that he was acting in a supervisory capacity, the raven darted down to nip the wolf-dog's hindquarters or ears with his sharp little beak.

About six miles west of the sprawling ranch there was a series of gradually rising hills off slightly to the south, with thick clumps of mesquite and stunted scrub trees picturesquely spotting the landscape. John Cooper rode along easily in the saddle, not wanting to tax the palomino. Catarina would be expecting him for dinner this evening, to be sure, and they had much to say to each other. He must remember to be especially tender with her, now that she was bearing another child. How she had changed, and how their love had become deeper and richer and stronger since they had moved from Taos!

Suddenly Lobo picked up his ears and halted, uttering a low growl and baring his teeth. John Cooper reined in the palomino and called, "What is it, Lobo? What's the matter?"

Then, as he stared in the direction in which Lobo's head was cocked with a fierce attentiveness, he saw near the base of one of the nearest hills a young gray wolf warily circling an older, shaggier male. Above these two, as if witnessing the battle, a female wolf and her little cub watched, the mother from time to time turning her head and nipping at the cub to keep it silent and at her side.

Now the young wolf suddenly sprang for the older one's throat, and as John Cooper turned his head farther to the left and southward, he saw that this was indeed a duel to the death between the leader of the wolf pack and his younger challenger. Some fifteen wolves of varying sizes and ages were nearby, their ears lowered and pinned against their skulls, their fangs bared.

Again Lobo growled, his ears tightly flattened, his tail thrust out stiffly, his hackles rising. "No, no, Lobo. Stay!" the young mountain man sharply commanded. If they remained silent and motionless, they would be able to watch the spectacle undetected.

The older wolf, the leader, had shaken off his challenger's first lethal charge, but John Cooper could see that the younger wolf's fangs had drawn blood from his rival's throat and shoulder. The challenger, with incredible agility, veered to his left and went straight for the leader's throat, this time hanging on with ferocious tenacity. John Cooper could hear the agonized scream of the wounded leader. The wolf tried valiantly to shake off his rival, but the latter's sharp, cruel jaws would not be dislodged. He staggered, then seemed to regain his strength and tried to bite back. But the younger wolf flung him down and, in the struggle, sank his fangs deeper into the leader's already bloodied throat. There was another hideous howl, and then the leader stiffened, convulsively kicking, and lay dead.

There was a chorus of barks and growls from the

watching pack to the south, and the triumphant young challenger lifted his bloody muzzle to the sky and emitted a long howl of triumph. Then without warning he charged up the hill toward the bitch and her cub.

"Let's go, Lobo!" John Cooper cried as he pulled "Long Girl" from the sheath and, holding Fuego's reins in his left hand, gripped the stock of his father's rifle in his right hand and fired a shot into the air. The reverberating echo startled the triumphant challenger, who whirled in his tracks and turned to see who dared interrupt his victory. Lobo raced ahead, snarling defiance. "*¡Mata, mata!*" John Cooper cried to Lije's savage whelp.

Now, not wanting to waste time reloading the rifle, he thrust it back into its sheath and drew one of the pistols from its holster, aimed it toward the pack, and pulled the trigger. The echoing shot scared the animals, and they turned and began to run toward the south.

The young wolf challenger turned back again toward the bitch and her cub, but John Cooper drew the other pistol and fired it and shouted, waving the now-empty pistol. Lobo headed for the challenger, who, seeing this buckskin-clad man on horseback and the ferocious Lobo galloping ahead of him, made a last defiant howl, turned tail, and raced after his fellows toward the south.

John Cooper made Fuego gallop toward the hill and then dismounted. He stood, his hands extended out in front of him, palms upward, to show the bitch that she had nothing to fear from him.

Lobo approached warily, wagging his tail, and the bitch growled a warning, glancing down at her cub and nipping it as it tried to move forward to greet the newcomer.

"Lobo, be gentle, like an *amigo, ¿comprendes?*" he said softly to the wolf-dog. The bitch had straightened now, staring fearlessly at him and at Lobo, and even her cub showed its tiny teeth and uttered a feeble little yowl to prove its valor, even against this giant, two-legged enemy.

John Cooper saw that the bitch's chest was bleeding through her thick, gray fur; undoubtedly the successful challenger had attacked her, doubtless to provoke her aging mate into this battle. The young mountain man glanced toward the south, but the wolves had already disappeared from view. Grudgingly he smiled, crediting the young new leader with a cunning that might be emulated by many a military leader or *polínca.* Then he knuckled Lobo's head and again said gently, "Be friends, Lobo!"

Lobo advanced very slowly, and once again the bitch bared her fangs with a soft growl. But Lobo began to wag his tail and now, very tentatively, crouching and cocking his head, lolled out his pink tongue and rasped it against the bleeding chest wound of the bitch. She whined softly, still trembling but less tense, although she made a pretended attempt at nipping him away from her. The puppy advanced now and sank its sharp little teeth into Lobo's paw. With an irritated yipe, Lobo cuffed the puppy with the wounded paw, sending it sprawling, and John Cooper could not help laughing aloud at the comical expression on the puppy's face, startled and yet angrily defiant.

"That's enough, Lobo, you've made a friend," he interrupted. "Come back now. We're going home."

Lobo uttered an impatient little whine, glanced back at him, and then stared a last time at the bitch. Finally, wagging his tail, he decided to return to his master.

As John Cooper mounted Fuego, he glanced back and saw to his surprise that the dead leader's mate and her cub were following.

He thought of Lije and the Dakota timber wolf, and how Lobo had resulted from their mating. Lobo had already made friends with the bitch and would doubtless want to mate with her. But suddenly he thought of something else. What if Jude and Hosea, both male Irish wolfhounds, should be mated with the wolf cub when it was old enough! That would assure him of always having a crossbreed as fierce and yet as tame as Lobo on their huge ranch. He was sure the cub was a female, and if he could somehow wean her away from her mother . . .

He took a leisurely pace back toward the ranch. From time to time he looked back, as if by accident. The bitch was following, sometimes veering off to this direction and then to that, but always coming along behind him with her cub.

He smiled to himself. This had been an outing to remember, and perhaps its omen for the future was an omen also for the admixture of settlers and relatives, of friends and companions.

Twenty-seven

John Cooper slowly rode back to the *hacienda*, while Lobo trotted placidly beside his master. From time to time the wolf-dog paused to look back and, observing that the mate of the dead wolf-pack leader was following from a distance with her cub beside her, uttered a contented little yipe and quickened his pace. The black raven, flapping its wings overhead, was clearly mystified by the situation; however, Fortuna did not attempt the customary game of pecking and taunting either Lobo or the wolf bitch. Finally, as if wanting some kind of explanation, Fortuna swept down and perched on John Cooper's shoulder, riding thus nearly all the way back to the ranch.

As this strange processional neared the large *hacienda*, the wolf bitch uttered a curious low whine and fled for safety, abandoning the cub. At the same moment, John Cooper heard the sound of a rifle shot and swore under his breath as he saw what had happened: one of the younger *trabajadores*, spying the wolf as he rode his mustang out to supervise the grazing cattle, had drawn his rifle from its saddle sheath, quickly aimed, and fired.

John Cooper wheeled Fuego round and galloped back to the little animal, whose ears flattened as it bared its tiny teeth. Dismounting, he ran toward the cub and lifted it up, discovering that it was indeed a female. Things were working out as he hoped: now the puppy could be raised with young Hosea and Jude, and either of the pedigreed Irish wolfhounds could mate with her. The resulting litter would have exactly the admixture of the two breeds that had produced Lobo. In addition, Lobo would be free to court the wolf bitch, and there would be no rivalry between Lobo and the young wolfhounds. It would be a happy solution, and hence, his annoyance at the overanxiousness of the young *trabajador* was quickly dispelled.

It was time, John Cooper decided, to provide a kennel for Hosea and Jude and the wolf cub. To lock them up in a shed, as he had done with Lobo, would tend to make them fearful and docile, which he did not want from the proud breed of Irish wolfhound. He told himself that he must speak to Miguel and see if some of the workers, who did not have too many tasks at the moment, could construct a kind of kennel. Also, there should be one for Lobo, whenever the wolfdog felt the need of rest, for he was noticeably aging. True, he still intended to give Lobo the full run of the ranch, as he would eventually with Hosea and Jude when they had had sufficient disciplinary training.

The little wolf cub yowled and struggled furiously as he cradled it in both arms. Fuego was docile enough and knew his master's wishes sufficiently to be able to ride back to the *hacienda* without being held by the reins; John Cooper had looped them over the palomino's neck and let them dangle freely so that he could devote both hands to this furry bundle, which was still savage for all its relative infancy. He stared down at the gleaming little yellow eyes, saw the bared fangs, and chuckled. "I'm going to keep you away from Lobo because he can go after your mother. You're still too young to be mated with anyone like Lobo. But you'll learn to play with Hosea and Jude, and I'm going to call you Mischief because that's what I'm afraid you're going to get into your first weeks here, until you can calm down and look over the place and decide it's not such a bad home after all. Yes, you'll miss your mother, but we'll fix up the little shed near the bunkhouse real cozylike, and Tía Margarita will get you milk and a little meat every so often to build your strength. And maybe, in about five or six months, you can take your pick of the wolfhounds for a husband. Oh, trying to bite again, are you? You think I've got no right to regulate your life for you—well, you're right about that. I don't think I'd take kindly if anyone tried to regulate mine, but I've got the advantage of being older and bigger, so you'll just have to put up with me for a while."

Nimbly dismounting, he again had to hold on tightly to the struggling wolf cub as she tried to disengage herself, biting and nipping.

Miguel Sandarbal hurried up, a worried look on his face: "*Amigo*, what have you got there? Not one of Lobo's get, I'll wager!"

"You're going too fast, Miguel," John Cooper said, chuckling. Meanwhile, Lobo exhibited intense curiosity and growled softly, crouching a little beside his master and fixing the cub with baleful eyes. "Stop that, Lobo!" John Cooper told the wolf-dog. "She's too young for you. You can go off and find the mother—she'll be coming around the ranch this evening, once she gets over being scared by that shot! Now go run off and play; I mean it, boy!"

Lobo understood from the tone of his master's voice precisely what was wanted of him. He moved away, but not without pausing and glancing back over his shoulder and uttering another soft growl to indicate that he was not entirely pleased with this disposition of the affair.

Now John Cooper turned to Miguel and explained how he had come about acquiring the wolf cub. The foreman, delighted with the turn of events, assured his friend that he would have some of his workers start on the kennel the following morning.

Within the week, the kennel that was built not far from the bunkhouse, sheltered by the shade of several oak trees, was complete, and John Cooper led Hosea and Jude into the structure, after first having had one of the workers make a closed-off small section for the wolf cub. "I don't want them to scare her too much, but I want her to get accustomed to them," he explained.

The wolf cub, Mischief, still tried to nip him whenever she could, but he knuckled her head, as he had always done with Lije and Lobo, and himself fed her a bit of jerky now and again, so that she would be confident enough to understand that he meant her no harm and would provide food. She seemed to take to her new quarters, and although she fussed and growled almost all the first day or two, when the gangling Irish wolfhound puppies were put into the larger section of the kennel, she began to accept them. As for Hosea and Jude, they were extremely inquisitive, poking their noses through the open slats of the closed-in section and occasionally being nipped on the nose by Mischief's sharp little teeth.

Lobo had disappeared the night that John Cooper had brought Mischief back, and did not return until two days later. John Cooper remarked to Miguel, "I shouldn't be surprised if Lobo went courting Mischief's mother. That's exactly the way I want it to happen. Lobo will be free to have his mate, and she'll give him a litter. My only worry is that they'll be three-quarters wolf and one part Irish wolfhound, and that might present a problem for training in the future. But I'll worry about that when the time comes."

Bess Sandarbal's lovely face glowed with happiness. She had had a plan, which received Miguel's hearty approval, that she knew would give great joy to Doña Inez, who had by now become her dear friend. The plan was to go to the older woman and suggest that she adopt the orphaned children whom John Cooper had saved from the burning house. Bess was well aware of the fact that Doña Inez wanted to have another child; her dream could come true if she adopted the American children and had Jorge Pastronaz perform the baptism and adoption ceremony in the ranch's little church.

So in the afternoon, after the children were dismissed from school and were playing under the warm late afternoon sun, she approached the older woman, drew her to one side, and said, "I have something I would like to discuss with you, dear Doña Inez."

"Please, haven't we agreed? Just Inez to you, *querida* Bess. I feel we are old friends by now, and as for an aristocratic title, all of us feel part of this new land and this new home, where rank does not matter at all."

"I think that's a very good outlook, because, you see, Inez, I feel myself very much an American. And although I know that you and your husband come from Spain and were of the nobility, you both are such natural, kind people, and you express yourself in my own tongue so well, that I don't ever notice the difference between us. To me, that's what being an American means. And I feel the same way about the workers, even though not all of them speak English."

"One day they will, as your school grows larger, Bess," Doña Inez smilingly proffered.

"I should like that very much! But here's what I was going to suggest. Those two little ones John Cooper and Miguel brought in from that burning house when they were returning from San Antonio—Miguel and I think that it would be wonderful if you and your husband adopted them. I'm sure that John Cooper and Catarina would agree with us."

"Do you really mean that, Bess?" Doña Inez's eyes were shining with happiness. She looked up at the sky and, clasping her hands, murmured swiftly and softly, "Oh, Blessed Virgin, You have heard my prayer—how marvelously simple

Your solution is, and I thank You with all my heart and soul, for my sake and for the sake of the poor little ones." Then to Bess she exclaimed, "I shall tell Diego at supper tonight. I am sure he would love to do that. He dotes on children, as you know."

And that evening over supper, having conferred with her stepdaughter and son-in-law, Don Diego's handsome wife turned to him and suddenly said, "Diego, *mi corazón*, would you like to be a father twice over and overnight?"

The former hidalgo started and nearly dropped his glass of wine as he regarded his wife with widened, questioning eyes. "What are you saying to me? Is this a riddle? Become a father twice over and overnight?"

"Yes, it is a riddle, but a very lovely, simple one. And I shall tell you the answer, *querido*. John Cooper and Miguel, yes, and your daughter Catarina and Miguel's wife, Bess, too, as well as myself, are in complete agreement—they have suggested that we adopt those two poor little ones."

"Are you serious? But I thought that perhaps John Cooper and Catarina would want to adopt them," Don Diego stammered.

"*Mi padre*," Catarina said, turning to him with a warm smile, "everyone here has seen how happy you and dear Doña Inez are with Francesca. So we all thought that your happiness could be tripled, and we know what wonderful parents you'd make for these poor little abandoned ones."

"My daughter, you give me joy in my old age. How considerate you are, how thoughtful!" Don Diego had to turn aside and blow his nose to hide his feelings, as he reached for Doña Inez's hand under the table and squeezed it. "If you really mean that, I shall ask our acolyte priest to perform a baptismal ceremony and one of adoption. And, of course, the next time one of you rides to San Antonio, a record must be entered in the governor's office of these new citizens of Texas territory."

"You'd best think of naming them, then, Don Diego," Bess smilingly spoke up. She and her husband had been invited for supper, and Miguel, who sat next to her, leaned over to kiss her cheek and whisper, "How proud I am of you, *querida!* Every day I give thanks to the good God for having sent you to me."

"Yes, Diego," Doña Inez said, blushing with happiness as she turned to her white-haired husband, "we must think of names that are appropriate."

Don Diego lifted his glass of wine, closed his eyes for a moment, and then exclaimed, "The boy should be named after Padre Moraga. We shall name him Juan Moraga de Escobar."

"That would be a wonderful tribute, *mi padre*," Catarina spoke up, emphatically nodding her lovely head.

"And the girl?" Doña Inez pursued, her eyes dancing with joy as she looked at her husband's radiant face.

"Now I shall overrule you this time, as well, my darling. You remember that when you gave me Francesca, you wished to name her after your sister. And I told you that I wished to name the child after your mother, Francesca. Well, this time I wish to name the little girl Dolores. But not in memory of my dead wife—you have so wonderfully become my wife in my rebirth, till I no longer mourn nor grieve. And I know that she in heaven looks down and sees our happiness and is glad of this. No, my Inez, I will name her Dolores because it means lady of sorrow, and surely this poor little girl, whose parents were needlessly slain, began her life in sorrow. The two of us, Inez, will do our best to give her joy through all her days henceforth."

"My Diego, your words are a joy to me. Yes, let it be Dolores then, with all my heart!" Doña Inez whispered to him as she leaned over to kiss him. And the aura of happiness and unity in this dining room was almost consolation for the absence of that intrepid young man who wished to be his own master and who had gone off to slay his own dragon of grief and sorrow before he could return to take his place at the Hacienda del Halcón.

On the next morning the young acolyte priest, Jorge Pastronaz, wearing clerical vestments, performed the baptismal rite and then intoned the formula by which Juan Moraga de Escobar and Dolores de Escobar became the legally and ecclesiastically adopted children of Don Diego and Doña Inez.

After the ceremony, John Cooper went up to thank Jorge and to admire a little painting which the young *trabajador* acolyte had himself created. It was an almost lifelike picture of Padre Moraga, kneeling before the altar of the church in Taos, and at the top of the altar, there were the wings of angels hovering over the kindly old priest.

Catarina, delighted to be teaching in the little schoolroom, was able to show her family the extent to which she had become a mature, responsible young woman. But there really was no need to prove anything, either to her family or herself.

Indeed, Catarina found that one of the greatest joys in her life was working with the children. If she had stopped to analyze this, she might have thought it was due to the loss of her mother and her home at a very tender age. She had been pampered by her father and Doña Inez, it was true, all the more so after her mother died. She had been willful and petulant and had oftentimes hurt the people she loved, which only made her unhappiness grow.

Perhaps Catarina's own misfortunes had something to do with the particular interest she took in young Francesca. It was Catarina's goal, as both the little girl's teacher and her stepsister, to help Francesca overcome her shyness, to associate more freely with her cousins and the children of the *trabajadores*. It disturbed Catarina that the little girl was an indifferent student, sitting at one of the desks Teofilo Rosas had made for the children and idly daydreaming during the lessons. She was never able to answer the questions Catarina or Bess posed to her, and when she was asked to recite, she stammered and wrung her hands and looked thoroughly miserable.

So as the weeks passed Catarina worked gently and patiently with the little girl. At the dinner table, after all the children had been put to bed, she explained to her father and stepmother how their daughter was progressing, and they were delighted Francesca was in such capable hands.

"Do you know, my daughter," Don Diego began, putting down his dinner napkin, "you have a great gift. I believe one day your little school will achieve great renown, as you will. Those who come to settle in Texas alongside us will be grateful that you will be teaching their children."

Catarina flushed, and she exchanged a warm smile with Doña Inez, who squeezed the younger woman's hand.

Then one day there was a mishap that almost destroyed everything Catarina had worked so hard to achieve with Francesca. The little girl had been doing much better in her studies, and though she was still timid about reciting in front of the class, she bravely stood when she was called upon to read her lesson aloud. But today, as she read quietly from the history book that had been purchased in San Antonio, Carlos's young son, Diego, about the same age as Francesca, rudely interrupted her.

"Tell her to speak up," the boy angrily exclaimed. "I can't even hear her, and she's putting me to sleep."

"Now, Diego," Catarina said quietly. "It is impolite to interrupt like that. Besides, if you paid attention instead of making your little paper boats, you'd be able to hear her."

"I can never hear her," the boy persisted. "That's 'cause she's such a fraidy-cat and can't even speak up." He glared at Francesca, and then to the little girl's great distress, he made a face at her.

The tears rolled down Francesca's face as she stood helplessly, trying to be brave. Through her tears, she looked to Catarina for some assistance, and the young woman smiled gently and said, "You may sit down now, Francesca. You read your history very well." Then Catarina glanced angrily in the direction of her brother's son and continued the lesson.

Throughout the rest of the day she thought anxiously about how to assuage Francesca's distress. Little Diego had always been very hard and demanding on the daughter of Don Diego and Doña Inez, and Catarina realized the best way to remedy the problem was to see both children after school.

So that afternoon, when the other children were let out to play in the bright autumn sunshine, she asked Francesca and Diego to remain behind.

"Perhaps you can tell me, Diego," she said to the boy, who was fidgeting at his desk, his head lowered, "why you were so rude to Francesca."

The little boy, still restless, said nothing for a moment, then looked up at Catarina and grumbled, "I wasn't rude."

"Oh, but you were. You made Francesca cry."

"That's because she's such a fraidy-cat, and I don't like fraidy-cats." With this, he gave Francesca a menacing look, and it appeared as if the little girl was going to cry all over again.

Catarina thought she had lost control of the situation, and for a moment she began to doubt her abilities to deal with the children. But then she came up with an idea. She didn't know if it would work, but she intended to give it a try.

Turning to Francesca, the young woman said, "Tell me Francesca, now that Diego has had a chance to let everybody know what he thinks of you, why don't you tell us what you think of him."

The little girl looked very uncomfortable, and Diego continued to grumble. Then, after a long pause, Francesca stammered, "I—I think—Diego—is a—loudmouth."

The boy bristled at this, and rising from his desk, he said, "Oh, yes? Who says so?"

"I—I do," Francesca replied, becoming more sure of herself. "I think you are loud and have no manners, and—and—I never want to talk to you again." With this, she quickly rose from her desk and ran from the room.

Catarina waited expectantly as Diego watched Francesca storm out, then slowly turned to his teacher, a look of bewilderment and anguish in his eyes. "I—I," he began, "I didn't ever mean to get her so angry, Aunt Catarina. I—I just—" Diego could find nothing else to say, and he turned once again to look at the door.

"Why don't you go and apologize to her, then, Diego," Catarina said quietly.

"But she said she never wants to talk to me again."

"I bet she would if you apologize. I happen to know that Francesca loves you very much. She looks up to you, just like an older brother."

Diego looked confused and didn't respond for a moment. Then he said, "May I be excused now, Aunt Catarina?"

"Of course, Diego." She watched him leave the nursery room, and in a few moments she saw him outside in the courtyard, playing with the other children. Francesca was sitting by herself on a bench. Then, after what seemed like a long time, Catarina saw Diego walk up to the little girl. They talked for a while, and Diego reached into his pocket and gave Francesca one of his prized toy soldiers. Then, together, the two children walked over to where the others were playing.

Catarina suddenly felt a great sense of accomplishment and pride. Now she knew she truly had found her vocation.

Twenty-eight

By the end of the torrid summer of 1821, Stephen Fuller Austin had completed surveying the eastern section of Texas that was the future site of his colony, and had returned to New Orleans by November to arrange for the actual settlement. A prominent lawyer there advanced Moses Austin's resolute son the sum of four thousand dollars; in return, young Austin promised the lawyer half of the profits that would come out of the colony.

Now that his financial needs were no longer so pressing, Austin began to advertise for settlers, stressing the fact that proof of good character would be required of all applicants. His conferences with Governor Martínez had convinced him that what the Spaniards most feared were criminals, smugglers, and fugitives, who might enter Texas under the guise of peaceful homesteaders and foment dissension and violence.

Austin returned to Texas in December 1821, and was overjoyed to find several of the families he had selected in New Orleans already settled in the colony. The settlers had paid Austin the agreed-upon twelve and a half cents per acre, and now they were starting to build their houses. In many cases, men had left their families behind, planning to send for them later.

But the *Lively*, the schooner that had been purchased in New Orleans to sail for Texas with seventeen or eighteen colonists and cargo of seed, tools, and supplies, had not yet been heard from. Young Austin had instructed the colonists aboard the vessel to spend some time exploring the coast, then to land the vessel at the mouth of the Colorado. For some unknown reason, the landing had finally been made at the mouth of the Brazos instead.

Stephen Austin went down the Colorado at the appointed time to meet his schooner and was distressed that the ship had not arrived. The seed and supplies were badly needed by the settlers, and the colonists who were aboard the *Lively* would have been eagerly welcomed. But he would waste no more time in searching for this vessel, which, unbeknown to him, had disembarked on the other river. Accordingly down-hearted but not yet discouraged, Moses Austin's determined son planned to return to San Antonio in the near future to report to the governor on the progress of his colony.

Despite the absence of the ship, the whereabouts of which he had finally learned, Stephen Austin was enthusiastic about the very first settlements he had seen. Here was what his father and he both intended: men and women working their land, bringing up their children, leading a life of dignity, and affection, toil, and humility for the bounty of God. How, he asked himself, could even the most narrow-minded Mexican or Spanish authorities believe these people could possibly harbor any secret plots against the security of the new government? No, it was unthinkable; and he was certain the colony would prosper.

At the Double H Ranch, John Cooper had continued training Hosea and Jude, while noticing with approval that Mischief was growing sturdier and more docile in her new home with each passing day. The proximity of, and the familiarity with the two exuberant Irish wolfhounds had eased her wild nature and given her a sense of belonging.

As for her mother, John Cooper had occasionally observed the gray wolf just after sunset, standing far out on the bank of the Frio and uttering a mournful howl, particularly when there was a full moon. And on such occasions Lobo would prick up his ears, flatten his tail, and utter a low growl. Then, disregarding even his master's order, Lobo would race off in the direction of that howl. And a quarter of an hour later, straining his eyes through the darkness, John Cooper would see the two gamboling together, Lobo nipping at the she-wolf's flanks and hindquarters, she turning playfully to snarl and bite at him. He would outdistance her and make a wary circle near her, coming even closer, till at last the two would disappear in the darkness.

Early this December, a young *vaquero* rode to the ranch with a letter to Bess Sandarbal from her brother-in-law, Timothy Callendar, expressing his growing alarm over the news of harassing Mexican patrols. Timothy Callendar intimated that he planned to visit Bess by next spring, and if something could be worked out, he would like to investigate the possibility of settling down on land near his sister-in-law.

"Soldier patrols aren't too likely out your way, Bess," he wrote. "And the less I have to do with Mexican and Spanish soldiers, the better. It's true I'm a Texan by nature, but I'm American by birth, and I'd like to be with my equals and my only living relative, you."

The same courier carried another letter, addressed to John Cooper, from the six Texans whom he and the Jicarilla Apache had rescued from the sadistic Spanish lieutenant, Jaime Dondero. Ed Molson had run into Timothy Callendar on a trading trip to San Antonio, and when the latter learned that Molson and his comrades were also looking to resettle, he mentioned John Cooper Baines and the Double H Ranch. Callendar was delighted to learn that Ed Molson knew John Cooper, and Bess's brother-in-law promptly told him how he could reach the young mountain man.

The Texans were also increasingly distressed by the sporadic raids made by Mexican soldiers in Texas territory. Although Governor Martínez had welcomed them to San Antonio and given them to understand that in no way were they considered mercenaries or spies, they believed that an excellent precautionary move for the future would be to leave the heavily patrolled area near San Antonio. To a man they expressed to John Cooper their intention of visiting the Hacienda del Halcón possibly by March or April; meanwhile, they would try to quickly dispose of their holdings at a fair profit.

To John Cooper, this augured well for his plan of increasing the manpower and defensive strength of the huge ranch. Men like these, who had survived the Battle of Medina and known the cruelty of an enemy who hated them simply because they were Texans, would be even more valiant allies in the event an attack were ever made against the ranch.

Apart from occasional runs with Lobo—when the wolf-dog was not courting his savage mate—John Cooper remained on the ranch, to Catarina's great delight. They had become closer than ever now. She was four months' pregnant, but the outdoor life and her constant horseback riding and responsibilities with the school had given her a youthful suppleness, so that this pregnancy was not yet visible nor distressing to her. She had matured spiritually, as well, and as never before he felt that he could confide in her. All except one secret: the exact location of the hidden silver mine.

News of the new priest to replace Padre Moraga came early in December, when Benitay, the very brave who had ridden to tell John Cooper of the death of the old priest, galloped into the courtyard, dismounted, and seeing Catarina's husband squatting down and knuckling Lobo's head and good-naturedly chaffing the wolf-dog, hailed him: "*Halcón,* I bring you news from Taos, at the bidding of our *jefe!*"

John Cooper hastened to welcome the Apache with the tribal embrace. "It is good to see you, Benitay. What is your news?"

"That there is a shaman at last in the church of Taos, and his name is Padre Salvador Madura. He came to the church a moon ago, *Halcón,* but because the *indios* of the pueblo did not know how he would treat them at first, Kinotatay said that the news should wait, until the shaman had shown that he was not a shaman only for the *ricos.* But he has given food and clothing and *dinero* to the very poor of the pueblo, and Kinotatay says that he is a good man. Younger than the *wasichu shaman* whom we mourned but, like that one, straight of tongue and kindly of heart."

"This is good news indeed, Benitay. I will ride back with you to the stronghold to see my brother, and then I will visit this new shaman."

"That is good. All goes well with you and your people here?"

"Very well indeed, Benitay. Rest your horse and take food with me, and then we shall set forth for the stronghold. I'll take Lobo with me. He hasn't had a long outing in months now, and it will do him good." John Cooper thought to himself that by now the she-wolf had had her litter by Lobo, and also that with Lobo joining him in the journey to Taos, Hosea and Jude would ingratiate themselves still more with Mischief.

But as John Cooper and Benitay prepared for the return to the stronghold, the former suddenly decided that this would be the time to visit the hidden silver mine, to make certain that no one else had discovered it. It was still a secret that he would not share, even with the Jicarilla Apache—no, not even with his blood brother Kinotatay. So, somewhat lamely, he said to Benitay, "There are still some tasks I must do, and I must bid farewell to my woman, Benitay. Go on ahead of me, and I shall be at the stronghold no more than a day after your return. Tell my blood brother that I am grateful for the news he sent by you, and that I look forward to renewing our pledge of brotherhood and friendship, as with all of your people."

The Apache brave readily accepted this and, again embracing John Cooper as a token of friendship, mounted his mustang and rode off toward the northwest. John Cooper watched him disappear in the distance, and then went first to the little schoolroom to see Catarina, and then into the *hacienda* to bid his family farewell. He finished packing his provisions, then whistling to Lobo, he mounted his horse and rode off at a leisurely gait, wanting to give Benitay ample time to be well ahead of him.

Lobo was ecstatic at being allowed to accompany his master with no other distraction save Fortuna, his inseparable companion. The wolf-dog still showed admirable stamina, and that evening he proved that he had not lost any of his hunting skill when he killed a wild jackrabbit and brought it back to John Cooper, wagging his tail much as his sire Lije would have done. A wave of nostalgic remembrance made John Cooper fight back the tears: this brought back the memory, not only of Lije, but also of how boy and dog had earned their hunting outings in those placid days along the banks of the Ohio River, before John Cooper had found himself an orphan and with only Lije to comfort his agonized loss. He made a small fire on the slope of a hill that was obscured by tall, gnarled poplars, cooked the rabbit, and gave Lobo a generous portion.

Since the prospect of returning to the stronghold and thence to Taos to meet with Padre Moraga's replacement exhilarated him, he reached the mountain less than two weeks later, after making only brief stops to sleep and to eat sparingly from his provisions. He tethered his horse to a sturdy oak tree near the end of the winding trail, and he and Lobo began the ascent to the plateau above which was the ledge where he had first seen the skeletons of the monks and soldiers—the remains of the Spaniards who had guarded the silver mine so many years ago, before being attacked by Indians. On his second visit to the mountain, John Cooper had disposed of the skeletons and ancient weapons by hurling them down into the dense shrubbery hundreds of feet below. In this way, he had reckoned, no one else would discover the silver mine.

They reached the plateau, and as John Cooper clambered up the ledge, he ruefully observed that Lobo scrabbled with his paws and pulled himself up by sheer effort, till at last he stood beside his master, panting with exertion. Yes, as soon as it was possible, John Cooper would have to breed Hosea and Jude with the wolf cub.

Lighting an improvised torch, John Cooper went up to the slab that covered the cave entrance, and peered inside. The mummies of the Indian slaves still sat in macabre attention at that long table, on which he had first seen the silver ingots when he had discovered the mine years earlier. Padre Moraga had explained to him then that these Indians had probably been brought to mine the silver in the age of the *Conquistadores.* They had been left to die in the cave so they would not reveal the source of this vast wealth and had mummified in this almost hermetically sealed cavern. John Cooper could see that nothing had been disturbed, and that there were no footprints leading to the table save his own. He now went into the cavern, leaving Lobo outside by the entrance. The wolf-dog did not bark when his master disappeared into the mine, but patiently waited for him.

John Cooper found the opening to the mine shaft itself, and inside he saw all the old mining tools and the ingots of silver stacked along the farthermost wall. All was in order, and he returned to the main room of the cave.

In the eerie silence of the cavern, John Cooper thought again of the enormity of this secret he alone knew. He would be glad when there was someone in whom he could confide. He reasoned once again that this person would have to be someone not only of the highest moral principles, but also someone who would know how to use the silver for the greatest good. Perhaps the new priest in Taos would be just such a man.

Satisfied that all was well, John Cooper emerged into the open, much to Lobo's pleasure, and descended, mounted his horse, and rode off to the stronghold, two days' journey away.

Benitay had arrived the day before, and his welcome was warm and vociferous. Pastanari, the tall, handsome son of the former chief, Descontarti, had grown into a man, and there was a serenity to him which John Cooper had never before observed. Kinotatay smilingly explained it: "This valiant brave, who will one day be our *jefe,* is one of the young warriors who impatiently awaited your coming to us, *Halcón*, before he took his squaw to their secret wickiup."

"That's wonderful news, Pastanari! I only hope you will be as happy with your squaw as I am with my Catarina," John Cooper exclaimed as he clasped the young Apache in the tribal embrace.

"The girl is Numisari, daughter of Jirante, who is now our war chief," Kinotatay explained. "The other brave and his intended squaw are Numara and Daruma, who is one of the daughters of our shaman. This new shaman, who received the summons from the Great Spirit to take the place of the shaman who united your *cuñado* and his squaw who was called to the heavens, is a gentle man, much like the old shaman of Taos. He speaks of peace and of the friendship between tribes. It was he who united me with my Mescalero squaw, who gives me great joy. Tomorrow night, when the moon is high, you shall watch him perform the ceremony, and you shall be our honored guest at the feast, which celebrates both our joy in welcoming our blood brother back to us, and the blessing of these four lives which will then become two, inseparable for all their years upon the earth."

Later, as John Cooper walked out of the village toward one of the isolated summits of the Jicarilla Mountains, where Descontarti had often gone to commune with the Great Spirit, he and Kinotatay talked of the Jicarilla way of life. "We are at peace with the Mescalero, and no other *indios* seek to attack us, knowing our strength. I have made Pastanari the leader of our sentries who watch over the trail that leads here, and already he is behaving like a man wise in the knowledge of his duties. And this union with his chosen squaw will give him still more wisdom and peace within himself. I can say now that, if the elders of our council were to say that I must step aside as *jefe*, I would not hesitate to entrust Pastanari with the leadership of the Jicarilla."

"I have seen how much of a man he has become, Kinotatay," John Cooper replied. "And I am glad that your people are at peace. The life is good here in the mountains. But now, Kinotatay, tell me of this new shaman of Taos, who is called Salvador Madura. Is he an old man?"

"Not so old as Padre Moraga, *Halcón*. I would say that he has known fifty summers and winters, but he seems younger, and his words ring out and his eyes do not glance down when he speaks to someone. I have already heard that he has bought with his own money blankets and food for the poorest in the pueblo of Taos. That is why I had Benitay wait to bring you the news, till I was certain that here was a shaman who did not look down with scorn upon the *indios*."

"Then I shall hear his words and abide by them, if this is so," John Cooper gravely replied.

"I know what you are thinking, *Halcón*," Kinotatay observed after a moment, turning to stare about at the breathtaking sweep of sky patterned by the jagged peaks of the mountains on either side of him. "The ceremony that will bring Pastanari and the other brave their squaws recalls to you how, still in the dark of memory, Señor Carlos was bound to his beloved."

"It is true, Kinotatay. He mourns her deeply, and I am sure that he tries to observe the Apache custom, save that in his heart he will say her name, and surely that is not forbidden."

"No, my brother." Kinotatay made a wry face and looked away for a moment as he remembered his own loss: the death of his young son during the attack by the Mescalero eight years earlier. "I confess to you—and this is for no brave to hear—that, in the dead of night, sometimes the ghost of my son appears to me and his name sounds in my head, as in my heart, and this I am not ashamed of." He made an abrupt gesture. "What of Señor Carlos, is there news of him?"

"News that will sadden us both, Kinotatay. Miguel Sandarbal and I went to San Antonio some moons back for supplies, and as we returned southward near the Rio Grande, we met him at the head of a company of Mexican soldiers. He told me that he was under orders to drive away *americanos* who might have weapons and threaten the peace of the territory of Texas. This new government, whose leaders speak of a bloodless revolution and yet send out patrols to drive off and even to kill, I find most strange. I think that Carlos has been deceived, in joining the army of Iturbide in order to forget his grief."

"I can understand that. Many a brave who has lost one beloved to him seeks consolation in the onslaught of battle. Yes, and his grief would be the greater because of losing such a squaw—we speak dangerously because it is against our tribal law to speak this way of the dead, but it is only between us, *Halcón*."

"Yes, and neither of us will betray the other's confidence. We are blood brothers for life, Kinotatay, in thought as well as deed. And now let us go back and smoke the calumet to renew our pledge."

The next evening, after the great feast in which all the villagers of the stronghold participated, John Cooper sat with his legs drawn under him, beside the *jefe* of the Jicarilla Apache, and watched the exquisitely mystic rituals of marriage of Pastanari and his winsome young wife, as well as another brave, who wed to a small but piquantly featured, smiling girl in her teens. He watched as the shaman cut their wrists and tied them together, then pronounced the words that drove out all cold and wind and rain and made their lives inseparable. And he saw them ride their horses off to their secret wickiups, and he could not control the tears that filled his eyes at the memory of how not only Carlos had been wed thus to Weesayo, but how on their second honeymoon Catarina had urged him to let them both pretend that their first union came about through such symbolic fashion.

And in the morning, when he left the Jicarilla stronghold, it was his prayer that Carlos de Escobar would find a tender, sensitive woman who, though she could never replace Wessayo, might at least give him love and consolation in her own right.

Twenty-nine

John Cooper rode into Taos two days later just before dawn, having left Lobo and Fortuna back at the stronghold. Lobo knew the people of the stronghold and was docile enough to be trusted among them. And they in their turn spoiled him by tossing him bits of meat till he was gorged and sleepy. Indeed, at the end of the day, he lay sleeping with his muzzle resting on his front paws, and even the occasional taunting of Fortuna failed to disturb him.

John Cooper had taken a trail from the Sangre de Cristo Mountains that led to the outskirts of Taos, at the very end of the pueblo of the *indios*. He rode to the little rectory in which

Padre Juan Moraga had lived, tethered his horse, and knocked at the door. After a few moments a tall, robust, gray-haired man, with warm brown eyes and a gracious smile, opened the door and exclaimed, "Welcome, my son! I have not seen you before in Taos. But our church is open, if you wish to pray."

"I do, *mi padre*. But with your permission I should like to speak with you first. My name is John Cooper Baines."

"And I, Señor Baines," the priest spoke in Spanish as John Cooper had done, "am the humble servant of our dear Lord, Salvador Madura. Come in. I was just having breakfast, and I will ask my housekeeper, Soledad, to prepare a simple *desayuno*, only goat's milk and a little black bread. Of course there is no meat since this is the holy day of Friday."

"Thank you for your hospitality, Padre Madura. I will gladly share it with you. When men break bread together, speech comes more easily from the heart," John Cooper said, remembering the Spanish proverb. He had often heard Don Diego say this as a justification for providing fiestas for his *trabajadores,* during which he welcomed private conversation with each of his workers to hear their problems or any suggestions they might have.

"You speak our tongue very well, Señor Baines. Do come in. Ah, here is Soledad. The poor soul is deaf, but it is not an affliction." The tall priest smiled. "Sometimes, when I hear the petty wranglings in the marketplace and the hateful denunciations that one man makes against his neighbor, I think it would be a blessing to be deaf. But she reads lips—wait, I will tell her to bring more bread and milk and to set a place for you at the table."

John Cooper nodded his head respectfully toward the elderly woman, who recognized him and uttered a strident cry of pleasure, clasping her hands together, her wrinkled face aglow. Then her lips moved, and she exclaimed in her harsh voice, "It is good to see you, Señor Baines! You have heard the dreadful news of our beloved Padre Moraga? But Almighty God avenged his death, and sent us the good Padre Madura, whose servant I am honored to be."

"This I have heard already and from the Indians far in the mountains, Soledad. It is good to see you again. I pray you will have many happy years in the peace and contentment of this church, serving this man of God," John Cooper cordially replied.

Delighted, the old woman threw up her hands and, smiling to herself, hurried back to the little kitchen. Soon

John Cooper and the priest, sitting opposite each other eating the simple fare, were deep in conversation.

"I know you a little, Señor Baines," the priest smilingly declared. "When I came to this parish, Soledad told me how things once were in Taos under the rule of the former *intendente*, Don Diego de Escobar. She told me, too, how a young *americano* had been married by Padre Moraga in the chapel of Don Diego's *hacienda*, and what exemplary lives of Christian charity and kindness you and Don Diego led. I understand that you lived with Indian tribes before you came to Taos?"

"That is true, Padre Madura. Perhaps that is why I've always defended the Indians against those who believe them to be bloodthirsty savages."

"It is man's nature to seek to make someone who is humbler than himself a scapegoat for his own sins of envy and lust and hatred," Padre Salvador Madura gravely observed. "And when Soledad spoke of the kindness and the generosity with which the *indios* of the pueblo were treated while Don Diego was *intendente* here, she spoke also of the man whom I have since had reason to condemn as a sinner. Perhaps you have heard of a Don Esteban de Rivarola?"

"Yes," John Cooper guardedly admitted.

"I feel that I can trust you, Señor Baines. When I came here, Soledad showed me the paper on which that blessed martyr, Padre Moraga, was writing before he met his untimely death. It denounced this Don Esteban, the *alcalde mayor*, and it has been said that Don Esteban's death, by exactly the same way in which Padre Moraga died—an Indian arrow— was the justice of God. Myself, I do not pronounce on such things. But what I can tell you is that, since I have come here, I have found that the new *alcalde mayor* appointed by the governor is an evil, dissolute man who may well face excommunication himself if he does not change his ways."

"Why do you say this, Padre Madura?"

"Do not think me one who bears tales or listens to the gossip of the parish. But I will say this to you: I have had many visits from poor, elderly *indios* in the pueblo who complain of this Luis Saltareno. It appears that he has his *trabajadores* go into their village and bring them back to the *hacienda* to do labor, for which they are seldom paid. When they complain, they are given blows and curses instead of food or the pitiful sum promised to them. And, also, on two occasions since I came into this parish, fathers have told me that their daughters have been forced to serve as *criadas* in the household of that corrupt man, who allows his men the supreme outrage of taking their virtue. In so short a time as I have been here, my son, I am grievously distressed. And the *alcalde mayor* does not even come to church on Sunday to hear mass, doubtless fearing that I might denounce him from my pulpit. No, he has no time for God, and he doubtless knows that it would be a mockery and an hypocrisy to appear in the house of our dear Lord unrepentant as he is."

"It distresses me to hear that. I will tell you something in return, Father Madura. Both he and this Don Esteban were bitter enemies of Don Diego de Escobar, my *suegro*. They all but accused him of treason for giving assistance to down-and-out *americanos*, and they were always enraged by the kindness my father-in-law showed his workers."

"I give you my word that I shall not betray any secret you confide in me, Señor Baines. But I have gathered that you and your *suegro* live together far from Taos. No, you need not tell me where it is, though you have my promise I shall never reveal it."

"It is enough to say, Padre Madura, that we are raising cattle and sheep, bringing up our children, and building a community where there will be no hatred and no misunderstandings between Mexico and the United States."

"That news gladdens my heart. I would have you know that I am not one of those hidebound priests from the days of the Holy Inquisition, who would spy on you or who would pit one man against another to learn a secret that would undo you. No, my son. I myself am of the Franciscan Order, and as a young man when I came to my vocation, I was taught humility, poverty, chastity, and above all else, truthfulness."

"I am very glad that I came to Taos to meet you, Padre Madura. And I will tell you this: my *suegro*, Don Diego, and I have been blessed with material goods, and if there is need in the Indian village, you have only to send word to us, and I shall see to it that there will be food and clothing for the needy. You have heard of the Jicarilla Apache and their chief, Kinotatay?"

"I have, my son. He lives in peace, and I respect him."

"Then you have only to send a message to Kinotatay who will, in his turn, send a courier to me to bring me back to Taos with gifts for the poor."

"God will bless you for this, my son."

"Amen to that, Padre Madura. And now, with your

permission, I will go to the church and say my own prayers."

"Of course, my son."

An hour later, having said his prayers, John Cooper mounted his horse and rode back to the Jicarilla stronghold. He was still troubled that he had not been able to confide in the new priest; it was not that he distrusted Padre Madura, quite the contrary. It was only that with all the unrest in Mexico, the tenure of this new priest might be threatened. No, for the time being he must keep the secret to himself, even though it was far too vital to be known only to one man. If by some mischance an enemy were to find the lost mine, the power of that fabulous wealth could well be put to work against the already oppressed people of Taos and, for that matter, of all Nuévo Mexico and Texas.

John Cooper and Padre Madura would have been sorely distressed to know that this same day, Luis Saltareno, *alcalde mayor* of Taos, was already plotting his evil schemes. That evening, after John Cooper had headed out of Taos to fetch Lobo and Fortuna from the Jicarilla stronghold and then return to the Texas ranch, Luis Saltareno, bedecked in his finest waistcoat and breeches and new boots with silver buckles, was getting into his carriage. At his sign, two of his *peones* hustled a blanket-covered form into the carriage beside him, grinned, winked, and obsequiously inclined their heads in deference to the *patrón*.

"Has she been gagged and bound?" the *alcalde* demanded.

"*Sí, patrón,*" one of the *peones* ingratiatingly assured him.

"*¡Bueno!* Tell the coachman to drive me to the shop of Barnaba Canepa, *pronto!*" the bewigged *alcalde mayor* insolently ordered.

The carriage started off, moving toward the eastern edge of Taos and toward the edge of the pueblo, where the Christianized Indians lived. Luis Saltareno leaned forward and called out to the coachman, a burly *peón* in his early forties, Santos Filada, who acted not only as coachman but sometimes as abductor and torturer for the dissolute *alcalde mayor*. "Do you see where that lantern shines from a window? That's the shop. And you'll give me a hand with the *puta!*"

"*Sí, patrón, comprendo,*" the man hoarsely called back with a lewd guffaw.

The carriage stopped, and Saltareno slowly got out, stretching his legs and wheezing, for the night air was chilly and he had spent the last several nights in debauchery. He could not help thinking how fortunate he was to have inherited Don Esteban's former concubine, the *mestiza* Noracia. Thanks to her advice, he had sent ten of his strongest, well-armed *peones* to the *hacienda* of his dead friend, and they had kept at bay the terrified *trabajadores*, gone into Don Esteban's bedroom, and found the false bottom of that chest in which the former *alcalde mayor* had kept his silver and gold. Then after a careful search, they found the other concealed compartment in the chest, which neither Noracia or the *trabajadores* had found earlier. They had seized the chest, brought it back to their master, and three of them had remained, with loaded weapons, to take possession of the ranch and all its sheep, horses, and other assets. To all intents and purposes, therefore, this merchant, who had risen to the post second only to that of Don Sancho de Pladero of Taos, had virtually tripled his own wealth. But he had promised himself that when the new government was firmly entrenched and the revolution over, he would see to it that the estate of Don Esteban de Rivarola would become his own in all legality. Noracia had aided in that, wheedingly suggesting that if he were to forge a deed of transfer signed by the late Don Esteban de Rivarola, the transfer could be effected with no one's being the wiser. And she had most conveniently taken from one of the bags of money she herself had appropriated on that fateful night a tally sheet in Don Esteban's own handwriting and with his signature, which could easily be forged.

Now that he was wealthy beyond his wildest dreams, now that he had power and a beautiful, scheming woman to arrange all kinds of lascivious pleasures for him, Luis Saltareno felt he was on the threshold of ruling all Taos. It remained only to depose that silly old fool, Don Sancho de Pladero, as *intendente*, and then finally to pay back that scoundrel and traitor Don Diego de Escobar. Then he would be the sole master of Taos, and let any government in power in Mexico City be damned!

Grinning with anticipation, he advanced to the door and pounded on it. Meanwhile, the burly coachman descended from the carriage, reached in, and seized the blanket-shrouded figure, whose muffled gasps and groans protested against this rude hauling. Flinging the unknown captive over his shoulder, the coachman followed his master.

Again, Saltareno banged upon the door, and a querulous, cackling voice was faintly heard, "*¡Vengo, vengo, ahora,* have patience, *por el amor de Dios!*"

The door was opened, and a lantern cast an eerie glow on shelves that were filled with curious vases and jars. In them were dead toads, rattlesnakes, Gila monsters, curiously deformed lizards, and in another, the embryo of an owl, and in a jar beside it, that of a vulture. The coachman, adjusting his feebly struggling burden, crossed himself with one hand and muttered a prayer under his breath at this hideous vision, one born out of the phantasmagoria of an evil night.

Barnaba Canepa, now in his middle seventies, wizened, bent over with arthritis, with sparse white hair and a wispy goatee, his beady eyes blurred by growing cataracts, peered nearsightedly at his nocturnal guest. "Who is this who comes so late at night to disturb an old man's slumbers?" he cackled.

"It is I, Saltareno. I've brought you a present, you old devil."

"Ah, *señor alcalde mayor!* Come in, come in, you are welcome." Canepa retreated, bowing low, a fatuous grin on his shriveled lips, shivering with an obscene anticipation, the more odious because of his near-senility.

"Bring her in and unwrap her. Then go outside and wait for me, till I'm ready to go back to the *hacienda,*" the *alcalde mayor* gruffly bade the coachman.

With an obsequious nod, the burly *peón* carefully laid his burden down on the floor, then untied the rawhide thongs wrapped around the blanket, and pulled it away to disclose a girl not more than sixteen, clad only in a thin cotton shift, which came only to mid-thigh, gagged and blindfolded, with her wrists bound behind her back.

"This is Luisa," Saltareno declared. "I told you I'd reward you for your endeavors on my behalf. She's a *criada* of whom I've tired. She whines and snivels all the time, and she's much too religious for my stomach. But you, Barnaba, with your potions and your cantharides, will know how to make her serve you and straighten your bent carcass."

"Oh, how thoughtful you are, *señor alcalde mayor!*" The old man gleefully rubbed his hands and smirked down at the terrified girl, who, hearing these voices and these ominous words, tried frantically and uselessly to free herself.

Saltareno disdainfully sniffed and interposed, "Patience, Barnaba. There'll be time enough for you to amuse yourself with Luisa, once we've concluded our business. As I said, I make you a present of her. She tried to steal *dinero* from me and run away. And so I said to myself that, instead of giving her a good thrashing, the punishment would be far greater if I brought her youthful, delightful body to your malodorous shop and let you try to regain your youth. Which, of course, you'll do, with all your magic philters, *¿no es verdad?*"

"It is really kind of you, honored *excelencia*," the old shopkeeper wheezed, rubbing his bony hands as he blinked his eyes repeatedly to clear them, the better to see the enticing half-nudity of the young *criada* who lay on the floor at his feet. "And now, I'm at your disposal."

"Well then, I have some news for you, since thus far you've not been successful in tracing my detested enemy, that traitor who was once *intendente* of Taos, Don Diego de Escobar."

"But, noble sir, I've had spies everywhere, and all I've been able to find out is that the de Escobars moved to the west."

"Not so, and if you pay your spies for such false information, Barnaba, you're a bigger fool than I thought. Now listen: last week I had occasion to deal with one of those filthy *indios* of the pueblo. He's a young fool with ideas better than his lowly station, and he wished to ingratiate himself with me. He told me a curious story of how a friend of his, who was greatly in love with an *india puta*, managed to have that meddling old fool of a Padre Moraga intercede for the girl, when Don Esteban de Rivarola had taken her as hostage because her father had not paid his debt. Well now, when I questioned him and gave him a few pieces of silver, he told me something that interested me very greatly. It appears that this young *indio* and his squaw were sent to the stronghold of the Jicarilla Apache. And this young fool swore to me that he had overheard his friend say to the girl, 'In time, we shall be safe in Texas territory, where Don Esteban can never find us. There we shall be safe my dear one, living at the *hacienda* belonging to the man they call El Halcón.' Now, what do you make of that, you doddering old idiot?"

"*El Halcón*," Barnaba Canepa mused, then he screwed up his face into a hideous grimace to indicate his concentration. "Ah, yes, now I begin to remember! It was a name given that *americano,* that one who lived with the *indios* and who married that haughty baggage, Catarina de Escobar."

"Precisely! And where that *gringo* goes, he joins that traitorous *intendente,* whom I have sworn to bring to justice before the authorities. Why, look you, Barnaba, this Don Diego de Escobar tried to treat the *indios* as equals, as if they were *ricos, hacendados!* And I will say also that his successor, Don Sancho de Pladero, is as great a fool and Indian sympathizer, whom I hope also to oust from his lordly position. Now then, Texas territory is vast, we both know that. But if you succeed through any method of your spies or your own cunning to locate this *americano* and Don Diego, you shall have two more *criadas* to be your slaves and *mucho dinero!*"

"Ah, that's a reward worth working for, honorable *excelencia!*" The old storekeeper again rubbed his hands and uttered a cackling laugh. "I have some ideas which may be of service, esteemed *alcalde mayor.* Suppose I were to pay some of the pueblo *indios* to ride into the Texas territory and search out *El Halcón?*"

"That might take months upon months. Bah, your mind wanders, you think of the young flesh at your feet. Look away from her, Barnaba, and put your brain to work. I fear your age overcomes that keen mind of yours, which once had such cunning."

"Not so, honored *excelencia!*" the old man whined. "Wait, I have another thought. Perhaps you are right: the *indios* of this pueblo are too Christianized, too fearful of the power of the church to betray *El Halcón* and also this Don Diego of yours. After all, wasn't the *intendente* kind to them?"

"You tell me what I already know, you imbecile! I've a mind to take Luisa back—"

"Oh, no, *excelencia,* please—wait, something else—yes, now I have it!" Canepa wheedlingly pleaded. "Perhaps I might say to Don Sancho de Pladero that an important letter from Mexico City was mistakenly delivered to me, intended for Don Diego. I will say that I opened it by mistake, thinking it mine, and found that it was a summons for Don Diego to go to Mexico City to stand trial. And then, *excelencia,* I'd have my spies watch to see where Don Sancho de Pladero sent his messenger, follow that one, and thus locate your enemy!"

"And that's imbecilic as well, you purveyor of poisons

and love potions," Saltareno contemptuously averred. "The two of them were fast friends, and Don Sancho would not so easily be taken in by your lies. And he would ask you to produce the letter—"

"But of course, I'd forge it—" the old man plaintively began.

"Enough of this! Your mind wanders, as it always does. Well then, keep Luisa; I do not take back gifts. But understand this: set your mind to work in earnest. If you manage to help me find Don Diego, I promise you shall have many young girls and much silver. And I shall be *intendente* of Taos, with total power over this province. Remember that, Barnaba Canepa. And then I'll have the power to exile you forever, to let you die wandering on the plains where the Comanche or the Apache will find you and give you a slow death."

"Oh, no, honorable *alcalde mayor!* I promise I'll think of something, and quickly! I would never fail so generous a *patrón* as you!"

"See that you don't. And now I'm going. Faugh, the smell of your jars and vials turn my stomach, as you do." And with this, Luis Saltareno took out a handkerchief steeped in cologne and daintily put it to his nostrils as, turning his back on the stooped, wizened old man, he returned to his carriage.

Thirty

On the day before Christmas, in the year 1821, Carlos de Escobar found himself nearing the little hamlet of Big Wells near the Nueces River. Colonel Santa Anna was in command of the company of eighty armed soldiers, and riding on one side of him was Carlos, and on the other side was the liaison officer whom Iturbide had sent, Colonel Ramón Santoriaga.

They had been out on forays almost all month long, and during two of those raids on towns just north of the Rio

Grande, Santa Anna had ordered a search for weapons.
There were three Texans and two elderly homesteaders from
Missouri in one of the towns, and Carlos had found an old
Pennsylvania rifle, almost like John Cooper's "Long Girl,"
and two muskets. Santa Anna had peremptorily ordered, "The
owners are to be shot!" Carlos had protested in vain. The tall,
clean-shaven revolutionary leader had stiffened and snapped,
"Are you questioning my orders? Such insubordination re-
ceives a stiff military penalty, Teniente de Escobar!" And
then, with that suave, unctuous smile of his, and that soft
tone that had beguiled so many *ricos* and members of the
clergy, he said, "Come now, *mi teniente,* what does it matter
if we kill a few worthless *americanos?* Our great leader,
Iturbide, has ordered me to see to it that there is no revolt
and that there are no *americano* spies or soldiers hiding in
territory under the rule of our beloved, independent Mexico!"

And Carlos, clenching his teeth, quelling the mutinous
reply that had surged to his lips, had been compelled to watch
helplessly as a firing squad was selected. The five men had
died bravely, one of them crying out, just as Santa Anna had
given the order to fire by sweeping his rapier down, "Long
live the United States!"

Through this month-long journey which had made a
circular route of southeastern Texas, Carlos had been made
painfully aware of Santa Anna's great fascination for the
opposite sex. In nearly every town through which they passed,
the most attractive young women of the village put on their
finest dresses and wore what little jewelry they owned in
order to make themselves alluring to "the savior, the liberator
of Mexico."

In the little town of Spofford, a young, black-haired
widow had pushed herself past two sentries guarding Santa
Anna's tent and, falling on her knees, had embraced Santa
Anna's legs as she insinuatingly avowed, "My hero, you to
whom I pray for freedom, my husband died of fever, and I
wish to give my love to the man who will make all women
free in Mexico! I am yours, *mi coronel!*" And Santa Anna
had laughingly lifted her to her feet and then, whispering
something into her ear, had appeared outside the tent and
barked to his sentries, "Stand guard and admit no one till
morning."

Young girls and women who flocked to see the resplendent Santa Anna in his dress uniform astride a magnificent
black stallion also observed the poised, tall, handsome young

teniente. More than once one of the most attractive girls of the village had come up to Carlos and, putting her arm around his waist, whispered, *"Te quiero mucho, teniente. Mi casa es su casa."*

Carlos had courteously but politely declined their proffered favors. One of them, incensed by his refusal, had sneeringly put her hands on her hips and loudly declared, "Then you are a man who has no *cojones, señor teniente!"* And Carlos had turned crimson and walked away as the girl continued jeering him.

On this Christmas Eve, Carlos walked slowly outside the camp. Beyond him stretched the endless plain of Texas, with the occasional clumps of mesquite and scrub trees. It was fertile but not yet developed land, and there were no inhabitants for miles beyond. Never had he felt so lonely, but what most of all rankled in his soul was seeing the cause for which he had enlisted become tawdry and cheapened by senseless killings and needless raids on innocent people.

He uttered a long sigh and then shrugged. The die was cast. He had taken the commission of an officer, and desertion was unthinkable. It touched on the code of honor, and even if the leader was corrupt, the cause must still be just—he must think that, or else all that he had done was for nothing.

"Can you talk to a friend?" a pleasant, low voice came to his ears.

Carlos whirled, his hand to his rapier hilt, and then uttered a nervous little laugh: "Ramón, you surprised me. You came as quietly as an *indio*. But of course. The fact is, I want to talk to someone."

"And to a friend most of all, I believe. Carlos, I think I know what weighs upon your mind."

"Tell me, then. Put into words what distracting thoughts have been running through my mind for the past month," Carlos bitterly exclaimed.

Colonel Ramón Santoriaga, his friend and superior officer, put his arm around the young Spaniard's shoulders. "I will tell you, because your thoughts and mine are very nearly parallel. As you know, General Iturbide assigned me to follow Colonel Santa Anna. I cannot countermand Santa Anna's orders from a militaristic point of view, but I can make my own observations and report back to my own commanding officer, who is the head of our nation. I believe that Santa Anna wishes to supplant Iturbide, because I see in him a cynical opportunist, and a man who says one thing and thinks another."

"I know. And most of all, these women, these camp followers—"

"Come now, do not pretend to be a holy saint and an ascetic. Women are the natural preoccupation of soldiers, yes, even the married ones. Although for myself, I am true to my Mercedes, and I am not tempted."

"No more am I, Ramón. And this business of the sergeant-priest, this mockery, which I have seen three times performed since I rode with this company—it sickens me."

"I understand that. But you see, I, like you, saw in this revolution a chance to separate oppressed Mexico from haughty, indifferent Spain. When Iturbide proclaimed the independence of Mexico, I rejoiced. I had been brought up as a cadet, much like Santa Anna. I looked upon a military life as an honorable one. And then my commander assigned me to Santa Anna's forces. What I have seen is what you have seen, except that I have been a soldier longer than you, Carlos."

"Ramón, why these useless raids? Would it not be better to support General Iturbide in the provinces where there might be uprisings of hostile Toboso, or even rebellious villagers who do not understand that Mexico seeks recognition among the nations of the world?"

"There I agree with you. But General Iturbide is not an evil man; he is, in some ways, like you, an idealist, *mi* Carlos. Do not blame him for Santa Anna. He saw Santa Anna's military prowess and believed that he could employ it in this task of liberating all of Mexico. He also believed, because there were constant reports from the *alcaldes* of Texas territory and Nuevo México, that the *gringos* might take advantage of our time of change to take possession of land, to plan a military coup, which would endanger Mexico. I myself, from what I have seen all these past months, no longer believe this."

"Would you have given the order to shoot those five men?"

"No, Carlos. But this I say to you in the strictest confidence, as one friend to another and not as your superior officer: I thought that Santa Anna was a hawk. But now I see that, in reality, he is only a vulture, a scavenger who preys on the misfortunes of others, on the dead whom he creates with his brutal raids, whose only purpose really is to plunge the poor into deeper poverty. All these grandiose attacks of his on supposedly enemy villages and hamlets—alas, where the five men were shot could not be called an enemy outpost by the wildest stretch of the imagination!—all they do is succeed in furthering his own purpose, his selfish purpose of drawing new women to his camp, of surrounding himself with the trappings of one who has the dream of being an emperor. He might even be called the Napoleon Bonaparte of Mexico— and I should not be surprised if one day he himself would take that title, when he has won enough glory to dazzle his countrymen and to plunge an idealist like General Iturbide into the shadows of oblivion. Mark my words, Carlos, there are evil days ahead for Mexico."

"Your words do not cheer me on this night before Christmas, Ramón. There is a sickness in my heart. I do not have the zest for this struggle for independence which I brought to Mexico City when I was granted an audience with Colonel Agustín de Iturbide."

Again Ramón Santoriaga put his arm around Carlos's shoulders. Consolingly he murmured, "Patience, amigo. It is possible that a man may overreach himself if his ambitions are too selfish, and one day Santa Anna will do just that. Meanwhile, you and I are soldiers, and we obey. However, I have this good news for you. An hour ago, Santa Anna told me that he plans to return to Mexico City. He is anxious to present his report to our leader. At least, that is what he says. What he means, only the future will tell us."

The holidays had come and gone, and it was a time of great distress for the young lieutenant. Indeed, Carlos would have been still more disconsolate if he had known of the gala Christmas fiesta at the Hacienda del Halcón. There had been music, with Esteban Morales playing his flute, two *trabajadores* playing violins, and Miguel himself playing the guitar and calling out the dances. There was a steady *procesión morisca*, where dancers in two lines outside the church come together, bow ceremoniously, hold hands, and twirl each other slowly and sedately, then separate again. Miguel followed his beautiful yellow-haired wife as she danced with Don Diego de Escobar, and he winked at her and blew her a kiss with two fingers, yet without missing a note.

Tiá Margarita had outdone herself, and there were delicacies for everyone, as well as little decorated cakes for all of the children. And finally, Jorge Pastronaz gave a mass of thanksgiving for the bounty of *el Señor Dios* on Christmas Eve, Christmas morning, and just before midnight on the eve of the new year.

As the company of soldiers to which Carlos and Ramón Santoriaga were attached made its way back toward Mexico City, there was a bite in the January air, and the rocky landscape all around them looked bleak and desolate.

On a Thursday morning in the last week of January 1822, Colonel Santa Anna held court in his tent. There were two accusations of rape, brought by the elderly *alcalde* of the little village near where the troops had camped for three days and nights. Santa Anna summarily dismissed these charges and sternly warned the elderly man that the women of his village had practically flung themselves at the liberators. "If you seek redress in money or goods because of the immodesty of your *mujeres, amigo*," he avowed, "you will be liable to a charge of treason. You cannot expect to profit from, or exploit, these gallant men who protect your province and keep careful watch that the *americanos* do not menace your safety here. I have nothing more to say to you."

But there was another case that was brought before the opportunistic military leader; the accused man, a soldier, was marched in to face the baleful, tall, clean-shaven Santa Anna. The man's name was Bartoloméo Mirada, a burly, squat man in his mid-thirties, with a thick mustache and shaggy beard. He had twice been reduced from corporal to private on the grounds of intoxication and also because he failed to salute an officer. This time the charge was more serious: sleeping on sentry duty.

Santa Anna scowled at the document before him on the table, considered the burly culprit, and then drawled, "*Soldado*, is there any reason why I should not send you to the firing squad? You've been remiss in your duties. It's true we're not at war, but if we had been attacked and you had been the sleeping sentry, I myself should have taken a *pistola* and shot you down then and there without a trial."

The accused soldier glanced nervously at the two guards who flanked him, then leaned forward and wheedlingly replied, "I ask only a moment alone with you, *mi gran coronel*."

"If you mean to plead for your life and use excuses that I have heard a thousand times before, you waste my time as well as your own. Ask rather to have a priest shrive you, and that I will grant, for I am in the mood to sentence you to death at once," Santa Anna brusquely replied.

"But I have information that would be very valuable to you, *mi gran coronel*," the man insisted, his eyes wide and moist with a growing terror.

"Very well. Guards, go outside my tent and wait until I summon you back. All right, *soldado*, I shall give you exactly two minutes."

The sweating private exhaled a sigh of vast relief. "*¡Gracias, libertador!*" he gasped, crossing himself.

"Hurry. You waste the two minutes you have by useless flattery. What news do you have that would move me to spare your worthless life, *soldado?*"

"It is like this, *mi coronel*." Bartoloméo Mirada approached the table, gripped it with both hands, and leaned forward in a confidential manner, his words flurried and hoarse because of his terror of the firing squad. He was abjectly pleading for his life, but he was firmly convinced that what he had to offer in return would save it. "Eight years ago, *excelencia*, I entered the private army of Don Felipe de Aranguez, who was then aide to the Viceroy General Calleja."

"That alone does not impress me, *soldado*. You have used up nearly three quarters of a minute. I advise you to be brief and to the point." Santa Anna glowered at him, and then leaned back with a sadistic smirk on his cruelly large, thin-lipped mouth.

"Wait, *mi gran coronel*, I am getting to the point, I swear it! This Don Felipe had a good friend, a *hacendado* named Don Ramón de Costilla. And this *hacendado* owned many fine palominos."

"You begin to bore me, *soldado*. What has this to do with your crime of sleeping at your post?" Santa Anna angrily interposed.

"Please, *excelencia*, I am trying to tell you. You will see, once I have told you—I swear you will, on the grave of my mother!"

"Get on with it, then!"

"Gracias, *mi gran coronel*. Well now, there was a young *americano* who came to the ranch of this Ramón de Costilla and bought some of the horses. And he paid the *hacendado* in bars of pure silver."

Santa Anna's face lost its disdainful look, and he suddenly leaned forward, his eyes glittering. "Pure silver, you said, *soldado?*"

"As I stand here before you, I swear it! The purest of silver."

"Well, go on then, even though I do not yet see the connection."

"I beg of you, have mercy—when I have finished, you'll understand that the news I have for you will make you very rich, perhaps the richest man in all of Mexico!"

"Now that *does* interest me, *soldado*. Very well. You may take the time you need to tell your story—but be quick, man, be quick! I have duties to do, orders to give."

"*Sí, sí,* I will, I will! Now, *excelencia,* Don Felipe believed that the *americano* had found some secret treasure—he had said nothing to the *hacendado,* but Don Felipe instructed all of us—I told you that I was in the army eight years ago, remember—and he rode out to Taos to attack the *hacienda* where this *americano* lived. And this *gringo* was married to the *hija* of Don Diego de Escobar, who was then the *intendente* of Taos."

"I begin to understand a little of what you are trying to tell me, *soldado.*"

"Well, Don Felipe told us that we must attack the *hacienda* of this *americano*. But they were waiting for us, and they had the help of the Apache. Many men died in that raid, but I escaped, though I was wounded in the leg."

"But I still do not know where this treasure is, nor do I know how your news makes me rich, as you flatteringly try to make me believe."

Mirada was almost babbling in his frantic terror. "As a soldier for Don Felipe, you understand, *excelencia,* I obeyed his orders faithfully. We rode against this *hacienda,* and many of us were killed because the *americano* had already planned a defense against our attack. He had the Apache on the rooftops, and they killed us without mercy before we could find them. Don Felipe himself was killed, as I am told, but I had ridden off to the Sangre de Cristo Mountains sometime before that, as had a few of my companions who had not already been wounded or killed by the crossfire when we attacked."

"Get on with it, *hombre!* What is this treasure, and where is it?" Santa Anna impatiently demanded, hammering his fist on the table.

"You have a *teniente* who leads us, *excelencia.* I swear on the grave of my mother that he belonged to the *hacienda* that we attacked."

"A *tentiente,* you say? Whom do you mean by that?"

"It is Teniente Carlos de Escobar, *excelencia.*"

"A thousand *diablos* out of hell!" Santa Anna swore, his face twisted with rancor and malice. "And now I begin to understand you, *soldado*. You were driven off from finding the treasure, but you are ready to swear that you know Teniente Carlos de Escobar to be part of the household against which your former *patrón* directed his attack?"

"*Sí, sí*, what I am trying to tell you, *excelencia*," Mirada gasped as he took a bandanna from the pocket of his britches and nervously mopped his sweating forehead, "is that the *americano* and your *teniente* knew each other well, lived there together at the *hacienda*. They are brothers-in-law, and surely the *teniente* knows of the treasure of the *americano*."

"I see," Santa Anna pursed his lips and rested his chin on his left palm as he considered the sweating, nervous private. "And what makes you think there is treasure for my taking, *soldado*?"

"Because of what Don Felipe told us before we began the attack, *excelencia!* He said that his friend, Ramón de Costilla, had never before in all his life seen such pure silver cast into a heavy bar. And Don Felipe told us that he was convinced there were many more where that had come from, and that, if we caught the *americano*, we were to make him tell us where the rest could be found. But, alas, we had no chance. And Don Felipe himself was killed in a duel with this *americano*."

"Hmm, extremely interesting, *soldado*. And you are ready to swear on the holy book that this treasure which your *patrón* Don Felipe sought truly exists, and that my *teniente* must surely know of it?" Santa Anna pursued, his eyes avariciously glowing.

"By my hope for paradise, *excelencia!*"

"You have given me something to think about. It is good to lead the soldiers of an army, but it's even more important to be able to pay them. I count on General Iturbide's grant from the treasury in Mexico City to advance the wages of all your *compañeros*. Pure silver, in heavy bars, you tell me! And you say that my *teniente* is the friend and brother-in-law of the man who bought the palominos from Don Felipe's good friend and paid him with this fine silver?"

"It is true, I swear it, I wouldn't lie to you now, *excelencia!*" Mirada babbled, again crossing himself to show his feverish earnestness.

"I see. Yes, it's very possible my idealistic young *teniente* knows more than he has ever told me. Very well, *soldado*. I shall spare your life this time. But you'll have no more furloughs till the end of the year, *¿comprendes?* And I myself will see to it that you are given sentry duty for the next seven nights—and if I just once catch you sleeping, the firing squad will be called."

"Let the mind of your *excelencia* be at rest; it will not happen. I will be the most obedient and attentive of your *soldados!*" Mirada abjectly pleaded.

"Very well now, you may go. Tell the guards that I have instructed you to return to your quarters. The charges against you will be dropped—till I can personally investigate your story. And if it turns out that you have lied to me to save your life, *soldado,* you will wish a thousand times you had never been born."

"*¡Gracias, mi gran coronel!*" Bartoloméo Mirada saluted smartly and then left the tent, uttering another loud sigh of feverish relief.

Santa Anna sat back and lit a *cigarillo*. His eyes narrowed as he pondered on what the private had told him. And then abruptly he clapped his hands, and the two guards entered. "I have an assignment for you, *hombres*. From this moment on, I assign you to follow Teniente Carlos de Escobar. You will report to me as regularly as you can as to his activities, any journeys he makes, and if you are bright enough to overhear, what words he chooses in talking to this friend of his, Colonel Ramón Santoriaga. You will apprise me of any such conversations, is that understood?"

The two guards smartly saluted, then wheeled and left their colonel.

Santa Anna puffed at his *cigarillo* for a time, deep in thought. Then, rising from his chair, he went outside his tent and clapped his hands again. His orderly, Sergeant Julio Pérez, appeared at once before him, stiff and attentive.

"Go find the Teniente Carlos de Escobar, *mi sargento,*" Santa Anna purred. Then, watching the sergeant hasten off, he dropped the *cigarillo* and crushed it under his booted heel, a cruel little smile creasing his lips. The information he had just received might be false, but if it was the truth, then he stood on the threshold of becoming enviably rich and powerful. Yes, powerful enough to supplant even the acclaimed Iturbide!

A few mintues later, Carlos de Escobar, with the punctil-

ious sergeant at his side, approached his commanding officer
and saluted.

"Come in, *mi teniente*," Santa Anna invited. "*Sargento*
find some tequila and some of your best cigars."

"At once, *mi coronel!*" the sergeant deferentially ex
claimed.

"Make yourself comfortable, Teniente de Escobar. Yes
yes, sit down! Well now, you have done well on this cam
paign, I tell you this personally."

"I am honored," Carlos tersely retorted, stiffly sitting
before the bemedallioned, garishly uniformed commander.

"Come now, I suspend all rank between us. We are
friends, Carlos—may I call you thus?"

"You do me too much honor."

"Only what you deserve. Coronel Santoriaga has spoken
highly of you. And he reports directly to our great liberator
You have before you an unlimited chance at a military career
that may carry you to the very summit of rank and public
acclamation."

"I do not seek any ambitious post; I joined this army to
help free Mexico," was Carlos's noncommittal reply.

"You are one of these dreamers, but that is not to say
you are wrong. I admire you, Carlos de Escobar. It is true
that you have given me some concern because you seem not
quite cold-blooded enough to act in times of emergency. But
then I told myself that you have been with us only a limited
time."

"I should like to ask what you desire of me," Carlos
said.

Santa Anna stroked his cheek and chin, studying the
handsome young man before him. Then he smiled ingrati
atingly. "We have come upon a difficult time, *mi teniente*
Thus far we have accomplished the independence of Mexico
with little bloodshed. That is my wish—yet I know that
because you are very sensitive, you did not take kindly to
seeing the execution of the *americanos*."

Carlos flushed hotly, lowered his eyes, and bit his lips,
but said nothing.

"Come now, we are friends, you and I. I told you that I
had suspended all rank between us for now. Trust me. But
listen carefully. You are the son of a hidalgo, a man who was
once of great importance at the Escorial. Today, Spain no
longer exists for us who love our country of Mexico. And I
am sure that your father, as your mother—"

"I ask your pardon, *mi coronel,* but my mother died before my father and my sister and I left Spain," Carlos interrupted.

"I see, I see. Well now, do you still believe in our cause of liberating all Mexico, of helping the poor, of making this land rich and self-sufficient unto itself?"

"That is the cause which motivated me to join the army, *mi coronel,*" Carlos responded. He sat stiffly, not certain where this discussion was leading, but his personal aversion to the sensual opportunist was becoming increasingly hard to conceal.

"We have broken off all ties with Spain, *mi teniente.* But to run a government, we shall need money. Yet both His Excellency Agustín de Iturbide and I believe that through the enthusiastic and voluntary contributions of those who agree with our cause, as well as what revenues we can derive from the provinces, we shall be able to create a solvent government, where all men are equal."

"It is my sincere hope that you will achieve as much, *mi coronel.*"

"Exactly. But because we have not yet declared a Constitution, or had it ratified by any *junta,* we are still far from our objective. I am told, *mi teniente,* that you have in your knowledge the existence of a source of great revenue that would be priceless to us who seek freedom for our beleaguered country."

Carlos considered his interlocutor with a suspicious gaze. "I do not quite follow Your Excellency," he hazarded.

"I shall spell it out for you, *mi teniente.* It was brought to my attention that you know of the existence of a great deal of pure silver. If that metal were turned over to our cause, it would make us certain victors, and there would be no bloodshed, and our government could sustain itself. As one patriot to another, Carlos de Escobar, I entreat you to tell me what you know of this deposit of the precious metal. If you know your history, you will recall that the great Philip of Spain, well before he launched the ill-fated Armada against England, colonized the America of the South and, in such regions as Panama, sought to bring back tithes which would make the nation rich and strong. The English freebooters put an end to this. But here in this new world, I have learned that there is wealth beyond the dreams of that great Philip. And it is you, *mi teniente,* who can help me locate this fortune, and thus assure freedom to the needy and the oppressed."

Carlos lowered his eyes, thinking swiftly. Miguel Sandarbal had told him how John Cooper had purchased the palominos by the "accident" of digging up bars of silver. Beyond that, he knew nothing. But it was strange that Santa Anna should speak so knowingly, as if there were far more silver than even his own brother-in-law had told him. He became naturally suspicious and, as the eyes of Santa Anna narrowed and fixed upon him, finally hedged, "I assure you I know nothing more, except that my *cuñado* told me that, quite by accident, he had found some raw silver and that he had bought horses with it. And that truly is all I know, *mi coronel.*"

Santa Anna rose from the table, thrusting his right fist into his left palm and scowling. "You are an officer under my immediate command, Teniente Carlos de Escobar. This time I will reintroduce the rank between us, since it seems that you are not being honest with me."

"But I know nothing, truly, *mi coronel!*" Carlos protested.

"I shall let that pass. You may know more than you think—that is to say, an idealist does not always think of material things, but I assure you, *mi teniente,* that I do. We need *dinero* to sustain our cause and to make certain that the old regime of Spanish domination never returns to us."

"That is of course my hope."

"Good! In that event, your withholding from me information that would strengthen our independence would not be kindly taken, Teniente Carlos de Escobar. I warn you now that you must be as honest with me as I am with you. If this hoard of silver—and understand that I know only what I have been told, so that I cannot be specific—if this hoard of silver is known to you, and it has no legitimate owner, it is your duty as a patriot to divulge its whereabouts to me."

Carlos trembled with nervousness, for this interview was becoming irksome, and the underlying threat of Santa Anna's tone was so obvious that he could not overlook it. It confirmed exactly what Ramón Santoriaga had intimated to him, that the man before him, the hope of all Mexico, was not an eagle who would soar to the heavens, but rather a vulture who would be little more than a scavenger and would leave grief, death, and misery in his wake.

"Well then, I cannot read your mind, *mi teniente,*" Santa Anna concluded. "But if upon sober reflection, you can remember more than you have already told me, I urge you, in all honesty and patriotism, to share the secret with me. You would share with me the cheers of the populace; you would look back and you could tell even your grandchildren that you had been of prime importance in defending Mexico and strengthening it in its struggles for independence."

"I will think on what you have said to me tonight, *mi coronel*. May I ask a favor?"

"But of course. I have no fault to find with you, understand this at the outset. It is only my burning desire to liberate Mexico for my commander, Agustín de Iturbide, that leads me to press you to reveal all that you know and perhaps even what you do not know. Please believe me in this." Again Santa Anna smiled ingratiatingly.

"I should like to request leave, because as you well know, *mi coronel*, I have had no leave whatsoever since I joined the army of the liberation. I should like to go home, to see my children and my father and my stepmother, yes, and my sister."

"Certainly! You have earned it. Consider yourself furloughed as of this moment, *mi teniente*. And when you return, we shall talk again, *¿no es verdad?*"

Carlos felt himself tremble as he rose from his chair and tendered the smirking Santa Anna an impeccably impersonal salute. Then he left the tent and went directly to his own. There, his orderly, a private in his mid-twenties, effusively greeted him: "Does *mi teniente* wish some wine before he goes to sleep?"

"No, gracias, Eduardo. I wish only to go to sleep. It has been a trying day. By the way, I have just been given furlough by Colonel Santa Anna. I shall leave early in the morning, but there is nothing you need do. I can saddle my own horse, so I bid you sleep and wait until I return. Have no fear, I shall commend you to my commanding officer."

Thirty-one

The dreams of freedom and equality that had inspired many young idealists began to fade in the face of continued oppression and opportunism. And by now, Iturbide himself had begun to believe that his intrepid military commander in the field was a dangerous self-seeker whose campaign had won much popular favor.

Meanwhile, beyond the Texas border, the young United States had begun to experience its own turbulent struggle for a different kind of freedom. In Charleston, South Carolina, a freed black, Denmark Vesey, had led a slave insurrection that was soon crushed, resulting in a tyrannical system of slave control throughout the South.

And in this same year, Boston capitalists founded the town of Lowell, Massachusetts, on the Merrimack River, and established a cotton textile factory that would depend on the cotton-producing South for its profits. At the same time, James Monroe was about to recognize the Latin American republics in this, the second year of his second term as President of the pioneering young nation.

Far removed from all these events, Carlos de Escobar packed his gear and told his friend Ramón Santoriaga he had earned a furlough and that he expected to return to his duties by the end of February.

The sympathetic young colonel took him off to one side, and said softly, "A word of warning, *amigo*. Only the other day, Colonel Santa Anna invited me to his tent, served some of his finest wine, and asked me my opinion of your character."

"He did that?" Carlos arched his eyebrows and then gripped the colonel's wrist. "I begin to feel as if I'm in a kind of nightmare, Ramón. Do you know that he questioned me at great length about a treasure?"

"Treasure?" his friend echoed. "That was not part of my own discussion with our commanding officer. Explain yourself, Carlos."

"It's a long story, Ramón, and I shan't annoy you with it, only to say that I do not know anything about it."

"I hear you, *mi compañero*. But I have learned this much of our heroic commander: when one talks of *dinero* or beautiful women, he is all attention. He covets these for his own possession, and unless I am greatly mistaken, he values the former above all else. With money, don't you understand, Carlos, Santa Anna could dare to overthrow our liberator."

"Do you think he would do that?" Carlos gasped.

"I do. And when I reach Mexico City, I intend to tell General Iturbide that he has a great deal to fear from Santa Anna and very little to gain. I shall say also that it is wise for him to strike while the iron is hot and to make himself head of our new, young nation. Because if he does not, Carlos, I'm convinced now that Santa Anna will proclaim himself the true liberator of all Mexico, and there will be those who are duped into believing such braggadocio."

"Do you have any idea where Santa Anna will be by the time my furlough is over?"

"I only know that he marches slowly toward Mexico City. You will find us, though, never fear. But be careful. Keep your eyes open, and if you camp near any village where Spanish is spoken, keep your own council and do not reveal where it is you go."

"Yes, you are right. I am certain Santa Anna understands that I would try to go to my father, to my stepmother, and my sister—and also to my dearest friend, my brother-in-law. So I will be very cautious, and will watch behind me on the trail."

The colonel nodded without a word and gripped his hand in friendship. *"Vaya con Dios, mi compañero.* I shall say prayers for your safe return."

Thus it was that Carlos de Escobar, with a sense of burning anticipation and almost impatient eagerness, rode Dolor northward toward the Hacienda del Halcón. He could now see clearly that his overwhelming, self-centered grief had made him blind to all else. And that was why he longed to shorten the miles between himself and his family, especially the *americano*, who was not only his brother-in-law, but also the man who had saved his life and brought him to unexpected happiness and fulfillment.

Santa Anna's interest in this mysterious treasure puzzled him. He remembered what John Cooper had told him about the ingots that had been found in the shed. And yet surely there must be more to it than that. Perhaps John Cooper had found much more than what he had paid for the palomino from Don Ramón de Costilla.

He would ask Catarina. She, his playmate from childhood, and he, her cavalier since their earliest years together, were closer even than he was to John Cooper. And since she was beloved of John Cooper, she would doubtless know more than he himself possibly could. Yes, it would be Catarina whom he would ask.

And if she did tell about the treasure, what then? He would certainly have to inform Santa Anna about it. Or would he? Perhaps the one he should confide in was General Iturbide. Then he would be sure the great wealth, if there was indeed any, could be used for the right purposes, the cause for which he had left his family and friends. Yes, that was it! He would seek out the treasure, tell Santa Anna that the rumors had been false, and then follow his unit the rest of the way to Mexico City, where he would seek out General Iturbide and tell him the news. It was a dangerous scheme, to be sure, and once Santa Anna learned of his lieutenant's perfidy, he would become his enemy for life, but by then he would be under Iturbide's protection.

Now remembering his conversation with Ramón Santoriaga, Carlos halted Dolor from time to time and looked warily back, but he saw no one.

Yet behind him, some twenty miles to the south, the two guards whom Santa Anna had assigned to follow him rode without haste. They were cousins, in their early thirties, Mateo Consuegro, and Paco Olivera. Both were corporals though for this mission, they disguised themselves as *peones*, with sombreros and ponchos. Santa Anna had intimated that if they tracked the young lieutenant and induced him to reveal the mysterious cache of silver, they would both be prompted to *subteniente*. Moreover, they would be able to choose among the *mujeres* of those villages which Santa Anna would subjugate to the rule of independence. And he would even see to it that they received a stipend, a kind of lavish pension.

And thus it was that, his heart growing ever more joyous, Carlos headed for the Frio River and the Hacienda del Halcón.

As he neared the huge estate set in the fertile valley, and saw the landmarks of trees and river and hills, there were tears in his eyes. The lacerating memory of Weesayo made his lips tighten as he said a prayer inwardly for her soul.

Then, only a mile or two away from his reunion, he halted Dolor and began to plan what to do. First, he must arrange to meet Catarina in secret, and talk with her about this treasure and determine exactly how much she knew. If John Cooper were present, it would be awkward. No, he must somehow contrive to get to her before anyone else in the *hacienda* knew that he had returned on a furlough.

The sun was setting as he slowly directed Dolor toward the *hacienda* from the southwest. He realized there would be *trabajadores* in the fields. Perhaps he could intercept one and ask him to bring Catarina out to meet him here on the grazing land.

Luck was with him. There were a dozen workers in the fields, most of them mounted on horseback, supervising the placid grazing of the herds of sheep and cattle. He pulled the visor of his helmet down over his forehead to disguise himself, and, erect in the saddle, rode now quickly toward one of the gray-haired *trabajadores* who, puffing his pipe and seated on a tree stump, was watching the sheep. He recognized the man, Tomás Noradiara, and rode straight toward the sheepherder, who had his back to him.

"¿Qué pasa?—¡hola! A *soldado*—you startled me—wait now—your face looks familiar—"

"Shh, *amigo.*" Carlos put a warning finger to his lips. "I beg of you, *por favor*, Tomás, go find Señora Catarina and tell her that her *hermano* is here. But be certain that no one else hears you. Do me this favor, Tomás. You see, I want to surprise her. I have special news for her."

"Of course, young master! I will go at once. You will wait here?"

"Sí. And make certain that she does not tell anyone else that I am waiting for her here, ¿comprendes?"

The gray-haired sheepherder nodded and then hurried toward the *hacienda.* Carlos dismounted, holding the reins of Dolor and watching the sheep graze. Wryly, he thought to himself how simple it would be to be a four-legged animal, who had no interest in history or politics or revolution. He now turned toward the *hacienda,* several hundred yards away, and he saw his sister emerge, her cape around her shoulders, talking animatedly to Tomás, who gestured toward him.

He saw his sister glance back at the *hacienda,* and then begin to quicken her footsteps. He took a step forward, waiting, his heart pounding with joy. *Dios,* how he missed everyone here, and all the more now that he knew that he had chased a will-o'-the-wisp instead of the lofted banner of freedom.

"Carlos, *mi* Carlos," Catarina sobbed as she ran toward him. As the cape fell partly away from her, he could see that she was with child. And he put out a hand and compassionately exclaimed, "Do not hurry, *querida!* Oh, you don't know how glad I am to see you, Catarina, sweet little sister!"

She flung her arms around him and kissed him, and he wept, unable to suppress the long, pent-up emotions that surged within him all the weary, long miles across the Rio Grande to this blessed sanctuary—for such it was. Here there were no soldiers, only the beauty of the trees and the grass, the river and the sky, and the placid life of the sheepherder and the *vaqueros,* and the laughter of children, and the love betwen man and woman, and—

"Carlos, why did you ask Tomás to have me come out here alone? You can't know how much everyone in the *hacienda* wants to see you—most of all our father and, of course, Doña Inez!" Catarina exclaimed.

"Are they all well?" Carlos asked.

"Yes, they are well, but you have not answered my question. Why did I have to come out here alone to see you?"

"Listen, *querida.* This is very important. I'll return home soon enough, but first there are some important things I must ask you. Do you remember when John Cooper bought those palominos with bars of silver?"

"I think so. Why do you ask me this, Carlos?"

"Is John Cooper in the *hacienda?*"

"Yes, he was talking to Don Diego when I came out of my room after Tomás had come to find me."

"I see." Carlos frowned and pondered for a moment. "I must be honest with you Catarina. As you can see, I'm an officer in the army of freedom for Mexico. But we are poor, because we are not under the thumb of the *ricos* and the *hacendados.* So I said to myself that the sweet little sister I grew up with, whom I defended from that lizard when we rode from Mexico City to Taos to begin all over again, surely she would tell me the truth about the silver. It's most important, I swear it."

"Carlos, I can see how you've suffered. You're thinner, yes." She put out a hand to touch his cheek and uttered a little sob. "And we've missed you so, you'll never know how often we've talked at the table of you and wished that you were back home with us."

"Of course, dear Catarina. But please, if you love me, Catarina, tell me all you know."

"Is it really so important?"

"More than you know. If the money can be given to free the poor, the helpless *peones* and the starving mothers I saw when I rode to Mexico City to join the army, then it will make up for what I myself could not do."

"Listen—John Cooper took me back to the stronghold for our second honeymoon—"

"Yes, I remember that."

"—But before we went back to Taos, he rode to a mountain, quite a distance from the Apache stronghold. And he told me that he had found a treasure not only of holy relics, but also of much *dinero*. He did not tell me everything, but he did tell me this and made me promise that I would keep the secret."

"Can you tell me where this mountain is, *querida?*"

"Let me think." She closed her eyes and frowned, trying to remember. "It was to the south of the stronghold, and it was a very tall mountain and strangely by itself, with almost nothing around it. I remember that because it looked so imposing, so tremendously tall."

"Yes, I have an idea where it might be. Now listen, little sister, I must go there—"

"But Carlos, you must come to the house now! It would be cruel not to see your father and Doña Inez—"

"Hush, dear Catarina. I am under orders. Until I fulfill them, I can't come back. Trust me. You must trust me, Catarina. I'm going to go there now. I'm going to try to find that treasure and see if I can help free Mexico and give the poor families and the starving ones, the mothers and children, the old people, some little help. If there is treasure there, surely there's enough to share with these unfortunates. And now, Catarina, don't tell anyone. I promise I'll be back as soon as I've done what I have to do."

He kissed her and then mounted Dolor and rode off.

Catarina stood irresolute, tears in her eyes. She remembered all too clearly how John Cooper had told her that this secret should be shared with no one else, not even her father.

Suddenly with a cry of anguish, she called to the old sheepherder, "Tomás, Tomás, get me my mare! Go to the stable quickly, saddle it, bring it to me—don't tell a soul, please, Tomás, I forgot to tell Carlos something very important!"

Tomás shook his head, then shrugged and began to hurry back toward the stable. Catarina was trembling as she waited. The thought that she had betrayed her husband's trust pierced her like a sharp thorn, and she groaned aloud in her dilemma. She must overtake Carlos, tell him that she had made a mistake, that it was a different mountain, that actually she really wasn't sure where the treasure was ... *Oh, Dios, I must think of something that will make him believe me and not go to the mountain I described,* she told herself with growing desperation. *Oh, where is that stupid sheepherder— ah, thank God, he is coming at last!*

"*Gracias, viejo!*" she gasped as she hurried to take the mare's reins. "You needn't help me—go back to your flock, and remember, not a word to anyone, *por favor!*"

"*Sí, señora,*" he said, and then went off, mumbling to himself. *Aiii,* young people cared nothing for an old man's tired bones. All this haste, and why was it so important he tell no one? Sometimes there was no understanding people.

Catarina gritted her teeth as she hoisted herself into the saddle. Her advanced pregnancy made her feel awkward and cumbersome. *Santa María,* she prayed as she kicked her heel against her mare's belly, *do not let Coop's child be harmed because I try to ride like a man—I must, to overtake Carlos! Aid me, Holy Mother, and forgive my sin of betrayal—I thought only of poor Carlos and his suffering!*

As she arched back in the saddle, trying to ease the strain on her abdomen, she clenched her teeth as a wave of nausea seized her and her face was drenched with sweat. *Oh, Blessed Virgin, give me strength, do not let the baby be hurt by what I must do—understand my need, Madre de Piedad! I pray to you for forgiveness; grant me this one mercy!*

But already darkness was falling. Straining her eyes, she could barely see the tiny receding figure of Carlos's mustang, or the tracks of its hooves. It was useless—she could never overtake him now. And to go on might harm the unborn child, and that would be by far the most unpardonable sin of all.

Catarina wept aloud in the stillness of the swiftly engulfing night as, with a groan of despair, she turned the mare's head back to the *hacienda* and let it take an ambling pace. Her lips moved in anguished, silent prayer, first for the safety of the child within her, then for her husband's forgiveness, for she must tell him how she had broken her solemn pledge.

Thirty-two

The two corporals whom Santa Anna had sent to follow Carlos de Escobar had watched the meeting between him and his sister from a distance of a quarter of a mile away while hiding behind the screen of a copse of spruce trees. They had seen him ride off and had been aghast when they saw the young woman take the horse from the old sheepherder and begin to ride after him. Their relief was enormous when Caterina finally turned her horse and returned to the *hacienda;* they certainly had no need of the presence of a young woman to complicate their pursuit.

But now Mateo Consuegro voiced another concern, and tugging at his goatee, the corporal swore under his breath. "Damnation! In the darkness, we might lose his trail!"

"Not very likely," Paco observed. "It'll be night soon, and he's certain to make camp somewhere. And we'll see his fire, if he does."

"Come to think of it," Mateo grumbled, "we didn't take enough provisions with us from that last little village we stopped at."

"Be of good heart, *hombre*," Paco genially chuckled. "If we trace the *teniente* to his treasure and tell our illustrious *coronel* where it is, we'll have *dinero y mujeres*, and we can buy the finest food and tequila in all of Mexico."

They spurred their horses and rode northwest at a gallop, not so much wanting to overtake Carlos, as to stay within good tracking distance of him.

As the moon rose, Carlos glanced up at the sky and saw the twinkling stars. Far beyond was this mountain, the moun-

tain with the treasure of which Catarina had told him. A
treasure that would, Santa Anna had insisted, relieve the
poverty of the poorest villagers, and bring peace to a country
which would at last know its independence, just as the
Estados Unidos had done.

But Santa Anna would never know of the treasure. If it
belonged to anyone, it belonged to the people of Mexico, and
there seemed to be only one person who would give it to
them: General Iturbide.

He looked back over his shoulder, but the *hacienda* had
long since been engulfed in darkness. He felt momentary
qualms at having ridden off without at least seeing his father
and Doña Inez and, of course, John Cooper and his children.
Yes, and his own little son, Diego, named after his beloved
father and probably growing like a weed. And sweet Inez and
also little Dawn, the lastborn of his Weesayo—

There was a lump in his throat, and tears sprang into his
eyes as her name came back to him. During the long
campaign that took them over dusty, obscure little roads and
into even more obscure villages and hamlets, he had fought to
clear his mind of the memory of that night of horror. But the
brief, stolen moment with Catarina near the *hacienda* had
recalled his grief with a terrible freshness and gnawing
despair. How lonely he had become, with only a commission
and his fine uniform, giving orders to troops that very often
went against his very grain. What was the cause for which he
had gone to Mexico City to fight—was it really to be on the
side of those who rebelled against tyranny, brutality, and the
inhuman contempt for the have-nots? Or, in reality, had it not
been because he knew of no other way in which to assuage
his dreadful loss, the sudden shattering of the blissful life he
had known with that gentle Apache girl?

Now he knew, and could hear the bells of their secret
wickiup ringing in his ears, an illusion that made him rein in
Dolor and bow his head and give vent to a terrible fit of
weeping. And there was silence in the night around him, not
even the howling of a wolf or the baying of a coyote, not even
the twittering of night birds to take him out of this engulf-
ment of black despair. The wound had reopened, and the
pangs were torturing.

With an effort, Carlos drew a long breath and headed
Dolor onward. Catarina had told him that this isolated
mountain was to the south in the range in which the Jicarilla
Apache dwelt. And as he remembered the country she had

described, he figured that from the Hacienda de Halcón it would take almost two weeks' journey to get there.

Carlos was weary with fatigue, and wearier still in heart and soul, as he rode through the night, his face grim and unrelenting. He did not even stop for food or water till it was well after midnight. And then at last, when his muscles ached so intolerably that he knew it would be folly to ride on, he dismounted. The mustang, so much his faithful friend and companion during all these lonely months away from the Hacienda del Halcón, turned to nicker at him and then to brush his shoulder with its muzzle. He turned to Dolor, gently stroking the mustang's head and nose. "*Amigo,* you know what I feel, don't you? You're dearer to me than Valor was—may that gallant horse forgive my saying so. How faithful you've been all these months over all those winding roads, over hills and through desert, in the worst of weather. And you've never complained. One could ask no more of a comrade in battle than you've given me, Dolor. *Gracias, amigo.*"

He tied Dolor's reins to the stump of an old fir tree that had been shattered by lightning. And then, opening his saddlebag, he contented himself with a handful of dried corn, a sack of which he had purchased from an old woman in a little village some twenty miles southeast of the Hacienda del Halcón. He ate, also, two strips of jerky and drank water from his canteen, which he had filled at the Frio River before skirting the *hacienda* and sending the old sheepherder in to bring Catarina to him. Then, wrapping himself in his blanket, for the night air was chilly, he flung himself down on a patch of bare ground and fell fast asleep.

Mateo and Paco, seeing no campfire, rode slowly now, not wishing yet to come upon their quarry till he had led them to the treasure. Along the way, the two corporals passed the time speculating on how vast this treasure could be. Mateo was of the opinion that there might be a cave in which there was a chest left by some rich hidalgo who had come to this isolated land perhaps even a century ago. And again, there might be jewels, a king's ransom.

"If we find it, might we not help ourselves to a few pieces here and there, and a handful of the golden coins?" he hazarded to his companion.

"Do you wish to stand before a firing squad, *amigo?*" Paco remonstrated. Then he insinuated in a hoarse whisper, "We'd have to kill the *teniente,* so he wouldn't report us, if we did that, Mateo. But if there really is a chest full of gold and jewels, no one would be the wiser if we hid a little of it in our saddlebags."

"That's understood. We'll wait and see where the *teniente* takes us."

"What if he doesn't take us there?"

"Wait until the time comes, *amigo*. Then we'll decide what to do. Anyway, I'm aching from so many hours in the saddle. I think we can take a chance on sleeping a few hours. We'll do it in shifts. You wake me in three hours, and I'll do the same for you."

"Agreed, *amigo*." The two men tethered their horses to the branches of nearby trees, took out their blankets, and Mateo appropriated for himself the privilege of first sleep, while Paco stood guard.

An hour after dawn, refreshed and eager for the pursuit, they mounted their horses and rode slowly to the northwest. With the light of day, they could follow the tracks left by Dolor and congratulated themselves upon not having lost the man they had been sent to follow.

Lagging behind him at about a five-mile distance, Mateo and Paco grew impatient, as the second day gave way to the third, and the third to the fourth, until more than a week had passed. Their own provisions had almost run out, since they had eaten rather lavishly of what they had brought, not expecting so prolonged a journey. And Carlos had set a blistering pace, sleeping only a few hours a day. Fortunately, Mateo's skill with the knife enabled him to bring down a fat jackrabbit which, not afraid of him, had disdained to run for cover when they had come upon it. Mateo had at first reached for his musket, but Paco had grasped his wrist and shaken his head: "No, idiot! Don't you think the *teniente* will hear the sound of the shot? It will carry in this air, and he knows there is no hunter around. It will put him on his guard, and then he may try to outdistance us. Use your knife, *hombre!*"

Finally, toward sunset of the twelfth day, Carlos de Escobar halted his exhausted mustang and stared at the lofty peak of the isolated mountain. There could be no doubt of it now; it was as Catarina had described it. But she had given him no clue as to where the treasure could be hidden. Dolor had bowed his head and was snuffling from fatigue. A sudden wave of contrition came to the young Spaniard, and he stroked the mustang's neck, murmuring, "I shouldn't have taxed you like this, Dolor. It was much longer than I thought it could be. We'll rest this evening; and tomorrow, while you wait here, I'll try to climb that mountain."

By now his sack of dried corn was nearly empty, and there were only two strips of jerky left. In another, larger bag, he had brought along oats for the mustang, and he gave Dolor a generous portion, saving some for the next day.

Once again, wrapping himself in his blanket, he slept. But this time it was not a sleep born out of exhaustion, but one fraught with strange images, inexplicable dreams. He dreamed that he stood on the top of this mountain, with the wind blowing furiously against him, and that the sky was dark and ominous and was suddenly cleft asunder by a jagged bolt of lightning. And that there was a rumble of thunder and suddenly, inexplicably, the sun shone down upon him, bathing him in warm, beneficent rays. And a voice came to him, a soft, gentle voice that he knew and that made him tremble, even as he slept, for it was that of his dead wife, Weesayo.

And he heard her words as distinctly as if she had been there before him. "*Mi esposo*, the Great Spirit bade me comfort you. I am with Him and with my father. Our spirits are above you, and they cannot be seen by day or night, save in your thoughts. Do not grieve so, for it gives me anguish to know of your sorrow. And yet with it there is joy to know that you love me so, that you still remember and are tormented because I am not with you. Our children have my spirit, *mi corazón*. You must live for them. There will be another one to cherish and to love you, for you are good and honest, and I love you greatly, beyond the dream I had as a maiden of being mated with a brave whose life would be mingled with mine and fulfill me. Do not sorrow too long, for I shall be happy when you are happy, Carlos. And when you feel the rain from heaven, know that my tears are mingled with it, and that, when the sky is blue and the sun shines down upon you and you are happy, I am also. Did not the shaman say that each of us would shelter the other from the wind and the rain and the storm? Think of this, *mi corazón*. Do what is in your heart, be true to yourself, for that is how you won me; that is how I knew that the Great Spirit had sent you to my father's stronghold as my *esposo* long before each of us understood it."

When he woke at dawn the next morning, there was a strange peace in Carlos de Escobar's heart. He rose, and taking a scant handful of corn and a swallow from his canteen, he patted Dolor's neck and stared up at the formidable mountain. And he said to himself, half aloud, "I am near the stronghold. I am near the place where I met her who was my life, the Light of the Mountains. I must go there now, I am driven by her memory. I must see those good people who took me in as a stranger, who made me their blood brother, where I knew peace and joy because she was there."

He stared silently at the mountain again, and then a furious indignation seized him: "No, I will not look for that treasure. It was not meant for one man to have. If John Cooper knew of it and did not use it for himself, surely I shall not betray his trust. He keeps it inviolate for the poor and for those whom I sought to defend as a soldier. Let it be so. But it shall not go to General Iturbide, nor to any of those who hold power, for they only abuse it."

And as he said that to himself, the grief and anguish seemed to vanish, and his eyes sparkled and he straightened his shoulders and smiled for the first time in many weeks. Then, turning to the mustang, he excitedly exclaimed, "We'll go to the stronghold, Dolor! You've never been there, but there's freedom there, and truth and honor. Now I know why John Cooper lived with the Apache and felt such kinship with them. They spoke with a straight tongue, as does he; they did not cheat or lie or steal or try to deceive. What they believed in, you understood at once, for they did not speak of one thing and do another. They are not like Santa Anna, who talks so glowingly of freedom and equality for all men, yet who secretly lusts to lead all others and plunge them into a worse slavery than the poor *peones* knew."

Untying Dolor's reins, he mounted and rode away in the direction of the Sangre de Cristo Mountains and to the stronghold of the Jicarilla Apache.

From a distance of a quarter of a mile, Mateo and Paco had watched the young Spanish officer deliberating with himself. Paco had exclaimed, pointing to the mountain whose peak rose in the distance, "That must be where the treasure is. Wait a bit, he'll take us there."

But when they saw him untie Dolor's reins and mount the mustang and ride off, Mateo swore violently, *"¡Por los cojones del diablo!* Your fine *teniente* is riding away from that mountain. Why did he stay there so long, or can it be that the treasure is hidden somewhere else?"

"I don't know any more than you do, Mateo, and that is why we're going to follow him. And it is high time we both told him that the *comandante* ordered us to make him tell us where this treasure is," Paco abruptly decided.

They rode off toward the east, obliquely, so that Carlos would not see them, but they watched him veer to the northwest once he had skirted the mysterious mountain. Angrily, they followed him, cursing him for having led them on this wild goose chase when they were out of food and exhausted from the lengthy journey. And Mateo growled, "We owe him something, that fine aristocrat of a *teniente*, Paco! We're no nearer the treasure than when we started, and I'm bone-tired into the bargain, and hungry, too!"

"Patience, *mi compañero*," Paco urged. "I hate him as much as you do. But we have our orders, don't forget that. If he tries to trick us, we'll kill him, that's what we'll do. And the *coronel* will reward us for it, you watch and see."

"All the same," Mateo whined, "I'd rather find the treasure first, and then kill him."

"Stay back a little, but don't lose sight of him," Paco urged. "Maybe he stopped at that mountain just to throw us off the track—maybe he's really going to the treasure now. It's possible, you know."

"But he hasn't seen us, or even guessed if we're on his trail, Paco," Mateo irritably complained. "I tell you, when this is over, I am going to go to a *casa de putas* and get drunk for a week and not get out of bed all that time, *¡por todos los santos!*"

"*Caramba*, if this accursed *teniente* keeps on riding, my backside will be so sore from this bony horse that I'll not be able to enjoy a bed, even with a dozen *putas lindas* to look after me," his companion complained.

Carlos de Escobar had given Dolor almost the last of the oats in the sack from his saddlebag, caressing the mustang and assuring him that soon they would be at their destination. Then he rode on toward the Jicarilla Mountains. Now for the first time since he had said good-bye to his father months ago, there was a kind of calm determination in him, a certainty to which he clung, as a drowning man clings to a bit of floatsam to save himself. *The stronghold*: that halcyon place from which one saw the pure beauty of the sky and the sun and the moon and the stars, where the air was clearer and one's thoughts seemed sharper and more defined than anywhere else. The refuge where he had come for the first time with John Cooper and seen that gentle girl emerging from the wickiup. With a sudden illuminating radiance of spirit, he had known that here was the woman he loved, as he had never loved any other.

He leaned eagerly forward in the saddle, as he saw the base of the mountain and perceived in the distance the trail which led around and up its side. There would be sentries there, and they would remember him. He was the blood brother of Weesayo's father and that of Kinotatay, also, for he and his beloved wife had visited the stronghold shortly after their move to Texas, and Carlos had then enacted the bonding ritual with Descontarti's successor. These simple, honest people would set him right again, because here there was no struggle for power, no taint of corruption, no envious lust to be better than one's neighbors. If there was a yearning for superiority, it came only through proving one's service to the tribe. Well, he wore the uniform of the new Mexico, and it represented the cause of freedom.

Dolor seemed to sense his master's galvanized excitement, for he lowered his head and quickened his gait as they approached the beginning of the trail to the stronghold.

Mateo and Paco had begun to gallop their horses to catch up with Carlos. "At last, he's decided where he's going," Mateo exclaimed, pointing to the tiny figure of the mounted young Spaniard beyond them. "He's going to take us to the treasure! Let's hurry, Mateo," Paco excitedly urged, "Let's not lose him now. Damnation, when I think of the trouble this popinjay of a *teniente* has given us, I could cheerfully cut his throat for him."

"You can do that later, after he's shown us where the treasure is," Mateo sniggered, and drew his left forefinger across his throat in a meaningful gesture.

Their flagging horses, spurred on by the two corporals, gave what remaining stamina they had in cutting down the distance between their riders and Carlos.

As Carlos slowly ascended a treacherously steep area in the trail, the two men, now confident they were near the treasure, closed the gap to a few hundred yards. But then Carlos's horse lost its footing on some loose rocks and wheeled around in order to regain its balance. As it did, Carlos spotted the two men.

"¡Aiii, mi amigo!" Mateo exclaimed. "The *teniente*, he sees us, and just when we are near the treasure! Look, he is coming back down the trail to us! ¡Santa María! What are we going to do?"

"Don't worry, I know how to handle the *teniente*," Paco sneered, patting his pistol's butt. "Just shut up and let me do the talking."

Carlos reined in his mustang just in front of the two sheepishly grinning and profusely sweating corporals. "What are you doing here?" he glowered at them. "Have you been following me all this way?"

"*Señor teniente, el gran coronel* ordered us to accompany you to find the treasure. Have you found it yet?" Paco said ingratiatingly as he executed a hasty salute.

"I have nothing to say to you on that score, *hombre,*" Carlos coldly responded.

"But you're going up this trail on this mountain—is that where the treasure really is? You know, we have our orders, and Coronel Santa Anna told us to inform you that he is eager to have this treasure found, so that it can be put into the treasury of the independence." Paco's hand slid stealthily toward his pistol.

"There is no treasure here, *hombre*. This is the stronghold of the Jicarilla Apache. I go to see the chief. Go back to Santa Anna and tell him you have wasted your time. I have not been able to find any treasure, and I shall not look for it. Besides, it is not mine to give him. If God wishes, He will tell Santa Anna where it is," was Carlos's response.

He saw the faces of the men darken with anger, their lips curl with annoyance. With a shrug, he turned back and, spurring on Dolor, resumed his ascent toward the stronghold.

"*¡Hijo de puta, traidor!*" Paco snarled as he tightened his right hand on his holstered pistol, drew it, cocked it, and aimed it at the back of Carlos de Escobar. Grinding his teeth, he pulled the trigger. Carlos stiffened in his saddle, then fell forward on Dolor's neck, limply, without a word. The mustang, frightened, whinnied stridently, and then broke into a gallop up the winding trail.

"The dirty traitor, the bastard," Paco swore as he holstered the smoking pistol. "All this way for nothing. Not a *centavo,* and that means we won't be *subtenientes,* nor have all the women and *dinero el gran coronel* promised us!"

"What do we do now, *amigo?*" Mateo groaned.

"We go back to Santa Anna and tell him that his precious *teniente* is a traitor, and that we served him the way traitors deserve to be served, that's what we do." Paco brightened. "You mark my words, Mateo, we'll be *subteni-*

entes yet because of that. We have done what any good
patriot would do."

"But look, his horse goes on up the trail to the stronghold—he said there were Apache here—we had better turn
and head back fast, before they come down on us." Mateo
shivered as he looked up at the towering mountain. "I know
what Apache do to *mejicanos* when they catch them."

"So do I. *Caramba*, let's get out of here! And we'll have
to find fresh horses and some food on our way back, thanks
to that damned traitor," Paco swore.

Thirty-three

The ball had shattered Carlos de Escobar's shoulder
blade, and the shock and pain had mercifully made him
unconscious. Out of instinct, his faithful mustang continued
to ascend the winding trail to the stronghold. But by now the
first sentry had seen what had taken place and had made a
smoke signal, then uttered the sound of the crow. Above him,
on another ledge two hundred feet higher, another sentry
heard the signal and passed it on, till in a few minutes the
stronghold bristled with activity, and Kinotatay as well as
Pastanari emerged from their wickiups to await the news of
the identity of this unexpected visitor.

But when the first sentry saw Carlos's unconscious body
leaning forward over Dolor's neck, he gave another signal
that was passed on by sentry to sentry, till it reached the *jefe*.
And at Kinotatay's order, three mounted braves galloped
down the trail to intercept Dolor and to care for the seemingly lifeless rider.

When they came upon the mustang, Dolor whinnied and
pawed in the air, in defense of his master. One of the braves,
dismounting, soothingly approached the frightened, exhausted
horse and gentled it by talking quietly to it, while his two
friends carefully lifted Carlos down.

"He has lost much blood," one of them said to his

companion. "We must ride back quickly and see that the shaman cares for him. The ball went deeply, and it may have broken a bone in his back. But he still breathes."

"Even in the uniform of a *soldado*, I recognize him as the *cuñado* of El Halcón," the other brave declared.

Swiftly, the three Apache braves hewed off branches from tall young saplings that grew along the winding trail, bound them together with rawhide thongs, and made a travois onto which they carefully laid the unconscious Spaniard. And then the oldest of the three mounted his pinto and, glancing behind him, urged it on at a slow pace, while the two others followed, one of them grasping Dolor's reins and drawing the exhausted mustang on with him. Dolor, seeing that his master was cared for, docilely followed.

When they reached the stronghold, Kinotatay hurried forward, squatted down, and examined Carlos. "Take him to the wickiup of the shaman. And let Colnara care for him."

Carlos de Escobar slowly opened his eyes and uttered a groan of pain. He lay on his stomach, and twisting his head to the side, he could see light filtering in through the entrance of the wickiup. There was a throbbing in his back, and he felt weak and listless. His eyes, glazed and staring, fixed at last on the shaman of the Jicarilla Apache. Then he uttered a faint, contented sigh. He knew himself to be among friends again, after so many arduous, harrowing months.

Behind him, a tall young girl, no more than seventeen, with a round sweet face, her thick black hair plaited into a single long braid that reached nearly to her hips, looked to her father, the shaman. "It is the first he has made a sound since the sun rose and set four times, my father," she murmured.

"He will live, Colnara. Kinotatay has told me who he is and that he is beloved of our tribe because, though a Spaniard, he respects our ways. He who was my predecessor as shaman of the Jicarilla Apache united him and the daughter of the *jefe* who ruled us wisely before the days of Kinotatay. And her spirit passed to the heavens, blamelessly. This man had died a thousand deaths since then, Colnara. Be kind to him, be as gentle as she once was, and it will bring back good thoughts and his health and perhaps lessen his sorrow."

"I will do it gladly, my father. Our *jefe* has told me about this man, also."

The shaman beckoned the girl toward the door as he

said, "I will go now and talk with Kinotatay, Daughter." He led her outside, then spoke in a soft, kindly voice. "Look to his comfort. The ball lodged deeply, and it shattered part of the bone. Perhaps in time, with what I know, I shall try to extract it. Otherwise, it will stay within him and gather poison and do him great harm. But first he must get back his strength before this can be tried."

"Yes, my father."

The shaman left, and the young girl returned and knelt down beside Carlos, who rested on a thick pallet, upon which the softest blanket had been placed. His beard had grown and his face was pale and drawn.

As the days came and went, Carlos, unaware of the passage of time, gradually regained his strength. Colnara tended to him from early dawn until late each night, wiping away the sweat from his forehead, giving him cool spring water in a clay bowl, carefully feeding him tidbits of venison and mountain-goat meat in nourishing stews. And at her father's bidding, she dosed his food with the cinchona bark and other herbs known to the Apache to allay raging fever.

At times he was lucid, and he saw the girl in buckskin and beads attentively sitting beside his pallet. There were times when he wept and closed his eyes, for the sight of Colnara recalled to him his beloved Weesayo. And with the white feather in her hair, the symbol of her virginity, the image of her young, gentle, tender beauty stabbed at his heart. She was about to undergo the purity rites that would declare her to be the "Beloved Woman" of the Jicarilla Apache, just as Weesayo had once been.

By mid-March he was strong enough to have the ball that had shattered his shoulder blade extracted. He was given a strong herb that produced a dreamless slumber, and the shaman himself, with a sharp knife heated in the fire inside the wickiup, probed for the ball and removed it. The wound was plastered with mud and cinchona bark, and Colnara assisted her father.

Gradually his color returned, and in the last week of March, Carlos opened his eyes one morning to find Colnara staring intently at him. She blushed and looked away as he feebly reached for her hand.

"How long has it been? Am I still in the stronghold?"

"Yes, señor. It is the wickiup of my father, Marsimaya, who is shaman to us. I am his daughter, Colnara."

"Colnara," Carlos faintly echoed. "I do not know what the name means, but I thank you. I seem to remember—I do not know how long ago it was since I came here—that when I opened my eyes, you were always there."

"It is my duty. You are blood brother to Kinotatay. We know of you, Señor Carlos, and my name in your tongue would mean 'the hope of life.' "

"And that you have given me," he murmured. "It is strange, but I know that I have seen you before."

"As a girl, as a child playing outside a wickiup when you and *El Halcón* walked through our village. Yes, Señor Carlos, I have seen you often before. You are kind; you respect the customs of our people. And my father wishes to give you the gift of life. You must lie still, eat what I bring you, do what I am bidden to tell you to do, and soon you will be strong again."

"I want to be." He put a hand to the floor of the wickiup and feebly tried to raise himself, but Colnara shook her head and very gently urged him back onto the pallet.

"No, Señor Carlos, not yet. If you move too quickly, the new flesh that has grown to replace that which was removed may be torn, and the blood will start again. Do not be impatient, you have many long years ahead of you."

"How kind you are to me. Just—just as she—she was—" Carlos closed his eyes as he felt hot tears scald him. He did not try to hide them but lay quietly as he wept for what had been and what could never be again.

And Colnara herself looked at him, and her own eyes were moist as she touched his forehead and then said in a calm, soft voice, "You are not so warm now; the fever goes down. This is a good thing. Now you must sleep and rest."

A week later, when Kinotatay visited him, Carlos was able to sit up, and he seemed stronger and his color far healthier. "Kinotatay, I came here because my heart brought me."

"This I understood. It was because of her."

"Not only because of her, Kinotatay," Carlos said, and he went on to explain the grueling turn of events of the last several months, including his search for the treasure and the pursuit by Santa Anna's two soldiers.

"I hear you, my blood brother. Jocinde sent a signal to us that two *soldados* rode up to you as you approached the trail to our stronghold, talked with you, and that when you

rode on ahead toward us, one of them shot you down withou
warning. Why was this done, if you, an officer, were their
superior?"

"Because the man who is the leader of the army of
Mexico, Kinotatay, thought that I would lead him to much
dinero. And he sent those men to see where I would go, so
that they might find it and take it for him."

"I understand you. You need say no more. And so, after
your grief, you have found that being a *teniente* for the
mejicanos is not the answer for you either."

"No. I know now what I hoped for, and it will no
happen. When I am well enough, Kinotatay, I will go into
Taos and confess my sins to Padre Moraga. And then I shall
try to find some place to stay—I cannot yet go back to my
family. I have hurt them, and I am ashamed of myself."

"But, my blood brother, I must tell you that Padre
Moraga is no longer shaman in Taos. He was killed at the
order of Don Esteban de Rivarola, the *alcade mayor*."

"*Dios,* it cannot be!" Carlos gasped, his eyes wide with
incredulity.

"But it is so, my blood brother. But Don Esteban de
Rivarola paid for his crime. The Great Spirit took his life no
long after that. And there is a new shaman in Taos. He was
sent from Santa Fe."

"Then it is to him I shall make my confession, when I
am strong enough, Kinotatay. I cannot thank you enough for
this gift of life. They left me for dead, and I cannot remember all that happened after I felt the ball dig into my back."

"It is best to forget such evil things. Rest here and gain
your strength. We will talk again."

Thirty-four

Stephen Fuller Austin had gone resolutely on to San
Antonio in March. There he encountered shattering news, for

Governor Martínez was obliged to tell him that the officials at Monterrey had refused to recognize his authority to introduce settlers under his father's grant. Furthermore, the new government of Mexico was considering a strict colonization policy for Texas and the Californias. "In my opinion, *mi amigo*," the governor compassionately added, "you had best go to Mexico City and look after your interests. I will tell you frankly, things change almost daily there, and there is much unrest. If you have any influential friends at the capital, your best hope is to go there at once and urge them to consider your idea of a settlement."

"I'm grateful to Your Excellency." Stephen Austin courteously bowed, masking his distressed reaction to this unexpected news. "I wish you to be assured of my gratitude for what you personally did to entertain my proposal. But I am confident that if I can meet with the leaders in Mexico City, they will see that I mean to bring peacefully disposed homesteaders into Texas territory, who in no way will threaten the security of the new government."

"That is a point you must constantly strive to emphasize, *mi amigo. Vaya con Dios,* Señor Austin," the governor said as he smilingly extended his hand.

Stephen Austin rode back swiftly to the little American colony that had already been established in Texas. Without further delay, he appointed one Josiah Bell the leader of the colony, explaining that it was imperative that he absent himself and stay in Mexico City until some sort of compromise could be worked out with the government now in power. The agreement of the Spanish officials no longer pertained, since they had been overthrown in the revolution. And thus it was, still cheerfully optimistic, that Moses Austin's undaunted son set out for the capital. He reached Mexico City on April 29, 1822, and faced a confusing political scene. A quarrel had arisen between the *"Libertador,"* Agustín de Iturbide, and the liberal constituent Congress, and the situation was rapidly approaching a crisis. Scarcely a week later, Iturbide prompted a popular revolution and declared himself Emperor Agustín I, dissolving the hostile Congress and thus callously renouncing his idealistic formula of an all-embracing peace for Mexico. '

On the day that Stephen Austin reached Mexico City, Catarina gave birth to a girl, whom she named Carmen, in honor of Don Diego's long-since-dead mother. John Cooper had heartily endorsed this, believing that it might somewhat ease his father-in-law's grief over Carlos's prolonged absence.

Catarina, after much anguish, had said nothing about her meeting with Carlos and the information she had given him about the secret treasure. She was terrified of her husband's reaction, and her confinement during the final weeks of her pregnancy had been a mixed blessing. She realized that John Cooper would attribute her reticence and moodiness to the fact that she was nervous about giving birth, nothing more. But her period of confinement was also a private hell. Unable to continue her teaching duties, she had a great deal of time to think and feel remorse about betraying her husband's trust.

Indeed, the school had been closed for a month now. Bess Sandarbal had also been in confinement, and the week before Catarina's daughter was born, Bess had given birth to a son. Knowing that Miguel's father had been named Juan, she insisted that their new child bear this respected name. The middle-aged *capataz* knelt down beside the bed and reverently kissed her hand, his eyes glowing with pride and love.

But, as if these births were not enough excitement for the ranch, Don Diego and John Cooper were delighted to welcome the visit of Timothy Callendar, his wife, and two children. Bess was ecstatic at this reunion, urging the tall, genial man to stay with them as long as he could. But Timothy Callendar humorlessly chuckled and declared, "I'm afraid, my dear Bess, that when your fine husband and Mr. Baines saw me in San Antonio and suggested that I come out here, I hadn't yet discovered that *americanos* weren't really too welcome in that area. Santa Anna's men have staged a few raids against a good many of my friends, and one of them came very dangerously close to involving my wife and me." He turned to Don Diego and earnestly avowed, "I'd like to discuss the possibility, Don Diego, of settling down near you—that is, if land near here is available."

"*Seguramente,* Señor Callendar," Don Diego beamingly responded. "Indeed, knowing of Señor Austin's desire to establish a colony of settlers in the Texas territory, both my son-in-law and I are eager to welcome those families whose love for land and work would make them not only ideal neighbors, but also add to the defense of this *hacienda*." Then, his face sobering, he added, "I, too, like you, Señor Callendar, believe that the military leaders of the new Mexico will continue their harassment of the *americanos*. But they cannot expect to patrol everywhere at once, and we are quite isolated, as you know. Thus, the more families we have living around and with us, the stronger we shall be against any attack. As for the availability of the land in the vicinity, there are no claims that I know of and no land grants—and if there were by Spanish law, that no longer pertains. Enjoy our hospitality, then, with your lovely wife and fine young children, and at your leisure, choose a place to begin your new home. Our *trabajadores* will assist you in building it, you have my promise."

When Timothy Callendar learned that Bess had named her older son after him, he was deeply moved. And he confided, "You were a wonderful wife to my poor brother, Bess. Fact is, before we came here to visit, I sold my holdings so I'd be free to start a new life away from those hateful *mejicano* soldiers. And after what Don Diego said about my being welcome as a neighbor, I intend to be just that!"

By the middle of May, John Cooper and Miguel saw a small group of Conestoga wagons moving slowly toward the ranch, coming from the east. Ahead of the wagons, two men on horseback drove about fifty head of cattle. The young American and the *capataz* galloped up to meet them, and John Cooper recognized the Ames brothers, whose lives he had saved when he and a contingent of Jicarilla Apache had killed their relentless Mexican pursuers.

"Well, it's good to see you," John Cooper exclaimed as he leaned forward to shake first John's hand, then Henry's. "I received your letter, and I've been expecting you."

Edward Molson, riding a piebald pinto beside the wagon which his wife drove, galloped up now and enthusiastically greeted John Cooper and Miguel. "God, but I'm glad to see you again, Mr. Baines," he exclaimed. "That *dinero* you gave us staked us to a try again in Texas—we got back five years ago, but what with Santa Anna's patrols and the hostile redskins, we've had a rough go of it. Then I got word in San Antonio about Timothy Callendar's coming out this way to find his long-lost sister-in-law—"

"He's here ahead of you, and going to settle down with us, Mr. Molson," John Cooper interrupted. "And if you and your families with you are looking for a peaceful place, you won't find a better one. We'd like nothing better than to have you all as neighbors. And judging from that Kaintuck rifle you're carrying in your saddle sheath, I'd say your help would be mighty welcome just in case we ever do run into trouble. Tell you what, why don't you drive your wagons over west, where you can see those cattle and sheep grazing, make them secure, then all of you come in and have a get together and a good meal with us!"

That evening, Don Diego instructed Tía Margarita to get the help of the *trabajadores* and hold a fiesta barbecue in honor of the six Texans and their families. There was music and dancing, and at the end of the evening Don Diego said to Edward Molson, "As my *yerno* must have told you already, señor, I would be delighted to have you and your friends and families settle down beside us."

"Why, that's mighty kind of you, Don Diego!"

"I am told you have set your wagons and your cattle to the west. Well, there is ample land, and no one has claimed it to this day. Why not accept the help of my *trabajadores* and build houses and a barn and stable for your horses and cows? And as neighbors, I promise you an equal voice in decisions which will affect the well-being of the Double H Ranch."

"Don Diego," Molson said in an unsteady voice, "I know, you're Spanish by birth—but darn it anyhow, you've got the guts of an American—better still, a Texan!" And the two men shook hands energetically.

Jack Williams, after leaving the *hacienda* to walk outdoors with his cronies, uttered a sigh of vast relief. "I'm glad our wandering's over, Ed," he admitted. "Juana's going to have a baby—and this time, by God, I aim to see it gets born!"

Thus, Don Diego de Escobar, an exiled hidalgo, and John Cooper Baines, who had begun life in Illinois as a destitute orphan, began realizing their plan of expanding the Double H Ranch so that it would become a strong, self-supporting community.

Mateo Consuegro and Paco Olivera rode back south in search of their commander. By this time, however, Santa Anna had been promoted to the rank of brigadier general and dispatched to Veracruz to head an enlarged regiment. The two corporals learned this news from a mounted captain of cavalry who, himself at the head of a small company, had been put in charge of suppressing revolt among groups of unfriendly Toboso Indians. The company had taken up quarters a few miles south of Santa Anna's camp at the time when Paco and Mateo had been ordered to follow Carlos de Escobar. At first, the captain believed the two corporals might be deserters who had lagged back to plunder and rape, but when Paco informed him that he and his companion had been commissioned by none other than Santa Anna himself on a secret mission and cited the name of the traitorous lieutenant, Carlos de Escobar, whom they had killed, he wrote out a pass that would prevent their interrogation or arrest by any military patrol they might encounter on their way back to Veracruz.

Consequently, it was many weeks before they caught up with the new brigadier general.

They found him in his tent, staring at himself in a silver-framed mirror and self-consciously adjusting the garish medal he had received from the hands of Emperor Agustín I himself. When they were announced to him by his orderly, he cast the mirror aside onto his cot and excitedly exclaimed, "Come in, *soldados!* Well, it's taken you long enough."

Paco, who had, with Mateo's approval, nominated himself as spokesman of the pair, ingratiatingly excused himself. "A thousand pardons, *mi coronel.* First off, we did not know that you had gone back to Veracruz."

"Well, that's understandable. But tell me now, what of this *teniente?* Did you learn where the treasure is?"

"I regret to inform you, *mi coronel,* that it was not possible."

"Before you continue, let me explain something to you, you imbecile," Santa Anna said, puffing out his chest like a pouter pigeon. "If you have been in the army any time at all, you should recognize my insignia. I am no longer your *coronel,* but a brigadier general. You will address me, therefore, both of you, as *mi general.*"

"I beg my general's pardon, a thousand times over! But I am happy, for one, to see that our glorious nation recognizes the genius of Your Excellency," Paco fawned.

Santa Anna smirked and again adjusted his medal. "Now get on with your story, and be quick. I have waited months to have news from you two dogs, and now you come into my tent to tell me there is no treasure."

"No, *mi general*," Paco diplomatically amended. "I did not say there was no treasure. I said only that we did not learn of it from the Teniente de Escobar." The corporal went on to explain how he and Mateo had followed Carlos, first to the *hacienda* and then to the mountain range, and how they had been "forced" to kill the young man.

"Imbecile, *ladrón*, fool!" Santa Anna stormed, and slapped the astounded Paco across the mouth. "The two of you were well armed. You should have overcome him, applied torture if need be to wrest the secret from him. And now it is lost with him."

Paco bit his lip and bowed his head, fearful of Santa Anna's wrath, while Mateo, not without alarm for his own skin, gulped and cleared his throat.

"Let me think a moment," Santa Anna mused aloud. "I know that Teniente de Escobar was the *cuñado* of this *americano*. And if he stopped at the *hacienda* of which you told me, it could only be that of his *cuñado* and his own sister, who is the *mujer* of this *americano*. Well then, you will tell my orderly exactly what you know of the location of this *hacienda*, and he will write it down. It is quite possible that if I have that ranch watched, the *americano* will lead us to the treasure. And from what I was told by a rascally private who ought to have been shot, it was the *americano* who himself found the treasure and used some of it to buy the finest Arabian horses from a certain *hacendado*. Well, I cannot find too great fault with you, *soldados*. You are not officers and therefore cannot be expected to have their brains and cunning. I shall reward you both by promoting you to the rank of *sargento*. And if one day the treasure is recovered, I shall see to it that you receive an additional reward. As from this moment, you are attached to my regiment. You will report to Coronel Santoriaga to learn your duties. You may leave now."

Vastly relieved, both Paco and Mateo saluted, babbling effusive thanks for their promotion, and hurried out of Santa Anna's tent.

The wily brigadier general sat on the cot again and took up the mirror and studied his reflection. Then he grinned wolfishly. "Our worthy emperor has a maiden sister," he said aloud to himself. "If I were to court her and wed her—even though she is sixty, from what I am told, and ugly as an armadillo—I would be one step closer to that throne which Iturbide has carved out for himself. And I alone am truly fit to sit upon it, as one day I shall. With the help of *Dios*, to be sure—and also with the help of that treasure of the *gringo*."

Thirty-five

--------◆--------

Carlos de Escobar had lost weight and was still weak from his wound. The shaman's daring removal of the ball—though undoubtedly it had saved his life—had plunged him, for some weeks thereafter, into a kind of listlessness. Part of this, to be sure, was his own disillusionment with the cause with which he had allied himself in the desperate hope of forgetting his personal tragedy. The will to live, always so strong within the handsome young Spaniard, had dwindled, torn by self-recrimination and the brooding despair over Weesayo's purposeless death.

It was not till this August of 1822 that he was at last strong enough to ride horseback, to join the competitive sports of the Jicarilla braves with the bow and arrow, the lance, and their own version of a kind of lacrosse, which was not far removed from the ancient Creek game of *tokonhay*.

Kinotatay had shrewdly instructed the braves to welcome Carlos into their sports, to praise him, to show respect—which, after all, was surely due to the blood brother of the *jefe* himself. And he said to Pastanari, "He must take his own time to choose the path on which he will go, Pastanari. But I will tell you this—the maiden Colnara would not cast away the arrow if he were to plant it before her and ask her to become his squaw."

"Do you think he will do that?" the son of Descontarti eagerly asked.

"In my heart, I do not think so. His mind and his spirit are still linked to her who was the Beloved Woman. Colnara can only remind him of her, and it would be the thought and the image of that Beloved Woman that would draw him to Colnara, not Colnara herself." He shook his head again. "He would have grief mixed constantly with his love, though Colnara is sweet and gentle and would truly respect and comfort him. Have you not seen how attentively she waits on him to make certain that he eats, changing the bandages and putting the healing bark upon that terrible wound that nearly sent him to the Great Spirit? Yes, she would willingly be his squaw, but I do not think he would want this, and it would not be good for either of them, if he were to take her as the ghost of the one whom he met here and loved and who bore his children for him."

Thus gradually, thanks to the exhilarating life outdoors high in this mountain stronghold, Carlos de Escobar began to examine himself and his life in the light of what had happened to him since he had impulsively decided to abandon his family and friends and join the army of Iturbide with its petty envy and greed and arrogance. The warmth of fellowship that the Jicarilla Apache people extended to him made him increasingly conscious that he could not shut himself off as a hermit any longer.

As soon as he was well enough, Carlos had asked to see Tasumi, the brave who had been with him when he had avenged Weesayo's death. The reunion was a painful one, but the middle-aged Indian was heartened by the new determination and fortitude of the Beloved Woman's *esposo*. He now saw, as did all the other Apache, that the young Spaniard had regained the will to live.

Carlos, too, realized that he would be able to resume his life, but first he had to avow what had been in his heart and mind to someone who would understand it. And that was why, on the last day of August, he went to the wickiup of Kinotatay and asked, "Will the *jefe* of the Jicarilla speak with me as to a friend and a blood brother?"

"You do not need to ask, *amigo*." Kinotatay gestured to the young Spaniard to seat himself on the blanket beside him. "I had hoped that you would come to me well before this. Each day I have watched to see that you grow stronger, that your wound no longer troubles you, and now I say to myself that you have decided what you will do in the days ahead."

"Yes, my blood brother. I must go to Taos and talk to the priest. You told me that Padre Moraga had been murdered."

"Yes, *mi hermano*. In his place, there is another shaman of the white-eyes, Salvador Madura."

"Then I shall go to Taos and talk with him."

"Will you go back to the *hacienda* of *El Halcón?*"
Kinotatay stared intently at Carlos.

"It is not yet time. I have much to think about and to do
before I can go back."

"But in all this time, you have not even asked me to send
a messenger to the *hacienda*. I would have done this without
your bidding, but I knew that you have a reason for not
wishing them to know what had happened to you. I said to
myself that you did not wish to cause them sorrow to learn
that you had been shot by *soldados* of your own side."

"That was only part of it, Kinotatay."

"And after you see this shaman, what will you do then,
mi hermano?"

"I don't know. Perhaps I'll go see Don Sancho de
Pladero. He is my father's good friend. Perhaps I shall stay
with him for a time, until I know what to do."

Kinotatay put a hand on Carlos's shoulder and very
gently, almost paternally said, "You would be welcome here
to live with us, if that is in your heart. There is one here who
cared for you when you had the fever, and she would not
refuse, if you were to place the arrow before her father's
wickiup. He too knows that your heart is good, and that you
love and respect our people and our ways."

Carlos looked away, and a shadow darkened his handsome face. He chose his words carefully before replying, "She
is sweet and good. She is too young to know that a man who
is only half a man cannot hope to give her a whole life. I am
not for her, Kinotatay, nor is she for me."

"Yes." Kinotatay sagely nodded. "This I foresaw you
would think. She would remind you always of her whom you
first met here and loved."

Carlos shuddered and covered his face with his hands.

"She will wed one of our braves, then. But I will tell her
father how grateful you are for the comfort she brought you.
It will be a great compliment. You are well thought of in this
stronghold, *mi hermano.*"

"I will leave tomorrow, Kinotatay. I have no words to
thank you for having kept me here all this while." Carlos
smiled ruefully. "I have not earned my meat and salt."

"Between blood brothers, one does not speak of such
things. You are not a *trabajador,* and I am not the keeper of a
posada," Kinotatay said, quietly smiling. "Tonight we will
have a feast, and our shaman will make incantations to the
Great Spirit to send you from us well and strong and to guide

your footsteps to what awaits you beyond the stronghold."

Dolor was eager to see his young master as Carlos approached and saddled him. The mustang nuzzled at Carlos's shoulder, and Carlos uttered a happy laugh. He still wore the uniform of a lieutenant, with holstered pistols, his rapier in its sheath attached to the sturdy belt, and his helmet with its insignia of rank in the center, as well as the epaulets on his shoulders. As he sat in his saddle and flexed his muscles, he felt no pain from the wound. The shaman had healed him. Or, at least, he had healed his flesh. It was for Padre Madura to try to heal those secret lacerations of his mind and spirit. He raised his hand in farewell to Kinotatay and Pastanari, and then rode down the winding trail to the base of the mountain of the stronghold and on toward Taos.

By early morning of the third day, coming in by the eastern side of the pueblo, he observed that little had changed. There were the adobe *jacales,* and there beyond the plaza were the shops and the church. He did not wish to be seen as yet, till he had met the new priest. Thus, he headed Dolor toward the back of the church, down a side passageway which led to the little yard and the rectory.

As he dismounted and tethered Dolor, he saw the deaf old housekeeper watering the little garden. He advanced slowly, not wishing to startle her, and when she looked up he smiled graciously, doffed his helmet, and gave her a low bow. Then he said, "I wish to see Padre Madura. Tell him it is Carlos de Escobar."

She had read his lips, and in her harsh voice she exclaimed, "He is at his prayers, Señor de Escobar. I will go in, and when he has finished, I will tell him. Come into the rectory and be comfortable."

"Gracias." He followed her into the study where Padre Moraga had written his last letter and patiently sat down and waited. The old housekeeper hovered about him, then finally asked, "If the señor wishes, I can bring coffee?"

"No, but thank you. I shall wait here. Thank you for your kindness." The smile she gave him made him feel strangely at peace, and he waited there in the silence for nearly half an hour until the priest entered the study.

Carlos sprang to his feet, made the sign of the cross, and bowing his head, declared, "It is good of you to see me, Padre Madura. I am Carlos de Escobar, the son of Don Diego de Escobar, the former *intendente* of Taos."

"I was told of your father. He is well?"

"Yes, I think so," Carlos replied, then asked, "Could you hear my confession, Padre Madura?"

"Of course. Come with me into the church." The priest studied Carlos a moment, then added, "By your uniform, I guess that you are attached to the forces of Iturbide."

"Yes, *mi padre.*"

The priest sighed and shook his head. "He now calls himself Emperor Agustín I. When the Corsican Bonaparte began what he called his fight for the liberation of the oppressed, he, too, declared himself emperor. It is not a happy analogy, my son. But I digress." He opened the door and entered the church, and Carlos followed, crossed himself at the sight of the altar, and then went directly to the confessional booth.

The young Spaniard began with the ritual of humility, "Forgive me, *mi padre,* for I have sinned."

"My son," Padre Madura said from behind the screen, "the sinner who confesses and is repentant will be welcomed into heaven, even as was the thief on the cross. I shall hear you, my son."

"*Mi padre,* I—I shall start with what happened to my wife, who was Weesayo," Carlos began. Slowly and agonizingly, he told of Weesayo's death ... of how he took vengeance ... of how he left his family and joined Iturbide's army ... of Santa Anna's raids against innocent settlers ... and finally, of how he came to his decision to leave the stronghold and confess his sins. "Now that I am well again," Carlos continued, "I come to you to tell you all this and to ask your help, Father, as well as to make restitution for my sins. Sins of murder, of selfishness, and of having been untrue to my family."

"Our dear Lord says 'Thou shalt not kill,' it is true, my son. And yet, knowing what you have told me, I do not think that He will damn you to the fires of hell for the vengeance you took. Also, men often do foolish things when they are under the influence of those who prey upon their grief, who, knowing their despair, seek to turn it to their own selfish profit. I speak of Santa Anna, because I consider him a satanic individual, a true demon. He is not a soaring eagle of liberty of the Mexicans; alas, he is more the vulture."

"*Mi padre,*" Carlos exclaimed, astounded by such words in the confessional booth, "you have said what my close friend, Colonel Ramón Santoriaga, told me just before I rode to see my sister. But all the same, *mi padre,* I am not yet at peace; I do not know what I must do."

"Go back to your family, my son. Have you sent them word of what has happened to you?"

"No. It is true that I could have had the *jefe* of the Jicarilla Apache send a messenger to them, but I did not wish it, not until I had absolved myself of the dishonor I had brought them. I have disgraced them, *mi padre.* I made them mourn my departure, abandoning them as if they were only strangers to me, all because of my grief for my dead wife. I told myself that it was justified because I would fight for a cause in which I believed with all my heart. And when I found that it was far from that, the weight of the dishonor I brought upon them became an even heavier burden, as it is now, while I kneel before you, *padre.*"

"You must somehow let them know that you are alive and well, my son. It is cruel, if you care for them at all, to keep this long silence. They do not think that you have disgraced them. And from what you tell me, I do not see dishonor. I see a young man torn by grief, a dreamer and idealist, a good man with a warm heart—the fact that you have lived with the Jicarilla Apache proves this to me, more than your words could—and you must not scourge yourself for not being perfect. What man, born in sin from the first sin, can be that? Even the Son of our dear Lord knew that man is frail, a weak vessel, tested in the crucible of life and all too often found wanting. You have whipped yourself enough, Carlos de Escobar, and your soul bleeds from it. God does not demand this from you. God is a God of love, and such a sinner as you claim yourself to be is welcome in His sight. Pray, my son, pray steadfastly that you may be reunited with those who love you. You will not forget her whom you loved so deeply; she will be with you always. But, in time, even that agony will lessen, and there will be new life to occupy you. She herself would wish this."

As he was absolved, Carlos's shoulders shook with his hoarse, choking sobs. He had not believed that this new priest could be so gently compassionate. And when he had controlled himself at last, he crossed himself and said, "I am glad that you have been sent to Taos, *mi padre.* You do not know how I needed this time with you, or what you have done for me. I will go now to see Don Sancho de Pladero. I wish to stay there with him for a time, until I go back to those who, as you say, love me—I pray *Dios* they still will."

"Be sure of it, my son. May the blessings of our Lord be with you always."

"Amen, *mi padre*." Again, Carlos made the sign of the cross and left the church.

"By all the saints, Carlos, it is good to see you!" Don Sancho de Pladero gripped the young Spaniard's hand with both of his and shook it warmly. "That uniform becomes you, but you're thinner than I remember—"

"Yes, and a good deal wiser. And also, Don Sancho, a widower."

"A widower—oh, yes, I had learned this grievous news sometime ago, when Padre Moraga journeyed to your ranch to give the memorial service. I am truly sorry."

Carlos said nothing. Finally, in a soft voice he asked, "How are things in Taos?"

"I will tell you this at once, Carlos. Your father still has enemies here. It is true that Don Esteban de Rivarola, who was *alcalde mayor* and who hated your father and wanted to denounce him for treason because he was kind to those poor *americanos,* at last went to hell, where I'm sure the devil prods him daily with a molten pitchfork. But in his place, we have that detestable rogue Luis Saltareno." Don Sancho grimaced. "He was appointed to replace Don Esteban, you see. So I must hold council with the scoundrel, who daily fancies himself to be even more powerful than an *intendente.* And to add to all this, with the chaos that is going on in Mexico City and with this emperor business of Iturbide's, nothing is done."

"I heard that Colonel Iturbide has declared himself emperor. But I was under the command of Santa Anna, Don Sancho, and I'm now convinced that he intends to oust Iturbide and make himself the first man of all Mexico. And I regret now that I did what I did. To wear this uniform is dishonoring, because it was Santa Anna who commanded the soldier who wore it, if you take my meaning."

"Yes, I have heard that he's a devil incarnate."

"But you were saying that my father has enemies in Taos?" Carlos questioned.

"Oh, yes, of course. The fact is, as I started to say, this Saltareno hates your father even more than Don Esteban ever did. And I have the feeling that he's been watching me like a hawk. I wouldn't put it past him to have spies see where any of my *trabajadores* might ride off to. However, there has really been no news to send Don Diego, so none of my men have ridden to your *hacienda*."

"I understand. Yes, I remember Luis Saltareno very well." Carlos finally unburdened his heart and told Don Sancho all about the death of his wife and his disillusioning experiences in the Mexican army. "Well, that's enough of my sorrows, Don Sancho," Carlos concluded. "I didn't come here to burden you with them. But I'd be eternally grateful if I might stay here with you and your family for a time. So much has happened that I don't think I'm quite ready to return to Texas."

"Of course," Don Sancho exclaimed, "you may stay as long as you wish as my guest, and I'll be delighted to have you. So will Doña Elena. And of course, you remember my son, Tomás, and his sweet wife, Conchita. Oh, the two of them have made me the happiest man in the world with their children. And Tomás is as good a *capataz* as you'll find, either here or in this Nueva España they call Mexico now, believe me."

"You know," Carlos now said, "since I can't abide idleness, I'd ask the privilege of working with your horses, or even helping Tomás with the sheep."

"You, with the sheep?" Don Sancho guffawed. "I can remember how Don Diego used to tell me that you detested sheep, and that you certainly didn't want to inherit a flock. And I have a very large one, thanks to your father's generosity, as you well remember. No, don't worry about earning your keep. It will be my pleasure. Besides, if you have been to Mexico City, you can tell my charming wife, Doña Elena. She, by the way, is also a joy to me in my declining years. The misunderstandings we had in the past have long since left our household. I have much to thank God for."

"Yes, and I pray I may be as fortunate as you one day," Carlos slowly said.

have ridden to your *hacienda*."

"I understand. Yes, I remember Luis Saltareno very well." Carlos finally unburdened his heart and told Don Sancho all about the death of his wife, his faked allusion

Thirty-six

It was nightfall of the same day of Carlos de Escobar's visit to the *intendente* of Taos. Noracia, the beautiful *mestiza*, had assumed the role of stewardess and housekeeper to the pompous little merchant, Luis Saltareno. Thanks to her shrewd advice, he had more than doubled his own personal wealth by taking over the estate of Don Esteban de Rivarola. By dint of bribing a group of ruffians, who would be loyal to anyone who paid them in good silver, and also through his power as *alcalde mayor*, he had managed to acquire the luxurious *hacienda*, the stables, and some fifteen of Don Esteban's *trabajadores*. He chose three of the brawniest rogues who had once served Don Esteban and appointed them as foremen. They were to report to him monthly, and one of them, who was able to read and write, Pancho Sortomar, was ordered to bring a monthly ledger sheet, which would show the number of ewes, rams, and new lambs born to the flock, together with an itemized statement of the sale of wool. It was true that the market for wool had declined, mainly because of the upheaval throughout all Mexico, but the revenue was still sufficient to enable Luis Saltareno to import the finest wines from the Canaries, silks and velvets in which to dress Noracia, and elegant furniture, so that his own *hacienda* would, as the *mestiza* slyly urged, be worthy of so magnificent an *alcalde mayor* as he.

Much to Saltareno's surprise, his majordomo had announced that an old rascal, bent over and wearing a tattered cape and a wig too large for him, was demanding entrance. The old shopkeeper, Barnaba Canepa, was an unexpected visitor and, because of his even more unexpected news, an extremely welcome guest.

Canepa's profits from the sale of his love potions and, as always, the secret poisons that occasionally a disgruntled woman would buy at a high price in order to dispose of a

309

faithless lover, had led him to be less miserly in his declining years. Too, the obscene joy of possessing a teenage slave girl, Luisa, the gift of Saltareno, had emboldened him to purchase a small carriage. He had compelled Luisa to learn how to drive it, and it was she who had driven the two piebald mares, attached in harness, to the *hacienda* of the *alcalde mayor*.

"Well, you old devil, I must say this is quite a surprise! Though I much prefer it to going to that stinking shop of yours, with all your reptiles and monsters and fetuses in those pickling jars at the back," Saltareno sneered. He held out his goblet with a fatuous smile, and Noracia, in a red velvet gown that was daringly cut to show the cleft of her superb bosom, swiftly moved to the cut-glass decanter and filled it to the brim, then moved over to the old shopkeeper to fill a goblet for him as well.

Canepa adjusted his spectacles and cackled as his cataract-blurred eyes squinted to observe what they might of the satiny, tawny flesh of the *mestiza*. "Luis, you see I'm not dead yet, thanks to your little gift of that *india puta*. And I'm not blind yet, either, though you might think it—your charming Noracia makes me feel young again."

"You didn't come here to discuss the charms of my stewardess and housekeeper, Barnaba. Now what is it? I've had a busy day, a meddlesome and disgusting day with that fat old fool Don Sancho de Pladero," Saltareno irritatedly declared.

"Do you remember when you came to my shop the last time and you promised me a reward if I could find a way to discover the whereabouts of Don Diego de Escobar?" Canepa slyly proposed as he took a hearty swallow of his wine.

"Of course, I do, you imbecile! And some of the ideas you had for finding him struck me as being remarkably stupid for an old man who is supposed to know everything that happens here in Taos and the environs," Saltareno sneered.

"Ah, Your Excellency, this time you won't think me so stupid," Canepa cackled. "You remember that we had the annual fair here at Taos in July."

"I should, you bag of bones and foul-smelling jars—I helped preside over it. If you've only come to drink my best wine and to ogle my delightful Noracia, you're imposing on what was never really much of a friendship to start with," the merchant spat out.

"Maybe I can refresh your memory, Your Excellency. Maybe you would like to be *intendente* of Taos, too?"

"Of course I would. It's no secret. I could do better than Don Sancho de Pladero without even trying. But what has all this to do with the fair at Taos?"

"Because, Your Excellency," Barnaba Canepa said, lowering his voice to compel his hearer's full attention, "there was a Comanche there, of the same tribe as Sarpento. He had brought a *gringo* male slave and sold him, and someone sent him to my shop because he wished to buy one of my swiftly acting poisons. In the tribe, I gathered from his broken Spanish, there was a brave who wished to take a squaw, a girl whom this Comanche desired. He had more horses and more *dinero,* and so he would probably win her. But with this poison, once the other man was dead, he could—"

"By the infernal, get to the point!" Luis Saltareno exploded.

"I come to it, Your Excellency. Now this brave, who called himself—dear me, what was it now, these horrible Indian names—oh, yes, Masquerna—he told me a very interesting story. His chief, Sarpento, sold a yellow-haired *gringa* at the fair in Taos some years ago. And it was this same Don Diego de Escobar who is your enemy who bought her and freed her, so that she could marry the *capataz,* Miguel Sandarbal."

"That's interesting. But how does this tell me where Don Diego is?"

"Wait, wait, give me a moment more—and ah, Noracia, if you could spare a little more of that wonderful wine for a poor, tired old man whose throat is dry," Canepa said, holding out his goblet with a pathetic look. Saltareno impatiently snapped his fingers, and the *mestiza* promptly filled the goblet. "Thank you, a thousand thanks! Well, Masquerna told me that about two years ago, he and some of the *indios* of the tribe went into the Texas territory to hunt. Their luck was bad, they had no game, but they came near a large *hacienda.* And a *gringo* and the very same *capataz,* Miguel Sandarbal, rode out with some of their *trabajadores* to see if they had come for war or peace. This *capataz* sold the Comanche two fat sheep and two steers for meat for the hunting party, at a very good price. And the *capataz* told Masquerna that the *trabajadores* of this *hacienda* wanted peace with the *indios* and would not drive away their buffalo, or other game."

"Do you mean to tell me that this Masquerna knows where that ranch is?"

"Well, not the exact location, but close enough. He said it was west of San Antonio, in the valley near the Frio River."

"And you waited all this time before you told me this?"

"Well, you were not very flattering to me when you visited my shop. Besides, I wanted to be certain that I could find this Masquerna again, if you wished him. Now my thought, *excelencia*, is that Masquerna might ride to his chief, Sarpento, and their braves could attack the ranch of this *gringo*. For that is where Don Diego de Escobar lives, I am sure of it."

"Yes!" Luis Saltareno whispered, his eyes glittering with malice. "And how will you find this Masquerna? Will he not have gone back to his tribe?"

Barnaba Canepa kept the merchant waiting for his answer while he finished his wine and then leaned back, uttering a derisive cackle. "*Excelencia*, I owed you a little something for treating me with such contempt in my poor shop. I do not have your wealth, but I have intelligence, which is sometimes more valuable than wealth. I told Masquerna that there was someone in Taos who would give him much gold and his chief as well, if they would do us a service. I told him that there was a ranch where there were many *mujeres*, and horses and cattle and sheep as well for the taking. And that they could take the *trabajadores* of that ranch by surprise, if they would attack. I told Masquerna to come back in two moons to my shop, and I would give him some gold to show that I was in earnest. And so, this very day at sundown. he came to the back of my shop and bade me redeem my pledge." The hideous old man sniggered and winked. "I promised that he would sleep with Luisa when I returned. Oh, yes, he is still there. No doubt drunk on some *aguardiente* I gave him, but he waits your bidding. But first, *excelencia*, you and I must come to terms. In return for this information. which you have waited years to obtain without success, do you not think that I should be well rewarded?"

"Yes, yes, you old devil! For the chance of killing Don Diego de Escobar, I'd pay the ransom of a king—but wait, not so fast, Barnaba!" Saltareno halted his exuberance and, craftily stroking his chin, considered the stooped old shopkeeper. "What do you wish?"

"Why, it's common knowledge that you as much as stole Don Esteban de Rivarola's fine estate, *excelencia*. Wait a bit, don't be angry with me. You know it's the truth. And you're wealthy enough; you don't need all that. As for myself, my old bones are tired of that damned little shop and, as you say, the smelly jars and the poisons and all the rest. I'd like to live my last few years like a hidalgo. Now, if I were to be permitted to move into the *hacienda* of Don Esteban, and if I had two or three more *criadas* like the charming Luisa—"

"Very well. Tell this Indian that I will give him the gold if he carries out the deed. And when I have word that Don Diego is dead, here in the presence of Noracia, whom I trust more than I trust you, I promise that you shall live in the *hacienda* of Don Esteban de Rivarola and that you shall have as many *criadas* as you wish."

"Done! Your hand on it, *excelencia!*" Barnaba Canepa exclaimed as he hobbled out of his chair toward the *alcalde mayor*. With another grimace, Luis Saltareno extended his hand in the unholy pact.

The day after his meeting with Luis Saltareno, old Barnaba Canepa sent word to the *alcalde mayor* that he had talked with the Comanche brave, Masquerna, and that the latter had agreed that his chief, Sarpento, would surely accept the plan to attack the Hacienda del Halcón. The gold that Saltareno had agreed to pay Sarpento was much needed by the tribe, Masquerna indicated. But he told the old shopkeeper that he did not think the attack could be staged until after Sarpento had come back from the annual January fair in Chihuahua.

This crafty, treacherous Comanche chief had once very nearly been ousted by his people, who had mistrusted his leadership. He had purchased some guns and ammunition that had proved defective, but to compensate for that he had sold *americano* male and female slaves at the fair in Taos, and also in Chihuahua, at handsome prices, which had benefited his people. And Masquerna had further told Barnaba Canepa that Sarpento now held as prisoners two *gringo* couples, as well as two teenage orphaned girls captured in raids along the southeastern part of Texas. He would surely sell these captives and return to his tribe with the *dinero* to bolster his command over the braves, and only then was he likely to launch a fierce attack on a well-guarded ranch. It would take at least fifty braves, well armed. Also, Masquerna had shrewdly hinted that Sarpento would assuredly wish some payment in advance as a guarantee of goodwill.

Luis Saltareno sent one of his *peones* back to the old man with a sack of money, amounting to five hundred *pesos*. Although he was impatient to have his revenge on Don Diego from that incident in the *intendente*'s court, when the latter had given a verdict for the old Pueblo Indian against him, he perceived that a surprise attack in February, when the weather would be bad, might conceivably have more of a chance at success. And it was this message that he had Barnaba Canepa convey to Masquerna, who immediately set out for the distant camp of his *jefe*.

Tom Prentice, brother of Amy Corland in Taos, had not seen his sister in many years, and now, more than ever, he was impatient to do so. Twenty-four, black-haired, and tall, Tom had matured and had been promoted by Miguel Sandarbal to assistant *capataz* of the remuda of horses used for the riders who drove cattle. Tom also held the post of trainer of the new horses for the household and for the workers. Five months ago, he had married lovely Rosita Portola, the nineteen-year-old daughter of a middle-aged *vaquero* on the ranch, and she was going to bear his child early next spring. This was news he must tell Amy, and, too, he wanted to bring back a present for Rosita. The shop that his brother-in-law, Frank Corland, and his sister ran in Taos would have an abundance of lovely things to choose from, such as a hand-worked silver bracelet with symbolic Mexican designs or a necklace of semiprecious stones. He was very much in love with his wife, and he had never been happier in all his life. Miguel Sandarbal had seen to it that his wages had been increased as the result of his excellent work.

The *capataz* had been confined to his cottage with a bad cold, and Bess was concerned that it could possibly spread to his lungs and perhaps be even more serious. Also, there was a chance that the children might catch the cold, so Catarina insisted that they move into the *hacienda* and that she would look after them.

So Tom Prentice went directly to Don Diego to ask the latter's permission to visit his sister in Taos. The former *intendente* generously acquiesced, but warned Amy's brother that, as in the past, he should be very careful about the route he took, so that no spies in Taos could possibly trace him back to the Hacienda del Halcón.

Tom rode off on one of the spirited geldings he himself had trained, his saddlebag packed with ample provisions for the long journey. He entered Taos and went directly to the little shop in the town square. Amy was overjoyed to see him, and Frank was most hospitable. And when he told them, his chest swelling with pride and his handsome young face aglow, that he was both a husband and soon to be a father, they made a great fuss over him. Amy cooked some of his favorite foods, remembering that she had helped her mother in the kitchen before they had started out on that fatal journey that had cost the lives of her parents and made her and Tom captives of the Ute chief, Ortimwoy. And Frank insisted on giving him an exquisite hand-tooled silver bracelet and refused to take a *centavo*.

Amy told Tom how she and Frank had yearned to visit him at the ranch in Texas, but with one thing and another, they had not been able to get away. "Business in the shop has never been better," Amy explained, "and my little ones take up so much time. And would you believe it, Tom, I'm expecting again!"

"That's great news, Amy, Frank. Congratulations." Tom kissed his sister and shook his brother-in-law's hand. "It looks like we're sure becoming a big family!"

"I guess you might say we've got our own colonization project going right here," Frank humorously put in.

"Well, it's a big country," Tom said. "There's room for everybody."

Wanting to return to the Hacienda del Halcón as soon as possible, Tom took his leave of Amy and Frank late that very same evening and galloped out of Taos along the trail that led past the Sangre de Cristo range. But it was about this same time that the Comanche brave, Masquerna, finally left Barnaba Canepa's shop. Since the old storekeeper had told the brave that during the last few years he had watched for couriers who might have come from the Texas home of the former *intendente,* and also since Masquerna's destination was some fifty miles southwest of the ranch of the *gringo,* where he knew that Sarpento and his braves were making camp and preparing for the winter hunting, he decided to follow the sturdy young man on the black gelding. It might be, Masquerna thought to himself, a messenger. He would then be able to get a look at the ranch first and determine how it was situated and how well it was defended.

Tom Prentice did not observe that the Comanche rider was anywhere near him. Overjoyed with his reception by his sister and brother-in-law, and eager to see his sweet Rosita and give her the bracelet, he first thought only of urging the gelding on at a gallop, as long as its stamina would hold out But then he remembered Don Diego's warning to make sure that no one tracked him. So the next time he stopped for a short rest and gave the gelding oats, he carefully took the precaution of walking back to see if anyone was following However, Masquerna, like all the Comanche, was an expert tracker and a superb horseman. He had stayed well behind Amy's unsuspecting brother, and so there was no sign of his pursuit.

From the top of a hill obscured by spruce and fir trees, Masquerna watched as Tom rode back to the large ranch house with its many buildings clustered around it. He also saw where the six Texans and their families had built houses and two barns to flank the huge acreage of the Hacienda del Halcón, and for a moment the brave wondered if such a substantial-looking settlement could be successfully attacked. But any doubts quickly vanished when he realized the inhabitants of the ranch would be taken by complete surprise by the most feared and fearless Indians in the land: the great Comanche.

Masquerna grunted his satisfaction at having tracked young Tom Prentice to this large *hacienda;* there was no doubt this was the place that his *jefe* was to attack. Having already hidden away a few gold pieces out of the money he had been given to take to Sarpento as advance payment for that attack, he turned the head of his pinto and rode toward the Comanche camp.

Thirty-seven

A week after Carlos de Escobar had arrived at the *hacienda* of Don Sancho de Pladero, the latter, abetted by his sympathetic wife, at last persuaded the young Spaniard to have word sent to his father and Doña Inez that he was still alive and well. Hesitantly, Carlos agreed to this, but stipulated that the message should say only that he still wore the uniform of an officer and should, under no circumstances, reveal his presence at the de Pladero ranch. Thus, the following Monday, Enrique Soldado, a *trabajador* who had several times borne messages from Don Sancho to his old friend, rode off toward the Hacienda del Halcón. He had been told by the *intendente* to be extremely vigilant as always, in the event he was being followed, but what neither man knew was that the enemies of Don Diego, as well as the Comanche, had found out all they needed to know about the location of the Hacienda del Halcón.

Thus the leave-taking of the *trabajador* went unnoticed by those who wished to harm Don Diego and his family, and Enrique arrived at the *hacienda* about two weeks later. He was ushered into Don Diego's study, given a warm welcome, and invited to stay and rest for at least a couple of days. Don Diego also promised him a fresh horse, for the gelding that the *trabajador* had ridden was exhausted.

When he opened the letter, Don Diego uttered a cry of joy, and Doña Inez anxiously came to him, drawn by the sound. "It is my son, Inez! He is alive and well, and he is still in the army. Don Sancho writes that he received word from Carlos through a soldier in Taos, and that he is relaying the greetings to us—but Carlos says no more. Devil take the scoundrel, why did he wait so long to ease our worries about him?"

"Is that all it says, *mi corazón?*"

"Yes, regrettably." Don Diego scowled, crumpled the letter into his hand, and then, regretting the action, smoothed it out and read it again. "What would it have cost him to tell us where he is? Well, at least we know he had not been harmed in battle, or become a prisoner of the royalists. At any rate, I am grateful to your master," he said, turning to address Enrique Soldado, "and I shall send you back a gift for his wife, together with my letter of thanks. Go to the kitchen, *hombre,* and ask Tía Margarita to give you the best food she has to offer. And tell her to serve you good Madeira, the kind we reserve for our most important guests."

"*Gracias,* Don Diego, you are too kind to a humble *trabajador.*" The messenger bowed his thanks.

A few moments later, Catarina, leading the children out of the schoolroom to play outside for a while, saw her father and stepmother in conversation in the study and cheerily greeted them. Don Diego waved the letter. "We have just had news from your brother, *querida!* Don Sancho sent it by messenger, who just now came with it. He is still an officer, he is well, but he did not tell us where he is. What a rascal your brother is, worrying us so!"

"But at least he hasn't been harmed, and that's the best news of all," Catarina declared. "Perhaps he'll be home in time for the holidays. That would truly be wonderful!"

As this long, hot summer drew to its close, Catarina was tormented by the secret she had kept from John Cooper. Even though she rejoiced in his affection for their new child and shared his pleasure in having mated Hosea and Jude with the yearling Mischief, who had produced a litter of six whelps, she realized that she had betrayed his trust. She often went to the little chapel late at night and prayed for forgiveness for this deceit, knowing she should tell her husband, cost what it might. Yet she feared a confessional might disrupt this perfect harmony they had at last achieved, and so she kept silent, even though her conscience gnawed at her.

She did not know whether Carlos had found the treasure; perhaps, and this thought terrified her most of all, he had actually found it and perhaps someone had followed him and would kill him for it. Or again, he might have given it to the leader of the liberating army of Mexico, and then there would be nothing left for the poor of Taos, for the *hacienda* itself, and for the comforts of the *trabajadores*.

In the early weeks of autumn, John Cooper and Catarina and little Andrew said their farewells. The young mountain man was preparing to go with Miguel and fifteen of the sturdiest *trabajadores* and *vaqueros*—or cowboys—on the largest of the cattle drives so far at the Double H Ranch. The fall roundup had brought in nearly three thousand head of cattle, all of which had been branded with the distinctive new HH insignia that had been designed for the ranch by the Pueblo Indian, Taguro. With so many animals gathered, John Cooper and Miguel had decided to take a thousand head on the trail now, rather than to wait until the customary spring drive to market.

"How long will you be away, *mi corazón?*" Catarina anxiously asked as John Cooper stooped and caught up in his arms the curly-haired Andrew, while the boy playfully ruffled his father's hair.

"We should be back in two months, *querida*," John Cooper said. Then putting his sturdy son down on the ground, he said to Andrew, "It won't be long before you're riding with us, and maybe one day you'll be boss of all our herds."

"I'd like that a lot, Pa," Andrew said, grinning.

"Well then, right now you can look after your ma while I'm away, and you do a good job of that, mind you son." Then John Cooper rumpled Andrew's hair, kissed Catarina, and went to say good-bye to his younger son and daughter, as well as to the other members of his family.

Miguel and John Cooper rode at the front of the line of cattle on the way to New Orleans. Flanking the herd at various points along the column were Esteban Morales, Tom Prentice, and the *trabajadores,* as well as the newly arrived Texans. They went by way of San Antonio, and there was good grass for the cattle to graze on and fresh water for them to drink as they crossed the Colorado, the Brazos, and the Sabine rivers on their four-hundred-mile trek. This time they encountered no Mexican army patrols, and neither John Cooper nor Miguel once mentioned their earlier encounter with Carlos. John Cooper looked forward to the time when there would be no more army patrols, when there could be many cattle drives throughout the Texas country, as more and more settlers built homesteads in this fertile land. He also looked forward to the time when the cattle drives of the Double H Ranch would be even larger still, with maybe as many as ten thousand head of cattle.

John Cooper also thought about the silver, and he wondered if perhaps the time had come to deposit it all in the bank in New Orleans. It was simply too dangerous to leave it untended; with all the unrest in Mexico, it would be safest to have it locked up in a vault. John Cooper believed Padre Moraga would have approved of this idea, and so he decided that when he arrived in New Orleans, he would speak to the banker with whom he had already deposited several of the ingots.

It took forty days to reach New Orleans, and there, John Cooper and Miguel supervised the herding of the shuffling, snorting Texas longhorns into the riverfront stockades, from which they would be loaded onto cattle boats bound for the West Indies and the East Coast. John Cooper had negotiated with the Creole factor, Fabien Mallard, for the transference sale of his cattle, and that afternoon he received a draft of ten thousand American dollars.

"Now we're really in business, *amigo,*" John Cooper told

Miguel with a boyish laugh. "This is just the start of what's going to come. The next step is to go to the bank, where this will be safe and will be a legacy for all our children."

Later, John Cooper was ceremoniously ushered into the office of Eduard Beaubien, of La Banque de La Nouvelle Orléans, and he was greeted by the banker. "May I felicitate you, Monsieur Baines. Your account begins to grow, and it is a compliment that you place your trust in us. *Je vous assure, parole d'honneur,* that trust will never be misplaced."

"I'm sure of it," John Cooper replied, "and that's why I'd like to talk to you about an idea I have in mind, Monsieur Beaubien. You know that I've put into your bank several bars of silver from a mine I found some years ago. I'm wondering if you would accept as many as twenty or thirty of those bars. I'd feel safer if they were in your vault, rather than in some isolated place."

"Of a certainty, Monsieur Baines. Once again I am honored by the confidence you have placed in our bank and in myself."

The two men shook hands, with John Cooper explaining that he would see the banker again on one of his next trips to New Orleans, when he had decided how he would transport the silver. Then he left the bank and rejoined Miguel. They and the other men would spend the night in a New Orleans hotel, then be on their way early the next morning to begin the return journey to the Texas ranch.

Thirty-eight

Taos still basked in the drowsy aura of the past. True, news had come of the revolution and that Iturbide had declared himself emperor. And there had been fewer orders from Santa Fe and still fewer from Mexico City. Yet generally, there was little change in the daily routine of this small town dwarfed by the majestic, snow-capped Sangre de Cristo Mountains.

For Carlos de Escobar, the sight of those mountains, as perhaps nothing else might have, began to restore the brighter memories of his young manhood. How adventurously he had come to Taos, all the way from Madrid, wanting no part of court intrigue and ceremony, and surely not the placid life of a sheep rancher! The exhilarating freedom of riding Valor into the mountains and hunting, being his own master, away from all the foppish *caballeros* and their pretentious little games of courting señoritas. His friendship with the rugged Miguel Sandarbal, without the slightest distinction of class. And lastly, the meeting with John Cooper and then that breathtaking moment when Weesayo had stepped out of her father's wickiup and their eyes had met for the first time.

And now that he was enduring the bitterness of his own self-condemnation for having been duped in his idealism, he could think of her, the Beloved Woman, without the torturing agony that had festered in him all the weary months south of the Rio Grande. This pure air, the magnificent stretch of sky, the riding on horseback, the candid hospitality offered to him by young Tomás and the latter's father, Don Sancho, as well as his thorough recovery from his debilitating wound, had drawn him back once again into the circle of the living, as the wound of his spirit was healing.

Tomás de Pladero had matured, also. When he had found the courage to stand up to his domineering mother and to resolve that he would marry the orphaned *criada*, Conchita Seragos, he had cast aside for all time the role of humbly subservient son and became his own man. And the love Conchita had given him, and their children, together with his mother's own transformation into a loving and devoted wife to his father, and an ally to him, had completed his transfiguration. He now rode horseback with Carlos along the trail that so often the latter had taken when he had gone hunting or journeyed with John Cooper toward the stronghold.

And Carlos, for his part, even found an interest in Tomás's imaginative suggestions for improving the quality of wool of his father's huge flock and of marketing it at a better price. As *capataz* now, Don Sancho's capable son had won not only the respect but the love of all of the *trabajadores* because of his generosity. There wasn't a man who could forget how he had fought the sadistic *capataz* José Ramirez for Conchita, and then had married one of his own and showed respect and love that would not usually be associated with the son of an aristocrat. He worked side by side with them, and he demanded no more of them than he himself could do—and Carlos, always a free spirit in his own right, found himself liking Tomás de Pladero almost as much as he did John Cooper Baines.

Also, he discovered that it had considerably eased his mind that he had agreed to let Don Sancho send a courier to let his father know that he was in good health. He did not know when he would go back, but at least the news would ease his father's anxiety—and he really had no desire, at any time, to have brought that cross upon his father. Even as a boy, when he had seen the hypocritical and artificial life of the court of Madrid, he had appreciated his father's manliness and honesty, and it had become part of his own creed.

And then, this first week of November, as he rode out on a bright, crisply cool morning along the mountain trail with Tomás, the latter casually remarked, "My father's expecting a guest by the end of this week, Carlos. She will stay with us for a time."

"Oh?" Carlos politely eyed his friend.

"Sí, mi amigo. She is Teresa de Rojado. My father knew her father in Madrid, before she was born. They remained close friends even after my parents moved to Taos, and her father wrote often to mine, telling him all about his daughter. She was married to a diplomatic envoy of the court, Don Ferdinand de Rojado. When Napoleon put his brother on the Spanish throne, she and her husband went to Cuba, where he was attached to the viceroy-general's staff. He died of fever last year, and my father wrote, inviting her to visit us. I understand she has no special love for life in Cuba and welcomes the chance to see this new country and perhaps even to settle here, if it is possible."

"She would find it certainly more beautiful than Cuba. Look at those mountains with their snow-covered peaks, Tomás! And the blue sky, and the pure air—and see the trees, and there, a deer is scampering up the slope to the ledge and looking down at us. It's a beautiful country."

Tomás smilingly nodded. "She may even join us riding, from what my father tells me. She's an accomplished horsewoman, and she knows how to use a foil and a pistola. And yet she was educated in the convent, which only shows that one adapts oneself to one's surroundings—just as I have."

"Yes, that's surely true, Tomás." Carlos looked at his friend and nostalgically chuckled. "I can remember when you and I were neighbors and my father was insisting that you marry my sister, Catarina. Personally, I wouldn't have favored you at all in those days."

"I wouldn't have favored myself, to be honest with you, *amigo*," Tomás grinned. "In those days Mother tried to regulate my life. Thank God, I didn't let her."

"You may well say that. But now you're a happy man. And you have a wonderful wife. I tell you, I'd take a girl like Conchita over every one of the aristocratic beauties left in Taos, no matter how blue-blooded their families are," Carlos smilingly confided.

That Saturday noon, Don Sancho's guest was driven to the *hacienda* in a carriage flanked by a platoon of mounted Mexican soldiers. Don Sancho himself came out of the *hacienda* with his wife and Tomás, with Carlos beside them, to open the door of the carriage and to hand down his lovely guest. Carlos caught his breath at the sight of her. She was perhaps twenty-seven, tall and slim, her dark brown hair done up in a thick chignon. Her eyes were as dark as her hair, her mouth firm and candid, her nose dainty and with delicately fluted nostrils that proclaimed an innate sensitivity. But there was nothing supercilious or aristocratic about her, for as soon as she was helped down from the carriage by Don Sancho, she turned to the coachman and in a clear, sweet voice declared, "I must thank you for a very pleasant journey. You drove well, you did not abuse the horses, and, also, you avoided most of the ruts in the road between Mexico City and here."

The startled coachman gaped at her, then flushed and made her a low bow from his perch. "A thousand thanks, señora!"

Teresa de Rojado now opened her reticule and distributed silver pieces to the military escort, saying, "I'd be grateful if you would all drink to my health at a *posada* and wish me success in this new land. I have come a long way, and you have helped protect me and make my journey pleasant. I'm very grateful to all of you."

A young lieutenant, stiff in the saddle, doffed his plumed helmet and made her a courtly bow from the saddle: "I wish I might look forward for the rest of my life, señora, to just such military duties as these. It was our joy to serve you, for you asked for so little."

"But then, *teniente*," she smilingly parried, "there is

nothing about me which presupposes I should have any right to special treatment. And yet you and your men accorded it to me. And for this I thank you. *Vaya con Dios*."

Carlos stared at her with disbelief. He had not expected to find so aristocratic a young woman—and one so beautiful in the bargain—taking the trouble to thank her escort and the coachman for a journey that, however polite she may have been in describing it, must surely have been arduous. After all, he could recall how long it had taken for his family to reach Taos from Mexico City, not counting their lengthy journey from the port of Veracruz to the capital, where Don Diego had first received his orders from the viceroy in his new post as *intendente* of Taos.

Don Sancho offered her his arm and led her into the *hacienda*. In the foyer, as he beckoned to a servant to take her cape and exquisite plumed hat, he introduced first his wife, then his son, and then turned to Carlos and genially declared, "Señora de Rojado, may I have the pleasure of presenting to you Carlos de Escobar. His father, Don Diego, formerly attached to the court of Carlos IV, was and still is my dear friend. He held the post of *intendente* prior to myself."

"It is a pleasure for me to meet you, Señor de Escobar." Teresa de Rojado smiled and extended her hand. Carlos took it and was about to bow his head and kiss it, when she gently interposed, "Please, Señor de Escobar, I am not a princess, and I am not attached to the court of Madrid. I'd like it much better if you would shake my hand."

For a moment the handsome young Spaniard gawked, speechless at this unexpected sally. And then his heart went out to her, and he made her a courtly bow, then shook hands as he would with a man, as he would with John Cooper himself. "I bid you welcome to Taos, Señora de Rojado. Tomás tells me that you're an accomplished equestrienne. I have a mustang, Dolor, that I trained myself. Perhaps, once you're settled in comfortably, you'd allow me the privilege of escorting you along the trails of those magnificent mountains."

"Why, certainly! I should like nothing better. Alas, I had to leave my own horse in Cuba, after my husband's death." Turning to Don Sancho, she said, "You've been so kind, offering your hospitality. If I may stretch it one mite more, would it be possible for me to ride one of your horses, if it is not in service?"

"But of course, Señora de Rojado, I'll see to it that you have the best horse in the stable," Don Sancho said, beaming. "And now, my wife will show you to your quarters. Refresh yourself and rest, and we'll have dinner when you are ready for it. How you brighten our household!"

"You are much too kind in flattering me so. And if I might say one thing more, Don Sancho—I know that you knew my father. I heard all about you, and he told me often what a good, kind man you are. I'd much rather have you call me Teresa, because—well, as you know, I'm a widow now, and I'd like to think back to the days when I was just a little girl, not due any special treatment. And I may say also that I mourned Ferdinand, but his death was a blessed mercy because he was in great agony. It was the will of our blessed *Dios*. Again, I am most grateful to all of you for welcoming me here so graciously."

As Doña Elena put a maternal arm around the young woman's shoulders and led her off down a corridor, Carlos stood staring after her. How refreshingly candid and honest she was, and how seldom it was that one saw an aristocratic woman refuse to stand on ceremony and not bask in all the vacuous amenities of etiquette. He told himself that he was going to look forward to riding beside Teresa de Rojado.

In her trunk, Teresa had brought a pair of foils and masks. Carlos, Tomás, and she had gone out riding along the trail that wound along the base of the Sangre de Cristo Mountains. On the third day after her arrival, when she rode back to the *hacienda* of Don Sancho de Pladero, her cheeks crimson from the cool mountain air and the exhilaration of her exercise, she declared, "I wonder if you, Tomás, or you, Carlos, know the rapier and the foil."

"I do, Señora de Rojado," Carlos eagerly spoke up. "My father had a gardener who once had a fencing school, a good, honest man by the name of Miguel Sandarbal. He is now our *capataz*, and he taught me how to use the rapier."

"Then perhaps you would please me with a bout when we return? Yes, this crisp, cold air is so much better than the humid atmosphere of Cuba. I find myself alive again. But I warn you, Carlos, my fencing master considered me quite expert. And by the way, I should be very grateful to you if you would call me Teresa."

"It will be my pleasure, Teresa," Carlos said, smiling. "And I may tell you frankly that my teacher, Miguel Sandarbal, was once considered one of the finest blades in all Madrid."

"Then it should be an exciting match. I want you to know, Carlos, that in no way must you try to win my favor by allowing me to win simply because I am a woman. I should look upon that as the act of an enemy, not a friend."

Once again, her forthright candor bedazzled the young Spaniard. He gaped at her and then burst into a hearty laugh. "By all the saints, Teresa, if you win, it will be because you have better swordsmanship and for no other reason."

"Excellent! That's the way I want it to be, a fair competition."

Half an hour after their return, Teresa de Rojado, in her riding breeches and boots and blouse, fencing mask shielding her exquisite face, faced Carlos de Escobar in the patio of the *hacienda*. The *trabajadores,* incredulously watching this unheard-of spectacle, were breathless as the two saluted each other, crossed blades, and the first clash of steel pronounced their engagement. The foils were buttoned, and at once Teresa attacked, lunging forward but from the side, so that she presented a poor target to her opponent's foil. Carlos saluted her, a mark of homage to the excellence of her style, and found himself dealing with a well-versed opponent. She was mobile, fluid of movement, supple as a reed, and the delight in this sport plainly showed in her bright eyes and smiling lips.

Carlos won the bout by the narrow margin of three hits to two, and when he flung off the protective helmet, he again saluted her by lifting the foil to his forehead and pressing it against it, the buttoned top high above him. "I salute you, Teresa. Your teacher must have been almost as good as *mi amigo,* Miguel Sandarbal."

"He was, indeed. I enjoyed it, Carlos. *Muchas gracias.*"

"*De nada,* Teresa," Carlos said, and he smilingly inclined his head in courteous acknowledgment. Laughingly, she gathered up the helmet and the foil, then marched promptly into the *hacienda.* He found himself staring after her, and his eyes glowed with admiration. He did not dream that there could be a woman so independently directed in her actions and speech. And what a refreshing relief it was to encounter someone like this, especially after being subjected to the greedy, scheming *putas* who had flocked to the military camp of Santa Anna, when he had been assigned to the latter's staff. Tomás, who had been unsaddling his horse and putting it in the stall, came out now. Discreetly, Don Sancho's son had kept away from the bout. As he approached the young Spaniard, he winked and said softly, "She's a beautiful woman, *amigo*. And she's a rare breed these days, at least for Taos."

"Yes. And for any other city in the world, I'm thinking," Carlos de Escobar raptly murmured.

Thirty-nine

Agustín de Iturbide, the self-styled Agustín I, had commanded the Congress to adjourn, and replaced it with a handpicked *junta* of forty-five men.

Stephen Fuller Austin, who by now had learned some of the basic principles of Mexican politics, patiently introduced himself to each of those members of the *junta* and proposed his plan for colonization. It would take many months before a final approval was passed, but Austin had vowed to stay in Mexico City until such legislation could be assured by a stable government. Already, he had begun to suspect that Iturbide's throne was a shaky one.

Brigadier General Santa Anna made his first visit to Mexico City since Iturbide had put him in command of troops to guarantee the success of the revolution. True to his promise to himself, the twenty-eight-year-old opportunist called at Iturbide's villa with flowers, candy, and a note penned in the most flowery language of love, and addressed to the timorous old recluse, María Nicolasa de Iturbide.

He presented the flowers and candy and epistle to her duenna, a dour-faced, white-haired old woman, but he was so ingratiating in his compliments that she simpered and blushed and hastened to her mistress, stammering, "The most handsome officer, mistress, I've ever seen in all my life—ah, don't I wish I were thirty years younger! But all of this is for you!"

When she read the letter, which, among other embel-

lished statements, declared that he had fallen wildly in love
with her because of her virginal purity and her honesty,
María Nicolasa de Iturbide blushed in her turn. She then
instructed her duenna to take a reply to the room in Mexico
City's finest hotel that Santa Anna had taken during his visit
to her brother.

There was an exchange of several letters in this manner,
each more stilted and affectatious than the previous from
both parties, and María Nicolasa spent her days and nights
dreaming about her dashing young suitor. When the emperor
himself paid a visit to the villa to inquire after his sister's
health, the duenna excitedly revealed the secret: Santa Anna
was courting her dear mistress and it was the most wonderful
thing she had ever heard of.

Agustín de Iturbide uttered a blasphemous oath under
his breath, for which he instantly apologized, since the
duenna was a devout *católico,* and then, when he was finally
ushered into his sister's salon, burst out, "María Nicolasa,
you're behaving like a child, at your age, too! Consuelo
Amarez has just told me of this incredible infatuation that
you and my brigadier general appear to have for each other.
Listen to me carefully—he is an opportunist, and he has
risen from the ranks of lieutenant to brigadier general in a
few short years. I begin to suspect that he would like very
much to replace me on the throne of Mexico. By marrying
you, if such an absurd event should regrettably take place, he
would be a member of my own family, and it would be all the
harder for me to demote or punish him for such insolence!"

María Nicolasa burst into tears and then promptly fainted. Swearing again and this time not apologizing for it, the
emperor summoned her old duenna to give his sister smelling
salts and then strode off to his waiting carriage and back to
the palace. A courier was sent at once to Santa Anna's hotel
room, commanding an immediate appearance of the brigadier
general before his emperor.

The interview was brief and vitriolic: "You are my
officer," Agustín de Iturbide declared loudly. "You are devoted to the army that strengthens my hold in ruling Mexico. I
forbid you to make a folly of this sacred cause and to
disgrace both yourself and me by paying court to María
Nicolasa. You are—yes, twenty-eight, I believe—you must
surely be aware that she is old enough to be your grandmoth-
er, *hombre!* Take your camp followers, your *putas,* but from

this moment forth I wish to hear nothing further going on between you and my sister. Is that understood?"

Santa Anna went down on one knee and bowed his head, flinging out his arms in a gesture of self-abnegation. "My emperor, forgive me. It is only because I am so awed by your power and wisdom that I thought—yes, foolish mortal that I am—an alliance with your beloved and respected sister would touch me with the same aura of wisdom."

"Well now, you needn't go so far as that." In spite of himself, Iturbide was swayed by Santa Anna's passionate avowals, and he smiled weakly and declared in a milder tone, "I am convinced of your loyalty, Santa Anna. Get up, man. Well, if you were truly sincere, I do not rebuke you. Only it is strange that a man of your virility and youth should be attracted to María Nicolasa. To the best of my knowledge, and of course I have known her all of my life, she has had only two or three suitors, and that was forty years ago. At one time she thought of entering a convent, but the discipline was too harsh."

"Forgive me. I promise never to discuss this matter again. I shall serve you faithfully, and all my energies will be brought to bear upon your enemies and those of our great country," Santa Anna said in a voice which he made tremble for effect.

He bowed himself and walked backward out of the salon in which the emperor had received him. All the while, he thought to himself, *This is an emperor? This foppish little man thinks to rule a country of so many thousands of soldiers and* trabajadores? *I will depose this pompous fool one day soon, and be the master of all of Mexico. For I know how to deal with heroes, as I do with scoundrels.*

Brigadier General Santa Anna thus decided that he had nothing to gain as the minion of a man who had equal rank with him and yet now proclaimed himself emperor of all Mexico. There would be no future with Iturbide, and his specious ploy to ally himself with the self-styled emperor through the courtship of the latter's elderly sister had proved to be a fiasco. Worst of all, Santa Anna correctly reasoned, it had created suspicions in his superior's mind as to his own reliability. Therefore, it was far better to take off the mask and to become Iturbide's overt enemy.

Late in the autumn of 1822, at the head of some four hundred soldiers, Santa Anna rode through the streets of

Veracruz, proclaiming a Mexican republic and demanding a revolution that would overthrow Iturbide's centralistic "empire."

This unlikely revolt at once produced unexpected stirrings of support, which the wily Santa Anna had counted on. Two liberal generals rode down from Mexico City to plot with the newly revealed champion of the federalist cause. And this alliance guaranteed the ascendency of the bright yet baleful star of the man whom Mexico City's last viceroy had described as one who would make all Mexico weep.

On January 3, of the new year of 1823, Stephen Fuller Austin had finally secured the passage of a general colonization law through which he could reverse the veto Governor Martinéz had communicated to him in San Antonio.

Yet because the courageous son of Moses Austin clearly perceived that Iturbide's power had begun to wane, he dared not leave Mexico City, lest the new government undo all that had been accomplished. By the beginning of February, Santa Anna's "idealistic" revolution had garnered such strength that Iturbide was forced to abdicate and flee to Europe, fearing that he might be tried and executed. As Stephen Austin had feared, the contract that he had just been given was made worthless by Santa Anna's revolution. But since he had devoted all his energy and finances to his father's cause, even this seeming failure did not totally discourage him. He waited, biding his time.

Ramón Santoriaga had received no orders from his commanding officer: Iturbide's sudden flight from Mexico had left the emperor with no time for such details of protocol. Thus, technically he remained attached to Santa Anna's regiment. And what he saw and heard of Santa Anna's plot with the two liberal generals further disillusioned him. He found himself thinking often of his friend, Carlos de Escobar, and mourning the latter's death. Santa Anna had told him that the traitorous lieutenant had been confronted by two of his couriers and urged to reveal the location of the treasure. When he had refused, they shot him. Ramón saw in this callous act another demonstrable proof of Santa Anna's opportunism.

When he could, he sent back letters to his lovely wife, Mercedes, in Mexico City. Knowing that they would be read by Santa Anna himself, he made no allusions to his growing distress in his present post. But since Mercedes had been the daughter of a language professor, and since they were both fluent in Greek, he concocted a code, using the Greek text of Homer and the *Iliad* to express his real feelings to her.

When he was once called in to spend an evening dining with the ruthless brigadier general, Ramón made a point of telling Santa Anna that he and his wife had won honors in Greek and often expressed their most intimate feelings— which, of course, should not be privileged to their children— in that language.

Santa Anna interpreted this in a bawdy fashion, and Ramón had to feign amusement at his commander's salacious jokes on the matter of conjugal relations and philandering. But this conversation only hardened Ramón's resolve to leave the service of this womanizing, chameleonlike schemer who could go over to the enemy on a moment's notice when it suited his purpose, and whose oratory was that of the devil quoting Scripture to serve his own venal purpose.

In one of his letters, which was sent to Mexico City early in January of 1823, Ramón urged Mercedes to sell their house and to take the children and stay with her uncle in Cuernavaca. He assured her that he would try to give her specific news when possible.

And now that the news had come that Iturbide had abdicated and fled the country, the idealistic young colonel knew that he could no longer follow Santa Anna's star. If anything, Santa Anna would seek to discredit him, perhaps to contrive some incident that would demote him to a lower rank—since, after all, he had been appointed by the now-deposed emperor. And during this first week of February, Ramón's decision to abandon his military career and seek a new livelihood, far from the aura of this scavenging vulture, was finally crystallized when, having penned a letter of resignation, he approached Santa Anna's tent to deliver it. The sentry, recognizing him, saluted and stepped aside. But the voices inside the tent were that of two of Santa Anna's subalterns, and Ramón could not help hearing what they were saying.

"Teniente Duvalos, and you, Capitán Valdez, I shall entrust you with a secret mission. You remember my faithless, traitorous *teniente*, Carlos de Escobar? He revealed to me the existence of a great treasure, which, had he delivered it into my hands, would have given us such freedom in our new republic as I have dreamed of since I was a boy and saw oppression."

There had been a sympathetic murmur from the two officers, and Santa Anna then continued in an ingratiating tone, "But when he refused to reveal the whereabouts of the treasure and my couriers shot him down because he had thus proved his treason to our glorious new republic, I determined that the treasure is known to his *cuñado,* a young *americano* who married the sister of this traitorous *teniente* of mine. As soon as I take command of the government of our beloved Mexico, gentlemen, I shall see to it that this treasure is made part of our national treasury. You can assist me. I shall give you orders, written and formal, so that there can be no question of your responsibility and of my authorization to you, to take patrols and seek out this *americano* and force him to reveal to you the exact whereabouts of this great treasure."

"You honor us, *mi general,* by giving us such a mission. We shall carry it out with all of our energy and patriotism," the captain enthusiastically declared.

Ramón Santoriaga ground his teeth and shook his head. Now he knew more than ever that he must resign as quickly as possible and, without Santa Anna's being any the wiser, make his way to that *hacienda* from which his good friend, Carlos de Escobar, had come. He must warn Carlos's father and stepmother—for to be sure, the young Spaniard had eloquently talked of his respect and love for Doña Inez—to be on their guard, for these patrols would harass and threaten them, until Santa Anna was satisfied as to the whereabouts of the hidden treasure. And he knew with a dismal feeling of total anguish that he would have to sacrifice his hopes for an honorable military career, since the treasure would not find its way into the national treasury of Mexico but rather into the coffers of this human vulture.

A few moments later, the two young officers emerged from the tent, saluting him. He entered Santa Anna's tent and, with a crisp salute, declared, "I wish to resign my commission. I have been away from my family for too long, *mi general.* Besides, the revolution is won, and it has been won without bloodshed. With your permission, I shall go back to my family in Mexico City."

"Coronel Santoriaga, I will accept your resignation. If truth be known, I was debating with myself, before these officers came to see me, as to the feasibility of officially ending your duties here as liaison officer. You know, of course, that your sponsor, Iturbide, has left Mexico. And it was as well for him, because he saved his skin. Very well then, make your plans and leave at your convenience. I have no further need of you, certainly not as a liaison officer."

Ramón saluted and left the tent. He did not trust the oily smile that his commanding officer had given him. And he said to himself that he would leave within a few days, and at night, when he could not be found and his route traced. He would make his way to the *hacienda* of his dead friend, Carlos de Escobar.

Forty

In some of the northernmost provinces of Mexico, the abdication of Iturbide had caused sporadic outbreaks of revolt. The always-warring Toboso seized the opportunity to raid small, undefended Mexican villages, carrying off women and young girls, slaughtering, and pillaging. Many of the Mexican soldiers who had been loyal to Iturbide, finding themselves without any central commander, saw their chance to become *bandidos* and joined the Indians.

At the Double H Ranch it was an unseasonably warm February afternoon, about a month after John Cooper returned from the cattle drive to New Orleans. The she-wolf, who still warily skirted the vast acreage of this sprawling Texas ranch, had given birth to a litter of cubs, and John Cooper enjoyed romping with Lobo and his whelps. When the mother was lonely for the wolf-dog, she uttered her plaintive howl.

But John Cooper readily saw that Lobo was slowly yet inevitably reverting to the wolf-strain by acting more belligerently when his young master sought to play with the cubs. Lobo was grayer and shaggier now, and there were other signs that showed he was rapidly aging. Also, there were many days and nights when he did not trot into the courtyard and seek his master for a romp. The allure of his faithful she-wolf mate would eventually draw Lobo away

forever from the Hacienda del Halcón. Thus, the cycle of life
was constantly renewed, and the strain of noble Lije that had
spawned Lobo would be preserved in the years ahead, thanks
to the kindness of the Missourian who had sent him Hosea
and Jude.

Although Hosea and Jude had successfully mated with
Mischief, only two cubs had survived out of her first litter of
six, a male and a female. John Cooper had the kennel
enlarged and sectioned off to provide quarters for these cubs.
The female would, when her time came due, mate with the
two exuberant young Irish wolfhounds. The young male John
Cooper had already named "Yankee," for this sturdy young
whelp, which would one day soon replace faithful Lobo, truly
symbolized the hearty breed of settlers making their home in
the new world of Texas.

John Cooper squatted down now, knuckled Lobo's head,
and murmured, "You've been faithful, you've helped us, and
you're free now. Go live your life, you've earned it. Be as free
as I've always wanted to be, with your mate. And here are
your whelps, your strong sons and your daughters, just as my
Catarina has given mine to me. From this moment on, be
your own master. That's the real purpose of life, and not all
of us can have it and appreciate it while there's still life
within us."

He heard from afar the plaintive call of the she-wolf,
and Lobo pricked up his ears, growled, and then, like a true
father, herded his cubs off in the direction of his mate.

John Cooper uttered a sad sigh. With the departure of
Lobo—if it were not today, it would be one day soon for
certain—another part of his early life was disappearing.

Catarina hailed him as she rode up on her palomino
mare. He looked up at her admiringly, for she was more
beautiful than ever. Maternity had not lessened the supple
agility of her body, though her face was fuller, and the love in
her green eyes was warmer and more steadfast. They were
easily accustomed to each other now, and yet there were still
those secret hours of fervent passion. But with these had
come a sweeter, more tender, and gentle blending of a
deep-rooted affection and of a communication that no longer
needed words.

"Did you send Lobo away for good, Coop?" Catarina
dismounted from her horse and stood beside him, a hand on
his shoulder.

"Just about, *querida.* You know, those two puppies

Matthew Robisard sent me have already given us a fine whelp to take Lobo's place, and a female that can be bred when it's her time. We'll always have these faithful dogs to protect us and to be part of our family, Catarina. I like that. I think Lije would have liked it, too, if he'd known it."

"I'm sure he would have, darling." Catarina looked down and bit her lips, her fingers digging into her husband's shoulder. She could no longer hold back the confession that she had kept within herself all these long months. She only hoped that he wouldn't hate her too much, that he wouldn't ask why she'd kept it a secret all this time.

"Ouch, honey, you're hurting me. What's this all about?" He turned to her with a quizzical smile and put his hands to her slim waist and kissed her on the mouth.

"I've something to tell you, Coop—I'm ashamed of myself that I haven't told you before. And if you hate me, if you even whip me, you'll be justified."

"Whatever in the world are you talking about, honey?"

Suddenly Catarina knelt down, took John Cooper's hand, and kissed it. "Forgive me, *mi esposo.* I—I told Carlos of the silver mine."

"You did what?" he echoed.

"Yes, Coop. He rode here from across the border many months ago, but he didn't tell me that he was coming. He sent old Tomás into the *hacienda* to find me and to bring me to him. And then he told me that the treasure would buy the *libertad* of Mexico. I believed him—and now I'm not so sure. I don't trust this Santa Anna who now rules Mexico. And besides, I had no right to tell him, not after you'd sworn me to secrecy."

"I wish to God you'd told me that Carlos was here—if only I could have seen him for a few minutes, I could have—" John Cooper began, then ground his teeth in nervous frustration. "Please don't do that—get up, Catarina. If Carlos asked you and he felt the real need, I can't really blame you telling him—anyhow, I didn't tell you exactly where it was. It's a big mountain, and he'd have had to look a long while before he found it—and it's very possible that, even if he went there, he couldn't have found it."

"Y–you—you're kind to say that—" she faltered, then asked anxiously, "What are you going to do, *querido?*"

"I've got to ride off to Kinotatay and ask him to send his braves to guard the mine until I can do something about it. I didn't even tell the new priest in Taos, Padre Madura, about it. Only Padre Moraga and I knew exactly where it is, you see, Catarina." His mind raced furiously as he thought the silver should be placed in a vault as soon as possible.

She was crying softly now, and she linked her arms around his neck. "You're sure you don't hate me too much?"

"No, honey. You were loyal to Carlos; he was in trouble, and I can understand why you did it. I don't think any harm's really done, but I've got to make sure. No, I'll never hate you, Catarina. I'll love you all my life, I think you ought to know that by now."

In a paroxysm of weeping, she flung her arms around him and kissed him ardently.

Then, just as he was about to disengage himself, he heard the sound of muskets and rifles, and the bloodcurdling yells of Comanche braves on the attack.

"My God, it's the Comanche, Catarina! Get back into the house and look after the children. I've got to tell the *trabajadores* and Miguel. I can see them now, to the south, coming out of the gullies and the bushes. They're going to hit the *hacienda* itself from the rear—hurry, Catarina! Wait, give me your horse, and I'll go ride off to the bunkhouse. Tell Don Diego and Doña Inez to stay inside and not get anywhere near the windows!"

Catarina, crouching low, ran for the *hacienda*, while John Cooper leaped astride her palomino mare and galloped toward the bunkhouse, shouting, "¡Los indios, los indios, protéjanse! Trabajadores, get your guns and take cover!"

The first shadows of twilight had begun to fall, and John Cooper could make out clustered groups of Comanche horsemen, almost naked save for breechclouts, their bodies gleaming with the yellow and red of war paint. They had forded the Frio River at its shallowest point about a quarter of a mile to the southeast, and were gathering to make a widespread attack at the back of the *hacienda*.

To his right, he could see the distant houses of the six Texans, which formed a western boundary to the great Hacienda del Halcón. Dismounting, he hurried into the bunkhouse, where Miguel Sandarbal was yelling, "To the weapons shed, *mi compañeros!* Take *pistolas*, muskets, rifles, and plenty of ammunition. Some of you climb on the roof of the *hacienda* and keep out of gunshot. They seem to be coming from the south." Then, turning to John Cooper, he demanded, "How many do you think they have?"

"At first glance, I'd say almost a hundred. And they're all painted with red and yellow—"

"Sounds like the colors of Sarpento," Miguel growled, remembering Bess's abduction by the chief years ago. "If that's true, I've a score to settle with him."

"Leave him to me. You place your men where they'll do the most good." John Cooper clapped the foreman on the back and then hurried out of the bunkhouse to the weapons shed. When he did not ride out to hunt, he kept "Long Girl" in its sheath hanging from a hook in the wall, and he swiftly loaded it and strapped on a powder pouch with balls. In addition, he buckled a belt with two holstered *pistolas* around him and put his hand to his neck, where he carried the long, deadly Spanish dagger.

Then, emerging from the shed, he ran toward the corral and, putting two fingers to his lips, emitted a shrill whistle. Lobo could still be valuable as a defender. He whistled again, and the black raven, Fortuna, perched on the top of the weapons shed, flew down to grip his shoulder with its sharp claws and uttered a shrill caw.

"That's right, Fortuna, call Lobo back! We can use all the help we can get!" he exclaimed.

From the distance he heard an excited growl, and he whistled again, then called, "*¡Mata, mata!*"

In a few moments, the wolf-dog, panting and growling, raced in from the darkness and stood beside him, wagging his tail. "Good boy, good Lobo!" Already he could see that Miguel's brusque orders were being carried out. A dozen *trabajadores* had shinnied up to the roof of the *hacienda* and lay on their bellies, their muskets primed and ready, pistols lying beside them, while six others had stationed themselves on the low, flat roof of the bunkhouse. Lobo crouched, growling beside his master, waiting for the word to attack. Now the first wave of Comanche riders reached the back of the *hacienda*, veering off to both sides as, crouching over the necks of their mustangs, they fired their muskets and rifles and pistols into the building.

Answering fire from the rooftops of the bunkhouse and the *hacienda* felled eight of the first wave of attackers, and the riderless horses galloped on, foam-flecked, their eyes rolling, whinnying stridently in their alarm at the sounds of gunfire.

Miguel came out into the courtyard now, armed with a musket. "That was a good beginning, *amigo*," he panted.

Then there was another volley of musket fire, and Miguel, uttering an oath, clapped his hand to his shoulder, then drew it away wet with blood. Glancing at it hastily, he growled, "It's only a scratch, *amigo!* We've guns and ammunition enough to hold them off, even though we've only half as many men."

"See over there by the creek, if you can make it out. The Comanche are moving closer to the house. Wait, there's a fire arrow!" John Cooper cried, as suddenly there was an arc of flame and an arrow whizzed into the adobe side of the back of the *hacienda*. Cupping his hands, he cried out to the *trabajadores* atop the *hacienda* roof, "Keep firing over toward the creek, at about waist-level, *amigos!* Watch for those arrows, they'll show you the direction of the Comanche!" Hardly had he spoken, when there was a furious volley, followed by distant howls of agony, as the balls found their mark in several of the attackers.

Roused by the sound of gunfire, as well as the unearthly war whoops of the Comanche raiders, the young Ames brothers had seized their rifles from the mantlepiece, hastily loaded them, and ran out into the dusk. Kneeling down, they saw the shadowy outlines of mounted riders and, squinting, pulled their triggers. One of the Comanche braves threw up his hands and fell backward, toppling to the ground, as his mustang raced on. Malcolm Pauley, Jack Williams, and Edward Molson had also come out of their houses to aid their friends, their rifles primed and ready. Ben Forrester, strapping on a brace of *pistolas* and seizing his musket, hastily loaded it and ran out to aid his compatriots. But the Comanche, in a second wave of some twenty braves, were now attacking the southeast side of the *hacienda* and the bunkhouse. Once again, the marksmen on the roof leveled their muskets and rifles and fired in a thunderous volley. A Comanche brave nearest the *hacienda* lifted his rifle and pulled the trigger, and one of the *trabajadores* kicked convulsively and lay still in death. But nearby, two braves were flung out of their saddles by the accurate fire and lay sprawled on the grassy soil about fifty yards behind the house.

Miguel had taken three *trabajadores* with him to guard the corral, and now, out of the darkness, five Comanche braves rode in from the east, having completely flanked the bunkhouse. One of them hurled a lance, which took a young *trabajador* in the throat, but Miguel, leveling his pistol, killed the Comanche with a single shot. The dead worker's two compatriots fired their muskets and two more Comanche slumped dead over the necks of their racing mustangs. One of the surviving attackers headed directly for Miguel, lifting his lance, his teeth bared in a savage grimace of hate. The *capataz* lunged to one side as the Comanche thrust the lance down at him, and then leaped, clutching the brave by the throat and pulling him down from his mustang. They twisted and thrashed on the earth, as Miguel, his left hand gripping the Comanche's windpipe, groped for his knife with his right hand, dragged it out of its sheath, and plunged it into the warrior's heart.

More fire arrows came whizzing from the direction of the tall reeds by the creek, and one of them ignited the dry thatch roof of a small shed near the *hacienda*. As one of the *trabajadores* on the roof leveled his musket, another fire arrow took him in the chest. With an agonized shriek, he dropped his musket and rolled off the roof, to fall with a heavy thud upon the ground and lie gazing sightlessly up at the dark, cloudy sky.

John Cooper moved catlike to the western side of the *hacienda* and, kneeling down, aimed "Long Girl" at a shadowy figure on horseback coming out of the darkness. When the rider was nearly upon him, he pulled the trigger, and the Comanche threw up his hands with a scream and fell to one side as his horse raced on. But before he could reload "Long Girl," another rider, seemingly out of nowhere, bore down upon him, drawing back a feather-decorated lance and uttering the triumphant war cry of the Comanche. John Cooper rolled over and over to one side, hoarsely crying out, "*¡Mata, mata!*" Lobo, with a ferocious snarl, lunged, and his fangs sank into the lance arm of the Comanche. Frenziedly, the warrior tried to shake off the savage wolf-dog, while trying to rein in his mustang with his free hand. John Cooper then drew one of his pistols from his belt and fired, the ball penetrating the back of the Indian's skull. He toppled from the saddle, Lobo still clinging to his arm and growling and shaking the corpse, till John Cooper called him off.

Still another rider loomed out of the darkness, drawing back his bow and speeding an arrow toward the young mountain man. John Cooper had just time enough to leap to one side as the arrow whizzed by him, and then he seized the pistol on his belt with his left hand, leveled it, and fired. But it misfired, and John Cooper uttered a cry of pain as the pistol exploded, numbing his fingers and burning his hand.

His assailant swiftly fitted another arrow to the bow-string and drew it back, uttering a triumphant cry, as John Cooper threw himself again to one side in desperation. Then suddenly there was the sound of a musket, and the bow dropped to the earth as the Comanche stiffened in the saddle, his head lolling back. Then he pitched forward over his mustang's neck.

As he turned, panting, his heart pounding wildly, John Cooper saw Catarina standing, holding a musket, her hair disheveled, and he uttered an incredulous cry: "*Querida,* you could have been killed—"

"*You* would have been, Coop," she exclaimed breathlessly. "I wanted to help—I had to help you fight—oh, thank God I came in time to save you—"

"Get back to the house." Then suddenly he cried out, "Look out, throw yourself down, quick!"

From the corner of his eye he saw still another rider race down toward him, and he heard Miguel call out, "Sarpento!" The chief of the Comanche was tall, naked to the waist, his chest painted in yellow, black, and red, and he wore a red headband with an eagle's feather thrust through it to denote his rank. His eyes glittering and narrowed, his mouth cruelly tight, he lunged at John Cooper with his sharp lance. Heeding her husband's cry, Catarina had flung herself down on the ground with a sobbing cry of terror at her husband's peril. But John Cooper had gauged the distance between himself and the vengeful Comanche chief and, turning to one side, leaped toward Sarpento and pulled him down from the saddle. Lobo, snarling angrily, hurried up, but John Cooper pantingly exclaimed, "No, Lobo, he's mine!"

Using all his strength, the sturdy mountain man broke Sarpento's grasp on the lance and threw it to one side. With a snarl of rage, the Comanche chief tried to gouge out John Cooper's eyes with his left thumb and median finger, while his other hand plunged to the hunting knife at his side.

Turning his head to one side and gripping Sarpento's right wrist with both hands, John Cooper exerted all his strength until a shriek of pain attested to the fracture of the Comanche's wrist. Disengaging himself and springing to his feet, John Cooper drew the bone-handled Spanish dagger out of its sheath round his neck and flung himself down on the writhing Sarpento. Then, his left hand gripping Sarpento by the throat and raising his knife, he demanded in Spanish,

"Why do you attack us? We have done you no harm! Why do you send so many braves against the *hacienda?*"

"It was the *hacendado*—he promised me much *dinero* —" Sarpento gasped, his face grimacing with pain from his useless wrist. "It is finished, spare my life—your *trabajadores* have killed many of my braves—the fight is over—"

"Not yet, Sarpento! What *hacendado?* Who promised you *dinero* to attack us, and why?"

"It was—it was Señor Saltareno, the *alcalde mayor*—he said there would be much *dinero* and many *mujeres,* if we attacked your *hacienda.* He said that it was the *hacienda* of the traitor who was *intendente* of Taos—I did not think you were so strong here, you did not have so many men—*aiii*— enough, I surrender to you!"

"Too late," John Cooper muttered. Grimly, his face a stony mask, he thrust the dagger down into Sarpento's heart, and rose. And now he knew that Don Diego still had one deadly enemy left in Taos, even though Don Esteban de Rivarola had paid for his murder of Padre Moraga. Luis Saltareno, the *alcalde mayor,* had sent the Comanche raiders against the Hacienda del Halcón.

The remaining Comanche, realizing their chief was dead and having sustained heavy losses, rode off, disorganized, in every direction. They would not again threaten the Hacienda del Halcón. And even as they rode off, the *trabajadores* and the six Texans pursued them on foot, firing after them and killing six or seven of the survivors before they were at last out of sight in the gathering darkness.

John Cooper stood panting, shuddering with the aftermath of this savage duel. And as he stared down at Sarpento's agonized and hate-twisted face, he said to himself, "I must go back to Taos again and deal with the *alcalde mayor* myself."

John Cooper Baines met with the *trabajadores* who had defended the Double H Ranch and thanked all of them for their loyalty and courage in repelling Sarpento's attack. Miguel, jubilant at the outcome, moved beside the tall mountain man and murmured, "You've done me a service, *mi compañero.* Now I never have to worry that the man who killed Bess's husband and forced her into slavery will come back to steal her from me. I'm going to the chapel to pray in gratitude."

"I'm going there, too, *amigo,* but first I suggest we go and tell our wives everything's fine. We lost only a few men, but they lost dozens. I don't think the Comanche will ever attack the ranch again. They've seen that we've added new neighbors to flank each side of our boundaries, and all of them have had a hand in saving us."

"I can see now what you meant about having reliable neighbors, *mi compañero.*" Miguel extended his hand in friendship, and John Cooper solemnly shook it. "And I saw how your sweet señora saved your life with her musket. I held my breath there; I couldn't move, and I really thought that your life was in danger."

"Looking back now, I guess I was scared enough, all right," John Cooper said, grinning sheepishly. "But when you're in the middle of a fight, you haven't got time to think. Just the same, I'm going to thank God, too, that He made Catarina run out there with the musket, because if she hadn't, I might not be talking to you this way." Again the two men shook hands, and then John Cooper went back into the house in search of his wife.

Doña and Don Diego were huddled with the children in the dining room, but when they saw John Cooper they knew everything was safe, and they all ran up to him, expressing their great relief and gratitude. John Cooper nodded and smiled, patting the children and kissing his baby daughter, whom Doña Inez held in her arms. Then he kissed her, too, and vigorously shook his father-in-law's hand, then went off to his and Catarina's bedchamber.

Catarina had put away the musket, flung herself down on her bed, and given vent to hysterical sobs. As he crossed the threshold, he stared a long, silent moment at her, and then very carefully advanced, put out his hand, and stroked her hair. "Catarina, *querida,* don't take on like this. Everything is fine now. You saved my life. I will never forget that."

"I couldn't let that *indio* hurt you, Coop. But I'm so ashamed—you know what I mean."

"About telling your brother where the treasure was? Honey, please, forget all about it. No harm was done, I'm sure of it. There was no way Carlos could have ever found the mine."

She turned to look around at him, her face wet with tears. "Oh, Coop. But just the same, I failed you, and all these months I held it back from you."

"There's no reason to fret, sweetheart. Come on, let's go to the chapel, and we'll pray together. Come on, honey. Now stop crying, do you hear me?"

"Why—why—yes, *sí*, Coop," she tearfully faltered. He took her by the wrist and slowly, smiling all the while, led her down the corridor toward the chapel of the *hacienda*. Drawing aside the curtain, he made a gesture to urge her to go forward, and then drew the curtain. The room was beautifully furnished, and there was a peaceful quiet to it.

Catarina crossed herself, knelt down, and bowed her head. Her tall, handsome husband moved beside her, knelt down, and took one of her hands in both of his. He watched her attentively, and he saw how her lips moved silently in her secret prayer for forgiveness. He could feel tears stinging his eyes, remembering as he did the vivid contrast between the spoiled, self-willed young girl and, now, the mother, sweetheart, confidante beyond his most fanciful hopes.

He reached to take her both hands in his and brought them to his lips. Then, kneeling beside her, his eyes fixed on the three-foot carving of Jesus dying on the cross, he said gently to Catarina, "Look at that statue, *querida*. You remember how your father got it. It was just after he came to Taos as *intendente*. Don Sancho invited him to sit in the court and hear the cases. And there was a *rico* by the name of Luis Saltareno who had contracted with one of the Pueblo Indians to make this statue, and then the *rico* refused to pay him because he said the face of the Christ was ugly. Your father told Saltareno that we are taught that God made man in His own image. And if the Indian conceived of Him with the face of an Indian, it was only natural. Then your father gave the Indian some money and said that he would like to have this statue in his own house. When I heard that, I knew what a good man your father was. And I knew what kind of man Luis Saltareno was, too. And now, Catarina, I've found out that it was this same Luis Saltareno who arranged for Sarpento to bring his braves and try to attack us, so that Saltareno could pay back your father for showing favor to a poor, crippled Indian, instead of to him, who was so all-important. So you see, my darling, you mustn't keep blaming yourself for what you thought was betraying me, or anything like that. He"—nodding toward the statue—"knows who really sinned and who betrayed."

"Coop, Coop sweetheart, you're so good, you're so patient with me, I ought to have known better—"

"Shh, Catarina," he gently interrupted, again pressing both her hands to his lips. "Don't keep blaming yourself. You saved my life out there just now. That counts for a great deal more than keeping a secret. Let's pray here together, and I want you to pray that we'll have a wonderful long life together with our children and with our friends and neighbors. Tomorrow I'm going to go to Taos, but first I'll stop to make sure that the treasure is undisturbed so that it can continue to help the people who need it in the days ahead. There are going to be bad days, Catarina, because this man, Santa Anna, is going to take Iturbide's place and be worse than any emperor; I just know he will be."

"I love you so, Coop," she whispered through her tears.

He kissed her eyelids, and then for a long moment they knelt together in silence, their eyes on the Christ.

Forty-one

John Cooper took tender leave of Catarina and told Don Diego and Doña Inez that he planned to return to Taos to confront Luis Saltareno with the damning proof that the unscrupulous merchant had engineered the Comanche attack. He then saddled the palomino Pingo, packed his saddlebags with provisions for the long journey, and primed and loaded "Long Girl" before fitting it into the saddle-sheath beside him. He wore a brace of *pistolas* at his belt, and the bone-handled Spanish dagger hung in its sheath about his neck. Lobo was not around the *hacienda* this morning. Very soon, John Cooper reflected, Lobo would go off into the wilds for good with his chosen mate.

He rode off to the stronghold with a greater peace of mind than he had known in months. It was ironic, he thought, that the malevolent plot by which Luis Saltareno had sought to pay back his father-in-law for that humiliation in the court of the *alcalde mayor* so long ago had boomeranged against the dissolute merchant. Catarina's heroic act in shooting the Comanche brave was an act of devotion and love and even selflessness that augured for their lasting happiness in the long years ahead. And he did not fault her in the least for having told Carlos about the mountain in which the treasure was hidden. Now he had no further doubts that Catarina and he could weather the greatest tribulations and the most unexpected dangers, whatever they might be.

As he rode at a leisurely gait, pleased with the way young Pingo now seemed to show his wish to obey his master, even without specific orders, he thought of the self-imposed exile of Carlos. John Cooper knew that the torture that Weesayo's death had caused his brother-in-law had left an indelible scar. He could only pray that now, after Carlos had discovered that his military service to the new republic had not eased his anguish but only deepened it, Carlos would be guided back to those who loved him and would begin to take up the threads of his life and weave them into a purposeful pattern.

When John Cooper arrived at the stronghold, he conferred briefly with Kinotatay and told the Jicarilla *jefe* his plans. John Cooper decided that since the secret of the mine's location was already in jeopardy, its security could no longer be depended upon. As soon as he was able, he would transfer the silver to the bank vault in New Orleans, but in the meantime, someone trustworthy would have to guard the mine. Besides, if he himself should be killed—as, indeed, he almost had been—his friends in the Jicarilla stronghold would be the best ones to take over stewardship of the mine. He asked Kinotatay to choose two dependable braves, who would guard the sealed cave while he went into Taos to confront Luis Saltareno and denounce him as the instigator of Sarpento's ferocious attack upon the *hacienda*.

Kinotatay at once sent for two young braves and bade them to follow *El Halcón* and obey his orders, as they would those of their *jefe* himself. The two blood brothers said their farewell, and Kinotatay realized that as much as he wanted to, he could not betray Carlos's trust and tell John Cooper about his visit to the stronghold. So all he said was, "May the Great Spirit watch over you when you face this evil man. And may He send your *cuñado* back soon to the Hacienda del Halcón."

John Cooper and the two braves rode out of the stronghold and toward the isolated mountain. After more than a day's hard riding, they approached the site of the mine Tethering their horses, they climbed the nearly obliterate trail to the plateau, some four hundred feet from the mountain peak. From there they approached a steep rock face and found footholds to draw themselves up to the ledge where John Cooper had seen the skeletons of soldiers and monks who had once been guardians of this fabulous hoard.

The young braves, Yamato and Subarko, exchanged wondering looks as John Cooper led them to the huge slab of rock, weatherbeaten, with faded, curious markings upon it that had once been etched out of the stone by chisels and adzes. He beckoned to them, pointed to the moss-and-lichen covered edges of the slab, and then edged himself through the narrow aperture that extended higher than his own head.

He had brought his tinderbox with him and made an improvised torch, with which he lighted his way in this eerie mausoleum. In the storeroom off to the right was the stack of pure silver ingots, bars some eighteen inches long, two inches thick, and three inches wide. He took two of these and went back to the opening, squeezed out of it, and showed the ingots to the braves, who exclaimed with wonder.

"You will stay here and guard the entrance of this cave Yamato and Subarko," he told them, and they nodded. At John Cooper's suggestion, they had brought provisions with them before leaving the stronghold. "Kinotatay will send others to replace you, when my work in Taos is done. I thank you for your help. And I will see that part of this treasure goes back to your *jefe*, so that there will be food and clothing for the poor and the old in the stronghold."

With this, he descended the trail and mounted Pingo, then rode off to Taos.

Padre Salvador Madura gasped as John Cooper opened his saddlebag and drew out the two silver ingots. "It is time *mi padre*, for me to share this secret with you, as I did with Padre Moraga," John Cooper explained. "Years ago, before I left Taos, I came upon this distant mountain and climbed it There I found a plateau and a ledge below the steep peak. I found the skeletons of soldiers and monks, who had guarded the cave. And inside, there were many dead Indian slaves seated at a table, their wrists bound behind their backs with rawhide thongs. And on the table lay ingots such as these,

hich I've since taken. In another room, I found crucifixes
nd many other holy images made of this pure silver. I saw a
uge cross with the figure of Christ crucified upon it, set upon
 stand of gleaming silver, of wonderful workmanship. One
ay, when your church is no longer under the rule of either
panish or Mexican authorities who interpret their laws as
uperior to those by which you serve the people of Taos, I
vill bring it to you for the church."

"This is incredible, my son. And Padre Moraga kept this
ecret as a holy trust, for he left no written message about it.
Iis old housekeeper, Soledad, let me see all the papers in his
lesk. We did indeed find some silver pesos in one of the
lrawers, but none of his papers made mention of this trea-
ure."

"I'm sure of that, *mi padre*. And I wanted to be sure,
before I made you privy to it. I know now that you are a
good man, and that you love the poor and the needy, just as
he did. I have decided that I will put the silver in a bank vault
n New Orleans, where it will be safe for all of us. But now I
bring you these two bars, Padre Madura, for the poor of
Taos. Ignazio Peramonte, who has the leather shop in the
public square, and who is the *sangrador* for *los Penitentes,*
will know how to melt them down and how to exchange their
worth for the pesos that buy the food and clothing and shelter
for those who are deprived of it."

"Yes, I know of *los Penitentes,* and also Peramonte, who
has been elected their new leader now that Padre Moraga is
gone. And I will see this Ignazio Peramonte, and God will
bless you for your kindness and thoughtfulness, my son. And
now I have news for you that should make you rejoice—
Carlos de Escobar lives in Taos."

"Here, in Taos?" John Cooper wonderingly echoed.

"Yes, my son. He came to me and made his confession.
He has left the army, but he does not want to go back to his
family yet. He feels, wrongly, I believe, that he has disgraced
them."

"But of course he hasn't!"

"I know," the priest said, his voice gentle. "But in his
grief, he flagellated himself because he was imperfect. Your
brother-in-law is a guest of the de Pladeros. He still punishes
himself, but it is my daily prayer that his grief and this sense
of guilt will soon be lifted from his heart, that he may resume
his useful life among those who love him."

"I pray for that, too, *mi padre*. And I mean to se him—what you tell me makes me very happy. Yet, I have on thing to do before I go to him."

"And that is, my son?" Padre Madura looked question ingly at John Cooper.

"When I first met you, *mi padre*," John Cooper ex plained, "you said to me that even though Don Esteban d Rivarola had paid for his sins, there was still another man i Taos who was as evil and whom you had thought of threaten ing with excommunication."

"Yes. The *alcalde mayor*, Luis Saltareno," the pries said, his eyes narrowing with anger. "I have heard that he ha somehow appropriated the estate of Don Esteban de Rivaro la, and so his material possessions make him the richest mar of our little town. And he uses this wealth for power, for hi own gratification of carnal lusts. Don Sancho de Pladero, th *intendente*, whom I have met and whom I respect for hi decency, has done what little he can to alleviate the sufferin of the oppressed here in Taos."

"I will tell you something else, *mi padre*. Recently, ou *hacienda* was attacked by renegade Comanche, under th leadership of Sarpento, and we managed by God's help t drive them off. I fought Sarpento myself, and before he died he confessed that it had been Luis Saltareno who had offered him *dinero* and *mujeres* if he had exterminated us all. And that is why I shall go from your church—asking for your blessing—to challenge Luis Saltareno to an honest, fair duel between us. I mean to avenge the dishonor he has all these years inflicted on my father-in-law."

"You have my blessing, Señor Baines. But I should warn you that even though the duel you seek will be fair and honorable, such a concept will not bind the *alcalde mayor*. Be sure that he will try to trick you, perhaps have some of his own *peones* watch the duel from their hiding place and, if you win or seem to be winning, they will try to kill you."

"I'll have to take my chances, *mi padre*."

"God will defend the right, as He always does. And He will bless you for this act of charity which you have per formed. And I give you my word, the secret you have come to share with me today will be known to no one else. Humbly, I thank you, in that you consider me as trustworthy as you did my predecessor. I will keep faith with you, Señor Baines." The priest put out his hand, and John Cooper heartily shook it. Then, after going into the church, kneeling down, and praying, the young mountain man crossed himself and left the rectory. Mounting Pingo, he rode to the elegant villa of the arrogant *alcalde mayor*. Lifting the brass knocker, he rapped it loudly, till the old majordomo irritatedly opened to him and exclaimed, "My master is not expecting you. He is at his siesta."

"Tell him that I bring him a message from Sarpento. He will know what that means," John Cooper replied.

The majordomo stared at the tall, blond young man in buckskin, nervously glanced at the holstered *pistólas* strapped round the latter's waist, cleared his throat, and then hurried off to inform his master. John Cooper waited, his arms folded across his chest, his face impassive. He was in full control of his temper, though the realization that this spiteful man had launched murderous Indians upon the ranch, and thus threatened the safety not only of his own beloved Catarina and their children, but also that of Don Diego and Doña Inez and the families of all the *trabajadores,* had filled him with a cold, merciless anger.

At last the majordomo returned, fawning and ingratiating, as he bowed low to John Cooper. "Please be kind enough to enter, señor. My master wishes you to take some food and wine with him in his bedroom."

"As to that, I've already eaten, and I'm in no mood for wine. Lead me to him," John Cooper abruptly declared. The majordomo blinked, startled by this rude rejoinder, but hastened to escort the visitor down the spacious corridor to the ornately furnished bedroom of Luis Saltareno.

Noracia was seated on a hassock, wearing a lace-trimmed chemise of exquisite cream-colored silk, over which she had drawn a blue velvet robe; on her feet were hand-worked leather sandals of the finest quality, imported from a shoemaker in New Orleans whose wares were in fashionable vogue and brought a high price. Saltareno, still reclining in his bed and wearing only a red velvet robe, was savoring a cup of chocolate. On a tray beside the bed were plates of *quesadillas,* melted cheese and cooked chopped onions between two tortillas; *burrito de carne asada,* beef chunks with tomatoes and onions; and *huevos con chorizo,* eggs with sausage, from which he had already liberally helped himself.

At the sight of the buckskin-clad young man, he scowled and demanded, "I'm told you bring a message from Sarpento, the *jefe* of the Comanche. Are you a renegade, dressed like one and a member of his band? I should say rather a *Comanchero,* perhaps?"

"Neither, *señor alcalde mayor,*" John Cooper tersely retorted.

"Oh?" The gray-haired merchant eyed him suspiciously. "Then I might ask how it is that you, a *gringo,* would have such commerce with Sarpento as to bring me a message from him."

"I bring you his death message, Señor Saltareno," was John Cooper's incisive answer.

The *alcalde mayor* dropped his glass of wine, staining the fine linen sheets of his four-poster bed. Then, lifting himself from the pillows and swinging his legs out of his bed, he rose to confront the buckskin-clad young man. "He's dead, you say? And he had a message for me?"

"Indeed, Señor Saltareno. He told me that it was you who hired him to bring his band and attack our ranch. My name is John Cooper Baines, and Don Diego de Escobar is my *suegro.*"

"Ten thousand devils out of hell!"

"They are possibly even now prodding Sarpento with their pitchforks, I should judge," John Cooper calmly observed. "We fought together, and I killed him with this." He pointed with his right index finger to the Spanish dagger hanging around his neck. "All these years since we left Taos, Señor Saltareno, you've been seeking Don Diego, declaring him a traitor. But the traitor is you, not Don Diego. You resented from the first the way he stood up for the poor *indios* of the pueblo here. You hated him because he was kind and decent, a man who would not betray American traders or the survivors from the Battle of Medina, to have them sent to prison, or shot before a firing squad. But this time you went much too far. I respect the Comanche tribe. They are great horsemen; they are clever, and there is no dishonor in fighting them, when one must. But you chose a *jefe* who himself was greedy for the *dinero* and *aguardiente* and the *mujeres* he could make off with, and what you wanted was to have Don Diego killed—and a great many other innocent people, including my own wife and children."

"Now a moment, I beg of you, Señor Baines," Luis Saltareno indignantly protested. "He resigned his post as *intendente* under a cloud of suspicion; he did not tell either the governor or the viceroy where he was going; and he most likely took the tithes with him, which should have been sent for the expenses of the crown, a just tax levied upon the province of Taos."

"And that is an outright lie, Señor Saltareno," John Cooper angrily interposed. "Don Diego de Escobar is one of the most honorable men I have ever met. Nor does he need to steal the revenue which belongs to the rightful government. But he cannot be here to face you and answer your false charges. I am therefore here in his place, and I challenge you to a duel."

"Very well!" Saltareno hissed between his teeth. "But the dueling code declares that the one challenged shall have the choice of weapons."

"It doesn't matter to me."

"In that case, Señor Baines," Saltareno sneered, "I choose rapiers. And if you will give me a few moments to dress, I shall be at your disposal in the patio. Noracia, querida, will you tell our majordomo to bring two rapiers to the patio, and tell Batista that I shall require him to act as official witness to our encounter."

"At once, mi Luis." Noracia gave him a dazzling smile and walked seductively past John Cooper, detailing him swiftly with narrowed eyes. Saltareno now turned to the young American. "You may accompany her, Señor Baines. I shall dress myself with haste, and join you. I regret that I have no priest in my casa, or I should send him to you to make your peace with el Señor Dios. You see, I am considered an excellent swordsman."

"I have already seen a priest, Señor Saltareno. And I've made my peace with God. I suggest that you get dressed, because I don't care to waste any more time and words with you."

"Oho, a most courageous speech, and you have the bravado of a young cockerel," the merchant chuckled. "Well then, since you're so eager to die, I'll hurry my dressing. In the meantime, you may go out to the patio and await me."

Without a word, John Cooper turned and walked out of the bedroom, down the corridor, and toward the door that opened onto the wide courtyard. The old majordomo, Maximilian, was already there, holding a long case lined with brown velvet in which reposed two rapiers, with basket hilts magnificently wrought of Damascus steel. Noracia had seated herself on a decorative marble stool near an ornamental fountain that stood in the middle of a hollowed-out square, six feet by six, and watched intently. The patio had been covered with a glazed tile that the wealthy *alcalde mayor* had had imported by mule train from Mexico City. John Cooper frowned with annoyance as he stepped out onto the tile, for he would have much preferred to fight on solid ground. He unstrapped his belt with the holstered pistols and walked over to Noracia. With a courtly bow that would have made Catarina giggle, he politely declared, "I'd be much obliged to you, señorita, if you'd hold this for me. I wouldn't want it to be said that I took any unfair advantage of Señor Saltareno."

She gave him a bold look and then a mocking little smile as she nodded. *"Con mucho gusto, mi caballero."*

He then walked back to the old majordomo and drew one of the rapiers from the case. He flourished it about in the air to get the feel of it. He had often watched Carlos fence with Miguel Sandarbal, who had been the teacher of that art back in Madrid and, indeed, inherited the shop from his own gifted father. Once or twice, Carlos had enthusiastically urged him to try his hand, and he had done so. Agile and with quick reflexes, he had shown that he could have readily learned to master this weapon by which gentlemen throughout Europe had defended their honor and saved their lives when beset by brigands or cutthroats. But although he knew that he was the veriest of novices, strangely he had no fear of the oncoming duel. Luis Saltareno was almost twice his age, and after having seen how greedily the merchant had lunched from those heaping plates of food in the bedroom, he was willing to take his chances.

A few moments later, Saltareno appeared, in doublet, breeches, and boots, as well as a fine cambric shirt with ruffles under the doublet and opened at the throat for comfort's sake. He made a short, sardonic bow toward his tall, tow-headed opponent and then strode toward the majordomo, took the rapier from the case, and made it dance about in the air. Then, adopting the classic style of the duelist, the left foot back, the left hand raised high in the air and the fingertips drooping forward, he chuckled, *"En garde, amigo!"*

John Cooper slowly approached. Then he remembered that Saltareno had told the beautiful *mestiza* to get Batista to preside as judge of this duel, but only the majordomo stood at one side.

Saltareno resumed his normal stance and scowled, then gestured with the rapier: "That dagger, Señor Baines, that was not to be part of the duel. Or I myself would have selected a dagger for the left hand, which is often practiced in the countries of France and Spain, especially between officers."

"It's a sentimental keepsake, if you don't mind, Señor Saltareno. I don't intend to use it. My word ought to be good enough for you—at least I've never set a Comanche band on unsuspecting people."

Saltareno turned livid with rage at this taunt, and his eyes narrowed. His left hand rose to caress his curly Vandyke as he considered a suitable reply. Then he shrugged, "You'll have little chance to use the dagger, even if you wished to, Señor Baines. And now, whenever you're ready, Maximilian, you'll give the signal to engage. Let's see how much you know, young cockerel!"

With this, he presented the rapier out straight, and waited as the majordomo drew closer, standing between the two protagonists and about five paces beyond. John Cooper had seen Carlos practice with Miguel enough to know this basic maneuver; he extended his blade until it clashed and slithered along the steel of his opponent.

"Engage and begin" the old majordomo exclaimed in a reedy voice, glancing nervously at his master.

Once again, Luis Saltareno fell into the classic duelist's attitude, and John Cooper imitated him. Swift and resourceful, the young mountain man knew that his only hope for survival with this unfamiliar weapon was to keep his eyes constantly on that deadly point and not to be misled by the feints and guileful poses that his opponent would assuredly assay. Now Saltareno lunged in tierce, and John Cooper defensively thrust the blade away and moved to one side.

"Very good," the merchant sneered. "You may give yourself one or two extra minutes to live, but that is all, Señor Baines." He suddenly pretended to lunge at John Cooper's throat, then, drawing back the rapier with more alacrity than the young mountain man would have supposed in a man of his age and girth, thrust wickedly at his opponent's belly. But John Cooper's keen eyes had followed the darting tip of the rapier and, as he drew back a step to avoid the first feigned thrust, leveled his rapier and so was able, at the sudden lethal thrust, to turn the blade aside again.

"I salute you!" the merchant again taunted him, retreating and lifting the rapier with the basket pressed against his mouth. "A good beginning, but I regret to say that it will have an unhappy ending for you. Yes, I'll readily admit it. I detest your *suegro*, as I do the fat, old fool of a Don Sancho de Pladero, who is no better and perhaps a traitor in his own fashion. Neither your precious Don Diego nor Don Sancho seems to realize that the accursed *indios* almost outnumber the good, Spanish citizens of Taos. And now that there is anarchy in Mexico and the controls from the provinces are meaningless, they must be held in check. The nonsense of treating them as equals is a dangerous policy. And now to your lesson, Señor Baines!" So saying, he whirled the rapier overhead, then lunged, only to draw back and lunge again at John Cooper's belly.

Infuriated by his opponent's insult to his father-in-law, John Cooper almost lost his concentration, and only by moving back and sweeping his rapier sideways was he fortunately able to parry that deadly thrust.

But in the energetic maneuver, Saltareno stumbled on the smooth tile, where a faint patch of rainwater glistened under the mild sun. In that movement, John Cooper glanced up and saw a bearded, black-haired, squat little man lying on his belly on the low flat roof of the villa, armed with a musket.

Now he understood; the order to Maximilian to have Batista act as witness had been a ruse—actually a veiled order for the peón to lurk there and, if his master should be in danger of defeat, to kill John Cooper. The *peón* hadn't known he was detected, but now as John Cooper moved back and tried to find a more secure position in order to meet his opponent's lunges, he thought desperately to himself that he must somehow eliminate the terrible odds that were all in favor of the corrupt *alcalde mayor*.

But again, this swift diversion of thought to the dire problem that confronted him cost him a moment's hesitation, and Saltareno, with a triumphant "Ha!" pinked his shoulder and drew blood.

John Cooper leaped to one side, glanced quickly at the wound, and saw that it was superficial. Yet the smirk on his opponent's face told him even more: that the *alcalde mayor* now felt that he could toy with this tyro at the rapier and kill him at will, prolonging the sport sadistically. And if by some miracle he, John Cooper, were able to hold his own, or even put Saltareno's life in peril, Batista's musket would doom him.

Suddenly he decided to take the initiative for the first time and, with a shout, waving his left hand, lunged at

Saltareno's thigh. The *alcalde mayor*, taken completely by surprise, stumbled back, but not in time to avoid being pierced by about an inch of John Cooper's blade. He let out a bellow of rage and riposted with a whirling flourish of his rapier that seemed to threaten a lunge at the young mountain man's eyes, and then, drawing back slightly, thrust toward his rival's heart.

But somehow instinct had guided the American. He crouched, as an Indian fighter might, and Saltareno's blade passed well over his head. At the same time, he thrust upward with all his strength. And just as the rapier transfixed the heart of the *alcalde mayor*, John Cooper leaped to his right and drew out the bone-handled Spanish dagger, just as Batista raised himself up and leveled the musket. He flung the dagger with all his strength and then hurled himself flat on the tile. There was an explosion of the musket, but the *peón* clutched at his throat, dropped the musket, which clattered on the tile below, and then rolled over onto his back and lay dead.

"*¡Bueno, bueno, muy hombre!*" he heard Noracia cry. And as he turned his head and lifted himself from the tile, he saw that she had drawn one of his holstered pistols and had been aiming it upward at the roof of the villa.

The old majordomo had uttered a cry of horror to see his master fall dead before him. Then at last he turned, hoarsely crying out, "I'll call the *trabajadores*—the *patrón* has been murdered!"

"Maximilian, if you do that, I'll kill you!" Noracia interposed as she felinely rose from the stool and came forward, the pistol now leveled at the dazed majordomo's chest. "You saw it, it was a fair fight. And you know what that *cobarde* did, telling you to have Batista be the witness— it was a good thing the Señor Baines saw him on the roof with the musket. Don't you understand, Maximilian, you're free—you and all the other *trabajadores* here, no better than slaves to that filthy brute! No one will mourn him in all Taos."

"It's—it's true—but—" the old man faltered.

"Call them, then," John Cooper interposed. "I know what she's trying to say. And all of you can be free. There will be a new government in Mexico soon, a stable one, I hope, and then the kind, just *intendente* of Taos will have a new *alcalde mayor*, who will treat people fairly. Call them, Maximilian."

The majordomo at last comprehended, burst into tears,

and then ran into the house. John Cooper stared admiringly at the *mestiza*. "I'm grateful to you, señorita."

"I was thinking of myself a little, too, if you don't mind, Señor Baines," she smiled broadly. "But I swear to you that I would have shot Batista if your dagger hadn't reached him first. I really didn't think you could beat Luis."

"I saw how much he ate, I saw his paunch, and from the wheezing of his breathing, I knew that he had to be short of wind. If I could only hold out for a time even his skill might not be enough—that's what I counted on," John Cooper confessed.

By now the servants had come crowding out onto the patio, and there were murmurs and gasps as they saw the *alcalde mayor* lying on his back, the rapier still buried in his heart.

"*Trabajadores,* you do not know me, but I am the *yerno* of Don Diego de Escobar, who was *intendente* here in Taos. This man, your *patrón,* called my *suegro* a traitor. I challenged him to a duel, and I killed him in a fair fight. This young woman who watched it, as well as your Maximilian, can tell you," John Cooper declared.

"It's so, *hombres,*" Noracia said, nodding, and the old majordomo feebly echoed, "*Sí, es verdad.*"

"I have cleared the name of Don Diego de Escobar. Never will it be said again in this *hacienda* that he was guilty of any treason. And you know your master, this man who lies dead before you. He abused the Indians and the poor—yes, even you, I'm certain."

As he spoke, some of the young *criadas,* hovering together and whispering to themselves, pointed to the corpse of the *alcalde mayor,* and their lips moved in imprecations. "Yes, I see already that most of you shed no tears over his death. You are all free now. Help yourself to his possessions, then go live your lives henceforth in freedom."

With this, he went to Noracia, took the belt with the holstered pistols, and strapped it round his waist. Then he took her hand and brought it to his lips. "I salute you, and I thank you, señorita," he said. And with this, turning on his heel, he quickly climbed up onto the roof to retrieve his prized Spanish dagger, then left the villa of Luis Saltareno.

Behind him, Noracia spoke again to the former *peones* of her dead protector: "All of what Señor Baines said is true, and all of you know it! You, Elena, and you, Sancha, and you too, Luz, he treated you like the worst of slaves, and you have every reason to spit at him there now. But you, *hombres,* and you too, *criadas,* if you leave, where will you work again? Who will employ you? Listen to me—the *intendente* Don Sancho de Pladero is a friend of this Señor Baines, and there will be no charge of murder, for it was a fair fight. And Taos is well rid of such an animal as this one!" She hawked and spat at Saltareno's lifeless body, and there was a shout of approval from one of the *trabajadores.*

"That's it, now we're all saying what's true and what we feel!" she continued, her eyes sparkling. "Let me stay here, and you will work for me. I will see that you are paid good wages. I know where this animal keeps his money, and this very evening, after supper, you will come to my room, and I will pay you the wages he has not given you in months. We can all be in this together, and we can have our freedom, too."

Another shout of approval rose up from the workers. Noracia's passionate display of indignation and anger had struck just the right chord; no matter what they had thought of her in the past, she had now clearly become their savior.

Forty-two

John Cooper mounted Pingo and rode away from the villa of Luis Saltareno and toward the church. He left the palomino tied to a hitching post in the public square and, this time, opened the front door and entered. At the back he saw a white-haired old Indian woman kneeling and praying, her gnarled hands clasped, her wrinkled cheeks wet with tears. He walked slowly down the aisle, seeing the empty pews and feeling the enormous, awesome silence. Little candles burned, their flames dipping, veering from side to side, or flickering valiantly, at each far side of the wings of the church beyond the altar.

As he saw the tall, straight figure of Padre Madura finishing the mass, he knelt down in the middle of the aisle, his hands clasped in prayer. He thanked God for the chance to pay back Don Diego for the latter's kindly acceptance of him, at such variance with the code of the grandee of Spain, to take an orphan from Shawneetown as the husband of his only daughter. This was the miracle of this new and changing land he was living in. It could not have happened in old Spain, land of the shadowy catacombs of the Inquisition, the secret peoples of the informers, who denounced man or woman who stood erect and defied the stultified tradition.

And as he knelt, he prayed for his father and mother and Ginny and Elsie, and that they would understand why and how he had changed. And he sensed that in no way had he betrayed his priceless heritage of the pioneer; and he thought that, if they could have been alive today, his family would have been eager to have as neighbors Don Diego de Escobar and his Doña Inez, and Catarina and Carlos, yes, and Miguel Sandarbal, as well. What he had learned from his years with the Indians was that all men were brothers. And this was the greatest boon of all for those who came to this new land in search of freedom.

He took his place at the far side of one of the front pews and waited until Padre Madura had genuflected for the last time. And then the gray-haired priest went toward the left and into the confessional booth, and John Cooper turned his head to see the old Indian woman hobble toward it, draw aside the curtains, and disappear. Then he heard the murmur of voices, and he was alone with his thoughts, his gratitude, and his hope for the future.

He had forgotten the slight wound; the blood had dried and there was only a slight twinge to his shoulder. After he had made his confession and told Padre Madura that Luis Saltareno had, in a fair fight, quitted not only his office of *alcalde mayor* but the debauched and selfish life he had led for all time to come, he would ride Pingo to the *hacienda* of Don Sancho de Pladero. And he would see Carlos and, with all the eloquence of which he was capable, urge his brother-in-law to turn his back on the shadows and the skeletons of the past and to walk forward with him into the sunlight of a new dawn, a new hope, a new beginning.

And when at last the old woman, crossing herself and genuflecting with difficulty before the altar, had left the church, he made his way to the confessional booth, drew aside the curtains, and entered, kneeling down and bowing his head in prayer. He explained to the priest all that had happened in the house of the *alcalde mayor*. He thanked God for his life, and asked forgiveness for having taken the life of another, and Padre Madura shrived John Cooper and blessed him.

"*Gracias, mi padre*," John Cooper said. "Now I shall go to see Carlos at the *hacienda* of Don Sancho, and take him back with me."

"I shall pray also that he will hearken to you, my son, and that joy will replace his sorrow. And I pray for the people of Taos, that in these difficult times, when there is revolution in the land, their belief in Him who watches over the least as over the greatest of us, and with equal love and understanding, will sustain them and strengthen them through the most troubled of times. I again give you my blessing, John Cooper Baines. And in the name of the people of Taos, I thank you for your generous charity."

He went out of the confessional box and into the dusty square, mounted Pingo, and rode toward the Sangre de Cristo Mountains and the *hacienda* of Don Sancho de Pladero. It was nearly twilight now, and he could see why these mountains had been named the Blood of Christ. To the west the sky was a violent crimson, and then, as the shadows deepened, it turned to a somber gray. The superstitious *Conquistadores*, who had first come to Nuevo México, had seen this and been awed by the phenomenon and had thus named it.

He rode into the courtyard of the *hacienda* of the *intendente* and one of the young *trabajadores*, smiling and gracious, hurried forward to take Pingo's reins and lead the horse to the stable. John Cooper knocked on the door, and Don Sancho de Pladero opened it, uttered a cry of joy, and embraced him. "I was just going out before supper to look at the sky and the mountains, John Cooper," the elderly hidalgo exclaimed. "How good it is to see you again!" Then suddenly the shadow of fear came into his eyes, and he muttered, glancing nervously around, "But isn't it dangerous for you to come this way into Taos, so openly?"

"No longer, Don Sancho. First, I must tell you that I rode to the villa of Luis Saltareno, by whose orders the Comanche *jefe* Sarpento brought his renegade warriors to attack our *hacienda*."

"He would dare such a crime? That man is evil, and he still hates your father-in-law, my dearest friend, Don Diego—"

"No longer, Don Sancho," John Cooper calmly interrupted. "I held him accountable for that crime, which is what you called it, and I challenged him to a fight. He chose rapiers as the weapon and, by luck, I won. Now the last deadly enemy—who was your enemy, too, for he boasted that he would denounce Don Diego as a traitor, and you, as well—can do no more harm, not to his *peones,* nor to the *indios* of the pueblo."

"But you're wounded, I can see the blood on your jacket—"

"A scratch, Don Sancho. I was very lucky." John Cooper grinned boyishly. "Padre Madura tells me that Carlos is a guest at your *hacienda.*"

"Yes, yes, by all the saints, and you shall see him this moment!" Don Sancho joyously exclaimed. An arm around John Cooper's shoulders, he led the young mountain man into the house and called aloud, "Carlos, come here and see a friend who is eager to see you!"

A door opened down the hall and Carlos de Escobar, no longer wearing the uniform of an officer in the army of Iturbide, emerged. He stopped short and stared at John Cooper, and then rushed toward him, and the two young men embraced.

"My friend, my good, dear friend," Carlos exclaimed, "you don't know how I've wanted to see you! I remember how before I joined the army I secluded myself in the mountains—it seems a lifetime ago—and when you came looking for me I almost threatened you. I've thought of that a thousand times over, and I've reproached myself. Can you forgive me? And my father and Doña Inez and Catarina—can they forgive me, too?"

"There's nothing to forgive, *mi compañero,*" John Cooper told him. "They're eager to see you. They've had so little news from you, except, a few months ago, that you were still alive."

"But what brought you to Taos, John Cooper?"

The young man briefly told of his duel with Saltareno, and Carlos, his eyes suspiciously moist, gripped John Cooper's hand.

"I owe you not only my own life, but the restoration of my father's honor, John Cooper," Carlos said.

"No, Carlos, there is no talk of debt or owing between us; there never will be. I'm part of your life now, you know, and I became that when I married Catarina. Your children are waiting for you, and Catarina has been taking care of them, but they miss their father. Will you go back with me?"

"Oh, *Dios,* yes, yes—"

"We'll go back tomorrow morning, then." He turned to Don Sancho, who was standing, rubbing his hands together and beaming, very close to tears at this reunion. "May I impose on your hospitality for tonight, Don Sancho?"

"You need not ask, John Cooper! *¡Mi casa es su casa!* Ah, here come Doña Elena and Tomás and sweet Conchita."

The young mountain man kissed Doña Elena's hand, shook hands with Tomás, and exclaimed over Conchita's serene beauty, kissing her hand and making her blush at his effusive praise.

Don Sancho hurried out to the kitchen to order his cook to prepare a sumptuous supper for his unexpected yet most important guest. And that evening, as they sat at the beautifully set table in the dining room of the *hacienda* of the *intendente* of Taos, John Cooper observed the spirited, stately beauty of Teresa de Rojado, and he noticed also how Carlos turned now and again to look admiringly at her across the table from his place beside the young mountain man.

John Cooper had saddled Pingo and thanked the young *trabajador* for having cared for his palomino so attentively. Don Sancho's cook had prepared ample provisions for his saddlebag on the return journey to the Hacienda del Halcón. And after he paid his farewells he said to Don Sancho, "It's true that you now are the only one who rules in Taos, and you are good and kind and just, like my own *suegro.* But now that Mexico has broken away from Spain, and now that Santa Anna has driven the would-be emperor Iturbide from his throne, I think there will be great unrest and perhaps even battles. In Texas I've come across many *americanos* who have suffered at the hands of the Mexican *soldados.* You and Don Diego are dear friends—I know that he would welcome you, as I should, if you would move to our ranch and become our neighbors. There is wonderful grazing land there, fresh water from the Frio River and from many little creeks around, and we have not been disturbed by any Mexican patrols. Besides, the settlers are coming to Texas, thanks to Moses Austin and his son. You and your family could begin a new life there, and you could live freely according to your conscience, and not have to worry about orders from Mexico City."

"I have thought about this, I will tell you honestly," Don Sancho replied. "Carlos has told us all about his experiences as a *teniente* under the command of that ambitious Santa Anna. Yes, I am beginning to think as he does, and as you do, John Cooper. Besides, I am growing old, and all I ask of life now is to watch my grandchildren grow, and to see how happy Tomás and Conchita are. Let me think about it. I will send a courier to you when I have made my decision."

And John Cooper knew that, when he told Don Diego this news, his father-in-law would be overjoyed indeed. Now he waited outside for Carlos, and as he turned to stare at the towering peaks of the Sangre de Cristo range, he thought of the stronghold of the Jicarilla Apache, and he reflected how fate had decreed that he should meet Carlos de Escobar and find love, a home, and a family in this burgeoning land, which was not yet part of the United States, but might be one day.

Carlos stood facing Teresa de Rojado in the little salon off the dining room. He tried to choose his words carefully, not wishing to offend her. Yet inwardly he knew that this was the woman, if there would ever be one, who could assuage the terrible emptiness of the lonely nights of grief, when he mourned the Beloved Woman, the Light of the Mountains. At last he said, "I'm going back to my home now, Teresa. It's in the Texas territory, a long journey from here. I want to thank you—you don't know how much I've enjoyed our riding together, our fencing."

"I, too, Carlos."

"Will you stay in Taos?"

She thought a moment, looking away from him, her face grave and sweet. Then she put out her hand and touched his and said very gently, "I think I know what you are trying to say. At least, I feel it. Carlos, I will be honest with you. Don Sancho told me of your great loss. But I have not told you of mine. My *esposo* was betrothed to me when I was only a girl of twelve. My father, whom I dearly love, arranged it. And so I was obedient, because I knew that my father was wise and good. In Spain, as perhaps you know, since you yourself are a *madrileno,* a daughter is dutiful and accepts her father's will as her own."

"Yes, I understand that."

"My husband was kind and considerate. He was, of

course, much older, but that did not matter. When he died, he left me wealthy, but that, too, is of no importance. That fortune is in the Banco de Habana, whenever I wish to claim it. Don Sancho was my father's friend, and when I wrote him of the news of my husband's death, he graciously invited me to come here. Besides, I wished to see the Estados Unidos.and also Nueva España."

"Yes," he said breathlessly, trying to remain detached and polite, yet desperately wanting her to speak and to tell him what was in her heart.

"Like you, Carlos, I was born in Madrid. I was brought up to believe that the Spanish way of life was the best in all the world. Now I see that Spain is no longer great nor wise nor even just. Spain, as you and I knew it, is dying, if it isn't already dead." She turned to one side, frowning in thought. "What will take place in Nueva España fills me with apprehension, because in a way it may be like Spain and its revolutions of the Peninsular Wars, when the dictator, Napoleon, tried to conquer all of Europe. I pray it will not happen in Nueva España, also."

She drew a long breath and turned to face him, her dark eyes intently fixed on his taut face. "I cannot be a parasite, Carlos, and for the same reason I cannot take the easy way. I grieve for my husband, and you grieve for your dear wife. There is thus a bond between us, and you and I both know what good friends we have become, what understanding we have had and what communication is between us. But the time is not yet, not for either of us. You know that in your heart."

"But I—"

She shook her head, and with a soft little smile that touched him to his very core and drew tears to his eyes in its exquisite poignance, she put out her hand and touched his lips with her fingertips. "No, do not say it. Now you are still grieving, and perhaps any girl who would be kind and friendly toward you would console you."

"But I swear it, that's not true—Teresa, no—"

"Hush, Carlos. For me, also, it would be very easy, because you are kind and good and brave, and, yes, handsome, too. It would be so easy to say 'I will make you forget her.' And that would be wrong, and each of us would come to hate the other, if we decided so soon, before our mourning can be put aside and we can look at life and begin again. Be patient, Carlos. If it is meant to happen, it will happen."

"Teresa, I—I won't say it, then. But I want to see you again. I will send word—I'll write letters—they'll come by messenger to Don Sancho."

"And I will answer them because you are my dear friend. And in the days when I was Don Sancho's guest and I was grieving, you brightened my life with your friendship, Carlos. At least, it is a good beginning. If anything is to come of it, we shall have nothing for which to reproach ourselves. Say good-bye to me now." She put out her hand as a man would, and Carlos needed all his self-mastery to keep from taking her into his arms and kissing her with all the anguished passion of his need, of his loneliness. Instead, with a polite smile, he clasped her hand and shook it. "*Adiós*, Teresa, may God go with you."

"And with you also, Carlos, *mi amigo*."

Reluctantly, he released her hand and then, with a deep breath, turned and left the salon.

Forty-three

They rode first to the Jicarilla stronghold, and on the trail Carlos told his brother-in-law everything that had happened to him since he had left the *hacienda* so long ago. They talked a little about Carlos's futile search for the hidden treasure, and John Cooper told his brother-in-law that Catarina had explained everything, and no harm was done. There was indeed a great treasure in the mountains, and for the present, the Apache would guard it so that it would never get into the wrong hands.

When they arrived at the stronghold, Kinotatay and Pastanari welcomed Carlos with a cordiality that deeply moved the young Spaniard. John Cooper walked with Kinotatay into the latter's wickiup as Pastanari affably led Carlos off to greet his beautiful young squaw, who was with child.

"I've told Padre Madura about the silver mine, Kinotatay," John Cooper declared. "And I gave him two of those silver bars to help the *indios* of the pueblo. There is treasure there to help your people, too, Kinotatay, if ever they are in need of it."

"I will order my braves always to guard the entrance to that mine, my blood brother. And each new moon I will send a messenger to your *hacienda* to tell you that all is well."

"I would not ask this, if all were well south of the Rio Grande, Kinotatay," John Cooper declared. "Carlos has told me of his experience as a *teniente* in the company that Santa Anna commanded. Santa Anna will make himself ruler of all Mexico before much longer. And he will need money to maintain his power, to buy soldiers who will be loyal to his cause. Carlos also told me about Santa Anna's spies who followed him when he was looking for the mine. They of course learned nothing, but Santa Anna will not forget that mine, not so long as he lives. And that is why I ask that you guard the treasure for me. It must be used for the good of the people, not for any one man who wishes to rule over others and make them his slaves."

"I pledge you my word, my blood brother. But do not be too long in coming back to us, even though the journey is long and tiring. Our people honor you, *Halcón*."

"As I honor them and you, my blood brother."

Don Diego de Escobar wept unashamedly as he hugged Carlos to him, and Doña Inez could not restrain her tears, either. Catarina had brought out the sturdy, young Diego and lovely Inez and little Dawn, and Carlos gathered them in his arms and hugged and kissed them. John Cooper turned away because his own emotions were overwrought at this joyous reunion. And he remembered how Carlos had looked and looked again at the lovely Teresa de Rojado. And when he had talked with her, he had told himself that here was indeed a young woman who could inspire and comfort his courageous, free-spirited brother-in-law.

Miguel was also on hand to welcome back his young *compañero*, and he embraced Carlos, then shook his hand, then embraced him again. Then turning to John Cooper, he exclaimed, "It is good to have Carlos among us once again, is it not, *mi amigo?*"

"That it is, Miguel!" John Cooper replied huskily.

Later, when they went out to the courtyard, Miguel told John Cooper that there had been no sign of Lobo for the past week. And the *capataz* added, "Sometimes, when the moon is full, I hear Lobo baying, and then I see the she-wolf and their grown cubs come out to join him. And they are always farther away from the *hacienda* than the time before."

"It means that Lobo wants to return to the free life, the free life which his mother's blood urges him to follow. And I'm glad of it. He's old, but he's been a loyal, true friend and a defender for all of us. Just as the whelp Yankee will be, although I hope that he'll never have to fight side by side with us against enemies who want to do us harm, Miguel."

"I'll say amen to that, *mi compañero.*" Miguel nodded and beamed. "So now there is no one left in Taos to hate my *patrón,* thanks to you, *amigo.* I owe you a great deal. You've done what I wanted to do, and you've paid my debt to Don Diego for me. God bless you and Catarina and your children."

"Gracias, Miguel."

On the very next morning, Carlos and John Cooper and Catarina went out riding, and Yankee, who had grown since John Cooper last saw him, loped along. As John Cooper glanced back, he found it almost uncanny to see how much this whelp looked like Lobo.

Suddenly, Catarina cried out as the three of them rode toward the Frio River, "There's someone coming on horseback toward us, and he's in uniform!"

"So long as he isn't leading a troop of soldiers, there's nothing to worry about," John Cooper wryly explained.

"Wait, I recognize the uniform and the insignia—*por todos los santos,* it's my friend, *mi coronel!*" Carlos cried. Then, his face aglow, leaning forward in his saddle, he spurred on Dolor to meet the approaching rider.

The two men met, and Carlos uttered a cry of joy: "Ramón, what wonderful good fortune—I'd hoped I'd see you again, but I never dreamed you'd ride here to find me."

"Carlos, I cannot believe it! They said you were dead—shot! Oh, it is so good to see you, my friend. I came here to tell your brother-in-law, the *americano,* and your father, too, that I've resigned my commission. You know, of course, that Iturbide fled the country. It is Santa Anna now, the vulture, who will be the scavenger of my poor country."

"Come, Ramón, you must meet my sister and my *cuñado!*" Carlos exclaimed, grinning like a boy. He wheeled Dolor back toward Catarina and John Cooper, who sat waiting as the two men rode toward them. "Catarina, John

Cooper, this is my good friend, Coronel Ramón Santoriaga," he told them.

"No, Carlos, I am only a citizen like you, and my name is now just Ramón Santoriaga," the affable young man amended. Then, inclining his head, he stared admiringly at Catarina and exclaimed, "My friend Carlos often told me what a beautiful sister he had, and now I see that he did not exaggerate. If anything, he did not do you justice."

"You have already made a friend in my wife, Catarina." John Cooper chuckled, extending his hand, which Ramón eagerly shook. "Let's go back to the *hacienda*. You must have ridden a long way, Señor Santoriaga."

"I'd be pleased if you'd call me Ramón. Yes, and it took a little doing. Many of the main roads are guarded by Santa Anna's soldiers, as a precaution against a possible counter coup by those troops still loyal to Iturbide, though their number is almost nonexistent by now, I'm certain."

"And your wife and children, Ramón, what of them?" Carlos demanded.

"I sent word to Mercedes to sell our house in Mexico City and to stay with her uncle in Cuernavaca, until I could send word to her."

"You know, John Cooper," Carlos said, turning to his brother-in-law, "Ramón was a wonderful officer. And there's no reason why he should stay near Mexico City now, because both of us found out about Santa Anna's duplicity and what he was really up to. I'd like to see him and his wife and children settle near us and be our good friends and neighbors."

"That wouldn't be a bad idea at that," John Cooper mused aloud. "He could actually train some of our *trabajadores* so that we'd have a kind of army of our own. When Sarpento and the Comanche attacked us, it was just our good luck that Miguel stationed the men in the right places, and we had better ammunition and weapons than the Indians. Well, we can talk about that over lunch this noon."

"There's something else I came to tell you—or at least, not knowing that you were still alive, your father," Ramón soberly averred. "I happened to overhear a conversation between Santa Anna and some of his subordinates, and he still hopes to find that treasure you were supposed to lead his two spies to. I tell you, so long as he lives, there'll be danger for all of you here."

"You're sure of that, Ramón?" John Cooper anxiously queried.

"Yes, indeed I am. He knows that you, *mi amigo*, are married to Carlos's sister, and, since he also thinks that Carlos was killed by those two spies, just as I did, he will turn his attention to you in the future."

"All the more reason then, Ramón," John Cooper retorted, "that you should live here with us and become the *jefe* of our private army. An army that won't be used for anything else except to defend the peace and security of our ranch here!"

It was the evening of April 14, 1823. In Mexico City, on this same day, the restored *junta* in Mexico City had ratified Stephen Fuller Austin's application under the terms of the Imperial Colonization Law. Immediately afterward, the *junta* had suspended the law. Now at last, the road was paved to colonization, to the acceptance of American family settlers in Texas. The dream of Moses Austin had at last been realized. Nonetheless, it would take almost another generation before Texas would declare its independence from Mexico, and eventually choose an allegiance to the young United States.

And in this same year, President James Monroe would issue his famous Monroe Doctrine in his annual message to Congress, declaring that the United States would neither meddle in European affairs nor countenance interference in the destinies of independent American governments by any European power. It was a declaration as significant as the Declaration of Independence.

Tonight, at the Double H Ranch, there was a great fiesta. Throughout the vast estate, with the scores of outbuildings and the houses of the *trabajadores* lit up inside, there came the sound of violins and guitars, flutes, and even the tinkling of a spinet piano that had been shipped from New Orleans to Corpus Christi, and then brought by *carreta* all the way to this fertile land near the Frio River. At the main house itself, Don Diego and Doña Inez presided, with John Cooper and Catarina seated beside them. Carlos de Escobar sat at his father's right, with Ramón Santoriago at his right, in turn. Ramón had accepted the offer that Don Diego and his son-in-law had made: to be in charge of training the loyal *trabajadores* in the basics of military defense against attack.

Before they had gone in to dinner, Miguel had asked

them all to accompany him on a short walk. At the foreman's request, workmen had been busy the last few days constructing two tall gateposts at the entranceway to the great ranch. But now what Miguel had to show them made them all stand in awe. Surmounting the gateposts was a large wooden sign in the shape of a hawk, on which was etched the double H insignia of the ranch. On one side was written Hacienda del Halcón, and on the other side Double H Ranch.

The sign had been made by Taguro, the young Pueblo Indian. He and his wife, Listanzia, had settled in comfortably on the ranch, and she had given birth to a girl whom she named Juanita, in memory of Padre Juan Moraga. The sign, which Taguro had made on his own time, was his way of showing gratitude to his benefactors.

Everyone was delighted with the gift, none more so than John Cooper and his father-in-law, who beamed as Taguro came forward and shook hands with them. Carlos, too, shook the Indian's hand, and said, "We have never met, but I want to tell you how pleased I am at what you've done for all of us. You have helped make my homecoming an even more joyous occasion."

The evening was warm, and the moon was full. After the lavish feast that had been prepared by Tía Margarita and Leonora and several of the wives of the *trabajadores,* the de Escobars and Baineses, accompanied by Ramón, went outside to enjoy the vast beauty of the landscape in a darkness illumined by the brilliance of the moon.

From a distance came the baying sound of a wolf.

"Look there, Catarina, you can just make out the shadows, there over by the copse of spruce trees near the creek," John Cooper murmured to Catarina as he pointed. "There's the she-wolf and her fully grown cubs. And do you hear that yowl? That's Lobo, answering his mate. They're all free now, and yet Lobo remembers how he guarded us. He'll never forget, not ever, that he was once part of our family and helped defend us."

Once again, the she-wolf lifted her muzzle to the sky and uttered a long, mournful howl. Lobo trotted up, wagging his tail, with a joyous yipe, as if he were still a young cub. And then he and his mate, followed by their whelps, trotted off into the darkness.

Bantam Books proudly presents
a special preview of the exciting
new novel from the producer
of WAGONS WEST and THE AUSTRALIANS.

A white-hot novel
By ROY SPARKIA

Enter the world of a spectacular new book, coming this November from the producer of WAGONS WEST and THE AUSTRALIANS. A white-hot novel of a giant land and the giant desires of those who dare to challenge it.

A world of forbidden temptations. Throbbing with the unbridled power of the river. Teeming with secret riches and exotic beauty. Ripe with the steamy pleasures of Rio swept up in the mad rush of love and intrigue during *Carnival* nights.

The playground of the greedy and the ruthless. Where savagery is untamed by time. Where terror saturates the skin like sweat and strikes as swiftly as the machete. Where every evil has its price and every kiss can be as fatal as the piranha's bite.

Now prepare yourself for the sensational opening pages of Roy Sparkia's thrilling novel ...

The Amazonian jungle rises lofty, silent, deadly, guarding its secrets passionately behind its sprawling riot of green life. Enormous enough to swallow all of England, France, Spain, Portugal, Germany, Italy, and half of the United States within its wild boundaries, this last of the world's great primal forests has been virtually unknown by man, untouched, unchanged over millions of years.

Then came the road builders . . .

First they came with axes and machetes to hack an opening through the tangled density for the survey stakes; at their heels came the chain saws, the dynamiters, the bulldozers, and the great monsters whose steel arms can clamp around a tree fifty feet high and pull it up by its roots. Next came the caravan of gigantic power shovels and crawler tractors—mechanized dinosaurs that gobbled away terrestrial obstacles within minutes. Then the bottom dump trucks, road graders, and finally the fifty-ton vibratory rollers to smooth and compact the road surface for automotive traffic. All growling, rearing, thundering, spouting plumes of poisonous smoke. Shaking the earth, frightening the wildlife, and driving the Indians from their ancestral homelands, pressing them ever deeper into the jungle.

The roadworkers labor in sweltering heat in twelve-hour shifts, around the clock, seven days a week. The drudgery lames their muscles, knots their stomachs, dries the saliva in their mouths while the sweat runs from their pores, draining bodily reserves of sodium and phosphorus that are never fully replenished by the wide-spaced meals of rice and beans with *mandioca*—and sometimes meat. The laborers are chronically exhausted, their minds closed inward in a gray blur as they mechanically perform the required motions of the job. Foot by foot they advance, never stopping. Slowly, but with the ineluctable certainty of another sunrise—or sunset.

But the jungle fights back...

Against billowing white clouds, the blue Learjet appeared to be but a misplaced speck of sky as it jetted an arrow-straight line above the forest.

In its sumptuous interior was a single passenger, a young man who was plainly a *branco*, one of the whites, and just as obviously of the moneyed class. Garbed in a suit of unbleached silk shantung, he was tall and rather roughhewn, with heavy dark brows, somewhat unruly dark hair, and blue eyes that could turn dark and stormy in anger: his face was both aristocratic and sensual. He sat close to a window surveying the vista below.

Viewed from five thousand feet, the world seemed to be an endless green ocean stretching in every direction. Beyond imagination, beyond human comprehension. The only tangible evidence of solid ground was a tenuous clay-red scratch bisecting the impenetrable density.

The red scratch vanished suddenly, engulfed by the forest, and the young man turned and called to the pilot.

"Pio, the highway seems to have ended. How much farther will it have to go to reach my land?"

The pilot shrugged. "I would guess about a hundred more kilometers."

"Then it should be only a few more weeks before it gets there."

"It could be many more weeks. Maybe many months. The jungle is not friendly to *civilizados.*"

Raul de Carvalho laughed. "You're a pessimist, Pio, like my old man. Maybe that's why he keeps you around."

Pio, a lean young *moreno,* half Indian and half Portuguese, worked for Raul's father, who owned the Learjet. Though Pio had virtually grown up with Raul as a childhood playmate on the de Carvalho cattle *fazenda,* never for a moment did he forget that subtle barrier between them: Raul was son of the master, and he was but an employee.

"Let me know when we reach the boundary of my land."

Minutes later, Pio called out, "Just ahead—at the bend of the stream—that is roughly the northeast corner of your property."

Excitement welled in Raul's chest as he stared down. It looked no different from the rest of the immense green panorama they had flown over, but it was—enormously different.

The huge chunk of jungle below, over a million acres, belonged to him!

Or soon would. On his thirtieth birthday, less than a week away, the deed to the property would become his, in accordance with the terms of his late grandfather's will.

Soon they were passing over the squared cleared area and an assortment of tiny oblongs that were the decaying old plantation house, the outbuildings, and the slave cabins. During the rubber boom, when Brazil had a total monopoly on the wild hevea rubber trees that were so plentiful, the plantation had earned huge profits, making his grandfather very rich before the boom ended —sliced off by competition from plantations in the Far East that had been grown from stolen hevea seeds smuggled out of Brazil. With his wealth, Raul's grandfather had moved to the Mato Grosso and become a cattle rancher, leaving the plantation to fall into disrepair, maintained only by a minimal crew who worked a few acres of the land for barely enough profit to pay their wages.

But that would soon end. Raul de Carvalho had big dreams for turning all those remote acres into a profitable kingdom. Very profitable indeed.

All thanks to the new highway that would soon be cutting across his land.

"I've seen enough, Pio. Better swing around now and head for Rio. It's important that I get there promptly at one o'clock."

"No problem, *Senhor* Raul."

Arriving in Rio by air, though he had done so countless times, was always a thrill for Raul. First came the gentle rocking of the plane from the powerful drafts that swept up from the fantastically peaked mountains near the coast; then came the fast slipping downward through layers of silvery mist before the rich fantasyland of the city came into view. On one side, satiny waterfalls, verdured mountainsides, cliffs serried with elegant houses. Gardens, terraces, volcanic eruptions of color, surrealistic effusions of crimson, blue, purple, and yellow flowers. On the other side, miles of pancake-gold beach, a ruffle of white froth separating it from the azure ocean, stately palms, gay-roofed villas, hotels, casinos, and finally the heart of the great city itself.

Unlike the average tourist, expectant of exotic sights, samba rhythms, beautiful girls in string bikinis, and a citizenry with a superheated zest for living, Raul was more attuned to the geographic beauty and the architectural splendor of this dream city. He drank in as a tonic the soaring grace of tall steel-framed buildings, the glistening walls of glass rising above tilted and gilded cathedral domes, the shadowed gash of the broad Avenida Rio Branco, the Monroe Palace, the copper-domed Municipal Theater, and the National Art Gallery. Won-

drous buildings everywhere. In the bay were miles of
moored steamers, freighters, and battleships; basins were
crowded with barges brimming to the gunwales with
colorful fruit.

The crawling trams, buses, sports cars, and people
thronging the streets lifted his spirits.

This was vitality! This was the heart of Brazil, a beautiful present and the promise of an even more glorious
future.

And he was a part of the surging forces that were helping to create it.

Speeding along the Avenida Atlantica behind the wheel
of his white Ferrari, Eduardo de Carvalho, Raul's
younger brother, soon shook off his worries. Problems
that could be cured by money were never too serious,
and he could always manage to get extra money. Never
from his father, who was always scolding him for his
extravagance, but as a last resort from his mother, if she
could get it to him without his father finding out.

Twilight was just beginning, like blue dust sprinkling
gently from the skies. His spirits lifted, as they always
did with the approach of evening and the anticipation of
unknown adventures ahead. He only came fully alive at
night, and where were the nights more glorious than in
this gay tropical city of wealth, gorgeous girls, and a
multitude of sinful pleasures? Rio, generally acknowl-
edged as the most beautiful city in the world, was as
much a part of him as the very air, food, and drink that
sustained him. On his left rose a wall of hills and shafts
of granite that ringed the city on the offshore side, opening seaward onto a crescent of ocean and wide beaches
that were thick by day with sun-browned bathers in
string bikinis and of such heartbreaking beauty as to
send the blood fizzing through his veins like champagne.
Rio, a blaze of color and desire by day; by night an il-
luminated necklace of jewels promising secret fulfillment
of illicit joys. And towering above it all, the Corcovado,

or Hunchback Mountain, with its giant statue of Christ sorrowfully overlooking this paradise of corrupt pleasures.

Ah, this was his element! Even the shape of the city, stretching out along the sandy shores of the ocean as it did, was said to be like a beautiful female basking in the sun, somnolent, enticing. Her head formed the downtown section, her hair streaming in northerly directions; the rising mounds of topography and curved shorelines from the residential areas of Flamengo, Botafogo, and Copacabana were supposed to make up her voluptuous torso; and her legs spread invitingly at Arpoador Beach, reaching out to enfold the neighborhoods of Ipanema and Leblon.

Eduardo's own beach apartment, as he often told his guests, was situated in the very center of the pelvic area.

By the time he reached the magnificent Leme Palace Hotel and turned his car over to a parking attendant, his mood was almost back to normal. Jauntily he headed through the crowded lobby to Le Cordon Bleu restaurant, and guided by the maître d', he found Raul and his fiancée seated at a palm-shaded table in a corner of the terrace overlooking the ocean.

Even as he was shaking hands with his smiling brother, Eduardo could scarcely hide his astonishment. One glance at the svelte girl seated at the table had stunned him. What perfection of face and figure! How had stodgy old Raul managed to capture this one? She had flawless milk-white skin and gleaming black hair that was severely coiffed to set off the delicate elegance of her features. Her jewels and ice-green gown had obviously been picked to enhance the brilliance of her green eyes that sparkled and seemed to mock him as she looked him over.

"Eduardo, I wish to present Odete Bandiera e Xavier, my fiancée. Odete, my brother Eduardo."

"*Senhorita,* what a delightful pleasure," said Eduardo with genuine sincerity as he took her outstretched hand and lightly touched his lips to the back of her fingers.

"My respect for my brother's good taste has risen a thousandfold."

Her laugh tinkled. "I have looked forward to meeting you, *senhor*. Raul has told me many nice things about you, but not that you are such a flatterer."

"I have many sins, but flattery is not one of them. Has Raul not told you about how bad I can be?"

"Oh, no. Raul is too much the loyal brother to say an unkind word. The bad things you must tell me yourself."

"It would be a great pleasure, *senhorita*—"

"Please! As my future brother-in-law, you must call me Odete."

"With pleasure, Odete—and you must call me Eduardo."

"Splendid," said Raul, flashing his grin at them. "It pleases me to see that you have both taken such a liking to each other."

There was a silver ice bucket on the table containing an open bottle of Cliquot's, from which a waiter had already poured a glass for Eduardo. He sipped at it nervously, wondering if his brother had sensed his powerful surge of attraction to Odete and was subtly warning him to cool it. Then he decided that Raul was much too straightforward for subtleties, too trusting to harbor suspicions.

Raul continued. "Shall we order? And after we have dined, I am anxious to talk about how my new plans will affect your future, Eduardo."

Eduardo groaned. "More work for me, no doubt."

"But at a higher salary."

Eduardo brightened. Plainly Raul was in a fine mood. He scanned the *cardápio*, noting that caviar Beluga Malossol, at 620 *cruzeiros*, was the most expensive of the appetizers, and he automatically selected that.

"I'll begin with the Beluga," he said, shoving the menu aside. "The rest I'll leave to you to order for me, Raul."

"I'll do the same," said Odete, adding with a laugh, "I must start practicing at letting my future husband do the thinking for me."

Raul beckoned the waiter and placed the order.

The caviar was followed by *gazpacho à Andaluz*. Conversation at this point, as custom mandated, was restricted to inconsequential or amusing topics, with no reference to business. Next came the entrée: *iscas de vitela com creme e batatas à Bernesa*, accompanied by *palmito*.

Raul ate voraciously. Eduardo ate with far less gusto, consuming but modest portions of everything. Odete only dabbled at her food, but she ordered *doces brasileiros*, Brazilian sweets, for dessert, with *cafézinho* and a sweet liqueur.

As the two brothers were finishing with coffee and brandy, Raul's voice turned serious. "Eduardo, I wished to speak to you on business matters tonight in front of Odete because all of our futures are necessarily affected by the plans we work out."

Eduardo laughed. "How different from our father, who would never dream of including a wife in a discussion of business matters!"

Raul didn't smile. "He hasn't changed in that respect—but he is still our father, and I still need his approval before I can go ahead with my plans for the energy plantation."

"But why? The property is yours." A sudden doubt clutched at Eduardo's hope for borrowing from Raul. "Have you had any trouble getting the capital you need?"

"No. Da Silva has pledged the money. My problem is father's disapproval—and his dependence on me to manage our Rio export office. He feels I will be letting him down. It is my obligation to prove to him that you are very capable of taking over as the new manager—"

"Me!" Eduardo was truly surprised and a bit dismayed. He knew his own inadequacies, and he dreaded responsibility.

"Yes. I am counting on you to prove that you can work just as hard as anyone else when it is necessary. We have good people on the staff who will help you. Up until now you haven't had a real chance, but I'm sure that once you have been entrusted with full responsibility, you will take hold and make all of us proud of you."

Eduardo saw at once that the position might well afford opportunities to get his hands on company funds—borrowed only temporarily, of course—when hard pressed for cash. To cover his nervousness, he turned to Odete with a wry smile. "So now I have to pay a heavy price to help along Raul's dream of becoming an agro-industrial giant—all this extra work piled on me! Talk him out of it, Odete. I'm sure you aren't looking forward to hiding away in the middle of the jungle with only the alligators, snakes, and bugs for neighbors."

She shuddered fastidiously. "I do not wish even to know about such things. Perhaps after a while I can persuade Raul to hire managers to run his plantation, and we can live in town."

"I must warn you, Raul can be very stubborn."

"But so can I—and I have months to work on him, since mama will never allow the marriage to take place too soon after our engagement is announced."

Raul laughed, taking it all in good humor. "And I, too, will have time to convince Odete that the jungle is the most beautiful place left on earth. She will learn to love it just as deeply as I do."

Eduardo spread his hands in mock resignation. "You see, Odete? Raul has always been a stick-in-the-mud who has no appreciation of the excitement and fun of city life."

"Can we consider it settled, Eduardo?" said Raul. "You will agree to take over the managership? I must know because tomorrow I am flying home to talk it over with father."

Eduardo sighed wearily. "I accept, brother, and I will try hard to justify your faith in me."

"Splendid. Now one more thing. I shall be away most of the time for the next several months, and I am asking you as a great personal favor to look after Odete and help do what you can to alleviate her boredom."

"It will be my pleasure."

Odete smiled at Eduardo. "And then you can tell me all the bad things about yourself."

"That would take a long time."

"Who cares how long it takes?" she said.

Raul had turned away to signal for the check, and for a moment Eduardo could hardly believe his eyes. She had winked at him before fluttering her eyes downward, sipping her liqueur through her smile.

Read the complete Bantam novel, AMAZON, on sale November 15, 1981, wherever paperbacks are sold.

TALES OF BOLD ADVENTURE AND
PASSIONATE ROMANCE FROM THE PRODUCER
OF WAGONS WEST

A SAGA OF THE SOUTHWEST
By Leigh Franklin James

The American Southwest in the early 19th century, a turbulent land ravaged by fortune seekers and marked by the legacy of European aristocracy, is the setting for this series of thrilling and memorable novels. You will meet a group of bold, headstrong people who come to carve a lasting place in the untamed wilderness.

THE HAWK AND THE DOVE: Book One

John Cooper Baines, living by his wits and braving the wilderness, is brought to manhood in an Indian village and moves on to New Mexico. There John meets the proud, exiled Spanish nobleman, Don Diego de Escobar, and his beautiful daughter, Catarina. Won by John's courage, she sees in him the strength to conquer a savage land. Together they plant the seeds of an empire that will change the course of history.

WINGS OF THE HAWK: Book Two

John and Catarina, pregnant with her first child, meet the challenge of establishing a prosperous ranch. Then John's discovery of a shocking secret and a fabulous treasure reaches the wrong ears. The family, which now includes their new son, Andrew, is suddenly plunged into danger.

REVENGE OF THE HAWK: Book Three

Coming in December, 1981.

Read all of these Bantam Books, available wherever paperbacks are sold.

FROM THE PRODUCER OF WAGONS WEST
AND THE KENT FAMILY CHRONICLES—
A SWEEPING SAGA OF WAR AND HEROISM
AT THE BIRTH OF A NATION.

THE WHITE INDIAN SERIES

Filled with the glory and adventure of the colonization of America, here is the thrilling saga of one of the new frontier's boldest heroes. He is Renno, born to white parents, raised by Seneca Indians, and destined to be a leader in both worlds. THE WHITE INDIAN SERIES chronicles Renno's adventures from the colonies to Canada, from the South to the turbulent West. Through Renno's struggles to tame a savage continent and through his encounters with the powerful men and passionate women on all sides of the early battles of America, we witness the events that shaped our future and forged our great heritage.

WHITE INDIAN, Book I

Renno is raised among the Seneca to become the mightiest of all braves. He faces many daring adventures among both the Indians and the white settlers.

THE RENEGADE, Book II

Renno—enlisted by the colonists in the cause of peace—finds romance and danger on a desperate mission to the King of England.

WAR CHIEF, Book III

Two hostile Indian nations and ruthless Spanish pirates stand in the way of Renno's quest to prevent a full-scale war in the Southeast and to win the love of a beautiful Virginia heiress.

THE SACHEM, Book IV

While his Virginia-born wife is on a perilous journey, Renno, now acting chief of the Seneca, is threatened by devious enemies.

RENNO, Book V

Renno and his brave warrior son must muster every ounce of courage to stop a bloodthirsty plot against the American colonies.

*Read all of these Bantam Books,
available wherever paperbacks are sold.*

★ WAGONS WEST ★

A series of unforgettable books that trace the lives of a dauntless band of pioneering men, women and children as they brave the hazards of an untamed land in their trek across America. This legendary caravan of people forge a new link in the wilderness. They are Americans from the North and the South, alongside immigrants, Blacks and Indians, who wage fierce daily battles for survival on this uncompromising journey—each to their private destinies as they fulfill their greatest dreams.

INDEPENDENCE, BOOK I

The wagon train begins its journey on Long Island. Among the travellers are Whip Holt and Cathy van Ayl whose lives are changed by the unseen forces of the vast frontier.

NEBRASKA, BOOK II

Although some members remain behind, many people in the wagon train brave their way against incredible odds as they continue courageously toward their destination.

WYOMING, BOOK III

Only the stalwart survive the hazardous trek through the Rockies—beset by savage Indian attacks and treachery by secret enemy agents on board the wagon train.

OREGON, BOOK IV

The wagon train members are pawns in the clash between three great national powers, all gambling on the riches that lie in the great northwest.

TEXAS, BOOK V

1843. The fledgling republic fights for its life against the onrush of Mexican soldiers. Some of the original wagon train members join the call to help in this struggle.

CALIFORNIA, BOOK VI

Gold is discovered in 1848 and its lure attracts friend and foe alike...in a mad scramble for new-found riches. But many lives become endangered as lawlessness overtakes the territory.

COLORADO, BOOK VII (August '81)

Now gold is found in Central City, and the frontier town of Denver becomes the magnet for hucksters, hustlers and many of the wagon train friends. Shocking events result from this highly volatile situation.

Read all of these novels in Bantam Books, available wherever paperbacks are sold.

★★★★★★★★★★★★★★★★★★★★★★★★★

GREAT HISTORICAL SAGAS OF AMERICA'S FIRST FRONTIERS

The Producer of the KENT FAMILY CHRONICLES now bring
you the WAGONS WEST and COLONIZATION OF AMERICA se
ries. These books are full of the spectacular adventure and ro
mance that followed America's first settlers as they struggle
in a new land.

The highly acclaimed WAGONS WEST series by Dana Fuller Ross

☐ 20419	INDEPENDENCE!	$3.2
☐ 20417	NEBRASKA!	$3.2
☐ 14849	WYOMING!	$2.9
☐ 13316	OREGON!	$2.9
☐ 13980	TEXAS!	$2.7
☐ 14260	CALIFORNIA!	$2.9
☐ 14717	COLORADO	$3.2

The thrilling COLONIZATION OF AMERICA series by Donal
Clayton Porter:

☐ 20349	WHITE INDIAN	$3.2
☐ 20362	THE RENEGADE	$3.2
☐ 14069	WAR CHIEF	$2.9
☐ 13681	THE SACHEM	$2.9

The new SAGA OF THE SOUTHWEST series by Leigh Frankli
Jones:

☐ 20096	REVENGE OF THE HAWK	$3.2
☐ 20556	HAWK OF THE DOVE	$3.2
☐ 14276	WINGS OF THE HAWK	$2.95

★★★★★★★★★★★★★★★★★★★★★★★★★

Buy them at your local bookstore or use this handy coupon:

Bantam Books, Inc., Dept. LE, 414 East Golf Road, Des Plaines, Ill. 60016

Please send me the books I have checked above. I am enclosing $_____
(please add $1.00 to cover postage and handling). Send check or money order
—no cash or C.O.D.'s please.

Mr/Mrs/Miss _____

Address _____

City _____ State/Zip _____

LE—11/81

Please allow four to six weeks for delivery. This offer expires 5/82.